HUDSON

D1153574

"I can easily divide my life into two parts—before her and after."

HUDSON

LAURELIN PAIGE

4201 6937

East Baton Rouge Parish Library
Baton Rouge, Louisiana

This book is a work of fiction. Names, characters, places, and incidents either are products of the author's imagination or are used fictitiously. Any resemblance to actual events or locales or persons, living or dead, is entirely coincidental.

© 2014 by Laurelin Paige

ISBN: 0991379667
ISBN 13: 9780991379668

All rights reserved, including the right to reproduce this book or portions thereof in any form whatsoever.

First edition May, 2013.

The following story contains mature themes, strong language, and sexual situations. It is intended for adult readers.

East Baton Rouge Parish Library
Baton Rouge, Louisiana

ALSO BY LAURELIN PAIGE:

Fixed on You (Fixed #1) – Amazon, Nook, iBooks
Found in You (Fixed #2) – Amazon, Nook, iBooks
Forever with You (Fixed #3) – Amazon, Nook, iBooks
Fixed Trilogy Bundle – Amazon, Nook, iBooks

Take Two – Amazon, Nook, iBooks
Star Struck – Amazon, Nook, iBooks

— CHAPTER —
ONE

I sign in on the form and hand the clipboard back to the volunteer manning the desk.

The young man's brows rise in recognition of my name. "Mr. Pierce!" He stands from his seat and sticks out his hand to shake mine. "I didn't expect it would be you representing Pierce Industries. I thought you'd send someone."

I shake his hand, out of politeness, then force a stiff smile. "Surprise." God, I hate small talk. Especially from this twenty-two year old ass-kisser who likely hopes this interaction will earn him employment at my company. I'm afraid it's not that easy to even get an interview.

He lowers his focus to the nametags on the table, searching for the one with the Pierce Industries logo. He hands it to me, and I pocket it. I refuse to wear it. I'm easily enough recognized without advertising it.

The man—nothing more than a boy, really—seems disappointed. Whether it's because I'm not as charismatic or charming as he'd imagined or because I dismissed the damn nametag, I can't be certain. Frankly, I don't give a shit. Once upon a time, his emotions would have elicited more interest from me. Now, they're barely a blip on my radar. I'll never understand them. No point in wasting my time trying.

His smile is professional as he gives me the portfolio for the evening's presentation. At the same time, I feel a small hand press into my back. I tense. I know that hand.

I glance behind me, confirming my suspicion as I start toward the lecture hall. "What are you still doing here? I gave you what you wanted."

"I'm already here. I thought I'd stay." As she trots to keep up with me, Celia's heels echo on the marble floor of the Kauffman Management Center, the house of NYU's Stern School of Business.

I stop at the door to the hall and turn to her. "You weren't invited."

Her lids flutter ever so slightly, and I know my words have stung. "*You* could invite me. We rarely see each other anymore." She lowers her voice. "I miss you."

My jaw ticks, and I let out a slow breath. Celia is the one person I've been advised not to spend time with. She's also the one person who understands me better than anyone else. It's a war I wage daily—being with her is akin to being a drunk in a liquor store. She tempts me to indulge in wicked ways, even if she doesn't intend to. And I'm certain that she usually *does* intend to.

But she's my only friend, if that's what you would call our relationship. Without her, I'm all alone.

"Fine; you're invited," I resign. I open the door and hold it for her to walk through. "I don't know why you want to be here. These things are boring as hell."

I follow her down a row toward the back of the room and take two seats in the middle. The hall is small, and there are less than ten other corporate representatives currently seated. We could easily move closer, but Celia knows me well enough to understand that I prefer to be removed from situations such as these.

She leans toward me, the scent of her too-strong designer perfume pervading my space. "If it's boring, why do you even come? You could send someone who's twenty rungs down the ladder from you."

I pause, deciding if I want to explain. The annual Stern Symposium is the only event of its type that I attend. While the majority of the presentations are dull, I've found a handful of stellar students in the mix. A good find is rare and not worth the two hours I spend here every year, but that isn't the reason I continue to show up. Any of my execs could come in my place and be a better use of time management.

Still, I insist on coming myself. Partly, I'm curious. I want to know the ideas and trends emerging from the top schools. It's an attempt to stay in touch, to remind myself how to be fresh and innovative like the MBA graduates that will present tonight.

There's also another reason I attend, a reason that's less tangible and harder to put into words. It's been eight years since I finished my own business degree. Then I went straight to managing my father's company. I've become known for my cutting edge corporate decisions, my contemporary workplace vision. But the truth of the matter is that everything was handed to me. I never had to fight for it or earn it like the students we will soon see. I'm ambitious and intelligent, but they have a passion and a fortitude that is intriguing. It inspires me. Most of them will do anything to make it to the top. They want to be me, to have what I have. They look up to me to show them how to get there.

And I look up to them.

Celia would never understand, so I simply say, "You never know what gems you might find." I pick up the portfolio from my lap and flip through it absently as I speak. "Don't blame me, though, when you have to fight to stay awake. And don't even think of trying to get me to leave."

"I won't do either. I'll be a good girl."

My eyes dart to her legs as she crosses one over the other. They're attractive, I'll admit. *She's* attractive. I'd be a liar if I said otherwise. But I am not attracted to her in that way. Not at all. It's likely a symptom of my inability to love, though I do take interest in other women. Women I don't know. I fuck them and have a good time, but that's all. Celia is the only woman besides my mother and sister that I know on any sort of intimate level. And as if she were a family member, I have not a speck of desire for her.

"I'm only here to be with you, anyway," she says now, wrapping her hand around my arm.

I flick my gaze toward her grasp, but don't shrug her away. "Stop saying things like that, Celia." As well as I know her, I've yet to understand her intentions by making statements such as this. She's smart enough to realize that I will never return any affection, and strangely, I don't think that's what she's after. She simply wants that same connection that I do—a kinship with someone who understands the dark fascinations that live inside her.

And I do understand her darkness. In fact, I'm fairly certain I birthed it in Celia. Time and again I try to remember if I saw it residing there before I subjected her to my cruel experiment. I can never be sure of the answer. How could I be expected to identify light when I dwell in total darkness myself? Now, even though I'm *better*, though I've resigned from the game, there is only black everywhere around me.

Still pretending to focus on the portfolio, I feel rather than see her look away.

"I'm sorry," she says in a low voice. "I just…I don't know."

A moment of pity grips me. "You don't have to explain. I understand."

The lights dim, and the president of the business program takes the stage. I drop the folder onto my lap, having garnered very little information about the night's presentations. I won't learn anything from that, anyway. If there's someone worth my time, I won't know until I hear him or her speak.

After the president speaks, the first presentation begins. I know there will be six students in all. That doesn't vary from year to year. Only the top students of the graduating class are invited to present. They are the cream of the crop. Stern isn't Harvard, but it's a Top Ten business school. These students are some of the nation's best.

As I promised, though, the evening is a bore. Also true to her word, Celia doesn't complain. She appears to be deep in thought, most likely concocting her next scam. The temptation to join her in scheming is great, but I push against the pull and focus my attention on the event. International trade seems to be the topic of the night, but there are a few differentiations—one talk is about the newest tax codes and how they can better benefit corporations. Snore. Another presents a variation on an old business model. It's an original idea, but not practical.

By the time the fifth student finishes, I've met my limit. I nudge Celia out of her reverie. "I'm ready to go," I begin to say, but stop myself before I get the words out. The woman ascending the stairs to the stage has caught my eye, and all thoughts of leaving disappear. Something about the way she moves is captivating—the wiggle of her hips suggests an undercurrent of sexuality, and her back is straight with confidence.

Then she turns toward the audience, and my breathe catches. Even here, twelve rows away, I can tell she's the most beautiful woman I've ever seen. Her dark brown hair falls just so around her face, accentuating sharp cheekbones. Her eyes are dark. Her short dress reveals long, lean legs. The modest cleavage of her outfit can't hide perfectly plump tits.

There's something else—something about her carriage that makes me sit up and take notice. And she hasn't even spoken yet.

"What?" Celia whispers, responding to the jab I'd given her. Or perhaps to the way I gasped at the sight of the angel before us.

"Nothing. Never mind." Our conversation was in conjunction with the introduction and I missed what the presenter's name is or what she's meant to talk about. I can't move my eyes for even a moment to check the program.

I'm mesmerized. Truly mesmerized.

She takes her place at the podium and begins her presentation, and I half expect my attraction to her to fade the minute her mouth opens. The opposite occurs. The sound of her voice sends a jolt through me, and I straighten in my seat. Her tone and demeanor ooze passion and authority, and also a touch of caution. For several minutes, I barely focus on her words. I'm too beguiled by her mere presence—by her smile, by her body language, by the way she furrows her brow when she refers to her notes.

And there's an air about her that I'm drawn to immediately. I sense that she's been downtrodden, but not broken. That she's known pain but emerged whole and strong. I scoff at myself—how can I know that from a few minutes of business talk? I can't. But I also can't shake the feeling that it's true. It attracts me more than anything else about her.

When I finally do catch her speech, I'm further impressed. Her topic is simple—print marketing in a digital age—but she's approached it with brilliant practicality, and I'm sure that every exec in the room is going to pursue her at the meet and greet after.

I make it a point to find her first. This, precious, precious, gem.

"Alayna Withers," Celia says quietly at my side.

"What?" I shake myself from the presenter long enough to see Celia reading from the portfolio folder.

She nods toward the stage. "Her name is Alayna Withers."

I bristle, irritated that Celia has noticed my interest. At the same time, a surge of gratification spreads across my chest. *I have her name!* It's a small thing and unfortunately everyone in the room has it as well. But I cling to it, this one bit of information I have about her. I say it quietly to myself. Let the sound of it settle in my ears. Let the texture of it swirl on my tongue.

The room is still dim, the stage the only place illuminated, but I feel the cloak of darkness around me start to dissipate.

Suddenly, I see light.

— CHAPTER —

TWO

Before

"Your serve is terrible," I shouted to Mirabelle. Overall, my sister had gotten better since last summer. The private lessons she'd had throughout the year had strengthened both her backhand and her volley. Not that I planned on giving her the satisfaction of telling her I'd noticed.

Mirabelle's eyes sparkled as she bounced the tennis ball in front of her. "My serve is fine. I'm winning, aren't I?"

She'd won the first match because I'd gone easy on her. I hadn't expected her to be as good as she was. "Only because I'm paying more attention to your god-awful posture than to the ball."

Her lips curved up. "That's your problem. You're easily distracted." She tossed the ball up, but instead of swinging at it, she let her racket fall to her side and her attention shot elsewhere. "Oh, hey. I didn't see you there."

I followed Mirabelle's gaze and found Celia leaning against the side wall of our private court.

Well, what do you know?

I wasn't sure yet if I was glad to see her or not, but when she grinned, I returned her smile easily. I hadn't known she was in the Hamptons, but I wasn't surprised to see her. Of course, she'd stop by. Even if our mothers weren't the best of friends, Celia would find a reason to see me.

"I was enjoying your game," she said to my little sister, but her eyes never left me. "Hope you don't mind."

"Yeah, well, it's over now. Huds, we can play later." Mirabelle stomped to my side of the court where she left her racket cover and began packing up.

"Mirabelle," I said, low, with a hint of warning. I knew she didn't care for Celia, but she didn't need to be nasty.

She ignored me. Giving me a final scowl, she said, "Enjoy the rest of the day with your girlfriend." Then she took off through the opening in the hedges toward the main house.

"I'm not his girlfriend," Celia shouted after her. Then she turned to me, a fist on her hips. "Why didn't you correct her?"

I tilted my head to the side, waiting for my neck to pop. Honestly, I was surprised that Celia *had* corrected Mirabelle. I would have thought she'd be happy about the title. As for me, I preferred to let people believe what they wanted to believe. It made life far more interesting.

But my fascination with human behavior was one I kept to myself, so instead I said, "Mirabelle's a hopeless romantic. She'll form her own opinion no matter what I say."

Celia looked back after Mirabelle for a moment then walked toward me as I wiped sweat off my forehead with a towel. "She still doesn't like me." Disappointment was evident in her voice.

"Sorry," I said. I suspected that only-child Celia had always sought after Mirabelle as a surrogate sister. Our families were certainly entwined enough to make a bond between them seem inevitable. For some reason, it hadn't happened. Why was that? Curiosity tugged at my subconscious, but I forced it away. I would ponder that further at another time.

Celia didn't appear to think there was anything worth pondering. "She's fourteen. I get it. I wish it were different, but I understand."

"She needs to learn some manners."

"And you need to learn to relax. I'm fine. I don't have to be her friend. I'm your friend." She peered up at me with doubt in her eyes. "At least, I think we're still friends. It's been nine months since I left for San Francisco and not a single peep from you. What's up with that?"

I shrugged as if my neglect had been accidental. It wasn't in the least. Before Celia left for college, she'd made it clear that she was interested in more than friendship. I was not. I'd decided it was best not to lead her on. Not because I cared about how she felt, but because her infatuation was a hassle. I'd ignored her phone calls and deleted her few emails without so much as skimming them.

Yes, I was an asshole. This wasn't news to me.

Now, though, I was surprised at how good it felt to see her. Not in any romantic way, but in a familiar way. She was family. She was home.

I scratched along my jaw, deciding not to answer her question outright. Against my better judgment, I extended an invitation instead. "Millie should have lunch ready soon. I can grab a shower and then we can catch up over sandwiches."

Celia frowned. "Actually, I can't today. I only got away for a few minutes."

I raised an inquisitive brow. Why would she stop by if she couldn't stay?

She didn't expound. Instead, she asked, "Will you be here all summer?"

For as long as I could remember, both of our families spent the summer in the Hamptons. It seemed strange to think she'd assume differently. But I supposed, being older, things changed. I had already been thinking it was time to get a place of my own. I didn't need to spend all my time off from school with my parents. This would likely be my last season at Mabel Shores.

"Yes," I answered. "Will you?"

"I will. And I'd like to see you." She cleared her throat and moved her focus to her shoes. "I came by today to tell you something. Um, something that I thought might make it easier for you to want to see me again."

I folded my arms across my chest. She had me intrigued. "What is it?"

She forced her eyes up to mine. "I thought you should know that I'm seeing someone. I have been all year. We're quite serious." She fidgeted, obviously nervous. Did she think I'd be jealous?

"All right," I said. "Congratulations." I was schooled in how to respond in situations such as these though I didn't feel congratulatory. I felt nothing.

She took a deep breath. "I thought that might be the reason you hadn't returned any of my messages. Because you were worried that I…that I still…"

I cocked my head, fascinated with how she'd finish the sentence or if she'd finish it at all.

She didn't, and after a moment of awkward silence, I couldn't help myself. I wanted to push her, wanted to see what she'd say, what she'd do. "That you still liked me?"

Her cheeks went scarlet. *Interesting.* "Yes. You did know, then."

I laughed. "Everyone knew, Celia."

She shook her head as if reconciling herself with the idea. "Okay, everyone knew. But it was a silly schoolgirl crush. I'm over it now. I have Dirk, and—"

"Dirk? That's his name?" Immediately I pictured a long-haired hippy, though Celia would never be serious about anyone not in her social class. It wasn't in her. He was likely proper and well-mannered and from lots of money, just as she was.

"Be nice, Hudson." But her admonishment came with a smile. "Anyway. I have Dirk and I'm really in love with him. I think he might be the one." She blushed again, and this time I could see that she was indeed over me.

Fascinating.

"That's…great." This time, I wasn't really sure what else to say. Wasn't certain what Celia wanted me to say.

She seemed to sense I needed more. "So you and I can go back to being friends. No more weird puppy dog eyes from me. And it shouldn't be a big deal. Okay?" She smiled hesitantly, hopefully, as if my answer were important to her. As if my *friendship* were something she thought was important.

I licked my lips, salty from my earlier exertion. There was no reason to say no. And I did enjoy Celia's company. "Sure."

"Awesome!" Her relief was tangible. "I'll call you. Maybe we can play tennis later this week? Or take the Jet Skis out or something?"

"Sounds good." It also sounded dull. But she was proposing a routine summer in the Hamptons. It was what we always did and doing it again made sense. I'd find something else to occupy my boredom.

A moment of silence passed between us until it extended past comfortable to awkward. "Well, then," Celia said, shielding her eyes from the midday sun, "I'd better be going."

Chivalry returned to me. "I'll walk you out." I draped the towel around my neck and gathered my racket cover. Then we started up the path to the main house.

We were quiet as we traveled. I escorted her all the way to the circle drive where she'd left her car parked. After opening her door for her, I leaned in to give her a peck on the cheek. This was standard for us. She was, after all, practically my sibling.

She placed a hand on my arm, her expression melancholy. "Thank you, Hudson. See you soon."

I watched after her as she drove off, wondering about the change in the dynamics of our relationship. Our mothers had been best friends since we were toddlers. Every major holiday and family function had been spent with the Werners. Our parents had even enrolled us in the same elite private high school. We knew each other well, though I seriously doubted that we'd have become more than acquaintances had we not been thrown together as we were.

She should have been the perfect pairing for me. A match made in heaven. We both came from money, were already close. Yet, I had never had the slightest inclination toward her. What was wrong with me that I couldn't feel anything for her? For anyone?

"Do you like her?" Mirabelle's small voice questioned from behind me.

I turned to find her sitting on the front steps, her arms wrapped around her knees.

My jaw tensed with irritation. I didn't share the emptiness of my emotions with anyone. "It's really none of your business if I do." I strode past her, into the house.

Mirabelle jumped up and followed close at my heels. "She's not for you, Hudson. She's petty and shallow and not good for you at all."

I kept walking, heading to the main staircase.

Mirabelle continued after me. "And you don't like her. I can see it in your eyes. You have no interest in her at all."

That was true, but it intrigued me to think my sister had noticed. What else did she see? What did she know about me? I stopped mid-step and turned to her. "If you already know I don't like her, then why did you ask?"

"I wanted to be sure you knew too."

Well, I do. I didn't say it aloud. I turned away from her and jogged the remaining steps to the upper floor, then disappeared into my room.

For the rest of the day, I couldn't stop thinking about Celia and her supposed boyfriend. My chest knotted tighter and tighter as I spun the information in my mind. It wasn't jealousy—honestly I didn't care one way or another about her love life. It was intrigue. Obsessive intrigue. It wasn't the first time I'd felt it, nor, I was certain, would it be the last.

The idea of love and affection consumed me. I studied it on every occasion that I could. I didn't understand it. I'd never been *in love*. I didn't believe it was even a real thing. I wasn't virtuous in any way, nor was I inexperienced. I'd dated a few girls. Or rather, I'd taken girls out to dinner and a movie with the sole intent of fucking them afterward. Sometimes I skipped the dinner and the movie and simply fucked. But I'd never had any inclination to spend any real time with anyone. I'd never had *feelings* for them.

And even though Celia had set her sights on me the year before, I'd never assumed that she felt anything deeper than the silly crush she spoke of. We'd both been cut from the same cloth. We knew the ridiculousness behind romantic notions.

Or so I'd thought.

Now, she said she'd found *the one*. The idea boggled me.

It also challenged me.

What was it that made someone think they loved another? Could the emotion be manipulated? Forced? I decided an experiment was in order.

It was unfortunate that the results might not be too favorable for Celia. But on the other hand, if love was truly a myth as I believed, maybe I was simply saving her from a lie.

I was sunning with my laptop by the pool when Celia phoned me the next day to set up a date to get together. Feigning previous plans, I pushed our meeting off until the next week. I needed time to plan before I saw her. I was meticulous with my experiments, and this time would be no different.

I tapped my fingers rhythmically on the keyboard as I schemed. After the failure of my last study, I was eager to find success. Perhaps *failure* was too harsh of a word. My results hadn't met my hypothesis, but I'd still gained information from the experiment, inconclusive as it was. I'd gotten the idea for the study after two classmates, Andrew and Jane, became engaged. They seemed to be lost for each other, dizzy in their haze of lust which they'd most likely mistaken for something more. I wondered—if they believed they were close enough that they should marry, did it mean their bond was unbreakable?

I set out to find the answer.

The three of us shared enough classes that it was easy to flirt with Jane in front of her fiancé. I did so casually at first, expecting some sort of reaction from Andrew. When none came, I upped my game. I touched Jane when we spoke, brushed my fingers against hers, played with her hair. I invaded her space. I whispered suggestive things to her—hell, dirty-as-fuck things that made her blush and her nipples stand at attention. A whole semester of this behavior and neither Jane nor Andrew had told me to stop. Shouldn't there have been accusations? If not at me, then at each other? Were they spoken behind my back, unbeknownst to me?

Or did the couple truly have enough trust and affection for each other to withstand jealousy?

Or maybe they were looking for a threesome.

The lack of a conclusive answer was why I'd considered the experiment a bust. This time I wouldn't settle for ambiguous results. Which meant I better start with a solid hypothesis.

I opened up my digital journal and started a new section which I titled *The Rebound*. It was a perfect follow-up to *The Engagement*. That study had tried to break up a couple without any prior history on my part. This time, the subject, Celia, had a prior infatuation with me. The question was, and I typed it in as I constructed it, *Could a prior infatuation affect the status of a new relationship, if the previous object of affection suddenly returned the emotion?*

Next, I entered in my hypothesis: *If the subject truly believes the affection is returned, then yes.*

How would I be able to tell if I'd succeeded? I paused to watch my younger brother, Chandler, do a flip off the side of the pool as I considered. If Celia believed I was interested in her she'd likely either a) tell me to back off, b) consent to a summer affair, or c) break up with Dirk.

I would not sleep with Celia—that was non-negotiable. I couldn't have sex with women that didn't attract me, and I most certainly wouldn't have sex with a woman that knew me personally. That would mean letting her get close. And I never let anyone get close.

The only success, I decided, would be a break-up in the relationship.

I entered that into my document and sat back.

Now, I simply had to figure out my intended process. This was my favorite part—coming up with the plan. My heart rate kicked up a notch with the thrill. I'd have to put some study into it. Casual flirting would not cut it with this subject—she was only *The Subject* in my eyes now; to think of her as anything else would weaken my objectivity. I'd have to make a real attempt to show affection. It would be a challenge, but with true effort, I was sure I could win the subject over. Perhaps I could watch a few romance movies. Or ask Mirabelle—she seemed to think she was an expert on romance.

As if summoned by my thoughts, Mirabelle plopped on a deck chair next to me, her pink and black bikini seeming very mature for a girl her age. At least we were in the privacy of our own backyard. Were we to have company, she'd be wearing a cover-up, if I had any say in the matter. And I always had a say in the matter.

"Whatcha doing?" She peered toward my computer.

I swiveled slightly so that my screen was out of her view. "Nothing of importance," I said. Then I changed my tune. "Actually, I'm working on a project. For a friend. Perhaps you could help?"

"Sure." She grabbed the bottle of sunscreen that I'd brought out earlier and began slathering it over her petite body. "What is it?"

While I was sure she meant to sound aloof, I noticed the hint of excitement in her few words. If there were any reason in the world to learn how to love, it would be for Mirabelle. She adored me, as many younger sisters adored their older siblings. But unlike other big brothers, I did not deserve it. Yet she still persevered in her faith and affection. For that alone, I endeavored to try with her in ways I refused to try with anyone else. I went out of my way to give her attention—played tennis with her, took her for rides when the chauffer wasn't available, protected her from our mother's drunken ridicule. Asking her advice was just as much about boosting her as it was about helping me.

"Well," I began, "he wants to know the best way to woo a girl—"

Her eyes widened in surprise. "And he asked you? Anyone with half a brain knows you know nothing about wooing anyone."

I bit back the sting of her statement. It was true after all. "Exactly. So I'm asking you."

"This isn't really for you, is it? You aren't interested in someone, are you?" She stopped rubbing the lotion into her arm and stared at me point blank. "You aren't trying to woo Celia, are you?"

I made it a point to never lie. Even in my experiments, I had vowed to remain truthful. It was the way I maintained a bit of dignity despite my manipulative actions. So I spun my answer. "Now why would I try to woo Celia? You said yourself she wasn't for me."

"Just making sure." She returned to massaging her skin. "Let's see, women love the artsy, creative types of attention. Like write her a poem or draw her portrait."

I blinked. I wasn't artsy in the least. "Go on."

"Then there's the easy stuff—sending flowers, buying jewelry, giving gifts—"

I typed as she talked.

"But those are really lame if you don't personalize them."

I looked up from my screen. "What do you mean by *personalize*?"

"Don't just give roses. Those are boring. Give flowers that you know she'll like or that mean something to her. The jewelry should be unique to her or something she's admired."

God, it sounded like romanticizing was going to require more detailed investigation than I'd expected.

"Basically, all a woman wants is for you to spend time getting to know her," Mirabelle said, confirming my thoughts.

I chuckled. "As if you know what it's like to be a woman."

"Shut up. A girl, then." She smirked at me, an expression she had down to a T. "You know girls are just miniature women, don't you?"

"I've heard that somewhere." I scratched the back of my neck, noticing sweat had gathered while I'd been sitting in the sun. "Then all I—" I caught myself and started again. "All my friend has to do is spend time with this girl?"

"And then show that he's noticed who she is." She frowned. "Does that make any sense?"

"It does." Actually, noticing people was one of my talents. While trying to understand basic human emotion and behavior, I'd learned to study people with a fine eye. The application of my finds was what needed work. "I'm sure my friend will appreciate this advice."

Mirabelle put on her sunglasses and settled back into her chair. "I wish it were for you though. You'd make an awesome boyfriend."

I forced a smile, swallowing the nasty taste in my mouth. "Tell you what— I'll save the notes for when I need them."

I needed them now, but not the way Mirabelle assumed. I'd never need them that way. She was a bright kid, but she was absolutely wrong about one thing—I wouldn't make an awesome boyfriend.

But she'd never know that. I never planned to get close enough to a woman for her to find out.

— CHAPTER —
THREE

After

It's been two days since the symposium at Stern, and I'm still thinking of the brunette beauty who entranced me that night. I've returned to the portfolio over and over to read her bio and stare at her picture. Her face is ingrained in my mind and I've not even seen her close up in real life.

I had *tried* to see her, of course. After ditching Celia, I'd rushed to the meet and greet, eager to find Alayna Withers. I intended to offer her a job on the spot. Whatever position she wanted, I'd give it to her. It was completely crazy and like nothing I'd ever done before, but there was something about her. I couldn't shake it. I couldn't lose the desire to know her.

Then she didn't show for the meet and greet. To say I was disappointed was putting it mildly. I was also enraged and confused. Enraged because she'd wasted our time. *My* time. Who didn't show to meet with the top professionals in the business? There were six candidates and ten execs. She would have received an offer. Hell, she would have received five offers. Ten, even. And I would have topped each and every one to make her mine.

There was where my confusion lay—why did I give a shit? I'm not a completely emotionless man, but nearly. The feelings I do have are tame, controllable. Practical. This irrational desperation for someone I don't even know—it rattled me. It rattles me now, these days later when my desperation has increased.

Never in my life have I felt this way about someone.

Is it sexual? An overwhelming need to get laid? It has been a few weeks since I've had a woman in my bed. Maybe longer. I haven't had the interest lately.

But now, as I study her picture and remember her assuredness, her vivacious-ness, my cock stirs.

I try to convince myself that's what my interest is—physical. Or that it's her mind. Maybe that's it—I'm intrigued by her ideas, her innovative way of thinking, so much so that it arouses me. Because what else can explain her effect on me?

I'm so consumed with figuring out the answer, so in need of exploring my fascination, that I called my investigator earlier in the day to look into her fur-ther. I told myself it was about business. Perhaps she didn't show up at the meet and greet because she'd already been offered a job. If I find her, I can counter.

But I know it's more than that because if she doesn't accept a job, I'll have to find another way to get close to her. I need to know if this preoccupation has staying power. It fleetingly occurs to me that the intensity of my fixation is very similar to the way I used to feel when starting a new experiment. I dismiss that notion immediately. This is different because for once I'm not interested in another person's emotions, but rather my own.

It's about damn time.

Though I'm not sure I like it.

Pinching the bridge of my nose, I lean forward at my desk and try to erase Alayna from my thoughts. My efforts are interrupted by the buzz of my secretary. "Yes, Patricia?" *Maybe it's my investigator now.*

"Your two o'clock is here. Dr. Alberts."

"Fuck." I hadn't meant to say that aloud. "Fine. Thank you. Send him in." I've forgotten about my appointment with Alberts, even though I've been seeing him regularly for over two years now. The truth is I don't want to remember my appointment. He's helped—I wouldn't be able to resist the temptations that I do if it weren't for him—but lately I'm restless. I miss the excitement of my old life. My days now are drab and endlessly the same. Perhaps it's why I'm so intrigued with Alayna Withers. Seeing her that night, I felt something for the first time in years. For the first time since I quit playing the game.

I stand and circle my desk to greet Dr. Alberts when he walks in. Though I don't need to, I gesture to the sitting area then take a seat on the edge of the leather couch, crossing a leg over the other. Alberts sits in the armchair as usual. This is our routine. He'll suggest I lie down, I'll politely decline. He'll pull out his electronic notepad and jot notes when I answer his prompts—the same prompts he gives me week after week. *How are you feeling? Are there any new life stressors? How will you deal with those? Have you had any inclinations to play?*

I'm bored before he's even begun, and I can't bear to go through the moves yet again.

He must sense my mood—or my constant shifting gives my anxiousness away—because he varies from the ritual immediately.

"What's on your mind, Hudson?" he asks.

I run the tips of my fingers across my forehead, contemplating the answer. I could blame my anxiety on work. There is much to be concerned with there, such as the rumblings at Plexis, one of my smaller subsidiaries, where I fear I'm losing control of the board. Before the Stern symposium, that was my major focus. After, Plexis is barely on my radar. How can I concentrate on silly business when I can't get the thought of deep brown eyes and a silky confident voice out of my brain?

That's what's on my mind—her.

But what could I tell Alberts about Alayna Withers? About a student I saw for twenty minutes at a business school event? Talking with him is supposed to help sort out my emotions, but these emotions are too vague and unidentifiable. Too intense and strange.

Instead, I choose to mention the detail of my last few days that will interest him the most. "I saw Celia."

"You did?" Alberts shows his alarm with only a slight raise of a gray eyebrow. "What were the circumstances of that encounter?"

"I'd like to say it was innocent. But it wasn't entirely." I run my hands through my hair while he waits for me to continue. "She called me. She's been using my identity to play someone—an employee of my sister's." I cringe thinking about how close to home Celia's game was with Stacy. And how I did nothing to stop it until the other night.

"Were you aware she was doing this?"

"Yes." I answer his next question before he has the chance to ask. "No, I didn't encourage it, but I was aware." I stand, needing to pace as I talk. "Celia asked me to help her wrap up the game. I agreed. I told her where I'd be and when. She made the arrangements for the rest to happen."

Glancing toward Alberts, I expect to see a look of disapproval. It's not there. The man is as careful with his emotions as I am.

Next he'll want to know why I agreed to help. It's an easy enough answer—the game needed to end. I didn't appreciate my name being pulled into her scheme and being available for her staged embrace was the easiest way to end it.

But that's not what he wants to know. "How did it make you feel? Playing again, after so long?"

I pause, considering his question. There had been a certain spark, a thrill that had run through my body as I'd kissed my childhood friend. Not because of the woman I'd been kissing or even because I'd been kissing at all, but because I knew the effect I was having on Stacy—on Celia's intended target. In the moment, I wanted to immerse myself in the feeling, wanted to grab it and hold onto it. It was feeling, for God's sake. Feeling, where I'd been void. All I'd have to do was stop fighting the impulse, and I could have the excitement back in my life. With Celia there, egging me on as she always did, it would have been so easy to fall back into our old patterns, to resume our games.

But all it took was the look in Stacy's eyes, the devastation she felt at my supposed rejection to remind me that my entertainment came at the price of others' emotions.

"There was a rush," I answer honestly. "Then it was over, and until now I hadn't given it a second thought." Even without the reminder of the consequences of the game, I would have abandoned any notion to play again when I went to the symposium. That brief spark with Celia had been completely obscured by the charge that jolted through me at the sight of Alayna Withers.

Alberts clears his throat and I look to find he's studying me. He narrows his eyes. "Then you aren't concerned that you'll be pulled back into the game?"

I let out a huff. I'm always concerned I'll be pulled back into the game. But am I worried that Celia will pull me back? "No, I'm not."

"Do you plan to see her again?"

My eyes widen when, for a second, I think that "her" refers to the brunette that's plaguing my thoughts.

But that's not who Alberts means.

"No, I don't plan to see Celia again." She'd like me to. She asks me over and over. I see her enough at family events as it is. Her presence isn't a temptation to me as my therapist believes, but seeing her is still not a good idea. She's a painful reminder of all the wrongs I've done in my life. Of all the wrongs I've done to her.

I resume my pacing, hoping not to go down that path of conversation today, not wanting to revisit my past.

"Hudson, sit down."

I'm surprised he hasn't requested this before. I sit, crossing my ankle over my bouncing knee. "Sorry. I have a lot on my plate at the moment." I take a quiet but deep breath that does nothing to relieve me.

Dr. Alberts leans back, a distinct contradiction to my own tense posture. "I don't sense that your anxiety has to do with your meeting with Celia. Is there something else you aren't telling me?"

It's on the tip of my tongue to bring up my strange reaction to Alayna Withers, but I'm again lost on how I'd phrase it. "It's nothing. Work is stressful." Work is always stressful.

Too late I realize I've opened the door to an old argument.

"I hate to beat a dead horse, Hudson, but if we met in my office instead of here, you'd have a chance to escape that stress, if even for a short time."

I throw him a glare. "If I had to meet in your office, I'd never pull myself away."

"That's a problem, Hudson. I've tolerated it for the past two years, but I feel we're at a point in your therapy that this will no longer work. If you want to continue with your recovery, you need to make it your priority. You must decide that pulling yourself away is more important, that your mental health is more important than the work you leave behind."

I feel my jaw twitch. I agree that my therapy is at a standstill. He's likely right that to progress further, I'd need to rearrange my current priority list. However, that's not going to happen. I have no desire to pull myself away. I don't believe that I am more important than the work I leave behind. I don't believe that I am more important than *anything*. And while working with Alberts has kept me from ruining other people's lives, it hasn't given my own life any more dimension than it had. I still haven't found a way to fill the emptiness that resides inside. At least the game was enough to distract me from that. Now I'm ever aware of my hollowness, of my inability to feel more than a dull hum of emotion.

In the past, when the topic to meet in his office instead of mine has come up, I've persuaded him to leave things the way they are. Today, I sense he won't let it go. And I'm not sure that I want to fight him any longer. I have the tools I need to continue on as I have without seeing him any longer. Could he fix me if I gave in? If I made more of the effort that he suggests I haven't before? I don't know. That's what I must decide. Either I play it his way, or I don't need him. I'm not ready to give a firm answer.

"Touché," I say. "I concede that this arrangement is no longer working. Perhaps we should end our relationship altogether." It's a manipulation technique, I know. Like a child pouting. If I don't get to play my way, I won't play at all.

But my psychologist is too good to fall for my tricks. "If that's what you want to do. You know this only works if you're a willing participant."

Part of me wants to cut him out of my life and move on, but I'm not comfortable with impulse-driven decisions. "I need to think about it."

"Do that. If you decide you want to meet with me again—in my office—than call my secretary and make an appointment." He stands, our session clearly over even though we still have another thirty minutes on the clock.

I suppose there's no point in continuing if I have no real interest in progress.

I get to my feet and shake his hand. "Thank you, Doctor."

"I hope I see you again," he says, the twinkle in his eye more of the look a grandfather would share with his grandson than a psychologist with his patient. He's fond of me. I wonder what he could possibly see in me to feel that way.

Maybe I haven't given him the chance I should.

Though I'm more concerned that if I did give him the chance, he'd still be unable to help me.

He's almost at the door when he turns to me. "Remember, Hudson, true progress only happens with work." With those words, he leaves me.

I shake my head in frustration. Of course I remember that. I've worked my ass off to get Pierce Industries to what it is today. If he thinks I don't understand the value of hard work, then he has no understanding of what I do, of what I am. But in the back of my mind, I know that he's talking about a different kind of work, and while I've already spent some time in the department of self-repair, I'm not sure that I'm willing to spend more.

At this particular moment of my life, the only thing I want to spend time on is finding out more about Alayna Withers.

The minute Alberts is gone, I pick up my phone and dial my secretary. "Were there any calls?" She knows not to interrupt me when he's here, and I'm hoping my investigator has called.

"No, sir."

I give a quick thank you and hang up, pausing only a moment before I'm calling him myself.

"Jordan here," he answers on the first ring. The man used to be Special Ops and I've found his skills are beneficial in many situations.

"Have you found anything out yet?" I realize I'm being impatient. I've only given him a few hours to look, after all.

"Not much. I'm still waiting for her medical history and complete background check."

Her medical history can't possibly inform me of anything useful, but the background check might. "What do you know so far?"

"The basics. Her full name is Alayna Reese Withers, born and raised in Boston. Her parents died in a car accident when she was sixteen. She lives between Lexington and Third, near the Waldorf. She got her BA in business at Boston University and is set to graduate from NYU with a Masters in Business next month. Right now she's working as an assistant manager at The Sky Launch."

The Sky Launch? I wrack my brain trying to place the name. "The nightclub?"

"Yep."

She can't possibly be planning to work at a nightclub after her graduation. She has to have another offer. "Can you tell if anyone else has pulled her information recently?" If she's got a job waiting, they'll have checked into her.

I hear muffled movement as if Jordan's cradling the phone on his shoulder while he looks for the answer. "The system says there was one other pull of her credit history. Yesterday."

"Dammit." I wonder which of my competitors was lucky enough to earn her *yes.* "Find out who ordered that." Then I'll prepare my counter proposition.

"On it."

"And call me the minute anything new comes in."

"Yes, Mr. Pierce."

I've just hung up when Patricia calls me again. I pick up the receiver to answer when my office door is flung open and Celia parades in.

"I'm sorry, sir," my secretary says in my ear. "I was calling to announce her and she just walked in."

"It's okay. I'll take care of her." I hang up, cursing under my breath. Celia's the last person I'm in the mood for, but Patricia isn't any sort of bouncer.

Celia slinks in and half-sits on the far corner of my desk. "You'll take care of me, will you?"

I ignore her suggestive tone. "Two days in one week, Celia. To what do I owe the *pleasure?*" I put enough bitterness in my final word that she can't mistake that there is anything pleasant about her visit at all.

Immediately I feel a pang of guilt. It's not Celia's fault that I no longer want to be around her, rather it's my fault. All of it, my fault.

She doesn't let my tone ruffle her. "Oh, come on, Hudsy. Don't be that way. I'm not the enemy."

No, she's not. I'm the enemy. She'll never see it, though, so it's my job to keep the distance. "Why are you here?"

There's a gleam in her eye when she smiles. "I have something that I know is going to interest you."

"Oh?" I sound bored, and I am.

"I'm serious. You're going to want in on this."

In on this? She can only be proposing a game. "Celia, I've told you, I don't play anymore." I shift my focus toward my computer screen, pretending to go back to whatever I was doing before she arrived.

She doesn't get that I'm dismissing her—or doesn't care. "You've told me, you've told me. Now I'm telling you, you'll want in on this."

I should kick her out now, pour out the bottle before I've even taken a sip, so to say, but I can't help myself. Even with my attention turned, my pulse has quickened and the moisture in my mouth has increased. Her eagerness is contagious. And I'm curious. Too curious.

I can't let her know. "I won't want in on anything. But since you're here," I casually turn back to face her, "what is it you're planning?"

Her grin kicks up a notch. "Look at you. You're dying to know. Your eyes blazed the minute you realized what I was offering."

I don't try to deny it—I *am* interested and even with schooled features, she can see it. I hate how well I've taught her to read people. I hate when she uses her knowledge to read *me*.

It pisses me off enough that I almost send her packing.

But curiosity wins out. She hasn't tempted me with her games in quite some time. Why now?

"Out with it, Ceeley." I cringe inwardly at the slip of her childhood nickname. She'll think I mean something by it that I don't. It's why I hate nicknames so much.

She stands and starts rummaging through her bag. "It's a basic scenario—make the girl fall for you and then deny her, watching her fall to pieces."

It had been our old favorite. No matter how many times we'd performed the experiment, it never failed to interest me. It was a marvelous study in the emotion called love, but somehow it never gave me any of the answers I was seeking.

I pretend the idea doesn't pique me in the slightest. "How original. What about that did you think would interest me?"

She smiles with confidence. "The girl."

I raise a questioning brow, but instead of answering me verbally, she retrieves a file folder from her bag and sets it on the desk in front of me. Then she waits for me to study it.

With a reluctant breath, I flip the cover open and move my eyes from Celia to the top sheet inside the file. Deep brown eyes and a warm smile meet me.

Celia's right—it is the girl that interests me. And I know before she says anything more that I will hear her out to the end. Because if Celia has the answer to getting closer to Alayna Withers, I am in.

All the way.

— CHAPTER —

FOUR

There are other pictures in the file Celia gathered and I want to survey them all, want to memorize every detail of Alayna Withers' expressions, her postures. I don't though, because I'm very aware of Celia's hawk-eyed stare. She's waiting for me to read the reports included, and I want to—I want to absorb it all.

But there's something else nagging at me to close the folder and end this now despite my overwhelming desire to act otherwise. I'm supposed to abstain from these games. That's not what's halting me. My hesitancy comes from a far more primal source—I don't want to share. I'm already irritated that Celia's learned things that I want to know. I wish I could horde the findings to myself, decide how I want to handle my fascination with Alayna on my own. Obviously it's too late for that, but I can try to dissuade my former partner in crime from pursuing this further.

I shut the file without reading on. It's harder than I imagine, still I manage it with as much indifference as I can muster. "Not interested."

I slide the folder across the desk to where Celia has perched herself. My pulse quickens as my fingers let go of Alayna's profile. I'm itching to scrutinize it with an obsessive pull that I haven't felt in years. *Jordan will find the same information,* I remind myself. I can wait. Patience has always been one of my most admirable traits.

Celia takes the folder into her hands. I try not to focus on it any longer, but my eyes flit to it more than once.

She stands. "I guess I was wrong then." Her tone says she doesn't believe that for a minute. "I'll have to keep this little prize for myself. You really are out of the game, aren't you?"

Celia's almost as good at manipulating as I am. It is both a blessing and a curse that I know her as well as I do—I can predict every move before she makes it. Unfortunately, she can also predict mine. She's the greatest chess opponent I've ever had.

I try to discern her next move now, or, rather, the move she predicts I'll make. She's letting me off too easy, which means she's not really letting me off at all. She wants me to ask her what she means to do with Alayna, and since that's what she wants, it's the one question I can't ask. Yet it's the one burning at me most.

On top of what I know she wants me to do, I have my own agenda: Whatever she has planned, I have to stop her. It's not an altruistic motive—it goes back to the not wanting to share. I don't want Celia to do anything to Alayna Withers because I want her all to myself. What I want her for has yet to be determined. I don't have any urge to play the woman. But I yearn to connect with her in some way and whatever that way is, it's not to include Celia.

So I have my work cut out for me in how I respond to my old friend. Terminate her plans without seeming to care what they are. I sit back in my chair and meet her eyes. "I'm out of the game, Celia. You know this. When will you accept that?"

I'm practiced in remaining aloof even when high stakes are on the line. I've often wondered if I could pass a polygraph test without being completely honest. I don't intend to ever be in the position to find out, but it is a curiosity of mine.

Celia laughs. "I'll never accept it, Hudson. I'd have to believe that people could change, and I don't believe that. Not fundamentally. Sooner or later you'll realize that it's killing you. You thrive on your experiments. They gave you reason to live. What else could replace that?"

I've asked myself that same question since I left the game. I've searched for replacements in the best and worst of places—work, exercise, sex, alcohol. Nothing has yet to satisfy me in the way that I need, but I'm not ready to give up looking.

I won't share that with Celia. "Life replaces it, Ceeley. Sooner or later you grow up. Even the people with enough money not to. Even us."

"Huh. You sound even more like Alayna Withers than I thought."

Here's where I slip. I make my grand mistake and I know it before I start speaking and yet I can't stop myself. "What do you mean?"

Celia's eyes light up and I understand exactly why. Just like that, I've shown my interest. I'm exposed and there's nothing I can do to take it back. She's won.

I try to convince myself it's a small victory, but without being aware of exactly where my disclosure will take me, I already know that it's not small at all.

"If you'd read the file," she says calmly, "you'd know."

So I'm stuck. Either I prod her to tell me or I ask for the file back. Both will expose my intrigue further.

Or I could ask her to leave. If I do, I'll have to let it all go. Forget my own agenda. Forget the woman with the brown eyes and the hold she has on me.

That hold, though, is unyielding. I can't let Alayna Withers go just yet. And if I usher Celia out, I will lose my chance to be privy to her plans. I've lost no matter what. Now I have to regain ground, take control of the situation.

I rise and head toward the elevator that goes only to my private loft, offering Celia a one-word directive as I do. "Upstairs." I don't look to see if she follows me. I know she will and sure enough, she slips in beside me just before the doors close.

"Just like old times," she mutters under her breath.

I swallow my disgust. It feels directed at her, but it's actually for me. It sickens me that I'm here again, that we're sneaking away to discuss matters that have nothing to do with business. As we arrive at the loft, I attempt to stifle the notion that this simple action means that I'm conceding to anything. "This is an inappropriate conversation for my office. That's all."

My attempt was futile.

"Exactly," she gloats. "Like all the conversations we've had here in the past."

I can taste the disgust again at the back of my throat, its bitter flavor very real in my mouth. Though the loft had been everything from a fuck pad to a place to crash after a long day at work, it was always first and foremost *our place*— mine and Celia's. Early in our gaming days, it had become our headquarters. We planned and schemed here. Used it as my address to keep our subjects from invading my personal space.

This isn't the same. I brought Celia up here to give her the impression she was winning. To lower her guard. It was my play. Only, the memories throw me off-kilter as well. I'm prepared for that. Sometimes you have to lose a pawn to save your king.

I head to the refrigerator. Without asking, I pull out a bottle of water knowing it's Celia's beverage of choice. I hand it to her and head to the bar to fix my own drink. This encounter requires Scotch. It's fortunate my schedule is free for the rest of the day. I quickly down two fingers of amber liquid and turn back to my guest. "Let me have it."

She sits on the couch. "The file or the story?"

"The file." I'm not interested in her story. It will be twisted to her liking. I take the file from her outstretched hand. She expects me to sit next to her. I take the armchair instead.

I open the folder again with a steady hand. Inside, I have the shakes. I have no idea how I'll be impacted by what's in here, but I fear I'm about to fall down the rabbit's hole. That's how much I'm affected by the mere idea of Alayna Withers. Settled into the leather at my back, I begin to read.

My eyes scan through the documents. There's the usual info—copies of her credit report, her birth certificate, a death certificate for her parents. I don't spend much time on these, only to note her age—twenty-six until November—and confirmation that she does indeed work at The Sky Launch.

Celia's quiet at first as I read. She knows when to give me space and when to push, but she can't help commenting when she sees that I'm looking at a copy of Alayna's latest paystub. "She's staying there. At that night club. Even after graduation."

I won't ask how she knows this. If it's true, and I'm sure it is if Celia's sharing it, I would have found it out too. "Why?" I ask instead.

"She wants to use her MBA to move up in management. Take over the place one day, was my impression." Celia takes a sip of her water. "I chatted with the owner there when I inquired about doing a redesign for them."

Celia's worked fast. I'm impressed.

There's more that she wants to say so I prod her. "And the owner just shared info on his employees?"

"That's the thing. He doesn't want to be the owner anymore. He's selling. Asked me if I knew any buyers and highlighted a couple of his key staff to incentivize anyone with interest. I told him I might know someone." She sits forward, excitement in her features. "There's your in, Hudson."

This news rouses me and I'm already looking for excuses to make the purchase. Isn't it good business? If you can't get the employee you want, then buy the employee's company?

Maybe I made that rule up. But I'm a leader in innovative business practices. It could still be an acceptable principle even if I did make it up.

Still, I'm not moved to action. I don't need Celia to pursue this route if I choose it.

I return my attention to the file.

"There's more," Celia taunts.

I ignore her. Then I see it, the information that Celia's hinting at. A police record. "She's been arrested?"

Celia scoots closer to me on the couch. "She violated a restraining order. Twice. Her brother's a lawyer and got her record buried."

"But you got it unburied. Let me guess—Don Timmons." Don is a cop that Celia's friendly with. She's toyed with his emotions for years, fucking him simply to get information when she wants it. He's out of her social class, something that would matter to her if she ever dated anyone seriously. But Celia doesn't believe in romantic engagements. Not anymore. I taught her that.

She crosses a leg over the other. "Don't look so judgmental. Don got what he wanted out of it."

I'm not sure why I'm judging her. That behavior is well in line with things I've done myself time and time again. Perhaps therapy has had a positive effect on me. Not that I have suddenly developed a conscience. My contemptuous attitude is a defense mechanism—if I don't approve of her actions, it will be less likely that I will want to adopt them for myself.

"Anyway, maybe the arrest is part of the reason she doesn't pursue another occupation. She may not want it uncovered and she knows that any decent corporate screening process would uncover it."

"It's possible." I make a mental note to get Alayna's arrest sealed permanently. I have people more influential than Don Timmons. And I don't have to blow them to get favors. Alayna's too brilliant to let a jaded past keep her from her full potential.

A part of me recognizes I'm lying to myself about my reasons for caring about this woman's future. My motivation isn't centered around her business career or how I might tap into her intellectual skills. I can't name the source of my motivation, though. So I cling to the lie as long as I can.

"On the other hand, the owner went on and on about Alayna's genuine love of her job. She seems to be really passionate about it. She has a vested interest in the club."

That reasoning resonates with me. Alayna Withers did not strike me as someone who lived in fear. Why did she get her degree in the first place? Because she wanted to make the club her own makes sense. She has drive. She has ambition. That was obvious in her presentation. My original shock at her choice of employment has been replaced with complete respect. This I can support. I want to help her reach that goal. It's admirable.

"But the arrest isn't the big thing." Celia brings me back from my thoughts with an enthusiasm that threatens to be contagious. "The cause of it is. She has a mental health history."

I turn once more to the papers in my lap and settle on the last section of documents. They consist of doctors' records, outpatient reports, a certificate of rehabilitation completion. It only takes a few minutes for me to puzzle out her history. Alayna Withers has a compulsive disorder most likely aggravated by the death of both her parents at a young age. She specifically targets her obsessive tendencies on men and relationships, leading to socially abnormal behavior such as stalking, vandalism, and disorderly conduct. According to her rehab report, she's been recovered for the past two years—a similar timeline to my own.

There's a part of me that's appalled by this information. The woman that stood in front of us at Stern was not fragile. She was confident and put together and in control. But I remember that strong sense that there was something more underneath her façade. I realize now that I had so easily recognized it because her carriage was so familiar. Strong on the outside, battling demons on the inside— she was, in so many ways, like me.

I close my eyes and massage the bridge of my nose. Is that the nature of my attraction? A kinship with this woman? I don't believe it's that simple, but, with this new information, I am beyond fascinated with her. I've often questioned if there was any recovery for someone like me. Can I really get better? Do I have any hope for a full and healthy life?

Celia was right. I want to experiment with this one more than any other she's tempted me with in the last two years. Our objectives, though, are in opposition. I can easily guess the nature of Celia's planned game. She wants to see if she can cause the subject to break again. See if Alayna will return to her past behaviors when pushed.

I, on the other hand, do not want to see Alayna Withers break. I want to see her survive. Because if she can, then maybe so can I.

I'm decided now. I won't let Alayna out of my sight. I will pursue her. I will study her. I will not play her.

And so it's time to make sure Celia doesn't either.

I shut the folder, stand, and hand it back to Celia. "This is not a game we're playing." My tone informs her that this is a closed subject.

Celia stands with a sigh. "That's too bad. I had a great scenario. We'd pretend that our parents want us to marry—best lies are closest to the truth, as you always say." In this case, it *is* the truth. "Your mother believes you'll never love anyone so you best marry me. You hire Alayna to be your girlfriend. To convince your parents to leave your romantic life alone. With all the pretending, the girl will fall for you. The scheme will end and we see what happens. Intriguing, no?"

I shake my head. "We're not playing."

"It would give you an excuse to get close to her. Don't deny that you want to. I can read you too, Hudson."

Without looking at her, I motion to the exit. "We're done here, Celia."

She sets her water bottle on the coffee table and starts for the door. "You're done, Hudson," she says as she crosses the room. "I'm not. I can play her without you." She turns back to face me. "But be assured, I *will* play her."

"Not this one, Celia. Find another play." I'm admitting too much interest in Alayna. It can't be helped.

"Yes, this one. The game's already in motion."

Panic grips me. Of course, I don't show it, except for maybe in the tightening of my jaw. "What have you done?"

She's triumphant, but she hides it as well as I hide my emotions. I only see it in the slight widening of her eyes. "I made an offer on the club."

I'm immediately put at ease. "There's been no time. The owner can't have accepted already." I don't tell her that I'll counter.

Celia lifts her chin to deliver her next words. "I told him my offer was good for an hour. He's had no bites in the year that he's had it up for sale. He accepted on the spot."

Fuck!

How did I not see this a mile away? I've grown rusty in my time gone while Celia's grown more calculating. She correctly assumed my weakness in this situation and secured her capital in advance of her approach. Fucking brilliant.

I don't even consider that she's lying. She knows I'll check on her declaration the moment she's left and she wouldn't risk that bluff. Besides, our code has taught us to be honest whenever possible. Practically, it helps keep your lies straight. Also, it makes the games more challenging.

I'm not sure how to move next—that's a rarity for me. I stall for time with a question that might provide me some insight. "Why?" I tilt my head, examining her. "Why do you care if it's this girl or the next?"

"Because *you* care if it's this girl." It's not said with spite. It's honest. It's raw.

I want to hate her in that moment. I want to loathe the way she's trapped me, the way she's baited me. The way she's already destroyed something that interests me like the child on the playground that stomps on the butterfly simply because another child has given it his attention. It's mean.

But I can't hate her. She doesn't intend to be vicious. I'm the one who schooled her to look for vulnerabilities and manipulate them to be advantageous. She knows no other way to connect.

Frankly, I don't know any other way myself. There is a longing for that deep within me. Dr. Alberts hasn't even begun to scrape the surface of that desire, but it is the one thing that keeps me from being completely sociopathic. I don't care for people, but I *want* to.

That's all Celia wants as well. "If you agree to play, I'll let you buy my offer out." She blinks. "Simple as that."

With her checkmate, the ball is in my court. I could still walk away. But Celia will play Alayna Withers. It's not a question in my mind. She's never backed down from a scheme once she's started it.

Then why should I care? I've let Celia play others since I've left our partnership, Stacy being the most recent example. I never made a move to stop that. Why should I now?

But I've already answered that. Because I'm intrigued. I'm bewitched. I'm beguiled. I am obsessed. Maybe this is the best chance to get close to Alayna. And even if I played the game, I wouldn't have to work toward Celia's outcome. I could work toward my own—to not break Alayna. It's the biggest of excuses, but there's nothing in the code about lying to ourselves.

There are other ways to fight Celia, I know. If I really tried, I could come up with another way to thwart her plans.

Knowing that is why I am completely culpable when I surrender so easily. There will be no battle. I will not counter Celia's sly move. I will not attempt to dissuade her from her game. I will not make another appointment with Dr. Alberts. I will not fight.

"How much is your offer on The Sky Launch?"

With a smirk, she gives me the information.

I square my shoulders. If I'm going down, I'll at least do it with pride. "I'll have my financial advisor draw up the check."

"Game on, then?"

My agenda is without point now. Even if Alayna Withers teaches me that people like us can survive, with this step, I've already proven that I can't.

I seal my entrance to hell with my assent. "Game on."

— CHAPTER —
FIVE

Before

"...and if Sherry doesn't tell him that she likes him, then he's going to end up with Marisa. Which is just wrong. Lance should be with Sherry. Don't you think?" Mirabelle poked my bare thigh with her toe. "Are you listening to me, Hudson?"

"I am not." Usually I didn't mind Mirabelle's babble about her friends, simply because the psychology of early teens and their so-called relationships was fascinating. But on this day, I had my own psychology I was working through, namely the psychology of Celia.

Mirabelle huffed in the deck chair next to me "You could at least pretend."

Though evening was approaching, the day was still warm. I'd yet to change from my trunks after my earlier laps in the pool. By now, the sun had dried them and my skin glistened from the sun's rays. This was one of my favorite pastimes this summer—soaking and simmering. Soaking in the rays while I simmered over my project.

"I *could* pretend," I said. "I didn't feel that was fair. If you want to keep chattering, that's fine with me." I moved my sunglasses down to the edge of my nose to look at her straight on. "But if you do, know that you're talking to yourself."

Mirabelle let out a sound of exasperation. "You are so mean!" Then she stormed off toward the house.

I'd thought I'd been pretty patient, actually. I could have told her to shut the fuck up, and I didn't. I looked at my watch. It was nearly six. I gave my mother seven minutes before she came out to scold me for picking on my little sister, on the day of her big party, no less. The berating hadn't even occurred yet and I was already tuning Sophia out. She'd probably already be half-drunk and half-bitch. Strike that, half-drunk and full-bitch. It was my mother, after all.

The party wasn't really as big as she liked to pretend. Not by Hamptons' standards—twenty families, various friends of my parents, including, of course, the Werners. Any minute Warren and Madge would show up with Celia. They were always the first to arrive at our end-of-summer parties. That meant I had very little time to finalize the details of that evening's part of my project. And as September was just beginning, I had only a handful of days to bring the entire experiment to an end.

I pushed my sunglasses into place and lay back down. I'd come far with Celia since I'd begun my study, though the progress was slow. Taking Mirabelle's advice to get to know The Subject, I'd spent hours upon hours with Celia. We'd played tennis almost daily and I'd taken her sailing on more than one occasion. She was maintaining her long-distance relationship with Dirk, and I let her talk about him to her heart's desire. I encouraged their affair, praised the silly tokens of love he sent her on a weekly basis, repeatedly remarked on the positive effect he'd seemed to have on her.

My interest and support put her at ease. She'd let her guard down.

And then I'd slipped in.

Subtly, I'd begun making comments that insinuated a feeling of envy on my part. First, of couples in general. "People in love are so lucky to have found each other," I'd say. Then I moved to envy of her and Dirk specifically. "You and he are lucky to have found each other." More recently, my allusion of envy transferred to only Dirk. "*He's* lucky to have found you."

Accompanied with a look of longing, that last one hit the nail on the head. How could she not believe I wanted her?

Nothing I'd said had been a lie—I didn't profess an emotion that I didn't feel. I'd simply manipulated the truth to appear otherwise. In some unexplainable way, I believed the omission of a lie kept my integrity. It also made the experiment more valid. Lies tainted the sample. Lies were easy.

My attempt to woo didn't rely only on words. I'd learned in earlier experiments that touch was an easy way to get closer to a subject. With Celia, I'd ignored the boundaries of personal space, brushing against her at every opportunity, casually stroking her skin whenever possible.

My actions had an effect on her. Her gaze lingered on me longer and longer, and soon she made her own excuses to touch me. Finally, after two months had passed, I made my big move. On the doorstep of the Werner's Hampton home, I'd leaned in for a kiss. She lifted her chin to meet me, wetting her lips as I slowly made my descent.

Half an inch from her mouth, I'd pulled away.

"I'm sorry," I had said with as much heaviness as I could lay in my words. "This is wrong. I'm sorry." I'd hurried to my car and raced off, her voice chasing after me to stop. I'd left her wanting. I'd left her yearning. For me.

Then I didn't call or see her for two weeks. The distance had an air of douche about it, but with the event of a broken kiss preceding it, I believed my behavior would seem understandable. Gallant, even. I hadn't wanted to destroy her relationship with Dirk, so I'd removed myself from her presence. Or, that was the scenario I'd attempted to create anyway.

Celia had tried to contact me, despite my withdrawal. But I'd refused every call and managed to avoid her visits to the house. Tonight would be the end of our "break." It was seemingly forced—both of us were expected at the party—but I had carefully planned my pursuit to escalate to this very evening. I felt confident about the set-up, yet there were still variables. Would she be angry with me? Relieved to see me again? Would she pretend our last encounter never happened? The variables didn't concern me. Their unpredictability was what made the experiment fun.

Approaching footsteps sounded over the stone walk to the pool. *Here comes Sophia. Right on time.*

I removed my sunglasses and sat up to face my mother's wrath.

But it wasn't Sophia. It was Celia. *Even better.*

I stood to meet her.

She balled her dainty fists and propped them on her hips. "Don't you think about going anywhere, Hudson Pierce. You're trapped tonight. You have to talk to me whether you want to or not."

Her tone said frustrated. Heated, for sure, but not angry.

Interesting.

I decided I'd be the one to play that nothing happened. "I'm not going anywhere, Ceeley," I said, purposefully using my childhood nickname for her. "I was merely standing to greet you."

She frowned, disbelief on her face. "Next you're going to pretend you haven't been avoiding me for two weeks."

I shook my head and shrugged, my gaze drifting behind her to nothing specific. It was a posture I'd perfected—dramatic and aloof. "Nah, I'm not going to do that." Then I pinned her with my eyes. "I can't pretend with you, Ceeley. Not anymore."

It hadn't been what I'd planned to say—it was a blatant lie. I'd planned on pretending with her as long as necessary, but as soon as I'd said it, I knew it was what the moment needed.

Celia's expression confirmed that it was the right thing to say. Her frustration melted off her features and she was left looking soft and off-kilter. "Then let's not pretend. Let's talk about this."

I wasn't ready for that. If she made a declaration of love or an intention to end things with her boyfriend, I'd be stuck for the rest of the evening playing that I welcomed those things. It was my parents' fucking garden party. I wouldn't be able to dump her and leave. And I certainly wasn't going as far as that would require me to go. I wasn't planning to even kiss her.

So I deflected. "How about we not talk tonight? Instead we just enjoy one of the last days of summer. We can talk tomorrow. Are you going to the Brookes' shindig?" I already knew her answer. The Brookes were our age. Twins—Thomas and Christina. Christina was one of Celia's friends. An entire house full of spoiled rich kids. No supervision. That was the more appropriate setting for the end of my project.

Celia's mouth turned up in an eager grin. "Of course I'm going. Christina would kick my ass if I didn't." She'd been hoping that the reason behind my asking was because I wanted to be alone with her instead.

It wasn't. "I'm going too. I'll meet you there. We can slip away when we don't have our parents breathing down our necks." I glanced toward the house, indicating how close our parents were at that very moment. "It will give us a chance to…" I hesitated, letting her mind jump to whatever conclusion she preferred before I finished with, "talk."

"Right." Her cheeks flushed and I was sure her thoughts had been dirty. "We'll…*talk*…then."

"Good." I let a brighter than usual smile cross my lips. "I see swimsuit straps under that dress. If you want to get in, I will too."

We played in the pool for quite a while. Soon other guests arrived and more of our peers joined us. Christina Brooke flirted with me, as she often did, though I refrained from returning the attention the way I normally would. There were several other attractive girls there as well—some that I'd even fucked on occasion. On any other night, I would have picked one and banged her behind the poolhouse.

But tonight Celia was there. Tonight the experiment was more important. So I ignored the eyes the other girls gave me, and I made sure to keep my focus on The Subject throughout the night. I wanted to be sure that she noticed I was looking, that she assumed I was attracted to her physically, though I wasn't. It wasn't that Celia wasn't pretty. Quite the contrary. She'd been a beautiful girl that had grown into an even more beautiful woman over the year we'd been apart. Her curves had filled out—her hips were full, her waist slight. Her breasts were on the small side, but firm under her bikini top. Her nipples beaded through the thin material under my frequent glances. Any other man would have been hard staring at her as often as I did.

But I wasn't just any man. Despite her beauty, Celia had never turned me on. I knew her too well. I cared for her as much as I was able. For me, emotions didn't go with sex. They were completely separate. Emotional attachment was for people you wanted to spend time with—there were few of those people in my life. So few I could count them on one hand.

Sex was something else entirely. It was for pleasure. For getting off. For releasing pent-up aggression. I'd explored the possibility that it was anything else very thoroughly. I'd fucked frequently. I'd learned how to please and how I liked to be pleased. I'd perfected technique, shaped myself into a skilled lover. Yet with all the encounters I'd had, I'd never discovered the association others had with emotion and sex. My findings only solidified my original hypothesis—they were separate things entirely.

Or I'd proven another hypothesis altogether—that I was incapable of that type of emotion. That I was incapable of love. That certainly wasn't a conclusion that I'd ruled out.

It was after ten when a bunch of us commandeered a lounging area set up specifically for the party. I sat on the loveseat, Celia at my side. Christina Brooke half sat, half fell at my feet. I imagined she'd gone past tipsy to drunk, but most of it was an act. She was looking for an excuse to lean against my leg. I didn't mind. I liked the way her hand held onto my thigh as her breast pushed through her tank against my bare shin. My view of her was fantastic. I could see down her shirt with ease. She was an extremely sexy girl with plump lips that I couldn't help imagining wrapped around my cock. I had a semi just thinking about it.

Celia cast an irritated glance down at her friend. "Everyone's drinking but me."

With difficulty, I shifted my focus from Christina to Celia. I couldn't let lust distract me. "I'm not drinking."

She scowled. "But you could get some if you wanted."

I looked around at the other guests our age. They weren't legal, but almost all were nursing an alcoholic beverage of some sort. Obviously the bartender we'd hired wasn't carding. "Why can't you get one?"

I wondered if she was afraid to leave me alone with Christina. The way my cock pushed at my briefs, maybe that was a valid fear.

"My father's guarding the bar. I have no shot." *Not the response I'd expected.* "He already told me he wanted to find nothing in my hand tonight but Diet Coke. And he checks. See?"

I looked toward the bar where Warren was perched, his back against the counter. Sure enough, his eyes were on us, though I had a feeling it was more because he was interested in my fraternization with his daughter than because he was concerned about her stealing a sip of wine. Warren Werner was the protective father sort. It occurred to me that my experiment might earn me a black eye from the man.

It would be worth it.

The project consumed me now. I realized that fully. I'd turn down a fuck-hot sure thing at my feet for a chance to prove my hypothesis. Was it really an experiment anymore, or a game? It was my obsession, that's what it was. Anything else I called it at this point was merely a label.

"I'm standing up now," I warned Christina. She mumbled something then lay back on the grass, likely on the verge of passing out. Her shirt pushed up and I glimpsed her bare belly. I allowed myself one mental snapshot to savor for later when I jerked off in the shower. Then I turned to Celia.

"Come with me. I don't believe the entire liquor cabinet was brought out to the patio. If it was, I know where my mother keeps her secret stash." I took Celia's hand and laced my fingers through hers. It felt warmer than I expected, and the shock of it almost made me let go. But I reasoned the sensation was likely caused by the filthy thoughts I'd been having about Christina.

I let the visions of sex fade from my mind as we walked toward the house. At the door, I peered over at my friend and winked. "Also, I have something I want to give you."

"You do?" Her eyes lit up. "What is it?"

"All in good time, my love." The manipulation of my endearment made me cringe. Especially when I saw the effect it had on The Subject. She literally glowed.

I was disgusted with myself. That surprised me, but I didn't take it to mean anything too enlightening. A decent human being would have felt it long before now. More proof that I was neither decent nor feeling.

Except I *was* feeling in that moment. Bitter disgust. It was ugly in texture and taste. I didn't like it. It was a hindrance to my goal. That drink would be good.

Ten minutes later as the bourbon from the mini-bar off the living room settled in my stomach, I reevaluated the weakness I'd felt shortly before. Perhaps it wasn't weakness, after all. It was more recognition of fact than a feeling. There was no doubt I was a disgusting person. No one who knew the extent of my thoughts and actions would disagree.

But there was no one who knew my inner psyche. My secret belonged only to me.

"Better?" I swirled the liquid in my glass before finishing the last swallow.

"Much." Celia downed her own drink, cringing as she took in the bitter alcohol. "Woo!" She held her hand out to me to steady herself. "Maybe I should have drank that slower."

"Here." I helped her to the couch. "Sit while I get your gift."

She settled into the upholstery. "It's not my birthday or anything. Why would you get me something?"

"Do I need an occasion? Besides, it's barely anything at all." I left her to head to the dining room where I'd stashed my gift on the china cabinet. I'd planned this earlier, and not wanting to be too sequestered with Celia, I'd made sure my present was near the party.

I gathered the items and thought briefly how I owed Mirabelle for the tip of gifting based on knowing someone. Celia hadn't declared a major yet. She'd spent long hours debating with me about what she should choose. Her heart longed to pursue art, but her parents would never approve of such a frivolous career choice. While I'd listened and consoled, I hadn't given much input. I appreciated art in all forms, yet I had not a lick of that kind of creativity, and how she could marry her passion with an occupation the Werners approved of was beyond me.

Then my mother hired an interior designer for our home back in Manhattan. By hand, he'd sketched out beautiful new concepts for our living room and den. The work he'd done was creative and artistic and completely something within Celia's capability. I'd researched programs at Celia's school and ordered some brochures. Then I purchased a coffee table book with photographs of contemporary designs from the last decade. These were the gifts I gave to Celia.

"It's merely an option." I sat and watched her look through the brochures over her shoulder. "You can take or leave the information however you like. I won't be offended if you think it's all shit."

She shook her head. "No. It's perfect. This idea is perfect."

I shrugged. But I was quite pleased with the results of my gift.

"Thank you, Hudson." Her eyes were wet and her face flushed, equally from the liquor as much as from my gesture. "I'm so moved. You can't understand."

"Really, it's nothing."

"Stop being humble. It's a lot. Thank you." She wiped a tear from her eye. Then she threw herself into my arms. "Thank you so much."

I paused for a moment before embracing her back. I hadn't expected her hug, but once I got over the initial shock, I was glad for it. Warmth spread in my chest, and I couldn't figure out if my satisfaction was from the progress I'd made in my experiment or from sincere care for my friend's happiness. Did I have that in me? To care whether or not good things happened to Celia?

It seemed that maybe I did.

So when she pulled back and found my mouth, I welcomed it. I kissed her genuinely, letting my lips move in tandem with hers. She tasted sweet and innocent and also in need, as if she'd yearned for this kiss for as long as I'd worked to get her there. Her urge was so strong it was contagious. I could have kept kissing her. I could have taken her to my room. I could have stripped her naked and learned her body and made her writhe, forgetting all about my experiment, abandoning everything I'd ever believed about myself.

I could have. But how long would it last? Until we'd both come and were spent? Longer, perhaps—a week, a month? Until she realized that I was cold and calculating? Until she discovered that everything that she liked about me was a façade? That everything she thought I felt was a complete and utter lie?

No. I could never let anyone know who I really was. No one could want me if they knew who I was inside. It was better that I could never love in return because I'd never keep anyone anyway. So I had to end it—the kiss. In the name of all that I knew I could never be or have or give.

Also, I had an experiment to conclude.

I broke the kiss and pulled away from her. It was easier than it should have been. She tried to reach for me again and I halted her. "Celia." My breath was ragged. "You have a boyfriend."

"Can't we pretend just for tonight that I don't?" Her eyes were hopeful, wanting.

But my stoicism had returned and her pleading expression had no effect on me.

I stood, brushing my hand through my hair. "I told you I'm done pretending." Done pretending with myself. I had to finally be honest. It wasn't that I suspected I was incapable of love—I *knew* I was incapable. If I wasn't, I would have been able to keep kissing Celia. And I couldn't.

She rose and stepped toward me, but froze when the sound of loud voices came from the kitchen. My parents' voices.

I hurried to them, Celia at my heels. At the archway to the kitchen, I stopped, peering around the corner to see what was going on. Along with my parents, I saw my siblings and their nanny, Erin.

"You don't think I know?" my mother was shouting at my father. "You and your whores."

I looked across the room out toward the party that thrived outside. All the windows were shut, thankfully. Likely no one could hear this going on inside.

"How many have there been, Jack?" my mother spit out. She was drunk. She was often drunk, but she generally was able to hide it. That she couldn't hold it together when we had company irked me to no end.

It had a more devastating effect on my siblings.

"Mom." Mirabelle pulled at the edge of Sophia's dress. "Stop yelling. You're making Chandler cry."

"Erin." My father motioned to the nanny. "Take Chandler up, will you? And Mira."

Mirabelle protested. "I'm old enough to stay up. I don't want to miss—"

"Go. I'll be up when I can." There was no disagreeing with my dad when he had that tone. Mirabelle followed Erin out the other kitchen door.

Then Dad turned to my mother, putting a hand on her upper arm. "Sophia, let's talk about this later."

She shrugged out of his grasp. "Just go now. Pretend to look after your children when you're really after that piece of ass. Everyone here knows you're fucking her."

"No one here knows anything." He corrected himself quickly. "Because there's nothing to know. You've had too much to drink, that's all. Planning this party has exhausted you. Lie down for a bit—"

My mother slapped him. Hard enough that it left a mark. "Don't you fucking patronize me. I know, Jack. I've known forever. And I don't want to hear your excuses anymore. You're going to fuck who you want whether I'm around or not, but I don't have to have it under my roof. Your skanks are no longer welcome in my house. *You* are no longer welcome in my house."

"Sophia." Despite his aching jaw, my father reached again for his wife.

"You can stay in the guest house from now on. Fuck whoever, whenever. Not in my house. Not in front of my children." She threw her hand in the direction that the nanny had gone. "And Erin's no longer on my payroll."

My father finally lost his cool. "It's not your fucking payroll, Sophia," he shouted. "I'm the one who brings the goddamn money to the household."

"Is that so? And just how is it that you have companies to run in the first place?"

"Yes, yes. You're right. I owe you every fucking thing I've ever earned. I forgot." This wasn't the first time I'd heard this argument from my parents. It had been my mother who had the money when they'd married. My mother who'd given him the companies that he'd turned into Pierce Industries. And she never let him forget it.

My father scrubbed his hands over his face. This seemed to calm him. "Look, you can yell at me about this all you want, Sophia. Tomorrow. Later tonight, even. But now, we have a garden full of guests that I'm going to tend to. With or without you." He turned away from her and headed toward the patio doors.

"I'm serious about the guest house, Jack. Don't even try to come back in here to sleep tonight," she yelled after him, but he was already gone.

I watched her as she fell apart. Her face contorted and she doubled over as if in physical pain. The sob she let out was shattering. This because of love.

Thank God I was incapable of that. My parents were the best example of look-what-you're-not-missing that ever existed. Maybe I owed them more than I thought.

"Do you think you should go to her?"

I'd forgotten about Celia until that moment.

"Not my problem." It was more callous than I wanted her to believe I was. I backtracked. "I didn't mean that. I just don't want to embarrass her by letting her know we saw that. I'll go in a minute."

"I'll help," Celia offered.

"No. No, let me. She's drunk. You don't need to deal with that." It was a humiliating scene. I hated that Celia had witnessed it.

I glanced toward her and found her biting her lip.

"Did your dad really…" She took a deep breath. "Did he really sleep with the nanny?"

It wouldn't have surprised me. I had little confidence in my father's fidelity. Really, I didn't blame him. My mother was not the easiest woman to live with. If I had to blame anyone for the lack of humanity that existed in me, I'd blame her. She taught me to be cold. She forced me to put up that wall.

But Celia didn't need to know all my family secrets. "I don't know," I mumbled. "Like I said, my mother's drunk. She doesn't know what she's talking about."

Celia cleared her throat in a way that let me know she didn't believe me.

Then her hand settled softly on my back. "I'm sorry, Hudson."

I forced myself not to tense under her touch. It was harder than it should have been. She'd touched me a lot recently, and it never bothered me before. Right then, though, when I wasn't in control of the connection, when I was on the verge of some kind of vulnerability that I couldn't explain—then, her hand on me was difficult to tolerate. But pushing her away would undo all the work I'd done that summer. So I endured.

Then the strangest thing happened—a wave of grief rolled through me like a bout of nausea. Like my mother crumpled over in front of us, I felt like any moment I could fall apart. I had a strong urge to turn to Celia, to let her hold me, let her comfort me. As if I were Chandler, crying at the sight of my mother's tears. It was the most concrete emotion I'd had in longer than I could remember. I was out-of-control. I was fragile. It was horrible.

I had to make it end. I had to get away whether it ruined all my work on the project or not. "I'm going to her now." I didn't turn around, didn't let Celia see what was in my eyes, too scared of what she'd find there. "I'm helping her to bed, and then I'm going to bed myself. I'll see you at the Brookes' tomorrow. Goodnight, Celia."

I took a step toward the kitchen and was stopped by Celia's hushed call of my name. I stayed but didn't turn to her.

"It's okay," she said. "It's okay to feel."

Fuck, what did she think she knew about me? It angered me, which only added to my grief. I wanted her to go, to stop assuming she understood. If this was what it was like to feel, I didn't fucking like it one bit. But she was right that it was okay. I would get control back. This wouldn't overcome me. I'd get past it.

Now if she'd just fucking leave, it would be so much easier.

But she didn't. "And I understand if you need to go through this alone. I'm here for you when you're ready, Hudson. I love you."

I nodded once, acknowledging her declaration. I didn't attempt to speak. I wasn't sure I could. Her words were at once frightening and exhilarating. They burned me and freed me and, above all, confused me. I'd wanted those words—they were the words that led to confirming my hypothesis. But there in that moment, they threatened to destroy my other theory. Because a part of me wanted to return those words to her. A part of me believed that I might be able to love her back.

The mix of so many warring emotions paralyzed me. The grief, the pain, the joy, the release. So, I simply stood there, frozen, unresponding.

In front of me, my mother recovered enough from her breakdown to right herself. I'd waited too long to help her. She was going to help herself. She did that by heading to the counter where she refilled her glass from a bottle of vodka that she thought she kept hidden from us under the kitchen sink.

I realized that was how she did it. When the cold-hearted woman that was my mother felt a shred of anything—which was rare—that was how she suppressed it. She drank. She drank to ease her torment. To quiet her sorrow. To kill her love.

I understood her motivation. But the pathetic creature she'd turned into because of it was not someone I ever wanted to be.

Right then I vowed that I'd be stronger than that. I wouldn't need alcohol to stop the feeling from creeping in. I could control it on my own. Just like I could control everything and everyone else around me. The greatest example of that was still standing behind me. Celia had just declared her love for me.

Clueless about the power of the moment or her impact on it, Celia whispered a goodnight. The *flip-flip* of her feet in her shoes told me she was leaving. The silence that followed said she'd left.

A slow smirk eased across my lips as the whirlwind of emotion dissipated inside me. As suddenly as I'd lost it, I'd regained control. The familiar numbness settled in my chest, replacing any semblance of feeling. My mother was drunk, but on her way to passing out. My father was a cheating asshole, but he handled my mother with as much skill as he was handling the party outside. Erin might be a slut, but she was doing her job tending to my siblings.

Nothing was falling apart. Everything was fine.

And Celia loved me.

I had to believe a break-up from her boyfriend was imminent. My experiment was nearly complete. Exactly as I'd planned.

— CHAPTER —

SIX

After

At a quarter past six, I approach Norma Anders' open door. As my chief financial manager, I'm not surprised to see her working after hours, but her assistant's presence is unexpected. He's leaning over the desk facing her, and their discussion is hushed. I knock on the doorframe to announce my presence.

Her assistant straightens immediately, and he moves out of the way so Norma can see me.

I catch her gaze. "I need to sign that power of attorney if you have it ready."

"Of course." She nods to her assistant. "Boyd, will you—"

"Certainly." The young man rushes past me to his desk, presumably to get the paper I require. I wonder briefly if he's always this anxious or only when the owner of the company stops by. Honestly, it's rare for me to venture down to Norma's office. She's usually summoned to mine.

Despite my infrequent visits, I'm relaxed in this setting. I don't wait for Norma's invitation to come in.

"Make yourself comfortable, Hudson," she teases after I'm sitting across from her. "I expected you to ask for this earlier this afternoon."

"I lost track of time." It's not entirely dishonest. I've had my mind on other things, such as my plans for later that evening, but I purposefully procrastinated making this visit. It's a waste of my time to spend hours signing for the acquisition of The Sky Launch. Giving Norma power of attorney to do so in my stead is practical. But signing the paper is, in very many ways, my official declaration that I'm pursuing this insane plan.

So I didn't request her to bring it by. I put it off until long after my secretary and most of the building had gone home. In the end, though, here I am. With my pen ready in my breast pocket, no less.

Boyd returns and hands a file to Norma. "If that's everything, I'll be leaving."

"Yes, right." She peers at her watch. "It is rather late. Thank you for staying. I'll see you in the morning."

"Right. Tomorrow, Ms. Anders."

A glance passes between them and I realize that the two are fucking. It's not likely obvious to most others, but I've studied human nature and relationships extensively. I know an "I-see-you-naked-on-a-regular-basis" look when I see one.

I don't mention it or let on that I recognize the situation, though. If I did, I'd have to be willing to reprimand Norma. Social relationships are not permitted between management and staff, and it's a terminable offense. But she's too valuable of an employee to care about something so unrelated to what I employ her for.

With Boyd gone, Norma opens the file and finds the paper I need to sign. She briefly looks it over before handing it to me. I don't read it. I sign and date where appropriate and hand it back.

"Are you sure you want to do this?" she asks as she takes the document from me. She's already putting it back in the file, knowing I'm not going to change my mind even though we're going to have a conversation about it.

"I'm positive." I'm not positive. I've never entered into a business deal with as much doubt as I have now. It's not the financials that bother me. Even if I lose money, it's too small of a company to even scratch the surface of my holdings.

"The price is reasonable enough, but, Hudson, this is not a good business investment." She's not trying to belittle my decision, I remind myself. It's Norma's job to question me.

"Is it a particularly bad one?" I should at least hear her out.

She scans through the prospect sheet regarding The Sky Launch. "Not necessarily. If you're willing to give it some time and attention."

"I am." *Too much* time and attention. I'm lucky everything else at Pierce Industries is running smoothly at the moment.

She closes the file and leans back in her chair, her elbow propped on the armrest, her chin held in her palm. "Why are you so set on a nightclub?"

"I own nightclubs in other cities." I have one in Atlantic City. Another in Miami and two in Vegas. This won't be my first venture into the industry, and as the current owner has assured me, the staff at The Sky Launch is self-sufficient. Whatever happens with Celia, I plan to have Alayna groomed to take over as general manager as soon as possible. Once that takes place, my involvement at the club will be minimal.

"Let me rephrase, why are you so interested in *this* night club? I could get some people looking, and we could find something else local that's going to take less of your time and be more profitable."

I dodge the suggestion. "How's your family?"

"I love how you think changing the subject will distract me from pursuing this. I'll make you pay by actually answering your question. My brother's home now. I wish I could say fully recovered, but that will take time."

Norma's brother had a breakdown recently and had been admitted to a mental hospital. While I normally try not to get involved with my employees' private lives, Norma had explained the situation so that she could get some emergent time off.

"He'll get there," I assure her.

"I know he will. And Gwen's still at Eighty-Eighth Floor." Her brows lift with an idea. "Now that's a nightclub you should look into buying."

She's not going to let it go until I give her a more satisfactory reason for wanting Alayna's club. "There's asset in The Sky Launch I can't get elsewhere." It feels wrong to refer to Alayna as an asset, though, legitimately, she is. "A star employee. I peg her as an up-and-comer in management and I want to be her employer when that happens."

Norma considers for a few seconds. Then she sighs. "I can't decide if you're being honest or blowing smoke up my ass. Whichever, you win. I'll stop giving you my two cents."

"You're one of the four most important people in my life other than my family. I value your opinion." Though I'm grateful that she's dropping this issue, I usually do appreciate her input.

"Really?" She leans forward, her elbows braced on her desk. "Who are the other three?"

I reply without missing a beat. "My secretary, my assistant, and my unofficial head of security." That's as good a title for Jordan as anything.

Norma frowns. "Isn't it sad that they're all on your payroll?"

"It's not sad. It's the way I like it." I brush invisible lint from my pant leg, not meeting her eyes. I don't find my relationships sad. I'm content. But is that how I want to live the rest of my days? Merely content?

Her frown remains. "Did I see Celia Werner here the other day?"

I don't like Norma's concern about my social life or lack thereof. It gives her an excuse to play matchmaker and I'm not interested in that at all. So I let her believe what she wants about Celia. It's easier. "Yes, she was here."

"You're not redecorating anything right now, are you?"

I don't answer, but my expression tells her that I'm not. It's the only work-related reason that Celia would be around—if she were handling a redesign of one of the offices.

Norma assumes as I guessed she would. "As much as I'm happy to see you with a woman in your life, I really wish it wasn't her."

Now that's what's sad—that Celia *is* the woman in my life. That my past has tied me to the person who I despise and look down on more than anyone...other than myself.

I stand, unwilling to continue the conversation. "Thank you for your help, Norma."

I leave quickly, as if by escaping the discussion I could escape the reality that the discussion centered on. But there's no escape from this reality. I've made my bed. Time to lie.

It's near ten that evening when I pull my car into the lot at Columbus Circle. My grip tightens around the steering wheel. I clutch on, pouring all my aggression into my grasp. Then I let go. The action helps center me. I'm anxious and I need to burn off some tension.

Really what I need is to go home and run a few miles on the treadmill. But I'm here already. So I get out of my Maybach and head toward the front doors of the club.

I've been to The Sky Launch twice before now. Both times were during the day, once with the seller and another time with my appraiser. I've never seen it in operation nor have I met any of the employees. Before I do, I want the opportunity to observe them in their environment.

That's my excuse for this visit. It's bullshit. I want to observe *Alayna* in her environment. I don't give a fuck about anyone else. The schedule posted to the wall in the staff room indicated that she was taking the next week off. Tomorrow is her graduation, so I assume she's using the time to celebrate. Tonight is my only chance to see her at work. When she returns, the transfer of ownership will be complete, and I will be her boss.

It's a weeknight and not yet summer, but there's a line outside the club. I manage to get in quickly—an expensive Armani suit is an automatic ticket into most anywhere. Inside, I spend a few minutes surveying the dance floor. The DJ is good and the layout works well. I glance up at the bubble rooms that circle the second floor. They're the highlight of the club. With a little emphasis, they'd draw an even bigger crowd. In fact, it's not hard to imagine how well the place could do with a few tweaks.

I catch myself brainstorming and stop. That's for Alayna. Marketing was her area of interest at school. After her presentation, I have a feeling her ideas for the club would blow mine out of the water.

Thinking about Alayna and her ideas, I can't wait any longer. I have to find her. The schedule I saw indicated she was to be tending the first floor bar. I make my way through the crowd that thickens as I close in toward the counter.

I spot her when I'm still twenty feet away.

In the days that followed the symposium—weeks now, three to be exact—I'd often wondered if I'd imagined the effect that Alayna Withers had on me. My sanity isn't exactly indisputable, after all, and the way I've obsessed over and transfixed myself on this stranger is indeed crazy.

But even across this distance, with the music blaring so loud that I can't hear her voice and the lights so dim I can't make out the details of her features—even now, she pulls at me with a magnetic force that is neither explainable nor rational. My eyes cling to her as though she were the only glow in a dark room. And isn't she?

She's swept away in her work. The way she shuffles around her fellow staff members to serve her customers—it's a dance, beautiful and mesmerizing. The smiles and nods she shares with those around her are so engaging that I'm instantly jealous of every recipient. I want her smiles. I want her nods. I want to engage her.

It's more than my competitive nature at hand here. It has nothing to do with my past games or experiments, though the feeling of exhilaration is identical. It's perplexing and I'm not a man who's easily confused.

I tear my focus away long enough to make it to an empty seat at the far end of the bar. Then my gaze returns to her. My constant staring will likely be attributed to a thirsty customer trying to signal the wait staff, but frankly I don't care what Alayna thinks of me just as long as she thinks of me at all. I yearn for her attention with such a deep ache. Yearn for the instant that she looks at me, connects with me. I'll turn down any service that isn't from her. I need to know if I have any of the effect on her that she has on me.

As I watch her, one of the other bartenders—a man that I imagine is David Lindt, the manager of the bar—gathers the staff around him. Soon he's distributed shots and all are partaking.

If I were really here to spy on my staff, this would be the episode that might grab my attention. Drinking behind the bar is not an acceptable way to run a club. However, though I can't hear exactly what's being said from my side of the counter, the cheers and hoots seem to indicate a special occasion.

From the way everyone's focused on Alayna, I gather it's about her.

"Woo hoo!" she screams, as if to confirm my thoughts. "Goddamn, that's nice!"

She's fun, I realize. Besides being smart and responsible, she knows how to enjoy herself. It's so different from me, so foreign that it should be a complete turn-off. Instead, it intrigues me more. As if that were possible.

Once the shots are consumed, the staff disperses. Alayna stays behind the bar. I'm more relieved than I want to admit. My relief is replaced with envy as she moves to embrace a customer. Who is this man? I've had Jordan tailing Alayna for the better part of two weeks. His findings have shown she has a limited social life, her outings relating only to work, school, and exercise—namely, running. There has been no evidence of a boyfriend or even a close friend. Has Jordan missed something important?

I strain to hear the conversation between the two. Quickly, I deduce that the man is simply a regular customer. My relief returns. Though I may have to step in if he continues to stare at Alayna's breasts the way he is. I don't blame him. They're exceptional breasts. I can't stop staring myself. But they should not be shared with the likes of drunk assholes who only want a quick fuck.

Thank God I'm neither a drunk nor someone who wants a quick fuck. Slow. That's how it will go with Alayna. I'll take my time when I fuck her and it won't be just a one-time thing.

Jesus, where did that thought come from? I hadn't planned to pursue Alayna sexually. It certainly wasn't part of Celia's scheme. But now that I've thought it, I can't seem to get the idea out of my mind.

It's her damn outfit. She looks like sex on legs.

I make a mental note to speak to Alayna about her wardrobe choices for work.

I manage to stop thinking about my cock by concentrating on the other information I've gleaned from my eavesdropping. Alayna has admitted she has no plans for her vacation. I don't like that. She should be celebrating her accomplishments. Furthermore, the hint of disappointment in her posture leads me to believe she wishes she had plans.

But I can't dwell on this. Because she's sliding down the bar toward me. Finally, her attention is mine.

"Now what can I get…you…?" Her words trail as she meets my eyes. The intense grip of her gaze on mine nearly takes my breath away. It leaves her speechless as well, her jaw slack as she takes me in.

Then I know.

I know that no one has ever looked at me this way. I know that this connection is not just one-sided, that she feels it too. I know that I scare her and fascinate her as much as she scares and fascinates me. I know that sooner or later I will fuck her, that she will enjoy it. That I will enjoy it. And somehow, with certainty that exceeds every other fact that I've come to accept in this space of seconds, I know that my life will never be the same again.

Eventually, I remember I'm supposed to be placing my order. "Single-malt Scotch. Neat, please."

She shakes her head as if snapping out of a haze. "I have a 12-year-old Macallan."

"Fine." A single word and I barely manage to rasp it out. She doesn't look at me while she pours my drink and I already miss the warmth of her eyes. Then, as she hands me my glass, I purposefully let my fingers brush against hers. I had to. I needed to know how it felt to touch her.

I'm rewarded with far more than the softness of her skin and the zing of electricity that passes between us. I'm rewarded with her shiver. It's visible. I *do* affect her. I'm more than pleased.

She's wary of me though. She yanks her hand away and scurries to the other side of the bar.

I wonder at her thoughts as I sip from my glass. Because of her history, I might assume she reacts to many men the way she did to me. Yet, I've watched her all night and she's seemed at ease with everyone *except* me. She is afraid of me, but I believe that fear has to do with herself. I've done nothing to frighten her, though I haven't masked any of the lust she's sparked inside me. Is that enough to throw her?

I'm seconds away from forming a theory. And then I force my thoughts in another direction. It is there that I finalize my intent with Alayna Withers. I will lead her through the stupid game of Celia's. I will participate as I've agreed. Separately, I will seduce her, because after the brush of her hand, I can't imagine not touching every inch of her with my fingers, my mouth, my tongue.

But Alayna will not be my *subject*. I will not experiment with her emotions. I will not let her break. If anything, this will be a study of myself. It will be an opportunity to see if anyone can break *me*.

As I solidify my plans, I nurse my drink and continue to watch her. Soon, she's left to manage the bar herself. She cleans the counters with what seems to be nervous energy. Then she looks toward me. It's a ray of sun escaping heavy cloud cover when her eyes find mine again.

She sweeps toward me and nods at my near empty glass. "Another?"

"No, I'm good." I don't need any more. I'm intoxicated by her presence. I reach in my breast pocket and pull a hundred from my billfold. I don't intend to accept the change.

She rings up my order at the register and I realize our encounter is nearing an end. I feel compelled to talk to her, to soak up as much of her as I can in the last few moments of anonymity that I will share with her.

I debate for a moment an appropriate conversation starter that will neither give anything away about me nor appear creepy. I remember the toast that was shared among the staff and choose to remark on that. "Special occasion?"

Her brow creases. "Uh, yeah. My graduation. I walk tomorrow for my MBA."

I already know this, but as I'm genuinely impressed by her, it's not hard to display admiration. "Congratulations. Here's to your every success." I lift my glass to her and then shoot back the last of it.

"Thank you." Her eyes are on my mouth and I can't help myself—I lick my lips and delight as her pupils dilate in reaction.

She reaches out to give me my change.

I almost change my mind about accepting it. It would be another opportunity to touch her, and I burn for that. But I'm already stiff as it is. I don't want to encourage my desire, not tonight. So I shake my head and say, "Keep it."

"I can't."

"You can and you will." It's not the first time I've tipped so generously, but it's the first time I've really cared that it be accepted. "Consider it a graduation gift."

"Okay." She concedes, but I sense that it's difficult for her. "Thanks."

Her surrender, simple as it is, arouses me further. She's turned from me now, but I'm not ready to let her go. "Is this also a goodbye party?" She faces me again. "I don't imagine you'll be using your MBA to continue bartending." God, those eyes. Those eyes find me, every time.

She hesitates. "Actually, I'd like to move up here. I love the nightclub scene." She seems to prepare herself for my criticism.

Three weeks ago, I would have given it. Now, I say, "It makes you alive."

"Exactly." She breaks into a smile.

"It shows." When I'd first learned she'd chosen to stay at The Sky Launch rather than use her degree in a more traditional way, I'd assumed that Alayna had an affinity with the club. Having witnessed her in this environment and comparing it to her presentation at Stern, I see it's even more than that. This place is a life force for her. She's struck me with her beauty both times I've seen her. Here, though, her beauty is transcendent.

"Laynie!" It's the drunk kid down the bar. Alayna leaves me to attend to him. I eavesdrop, cringing as he gives her his number. I wonder how many times she gets hit on in an evening. It bothers me more than I want it to. Once more, I curse her outfit.

Thankfully, she doesn't seem too interested in this guy. She throws his number away the minute he leaves, catching my eye as she does.

I could smile and nod and we wouldn't have to discuss it. But I find myself wanting to know, so I ask, "Do you do that with every number you receive?"

Really, I just want her to talk to me some more. Yet another way to demand her attention.

She studies me. "Are you trying to figure out if I'd throw away your number?"

I can't help myself—I laugh. "Maybe."

She smiles, illuminating the space around her. It's the kind of smile that some men would do anything to see as often as possible. I wonder what it would feel like to be that kind of man.

Then she leans on the counter toward me, and my gaze is pulled to the gorgeous curve of her tits. "I wouldn't throw yours away. I wouldn't take yours at all."

I manage to lift my eyes to hers. "Not your type?"

"Not necessarily."

I'm enjoying this conversation much more than I should. "Why then?"

"Because you're looking for something temporary. Something fun to play with." She leans closer and it takes all my strength not to look back down at her breasts, not to notice if her nipples are puckered against the thin fabric of her blouse, not to reach forward and brush them with my fingertips.

"And I get attached." She straightens. "Now doesn't that just scare you shitless?"

Scare me shitless? It turns me the fuck on. Everything she does and says is more fuel for a fire of desire that is slowly overtaking me. I'm beginning to think I'd do anything to be near her. Oh, that's right—I've already done anything.

And she assumes she's the dark one of the two of us. It's amusing.

"You, Alayna Withers, do anything but scare me." I stand and button my coat. I'm tempted to stay longer, but I've just dropped that I know her name. I shouldn't be here when she realizes. "Congratulations again. Quite an accomplishment."

Long after I've left, I feel her eyes on me. The warmth and life contained in her gaze clings to my body even after I'm home. Consumes me. I think about her while I'm in the shower as I stroke myself. I come fast and hard and still her presence cleaves to me like a second skin.

Needing to see her again soon, I decide to gift her a week at my spa in the mountains near Poughkeepsie. I'll have it delivered anonymously and then I'll join her there. I can meet her on equal ground. I can get to know her, spend time with her, seduce her. It would likely put Celia's scheme in jeopardy which is just an added bonus.

The idea thrills me and delights me as I think about it.

And then I let it go.

I know from experience that Celia is a worthy foe. Any violation of her plan on my part will result in retaliation. Though I don't fear what she can do to me, I am attached in this odd way to Alayna Withers. I care about what Celia can and will do to her. My protection can only be effective if I stay the course.

Though I'm a fairly humorless person, I laugh at my own attempt to fool myself. I'm not invested in this for Alayna's benefit. It's all for my own. I want to be close to the woman. I want to study the effect she has on me. I want to see her survive, but it's for my own selfish satisfaction.

Still, I decide to give her the spa trip. I'm not sure what motivates me to do so. I don't leave my name on the gift note so it's not about endearing her to me. I truly want her to go because I think she'd enjoy it. Because I want her to have a moment of pleasure in a life that has been less than easy. Perhaps I am capable of unselfish actions after all.

Or maybe I just know Alayna will have a better chance in Celia's game if she enters it pampered and well-rested. That's a more likely reason for my actions. I'm capable of manipulating the thoughts of many, but I can't convince myself that I'm a better person than I am, no matter how hard I try.

— CHAPTER —
SEVEN

I'm a composed man. Always in control. I've run meetings of disgruntled board members without forming a bead of sweat. I've bid on high stock investments without altering my pulse. I've played convincible mind games without batting an eye.

Tonight, in the presence of a woman I hardly know, I'm in over my head.

Perhaps I'm losing my touch. Or maybe I've just finally met my match.

Alayna enters the bubble room before me. Just yesterday, on her first shift after her vacation at my spa, I was introduced to her as the new owner of the club. We haven't yet had a chance to establish a working relationship. This is by design. I don't want her to see me as her boss or a business associate. I need her to see me as a man. As a potential lover.

So here we are in as close to a non-work environment as I can establish within the club. She's accompanying me while I eat dinner. The setup should feel to her like a date. However, it also feels like a date for me and that is why I'm a bit daunted.

At least we'll be daunted together.

Alayna flips the switch to indicate our bubble room is occupied. Then she hands me a menu. It's slightly amusing. She's not on-the-clock, and yet she's still on duty.

I gesture for her to take a seat. "After you."

She sits, and I watch her closely. Her knuckles are nearly white from gripping the table edge. Her heel is bouncing against the carpeted floor. She's nervous to be here—alone—with me. Frankly, I am too. But it's up to me to calm her nerves. And mine.

Jesus, I'm fucked.

I remove my jacket and take my time hanging it up on the hook behind me. This is when I get my shit together. I've only got one shot at pulling this off and if I don't do it right, the whole scheme is over before it's begun. And I'll look like an idiot.

One deep breath in and I'm ready to face her. *Game on.*

I sit across from her and throw down the menu she gave me. "I don't need this. Do you?"

"No, thank you, Mr. Pierce."

"Hudson," I correct.

"No, thank you, *Hudson*." The sound of my name on her lips and I'm already straining in my pants. "I've already eaten."

"A drink then? Though, I know you work at eleven." This is all a ruse. I've already ordered for us both. And I'm the one who needs the drink.

Alayna's tongue flicks across her lower lip. "Maybe an iced tea."

Now I'm thinking of her tongue flicking across my cock. "Good."

I press the button in the middle of the table that summons the waitress and my fingers crash into hers. Her touch, the stunning warmth in this brief contact—I must have more. She moves to pull away, but I don't let her and take her hand in mine.

She inhales sharply as I stroke my thumb along the back of her hand.

I lock my eyes on hers, noticing her pupils widen. I make an excuse about why I'm still touching her. She accepts it. From the look on her expression, she'll accept anything I say at the moment.

She's into me. This is good.

I'd worried that my harsh meeting with her the day before had ended her attraction. Admittedly, I'd been…not very friendly is one way to put it. It was necessary though. She'd been dressed provocatively—again—and I'd made a scene about it. I had to establish my authority in front of David. I had to show from the beginning that Alayna would not be my favorite as far as work was concerned—though she very much already was.

And I had to put an end to her wearing outfits that invited men to harass her. Maybe she could handle their advances. I could not.

Necessary as it was, the flare of anger that had sparked in her eyes afterward had concerned me. Now, as I caress her skin, and she practically melts in my hand, I realize my anxiety was in vain.

Also, I realize how nice it feels to touch her like this. Extremely nice.

My phone rings, interrupting our contact.

"Excuse me." I remove my phone from my pants pocket and silence it. I know from the ringtone who it is—Celia. She's likely checking in on my progress.

Fuck her. She's too eager and it pisses me off. I'll get back to her when I'm good and ready, if at all.

"You can take it if you need to," Alayna says.

"There can't be anything important enough to interrupt this conversation." It's a line and not a line all at once. Is it possible to play the game and be sincere at the same time? My script is very loose. I know where I'm supposed to end before I walk out of this room, but everything that takes place before then is improvised. In my past schemes, I'd study the subject and make educated guesses as to what he or she wanted to hear in order to get them to the finish. I artfully manipulated.

This is not like that.

Though everything I have said and done so far has set me up perfectly for my task, a great deal of it has come organically. It's genuine.

It's such a foreign arrangement that, again, I have the sensation of being completely fucked.

The waitress enters and I'm relieved for the break in my thoughts. She places my dinner in front of me along with a glass of Sancerre. Then she sets a glass of iced tea in front of Alayna.

Alayna's brow rises and I answer her unasked question. "I asked Liesl what you usually drank. If you had said you wanted something different, I wouldn't look quite so cool at this moment."

My play is working—she relaxes ever so slightly and gives me a smile. "Hmm, cool is not quite the word I'd use for you."

Well, this is intriguing. "What word would you use for me then?"

She blushes and takes a sip of her tea. I'm betting she was thinking something dirty. I'm desperate to find out.

But the waitress interrupts my quest. "Anything else, Mr. Pierce?"

"We're good." I wait until she's gone to return to my pursuit. "What word would you use for me, Alayna?"

She doesn't hesitate. "Controlled."

"Interesting." It's not what she was going to say. I take a bite of my sea bass, seemingly diverting my attention. "Not that controlled isn't an accurate description of me. But I had thought from the look on your face that you would say something else."

She doesn't respond and I'm more convinced that her thoughts were inappropriate. She moves her eyes to study the club below us. As I eat my meal, I study her. She's not as easy to read as most people I encounter. Or perhaps it's that I want to know more of her than I can scope out on my own. I want to know what she's thinking. What she thinks about me.

What the hell is that about? I can't remember the last time I cared about what someone thought of me. Yet here I am, not only craving to possess her body, but her mind as well. I want to be in her thoughts. I want her as consumed with me as I am with her.

At the same time, the idea petrifies me.

So I deflect. "I know why you agreed to dine with me, Alayna." Actually, I gave her no choice. But she likely has some ideas of why I've invited her here, and it's time to start weeding out the ones that are wrong. "I have to be honest with you. I don't intend to help you with your desire to make management."

In fact, I'd spent the earlier part of the evening discussing this very topic with David. I listened to him tell me Alayna's qualifications in depth. I let him *convince* me that promoting her was the best move for The Sky Launch. Only when I was sure he would move her along the career path that I wished for her did I tell him that I had no interest in being involved with the day-to-day operations of the club. We both left our meeting pleased.

Alayna, though, is fidgeting before me and I sense her disappointment in my proclamation.

I attempt to relieve her. "That doesn't mean you won't be promoted. David said you're quite capable, and I'm sure you'll get the position without my help. I may own The Sky Launch, but I am not your boss. David is your boss and will continue to be unless the business no longer thrives under his command."

She lets out a sigh and I believe she's reassured.

Now, with that out of the way..."But I didn't invite you here to discuss the club."

Her body tenses again. "Why did you invite me?"

It's the moment to drop my bomb. But I can't help but flirt around the other option that has probably crossed her mind. "Perhaps I like you."

It's not until after I've said it that I realize the depth of its honesty. I *do* like her. I'm often intrigued by people—not to the level that I am with Alayna, but there are those who do attract my interest. It's rare, though, that I like them. And I like Alayna. Quite a lot already.

She shudders, and I adore that I've flustered her. She takes a sip of her drink. "Perhaps I'm seeing someone."

Even more, I adore that she challenges me despite being thrown off-kilter. It helps take my mind off how off-kilter she's thrown me.

I know she's single because of my research, but I would have guessed it even without my spies. "You aren't. No man would let his woman wear the outfit you wore yesterday." Now she bristles, and I wonder if I shouldn't have brought up the encounter where I'd chided her. My thoughts wander to the tight-fitting corset—how her breasts spilled beautifully over the top. I wouldn't mind seeing it on her again. In private.

So I add, "Not in public, anyway."

Her eyes spark at the obvious innuendo I've made, yet her jaw clenches defiantly. "Perhaps I'm not into controlling boyfriends."

Touché. "Very well, Alayna." I cock a brow. "Are you seeing anyone?"

I've got her now. But she doesn't fold, and that's to be admired. Instead, she sits up straighter and borrows one of my favorite tactics—diversion. "That isn't why you invited me, Hudson. You have an agenda."

"An agenda." I stifle my laugh. She's so straightforward with me. It's alarmingly refreshing. "Yes, Alayna, I have an agenda."

I'm not prepared to share my agenda just yet. Or, rather, she's not prepared. I play my next card instead. "I presume you enjoyed your time at my spa last week."

I wish that I could leave the spa as an anonymous gift, wish that I didn't have to pull it into this game. But the truth is I'm afraid that she will not accept the even larger gift that is part of this scheme. I have to lay the path, get her comfortable with my wealth. If she can see that she's already taken advantage of what I can offer, then it won't be so out of her comfort level to concede to more.

"Oh, I didn't realize you owned...wait..." The moment she registers what I've admitted is clearly shown in her expression. "The gift was from you?"

"Yes. Did you have a nice time?"

"No. Way." Her mouth drops open in surprise.

"No way?" This isn't an answer to my question, I know. It stems from her awe. I'm glad now that I had to give this secret away. It makes me want to explore what other ways I can surprise her. Particularly ways that involve no clothing.

"I mean, yes, I had a nice time—a wonderful time, in fact—but no way could you have done that. Why did you do that? You shouldn't have done that."

"Why ever not?"

Alayna's eyes are wide and electric. "Because that's big!"

"Not for me." I'm not an idiot. I know how it looks. It was an extravagant gift from a stranger. She probably thinks I'm trying to get her in my bed. I am, but the gift was given independently from that.

"But for me it is. It's huge! And you don't even know me! It's completely inappropriate and unprofessional and unprecedented and inappropriate. And if I'd known it was from you, I never would have accepted it."

Despite her statement, I do not regret my actions. I'm a man with money. I'm not often generous, but I'm rarely refuted when I am. "It's not inappropriate at all. It was simply a gift. Think of it as a golden hello." I'm diverting again. Or trying to, at least.

The tactic doesn't seem to be working. "But you don't give gifts like that to women who work for you unless you're running an entirely different kind of club."

"You're overreacting, Alayna." Though she's actually quite adorable when she's this worked up.

"I'm not!" Her expression changes from frustrated to quizzical. "And what do you mean a golden hello? You mean, like a signing bonus?"

"Yes, Alayna." I've toyed with her enough. "That's my agenda. I would like to hire you."

"I already work for you and I'm happy where I am." She's startled and confused.

But I have her attention.

"Again, I don't feel that you do work for me. I am not your boss. I own the establishment that you work for. That is all. Is that clear?"

I relax when she nods. This is an important delineation for me. As her boss, I'd have the opportunity to work with her closely. However, I want her to choose that for herself. It has nothing to do with the scam Celia is playing—it's simply how I desire to interact with Alayna. I want our relationship to be unforced. I want it to develop naturally.

I'm a fairly humorless person, but that notion makes even me want to laugh. How can any of it be natural when every bit of it is a ruse?

Well, not *every* bit of it. Fuck, I don't even know anymore myself.

It's then I realize that now that I'm the owner of the club, Celia has nothing to trap me with. I could walk away from this here and now, couldn't I? I could spend time with Alayna on my own terms—ask her out on a real date, even.

But the idea is too absurd. I never date. And I know Celia—she won't give up that easily. Also, I'm not a person to make decisions impulsively.

"This wouldn't affect your employment at the club." I lean toward her. "Maybe hire is not the correct term. I'd like to pay you to help me with a problem. I believe you'd be perfect for the job."

"You win. My curiosity is piqued. What's the job?"

I have her exactly where I want her. I pause to heighten the suspense. "I need you to break up an engagement." God, how I've mastered the art of drama. It's pathetic; it really is.

She coughs. "Um, what? Whose?"

Leaning back, I reveal my bombshell. "Mine."

She gapes and I'm lost again in naughty thoughts about her lips. "Close your mouth, Alayna. Although it's quite adorable to see you flabbergasted, it's also very distracting."

Though she closes her mouth, I can see she's still aghast. I pass her my wine. She takes a swallow—her taste mixing with mine—and then speaks. "I didn't realize you were engaged."

She blushes as she says it and I have to look away. She's too delectable. I consider abandoning the scheme and focusing on seduction instead. But there's still a lot of groundwork to lay so I deny myself a little longer, and explain to Alayna Withers the strange relationship that Celia and I have found ourselves in. Though much is omitted, almost none of what I say is a lie. I tell her how our parents are friends, how they want us to marry, how my mother thinks there is no one but Celia for me.

I don't say that our parents' belief that we should wed is based on a relationship that Celia and I never had. The Werners and my mother—they've partnered Celia and me in their minds ever since that summer ten years before. That's not an important part of this charade, though, and it's a time I prefer to not think about. So I leave that out.

I leave too much out. Because she soon says, "I'm missing something."

I nod. "I suppose you are." I take my glass back from her and finish it off before clearing up the last detail. It's another truth—the most important truth of this scheme, and one that I've never been ashamed to admit. Until now. "Alayna, if there is anyone in the world who has any power over me, it's my mother." And Mirabelle, but that's neither here nor there for the moment. "My mother knows that I am…" I don't need to search for the word, but I pause anyway.

"…*incapable*…of love. She worries that I will…end up alone. A marriage with her best friend's daughter, at least, insures that won't happen."

I wish I had more to drink as a new doubt starts creeping in. Am I really incapable of love? Or was it merely an idea planted by a psychiatrist in my teenage years with no basis in reality? I've never cared to challenge the notion, and suddenly, out of nowhere, I wonder if I should.

But that challenge could threaten to disrupt everything I know.

So I quickly abandon it, and move on with the setup. I explain that if I were in love with someone else, our parents would be delighted. More than delighted—my mother would have a fucking heart attack. Or she simply wouldn't believe it. That is the more likely scenario.

At one point, Alayna narrows her eyes and asks, "So I'm supposed to be the floozy you're in love with?"

This amuses me greatly. There is nothing common or lowly about the woman sitting across from me. "No one would ever mistake you as a floozy, Alayna. Even when you dress like one." I was particularly naughty with that last line. It was an excuse to think of that corset one more time. Fuck, she was lovely in it.

She's not quite so happy with my comment. "Why don't you hire a real floozy to put on your charade?"

"My mother would never believe I'd fall for a floozy. You, however, have particular qualities—qualities that would make the story quite believable."

"What sort of qualities?"

Her patience is wearing. Frankly, so is mine. I can't skirt my desire for her any longer. I catch her up in my stare. "You are exquisitely beautiful, Alayna, and also extremely intelligent."

"Oh."

She's stunned. As am I. Because in her eyes, I see the reflection of my own want and I yearn to explore it further. Yearn to explore *her* further. Carnal fantasies fight for playtime in my conscience. The things I could do to her…

Not yet. Soon.

I break the eye contact. "And you're a brunette. All three make you 'my type' so to say." I don't date, but I do fuck. The women I fuck are beautiful. They are intelligent enough for me to make it through an evening in their company. And they are, by and large, brunette. I don't know if I like them dark simply because of preference or if it's got something to do with Celia being blonde. Whatever the answer, Alayna fits the bill.

She fits the bill so entirely that it's all I want to think about.

But there are details to work through. I lay out the hook of the scheme. Payment.

As I suspect, she laughs at my offer to pay off her eighty thousand dollars in student loans in exchange for her participation in the scenario. She doesn't realize that I've already paid it, and I'm sure if she knew, she'd be gone by now.

She isn't gone, though. She's still here listening intently to my every word, but Alayna isn't buying my proposition. I feared it would take convincing, and it seems I was right. It doesn't help that I'm distracted from my task. All I can think about is getting her beneath me.

But that's not the point of this meeting, I remind myself. My goal tonight is to get her to agree to pretend to be my girlfriend. The salary should have been the selling point. It wasn't, and I'm glad of that.

Still, she wants to know more. I'm glad of that as well.

"What exactly would you want me to do?" she asks. It's beyond her better judgment. She can't help herself.

I relax. My scheme hasn't caught her interest yet, but I'm near done trying to entice her to play the game I'm asking her to play. "Pretend we're a couple. I'd invite you to several gatherings where my mother would see us together. I'd expect you to hang on my arm and behave as though we're madly in love."

"And that's all?"

"That's all." That's not all I want, but it's all I had planned to ask tonight. My plans are on the verge of changing.

It's only because I'm studying her so closely that I notice her swallow.

"This pretend relationship—to what extent would I be expected to perform?"

I don't know if I'm angry or turned on that she's so nervous about the prospect of sleeping with me.

Turned on, I decide. The way her eyes dart up and down my body, the way her gaze keeps returning to my lips—I know she's as attracted to me as I am to her. She simply doesn't want to be considered a whore, and neither would I want that for her.

She'll have to become more comfortable than that if she expects me to give her what she wants—what she needs. I can tolerate innocence but I won't take ambiguity when it comes to a physical relationship. "Don't pussyfoot about it. You're asking about sex."

It's then that I make my decision once and for all. Though it isn't supposed to be part of the arrangement, though it's not what I meant for tonight, I have to have her and I can't wait any longer for her to know. "I never pay for sex, Alayna. When I fuck you, it will be for free."

Her eyes widen and unmistakably darken. She wriggles in her chair. I've revealed her weakness for me and she doesn't know how to react. She's helpless.

And I'm turned on as fuck at her discomfort.

"Maybe I should go," she says.

"Do you want to?" I know she doesn't. I'm inviting her to stay.

"I'm n-not sure. Yes. I think I should." She stutters her response.

It's sexy as hell. I want to hear her shaking and stuttering with my tongue in her cunt. I'm hard at the thought.

"Because you're uncomfortable with my proposition?" I can't stop myself—I have to make her squirm more. "Or because I told you that I'm going to fuck you?"

"I'm…yes. That."

I tilt my head, intrigued. Is she playing hard to get or is she ignoring the chemistry between us? "But I'm certain that's not a surprise to you, Alayna. You feel the electricity between us. Your body language expresses it quite well. I wouldn't be surprised to find you're already wet."

She blushes and I almost take her right here.

I flash a smile. "Don't be embarrassed. Don't you know I feel the same?" My cock grows harder and it's my turn to shift in my seat. "If you were to carefully read my body, you'd see the evidence."

Fuck my agenda for the evening. There's no use talking about it anymore, the only thing that interests me now is her—her mouth, her breasts, her long taut legs. It's my club and I could easily bend her over the table and drive into her, my balls slapping along the back of her thighs, her pussy clenching around me.

The only thing stopping me is that it's also where she works. It wouldn't be fair to her, so I must control myself.

But as uncomfortable as it promises to make me, I'm not ready to end this heated flirtation. So I don't. "Let's table my proposition to hire you for a moment and discuss this other thing further. Please understand that they are very separate from each other. I'd never want you to think my sexual desire for you was in any way part of a sham for my parents and their friends."

"I'm—I don't know how to react to someone stating they desire me." She's flustered. Surprised.

I'm at a loss. I frown. "Has no man told you that before?" Surely she knows how attractive she is. Her beauty goes beyond her physical looks—it's her aura, her carriage, the way her eyes shine and the way her forehead creases with worry. She is a combination of strong and weak—like a beautiful vase that has been shattered and glued back together so perfectly that you can only see the cracks when looking very closely. She epitomizes the rising of the phoenix from the ashes. Many a man must have burned up in her presence.

She fumbles with her glass. "Not in so many words. Actions sometimes. Certainly not so bluntly."

I almost curse at her admission. "That's a shame." How has no one recognized the preciousness of the gem before me? She doesn't recognize it in herself, even. It's disappointing. Heartbreaking, if I were the type who had a heart.

Without meaning to, I find myself reaching across the table for her hand. I stroke my thumb across her unbearably soft skin. "I plan to tell you every chance I get."

Now where the hell did that come from? But no sooner are the words out of my mouth than I know they're true. I'm breaking all my rules with this woman, acting outside my very nature. Maybe other men have survived her flames, but I fear I'm already burning.

She pulls her hand away. "Oh."

I see the wheels turning in her head. She's retreating. Fast. "I, uh, I'm feeling a bit overwhelmed. I need to go. You've given me a lot to think about."

She stands and I do too. I don't want her to leave. My pulse speeds up and there's sweat on my brow. Is this panic? It's an unfamiliar sensation, and I feel like I'm spiraling out of control.

I practically plead to Alayna to stay. "I wish you wouldn't. But if you must…"

She won't meet my eyes. "I've got to get to work."

She heads for the door, and I follow. Just as she places her hand on the knob, I press my palm on the top, preventing her from opening it. This is not in my script. This is not on my agenda. All I know is that I cannot let her leave.

I lower my head to her ear and it takes all I have not to nibble on her lobe. "Wait, Alayna." My cock stiffens as I breathe her in. Her scent is shampoo and bodywash and sweet musk—none of those flowery perfumes cover up her natural aroma.

Without premeditation, I speak, letting the words flow naturally. "I apologize for overwhelming you. That wasn't my intent. But I want you to know that whether or not you decide to help with my situation, I will continue to seduce you. I'm a man who gets what he wants. And I want you."

Then I can't help myself anymore—I do nibble on her ear. She gasps and leans her head to the side. With her neck exposed, I am a kid in a candy store. I nip and lick along her neck. She grabs my arm and that's my invitation to wrap my other arm around her. I palm her breast. She leans into my hand, and I feel her nipple pebble through her dress. All I can think about is sucking on it, pulling it with my teeth.

I squeeze her tit and nuzzle my face into her hair. "I should have told you earlier—you look absolutely beautiful tonight. I can't keep my eyes off you. Serious and sexy wrapped into one package." This isn't the most appropriate place for this, but I can't fucking stand to wait another minute longer. "Kiss me, Alayna."

Slowly, she turns her head toward me. I'm there to meet her. I take her mouth with mine, sliding my tongue in to tangle with hers. Her lips are soft and silky, but she meets my greedy ardor with equal fervor. I'm demanding, needing her to understand that this is how it will be with me—I will take the lead, I will dominate. Even when I'm as out-of-control as I am at the moment, I will guide us through the physical.

And her taste...

It's incredible. It's addictive. It's delicious.

I want to taste her everywhere. Want to trail my tongue along her navel. Want to suck on her clit. Want to lick the slit of her cunt.

We shift together, turning until our bodies are lined up. I grab her ass, drawing her closer, and she wraps her hands around my neck. God, I want her. I want her like I've never wanted anyone. I know I can't take her here, and yet I'm not sure I can stop. Especially when she starts grinding her hips against my cock. She's the matador waving the red flag, and I'm the bull about to charge.

But nothing about this is right. The location, the timing...most of all, the circumstances. This night is about the game. I don't want the taint of that overshadowing the glory of being buried inside her. Celia does not get an invitation into our bed.

Thoughts of Celia make it easier to push Alayna away. I keep my hands on her shoulders, though, keeping her at a distance. It would take only the brush of her body against mine and I'd change my mind about fucking her right now. We pant in unison as we recover our breathing, my eyes never leaving hers.

I see it when the disappointment and concern settle in. Wanting to ease her, I brush a hand down her cheek. "Not here, precious. Not like this." I wrap my other hand around her neck and press my forehead to hers. "I will have you beneath me. In a bed. Where I can adore you properly." This promise is the only thing keeping me gentlemanly. I won't have her tonight. But I *will* have her.

I trail my hand down to her bra where I know she keeps her phone. I feast on the curve of her breast as I remove her cell. I swipe her screen and call my own phone. I hang up as soon as it rings. I already have her number, of course, but I want her to see that I've gotten it legitimately. "Now we have each other's numbers. I expect you to use it."

I replace her phone inside her bra, my eyes lingering once more on the swell of her cleavage. My dick is so hard it hurts. It's a risk kissing her again, so I simply brush my lips across hers. "Call me when you're ready." Except I'm afraid she won't be ready as soon as I'd like, so I add, "Tomorrow."

I kiss her chastely and rush out. I will definitely need a turn with my hand tonight. Even two turns may not be enough to relieve me.

EIGHT

Before

I drove myself to the Brookes' party. Usually if there was a chance I might get drunk, I would have relied instead on a driver. But I needed full control that night—that required no drinking and an easy escape route. After the shaky ending to the previous evening, I'd decided it was time to wrap the Celia experiment up for good. I'd made it clear there would be no us until she broke up with her boyfriend. If she didn't offer to end things with him at this point, then I'd have to change my conclusion. Maybe her silly attachment was stronger than I thought. Maybe I was wrong.

But I doubted that.

I arrived after the sun had set and the party was in full swing. I wanted Celia waiting for me by the time I showed up. Part of me was surprised that she hadn't tried to call me to make sure I was still coming. Though, with the way she'd left things the night before, I bet that she was giving me space. I also bet it was killing her.

I parked my car far from the house so I'd be sure to not be blocked in. As I walked up the long drive, I noted that Celia's car wasn't there. It didn't mean anything. She could have been driven. She likely figured I'd give her a ride home. That wasn't in my plans.

I halted for a moment at the front walk. What exactly were my plans? If Celia decided she was breaking up with Dirk, I'd have to tell her it was all a misunderstanding, of course. But after that, when she was crying and quite possibly mad as hell—what then? I was consumed with wanting to know her full reaction. In my dream ending, she'd make a public display and I'd be a front row spectator. This was the most fascinating part of the entire study, after all. Emotions. How they weakened the strong. How they deluded the intelligent. How they transformed a person into someone unrecognizable. I had an advantage with Celia that I hadn't had with many of my previous studies—I knew people in her life well enough to be privy to the aftermath. I'd hear from my mother how quickly she recovered, whether or not Celia decided to get back with Dirk. I'd probably be on Sophia's shit list for it, but that would be an improvement from being not on her list at all.

But wait. I was getting ahead of myself. Celia hadn't even broken up with her boyfriend yet. No need to worry about the after when I was still in the before.

Inside the house, I grabbed a beer and found a group of acquaintances to sit with. Though I didn't plan to drink much of it, I needed the bottle in hand as a prop. It made me seem casual, relaxed. The less desperate I appeared to Celia, the better. When she found me and realized I'd had no urgency to find her, I suspected it would raise her own desperation. She'd invite me to talk. I'd shrug and go along. My aloof demeanor would force her to play her best hand.

It was only a guess. But it was calculated and I had a good deal of faith in it.

When nearly an hour went by, and I'd seen no sign of The Subject, I began to wonder if I'd overestimated my holdings. Had she decided not to come? Looking for her was out of the question. Inquiring about her would also give up some of my leverage. But if I were careful about the way I asked...

I hooked eyes with Christina across the room. She'd been trying to get my attention for the last fifteen minutes, and I'd pretended not to notice. But damn, I noticed. She was wearing a short skirt that rode her hips and a halter top so high that miles of skin showed in between. She oozed sex. Her fuck-me lips were painted with a light gloss that made them look like they'd just been licked. She was a distraction—a distraction that I didn't need.

But if anyone knew of Celia's whereabouts, it was her.

I played the staring game with her, exchanging lewd glances until she beckoned me over. I pretended to consider it. Then I made my way through the swarm of bodies toward her, hoping that the stiffy I was sporting wouldn't be witnessed by Celia. Maybe, if I worked the situation right, Christina could be my reward for concluding my experiment. Too consumed with my plans to think about my cock, it had been weeks since I'd gotten laid. Too long. I needed to be buried in pussy soon. And Christina Brooke was in possession of a more than acceptable pussy.

She leaned against the dining room archway as I approached, her eyes pinned on me. "Hudson Pierce." She said my name with a slow seductive smile. "It took you long enough."

I feigned innocence. "To get to the party?"

"To come looking for me." She wet her lips and my gaze immediately rushed to her tongue as it flicked along its path.

Damn, she was going to make it difficult to keep focused, but I tried all the same. "I didn't come looking for you. You summoned me."

"That I did." Her gaze flickered to my lips and back to my eyes. "And you came."

"No, I didn't. Not yet." Flirting was easy with Christina Brooke. I'd have fucked her in high school if it weren't for the fact she'd had a steady boyfriend. The boyfriend hadn't been a problem for me, but Christina had been loyal. She'd also been innocent then. The way her demeanor had loosened up since the summer before, I had to think college had stripped her of her naiveté.

And then all I could think about was stripping Christina of other things.

"Oh, such a naughty boy." Her grin was as wicked as my thoughts. "I sure hope that you haven't already chosen your target for when you do."

"And why is that?"

"Because I'd like to volunteer."

I stifled a laugh but kept my face straight. "That's funny that you think you'd have any choice in the matter." I placed a hand on the wall above her head and leaned in. "I mean, if you're my target, I'd hit it, whether invited to or not."

Her intake of breath was audible. "Damn. You just soaked my panties."

I glanced down at her tight skirt, imagining what sort of panties she was wearing underneath. Then imagining beneath the panties. "Maybe you shouldn't be wearing any."

"That could be arranged."

The banter was more than fun. It was getting me hot and making me forget my real purpose for approaching her. I dropped my hand from the wall and took a sip from the beer I was nursing, forcing my mind to switch gears. "Why are you alone anyway, Christina? I expected to see Celia hanging at your side."

She gave a bored shrug. "She was here earlier."

"She already left?" *Shit.* I'd been too cocky to think that she'd wait.

"She might be back later. She said she needed some recovery time." Christina swept her hair off her shoulder.

I raised a brow. What did she need to recover from? My nerves stood on end, concerned that I'd misstepped somewhere along the way. Self-centered thinking, maybe, but it didn't end my worry.

Christina answered my questioning expression. "She broke up with her boyfriend today."

My heart pounded in my ears. *Celia had broken up with Dirk.* It couldn't be that easy, could it? I'd been prepared for a confrontation. I'd been prepared to put on a good show of longing. The news was almost anti-climactic, but still very satisfying.

"Are you sure they really broke up?" I took another tug of my beer to hide my glee. That swallow finished off the drink.

"Yeah, I'm sure. She was here when he called." Christina took the bottle from my hand and set it on the buffet behind her. She waited until she was facing me again before she continued. "I don't think she was planning to dump him, exactly, but one minute she was saying hello and the next she was saying she was sorry it was over. Yeah, I eavesdropped, but she didn't leave the room, so I figured fair game."

"Damn." As if I'd judge her for eavesdropping. I could kiss her for it. And I would kiss her—very soon. A victory kiss followed by a victory plunge.

But first, there were too many unknowns. Celia and Dirk may have had a fight that had nothing to do with me. I needed more information before I could truly celebrate success. And I needed my source to give it to me without noticing I was prying.

With my hands free of the bottle, I moved into Christina, pressing her further into the wall. My dick hardened at the full body contact. "Why did Celia do that? I thought she was really into her boyfriend."

Christina chortled. "You did not. You thought she was into you." *So I had no need to cloak my interest after all.* "And she is. She dumped him because of you." She ground her pelvis against mine.

A surge of triumph washed through me. My pulse quickened both from the excitement of my achievement and from the knowledge that I was about to fuck and fuck hard. It was almost painful to draw out the celebration, but I also knew the pleasure of delayed gratification.

Christina traced a finger along my jaw. "Obviously, you don't return the feeling."

"And she thinks of you as a close friend, Christina. Obviously, you don't return that feeling." God, what despicable people we were. We deserved each other. At least for the night.

"Au contraire. I love her like a sister." She trailed her hands up the sides of my fitted shirt, sending sparks of electricity thrumming through my veins. "But she is not Hudson Pierce material. She could never handle you."

"And you think you can?" It was my turn to smirk. As if anyone could handle me. I was the one who handled people. Just like I was handling Christina Brooke. She may have thought she'd seduced me from across the room, but it was I who was in control. And when I took her, it would be on my terms.

But allowing her to believe she had the power was half the fun.

"I know I can." Her chin jutted forward in a challenge. Or she was hinting that she wanted to be kissed—probably a combination of both.

"Interesting."

"Is it really? Because I'll tell you what I think would be interesting." She grabbed me through my pants, and I grew stiffer in her hand. If she kept that up, I'd come right there.

That wasn't happening. I needed to get inside her. I needed to be balls deep. I needed to pound out the strange mixture of victory and self-loathing that was currently messing with my head. Waiting was done. It was time to act out my desires.

I leaned in to Christina's ear. "Unless it starts with my tongue in your mouth and ends with my cock in your cunt, I don't want to hear it."

Her eyes dilated as she peeked up at me under her long lashes. "Let's go to my bedroom, shall we?"

It didn't have to be a bedroom. It didn't even have to be private. "I'll give you two minutes and wherever we are in that time, that's where you're getting fucked."

She led me upstairs and to her room within her time limit. But just barely. As soon as the door was shut behind us, I was on her. My mouth mashed against hers in a bruising, erotic kiss. I plunged my tongue between her lips, immediately establishing my dominance. This would not be playful sex. This would not be sweet sex. This would be rough sex. This would be sex on my terms.

I broke the kiss long enough to pull her tank over her head. My hands palmed her breasts as I resumed my power over her mouth. She moaned as I bit at her lips. She sighed as I squeezed her tits. She yelped as I pinched her nipples. She loved it—every single minute of it.

I'd lost my virginity before I was sixteen, and in the three plus years that I'd engaged in sexual activity, I'd been broad in my exploration of technique and style. There were times that I fully enjoyed the idea of turning a woman on. It was a turn-on for me—not because I cared so much if my partner experienced pleasure but because it was a chance for me to exude my power. Like any of my experiments, I craved the dissection of cause and effect. I reveled in guessing what effect my actions would have on each of my lovers.

I knew how Christina would want it from her initial reactions to my dirty talk. She wanted me dominant and controlling. Fortunately, that was exactly the way I wanted to get off that night.

Without untangling my tongue from hers, I pushed her back to the bed. She started to sit, pulling me down with her, but she was not in charge of this experience. I was. I pulled away, exerting my domination and urged her to stand again. I turned her so her back was to me and nudged her down on the bed so that her ass was in the air in front of me. I placed my hands at the top of her thighs and caressed up to her ass, pushing her skirt up to her waist as I did. Her behind was round, plump, perfect for kneading. Perfect for biting.

Brushing the thin material of her thong aside, I swept my tongue across her cleft and then clamped my teeth into the flesh of her ass. She howled and my cock leapt. I danced my finger over her hole and found her wet and ready. Thank God I didn't have to put much effort into prepping her. I was eager to be inside.

I pushed her panties down to her knees. "Spread your legs," I commanded as I undid my zipper and pulled my jeans down just far enough to release my pulsing cock. Then, without warning, I shoved into her, filling her deeply with my first stroke. Shit, she was tight, and I realized she hadn't been as ready as I'd imagined. That was fine. She felt goddamn amazing—snug and clamped down around me.

Gripping her hips, I began to plough at a steady pace, my jeans falling further down my thighs. I watched my cock as it thrust in and pulled out. It turned me on more. This was my favorite position—going from behind. It was the most erotic view and decidedly less intimate than face-to-face. Plus, it just felt good.

"Please tell me you're on birth control." I'd been reckless to not put on a condom, but frankly, I was feeling invincible. The triumph of Celia's break-up, the way my plan had played out just as I'd planned, that I was fucking the girl of my choice in the way that I wanted—it was a powerful moment for me. I exhilarated in it.

"Yes. The pill." Her voice trembled and I slammed into her harder, faster, the sound of my balls slapping against her skin the sensual underscore of our intercourse.

"Of course you are. Because you're a dirty little slut, aren't you? You have to take precautions because you never know when you'll let yourself be fucked.

Whenever you get the opportunity." I didn't always go for the demeaning sex talk, but it was a nice touch when the girl was into it.

Christina's channel tightened around my cock. She was definitely into it.

"Say it," I demanded. "Tell me you're a dirty slut. Tell me you love to be fucked."

"I'm a dirty slut. I love to be fucked." She groaned it as much as spoke it, and immediately she grew wetter.

"Yes, you do love it." I let go of her hips and leaned over her body so I could be near her ear. "Now, Christina, you need to get ready to come. Because I'm coming soon and I'm not waiting for you. You're so good at being fucked, though, I don't think it will be a problem." I reached under her to rub her clit as I spoke. I wanted her squeezing my dick with her orgasm.

Whether it was my words or my rubbing, Christina complied, quickly erupting around me with a scream.

There, that was what I needed. I followed with a long, low grunt. My fingers returned to her hips, digging into her skin as I throbbed and pounded out the last of my climax.

I was still inside her when the bedroom door flew open.

Automatically, my face turned to see who our audience was. My eyes connected with familiar blues—Celia.

Could my night get any better? I'd thought the whole plan had ended perfectly before, but this was the real icing on the cake. Now, in this moment, Celia would realize that I didn't actually feel the emotions that I'd led her to believe I'd felt. I'd thought I'd have to have a conversation about it. But, oh, do actions speak louder than words.

Celia froze in her spot. Her eyes darted from me to Christina and back to me. It all seemed to take minutes, but in reality, only a few quick seconds passed before her hands flew to cover her eyes. "Oh, my God."

It was only then that Christina noticed our intruder. "Fuck! Celia." She moved to get out from under me, but I held her in place.

"I'm sorry." Celia's voice cracked. "I've made a terrible mistake."

She spun and headed out the way she'd come in.

I could have gone another round—I was hard again from Celia's interruption—and the last thing my cock wanted to do was withdraw from its warm cocoon. But I was desperate to draw more reaction from Celia. This was the final stage of the experiment—the recording of results. I had to know what she was thinking, what she was feeling. What she *thought* she was feeling.

Without cleaning up, I stuffed myself in my pants and gave directions to Christina. "Take off your skirt and panties and wait for me here. Next time I won't be so gentle."

She scrambled to obey as I left her. My cock throbbed, yelling at me to stay. My heart, on the other hand, beat wildly at the thrilling outcome of my experiment. The adrenaline and an ability to guess where Celia would go—to her car—allowed me to make up for the distance she'd put between us, though I didn't spot her until I was outside.

"Celia, wait," I called across the front lawn. I tried to sound urgent and panicked. I feared I sounded delighted.

She didn't turn to me but acknowledged me with her middle finger. "Fuck you, Hudson."

"Come on, wait." I ran to catch up. When I was close enough, I reached for her arm.

She snapped out of my grasp then spun around to face me. "What? What do you want from me?" Tears fell in torrents down her cheeks. Her voice was surprisingly steady considering. The look though, was off-putting. Her obvious heartache tugged at something in my gut, something I had no familiarity with.

I ran a hand through my hair, a bit thrown. A breath later, I managed to say something. "We were going to talk. I came here tonight to talk."

She laughed, her expression in complete contradiction to the flowing stream from her eyes. "That's fucking hilarious. You came here to talk to me and what? You couldn't find me so you *talked* to Christina instead?"

This was excellent. Her emotion was pure, raw. It intoxicated me in a way that very little else could. I wanted to bottle it, inhale it, take it in and process her feelings in depth. Since none of that was possible, I wanted to draw out as much as I could before she walked away.

I stepped toward her. She stepped back.

"What is it that I did wrong, Celia?" My voice was steady and controlled, in stark opposition to hers. "You act as though I owe you something. What exactly do you think is going on between us?"

A sob escaped her lips and she wiped at her tears with her hand. "I told you I loved you, Hudson. You kissed me."

Another step toward her. "*You* kissed me."

"And you insinuated that the only reason you stopped was because I had a boyfriend."

Ah, her side. The details of my cruel setup cited back to me like a melody I'd orchestrated but was only now hearing. It was beautiful.

I looked at my feet, hiding the corners of a smile. "No. No, Ceeley." I lifted my eyes to hers. "I'm truly sorry if you got the wrong impression. I was simply reminding you not to throw away your relationship with Dirk simply because you remembered how you once felt for me."

"How I felt for…?" Her eyes flared with incredulity. "That is not what happened. You were feeling things for me too."

"No. I wasn't." Here was the highlight of my act. My joy in performing it was a testament to my sadistic nature. I softened my expression. "I mean, I care for you. A great deal. I always have, I always will. I know that's probably hard to hear, but that's all I've ever felt regarding you."

I was good. I knew it. I felt it.

Except Celia didn't break the way I'd expected. In fact, her tears slowed and her brows furrowed in confusion. "What…what are you doing, Hudson?"

The way she looked at me, the way her gaze pierced through me—did she know? Had she figured out it was all an act? There was no way she could know. Who would guess that?

I paused too long before answering. "I'm trying to straighten out this misunderstanding."

She studied me. "No, you're not. You're running away." Her shoulders, which had sagged only a moment before, squared with renewed strength. She was the one who took a step toward me this time.

I was the one who stepped back.

"You're convinced that you shouldn't be allowed to feel anything or that having emotions will make you weak or something equally as ridiculous, and so you're pushing me away."

My calm was unraveling. Her words—they stung. They bit at me. They burned. And like the dragon who was angered by the meager attempts of humans to draw it down, I grew furious.

She took advantage of my setback. "Stop pushing me away," she pled.

The softness of her appeal, the sweetness in her eyes, the sincerity of her posture—it stirred me. There she was assuming things about me again. She wanted to see me feel? Well, I was feeling a whole shitstorm of rage. "You don't have a fucking clue what you're talking about," I hissed.

Her attack—because I refused to call it anything else—didn't waver. "Stop this, Hudson. Stop lying to me. Stop lying to yourself. This isn't who you are."

Fury spread through me so thick that it propelled me forward until I was in her face. "This *is* who I am, Celia. Don't you dare think you know something different. What you see is what you get."

"You're a fucking coward." Her voice caught and I savored the victory. To her credit, she didn't back away. "This was your chance to be a man, Hudson. I could have even forgiven your thing with Christina if you could just be honest now."

"You could forgive me?" My eyes widened in mock exclamation. "Well, hell. How will I ever go on without your pardon?" My voice was uncharacteristically loud. I didn't care. Venom was spewing from me whether I wanted it to or not—and I *wanted* it to. It was no longer about an experiment of emotion. I wanted to hurt Celia. She was the very example of how love weakened a person. She was pathetic. I loathed her.

I loathed myself for contributing to this creation.

"Scratch coward. I meant to say asshole." She was too kind to me.

I stepped back from her, not in retreat, but in disgust. I was consumed with it—the emotion wrapping around my insides like a cobra. "Jesus, you're really a piece of work, Celia Werner. What did you think was going to happen between us? You thought I was going to love you? You thought we were going to ride off into the sunset together? You're the one who needs to stop lying to yourself. That's a fairy tale, Ceeley, and I stopped believing in those a long time ago. It's time you grew up too."

I was done with her. Done with all of it. I left her there, crying on the edge of the driveway. I didn't turn back once.

The next two hours I spent alleviating my temper in carnal ways with Christina. I fucked her hard and long and unrelentingly until she was raw and I was numb inside and out. A quick shot of whiskey before I left the Brookes' kept the numbness clinging to me until I pulled into the driveway at Mabel Shores. I closed my eyes and rested my head for a moment on the steering wheel of my BMW Z4, a high school graduation present from my parents. I felt...tired. Exhausted. Drained. I certainly had notes to add to my log. My findings had been satisfactory, though not as precise as I would have wished. A part of me wanted to study further in this vein—would another subject react as Celia did, turning on me? Or was it her close relationship with me that produced the results I'd seen?

A bigger part of me never wanted to experiment with a subject so close to me again. It was too unreliable of a study. From then on, I promised myself, my research would be conducted further from home.

I'd been too distracted to notice Celia's car until I'd gotten out of my own. It was parked at the other end of the circle drive. Its appearance was ominous—I didn't like what it could possibly mean. I walked over to make sure she wasn't waiting inside. She wasn't. So I headed inside the house. The front door was locked, which meant if Celia was inside, she'd been let in before the house had been shut up for the night.

I intended to search for her but halted when I discovered Mirabelle curled in a ball reading on the main staircase. "Why are you still awake?"

"What's it to you?" She must have sensed that I was in no mood for her attitude because she quickly amended. "It's summer. I don't have a curfew. Or a nanny anymore, it appears."

Right. Erin was fired. Mother must have won that battle.

If we had parents that gave a damn, Mirabelle would have a curfew whether it was summer or not. "As long as you're up—" Might as well use her for information. "What's Celia's car doing here?"

My sister shrugged her slight shoulders. "She came by. I told her you weren't home and she said she'd wait for you on the patio. That was, like, two hours ago. She probably fell asleep out there."

"Fuck," I mumbled under my breath. I wasn't in the mood to deal any more with Celia that night. But it would be even worse to have to explain her sleeping on a deck chair in the morning.

I nodded up the stairs. "Get to bed, Mirabelle."

"I don't—"

"Get to bed."

"Fine." She stomped up the stairs muttering something about "never having any fun." I waited until she was out of sight before checking on Celia. Last thing I needed was Mirabelle as a witness to whatever was going to happen next.

The patio outside was empty, so I walked down to the pool to see if Celia had ended up there. She wasn't there either. I was about to head down to the beach when I noticed the lights on in the guest house. My father had stayed there after the party the night before, and that morning my mother had his things moved as well. Maybe Celia had wandered over looking for me.

I'd only taken two steps toward the house when the door opened. Celia walked out then my father appeared in the doorway behind her. From where I was, and in the dark, I couldn't be sure, but it seemed he wasn't wearing anything but swim trunks or boxer briefs. He held his hand out and he must have said something because Celia turned back to him. She took his hand. He pulled her to him. And they kissed. It wasn't a long kiss, but I knew that kind of kiss. It wasn't a first kiss—it was a thanks-for-the-fuck kind of kiss.

My stomach churned, and I looked away. I stepped back into the darkness both to remain unseen and to be off the pathway in case I puked—I'd rather do that on the lawn.

At some point, their kiss must have ended, because when I glanced back, the door was closed and Celia was halfway up the walk. She slowed the tiniest bit when she saw me, but she didn't stop. As she passed, I saw her more clearly—her lips were swollen, her hair and clothes a mess. We didn't speak a word to each other, but a conversation transpired nonetheless. With my eyes, I told her I knew. With her eyes, she told me we were even.

With our silence, we said that it was done now. *We* were done now.

It was a shared understanding. Soon she was gone and a few minutes later, I heard her car starting up in the driveway.

Then I walked down to the guest house. Celia and I might be done, but my father and I were not. He'd done a lot of fucked up shit before, but this I couldn't stand by without giving him my take on the situation. This was too low. Fucking his wife's best friend's daughter not one hundred feet away from where his wife slept? No wonder I had no sense of ethics.

The light inside the guest house was out now, but I knocked on the door lightly—light enough that he might assume it was Celia again and not his full-grown son. It didn't take long before he answered the door, and when he did, I was ready. I punched him in the face. Hard.

I left him cursing and holding his cheek. He didn't need any explanation for my behavior. He might have been an asshole, but he wasn't an idiot.

The night hadn't gone exactly as I'd planned. But I'd finished my experiment. I'd ended the drama with Celia. I'd learned more about how the idea of love affected human behavior. I'd even gotten laid.

If it had been such a fulfilling evening, why did I feel so fucking empty?

With my head throbbing and my chest heavy, sleep took its time to arrive. When it finally did, I dreamed I was in a fire, that flames licked at me, scorching me, robbing me of oxygen, destroying me. I woke in a sweat. *Fucking nightmare.* It held no truth in it.

In reality, I wasn't on fire. I *was* the fire.

— CHAPTER —

NINE

After

It's been two days since I first kissed Alayna. Yesterday, she came by my office and accepted my proposal. I was surprised, to say the least, as I'd thought I'd need more time to work on her. I was glad though, because I could then concentrate on the aspects of our relationship that interested me more.

After our arrangement was settled, I took her upstairs to the loft and made her come with my fingers and my tongue. The experience was unlike any other I'd had with a woman. While it wasn't the first time that I'd given pleasure with no expectation for the return, it was the first time it hadn't been about me. Usually, my focus is on my own skills. I'm studying, investigating. Watching and mentally recording how my actions cause the woman I'm with to respond. I love to try and find the trigger points. Love to discover how to make her come. It's intriguing. It's fascinating. It's also very self-centered.

With Alayna, however, my thoughts were not on myself at all except in the sense of how could I make it better for *her*. From her first moan, I became her slave. Everything I did after that was for her—for her pleasure, for her release, for her satisfaction. My entire being disappeared in the singular purpose of making her feel good. Though the episode ended with my cock rock hard and uncomfortable in my pants, it was the most fantastic sexual experience I'd ever had.

We made plans to meet this evening. I can't stop thinking about being inside her cunt. I'm so preoccupied by it that I've only half-heartedly addressed many of my other obligations—including Celia. I haven't spoken to her in days and she's eager for news. Not wanting that to disrupt my night, I figure I better speak with her before Alayna arrives.

Shortly after three, I walk out of my office, briefcase in hand, and ask my secretary to clear the rest of my afternoon. Then I come up to the loft through the main elevator so that even she doesn't know I'm still in the building. It reduces my chances of being disturbed.

Once in the loft, I make the call I've been dreading.

"It's about fucking time," Celia says in place of a greeting.

"Since when have frequent check-ins been a requirement?" I look longingly at my bar, but I'd prefer to have all my senses about me when Alayna arrives later.

"They're not a requirement. They're a courtesy." She's calmer, though. "Right now, I don't even know if this is a go or not."

"It's a go." I massage the bridge of my nose and a bitter taste gathers in my mouth. It's guilt that I'm feeling. While there are few emotions that I'm familiar with, guilt is one I know full-well. It's the monkey on my back. I carry it everywhere.

"Good." The satisfaction in her voice carries through the phone. "Then our first outing is this Sunday at your mother's charity event?"

"It is." I won't tell Celia I'm seeing Alayna before then. Nor will I tell her the nature of our time spent together for no other reason except that it's none of her business. I actually believe that Celia would approve—the more time I spend with Alayna, after all, the more likely she is to become attached. That is the risk I'm taking with my soon-to-be lover, but I have faith in Alayna.

Besides, I can't help myself.

Though not necessary, Celia and I have previously agreed that she will be present at the major events of our scam. I suspect she'll try to push her way in for more, and that I will not allow. "Is that all you need, Celia?"

"No. I'd like to hear the details."

I shake my head even though she can't see me. "I'm not sharing details. Not today and not in the future. I'm not checking in with you. You will not call me regarding the situation." I sense she's about to interrupt me, but I speak over her. "I've arranged things as you've requested, Celia. And I'll follow through, though I realize I have no reason at this point to do so."

"Because you own the club now? Hudson, you know as well as I do that I would find another way to follow through with my experiment." The click of her heels on the floor suggests she's pacing as she talks. "I'm invested in this project now. I won't let it go. It has such great potential. Frankly, I'm disappointed that you aren't as intrigued as I am by the emotional psyche of Alayna Withers."

I *am* as intrigued as Celia. More, I think, but I won't give her the satisfaction of confirming that.

So I divert. "I don't believe you're going to see the results you believe you are." Especially after spending time with Alayna. Every minute in her presence I'm more convinced that she's stronger than she looks.

Celia chuckles. "We have different hypotheses. That only intrigues me more. You know that."

I do know that. I also understand it. A memory flashes into my mind—a similar situation, a similar conversation. The subject was a woman who worked for one of Celia's design accounts. Her fiancé had flirted with Celia, rather innocently, at a company party. It was enough to interest Celia in a game. We devised a scheme where I told the subject that her betrothed had been unfaithful. It was my theory that the subject would forgive the indiscretion. Celia believed otherwise.

The scam had very little interest to me except for the difference in our theories. We fabricated proof that I presented to the woman. It was believable. In the end, the subject did forgive her fiancé.

But she also let me fuck her against the wall of the ladies bathroom.

She either didn't much value fidelity or it was a revenge fuck. Either way, I was pleased—my hypothesis had been correct. Celia's had been wrong.

Letting Celia know I differ in opinion about the predicted conclusion has only increased her invested interest in the experiment with Alayna Withers. It was a mistake, I realize now. I'm usually not so sloppy. Is it because I've been so long out of the game? Or is it Alayna that throws me?

I really have no idea.

A beep in my ear indicates a text has come through on my Blackberry. "Celia, I have a matter I need to take care of." Whatever the message is, at least it's an excuse to get off the phone. "I'll see you Sunday at the event."

I don't wait for her goodbye before ending the call. Then I check my texts. The message is from Jordan, who is now officially driving Alayna rather than simply tailing her. He's just picked her up and is bringing her to my building now. Bringing her to me.

I prepare for her the best I can, brushing my teeth and removing my suit jacket. Inside, I'm a ball of nervous energy. I don't remember the last time that I looked forward to sex with this much eagerness. College, maybe? High school?

No, I don't think I've ever been this anxious. That realization stops me in my tracks. Not wanting the situation to get out of hand—or to scare Alayna off—I decide that I'll go slow. When she arrives, I'll keep my contact to a minimum until we both have a chance to settle in. I'll order dinner first. We'll take our time moving to the bedroom.

I pace the floor by the front door in anticipation of Alayna's arrival. Minutes before I expect her, my phone rings. It's business—Roger Kingsley, a board member at Plexis. He wouldn't be calling on a Friday afternoon if it weren't important. "Roger," I bark as I answer. "What's going on?"

Roger proceeds to apprise me of the situation emerging at Plexis. Profits have been down, and some of the other board members are interested in selling. A sale would result in the dismantling of the company. A lot of jobs would be lost.

"The board is seriously considering this latest offer," he tells me.

"Fuck," I mutter under my breath. I loosen my tie and unbutton the top of my shirt, attempting to relieve the stifling feeling that's overcome me. This news upsets me. One of the few things I care about is my corporation. I do not want my employees screwed like this.

"It's not going to get better, Pierce," Roger says. "I know you're coming on Monday, but Grant and some of the others are planning to take a vote over the weekend."

I'm about to deliver another string of curse words when I hear her knock. *She's here.*

I open the door and there she is—gorgeous and flushed. Her outfit is on the modest side compared to the other things I've seen her in, though her striped shorts could be a little longer. Her legs are lean and toned, and I'm already imagining them wrapped around me.

Suddenly I don't give a damn about Plexis. I only care about her.

Somehow I pick up on my cue to speak in the phone conversation. "Roger, I don't want to hear that we lost this company because my staff wasn't able to foresee the possibility of separation." I hold the receiver away from my mouth. "Come in," I whisper to Alayna.

She enters, and I shut the door behind her. I turn to look at her. She's devouring me with her eyes and it sparks my own want. The energy that passes between us is thick and palpable. Jesus, I thought I was excited before. Now, I'm desperate for her.

Roger's in mid-sentence, but I'm done with this call. "Take care of it, Roger. I expect this to be resolved before I arrive on Monday."

I toss my phone on the table, my eyes still pinned to Alayna's. Silence blankets us. It's not uncomfortable, necessarily, but it's heavy.

"Hi," she whispers. She can't take the anticipation. She's nervous. And adorable. And sexy as all fuck.

I can't help but smile.

Then she's in my arms, her mouth crashing against mine. For the barest fraction of a moment, I remember my plan to go slow. And I quickly abandon it. She tastes too good, her tongue licking into my mouth, swiping across my teeth. She's as desperate as I am, and I'm determined to meet her needs.

I'm also determined to touch her. My hands find their way under her shirt, and soon I'm caressing her breasts. They're firm and perfect. Her nipples are already pebbles under her bra. I need her undressed so I can touch them and suck them. I need her underneath me.

But then that strange desire returns, the one from yesterday. The one where I want to make her feel good more than I want to find pleasure for myself. It's so intense that I forget the aching need surging through my veins.

I force myself to push her away. "Jesus, Alayna. I want you so bad, I'm not behaving."

"Hudson." Her voice is breathy and full of want. She steps toward me. "If this is misbehaving, please don't stop." She slides my shirt off my shoulders—damn, I hadn't even noticed she'd worked open the buttons—then leans forward and licks my chest.

Involuntarily, I groan. "At least let me take you to a bed. If you keep this up, I'm going to fuck you against the door." Now I'm thinking about fucking her against the door. Which would be goddamn hot as hell, but so not what she deserves.

"That doesn't sound like the worst thing in the world," she murmurs as I lead her to my bedroom.

I put door-fucking on my mental to-do list. "No, it doesn't." At the bed, I pull her into my arms and bury my face in her neck. "But I won't be able to savor you properly and I'll forever regret it."

And I *want* to savor her. I want to make her feel good. I know she's never been pleased the way I'll please her. Not because I think I'm a better lover than she's had—though that's probably true—but because I won't let it be any other way.

Now, I need her breasts in my mouth.

I pull her shirt off, my eyes widening at how fuck-hot she looks in her black lace underwear. But I want her naked. I unclasp her bra and toss it to the ground.

Alayna pushes toward me, seemingly wanting to hide. I can't have that. I have to feast on her with my eyes. I hold her so I can see her.

God, she's perfect.

"I imagined you'd have beautiful breasts, Alayna. But I had no idea…" I can't even speak. My eyes glued to her tits, I push her to sit on my bed. Then I kneel in front of her and feast with my mouth. Cupping her breast with a hand, I tease my tongue across her nipple. She takes a shaky breath, but this isn't going to do it for her, I realize. She wants it rough.

Thank fuck.

With a growl, I take her pink peak into my mouth, sucking and tugging, first one breast then the other. She cries out, gasping and clutching my hair. I could probably make her climax just like this. She's so fucking sexy with her sounds and her scent that I'm about to come in my pants.

I force my mouth to move down, kissing along her stomach. "You're so responsive. I could spend all day sucking your gorgeous tits." I push her down to the bed. "But there's so much of you to adore."

I remove her shorts and panties. She asks about her shoes. I glance down at them. They're at least three-inch heels. She looks so goddamned delicious wearing them—I want her wearing *only* them. "I want them digging into my back when you wrap your legs around me," I tell her.

She shivers, and I'm euphoric. I already learned she likes it rough. Now I know she likes to be dominated as well. I'd have given her whatever she wanted, but rough and dominant are how I like to fuck the best. Pleasing her is going to be easier than I thought. And a shit ton of fun.

"Lean on your elbows," I command. She does and I bend her legs up and part her thighs. *Jesus Christ.* I let out a long stream of air as I trail my hands up the inside of her legs. "You're so fucking sexy like this. All spread out for me." I see her cunt clench as I run my fingers down her slit. "You want me. Look how your pretty pussy throbs."

I want her too. My cock is pulsing.

But I barely notice it. My focus is completely on Alayna. I continue to tease her with my fingers. When I can't stand it anymore, I replace my hand with my mouth, licking her, tasting her, sucking her. She comes quickly, but I want her to have more. I want to give her more.

"Again." I plunge my fingers in her hole and fuck her with my hand while I suck and tug on her clit. She's close—I can feel her trembling under my tongue—so I reach my hand up and pull on her nipples. This sends her over the edge. Her cunt clenches around my fingers as she thrashes against the bed. I'm so mesmerized by her beauty that a part of me wants to watch her until she's ridden the entire wave.

But more than that, I want to be inside of her. I take off my pants and find a condom. She's still quivering by the time I climb over her. I lean on my forearms. "You're ready for me," I say, more for myself than her. My cock is pressing at her opening, and I know I can't hold back any longer. Yet, the moment I enter her, I fear I will lose everything of myself.

I *hope* I will lose everything of myself.

It's the hope that allows me to push my tip in. "Jesus, Alayna." I'm already in heaven and I haven't even fully entered her. "You feel so goddamn good."

She's so snug, so tight. I push her thigh back, widening her, and I slide the rest of the way in. "So good." Alayna's adjusted to me now. I pull out all the way slowly. I consider taking my time working up to a steady tempo. But that isn't how either of us wants it. So when I drive back in, I thrust hard.

She cries out, her face twisted in pleasure. I lean down and kiss her, fucking her mouth with my tongue as I continue to pound into her cunt. Though I'm lost in the complete ecstasy of her, I'm ever mindful of her needs. Soon she's rocking against me, writhing to meet each plunge. I need to get her where she wants to be.

Without slowing my barrage, I direct her to wrap her legs around me. She does, and the new position opens her up even further. The heels of her shoes dig into my ass. I'm so deep inside her.

And it's then—as my balls slap against her with each drive, as her body tightens and contracts against my cock, as I reach the peak of my own release—it's then that my fears and hopes are realized. I *am* completely lost in Alayna Withers. Figuratively and literally. Completely and inescapably lost.

She trembles beneath me. Does she know what I'm thinking? Is she as moved by this revelation as I am?

"I'm going to come," she groans.

"Yes. Yes, come, Alayna." Because I can't hold on much longer and I want to go with her.

I want to go with her wherever she goes.

Her orgasm crashes through her and I follow, shouting her name, flying with her. And I feel a release that transcends the climax of our sexual activity. A release of unspoken words. This moment we've just had together, it's the most I've shared with any woman. As though we weren't simply fucking but communicating. As though we'd invented our own language, and through it, I was finally able to speak emotions that I never knew dwelled within me.

Or I just had a really good fucking orgasm and I'm poetic with hormones.

I collapse onto Alayna, my head cradled in her neck. I hope it's more than hormones. I hope I'm not waxing poetic. Whatever the cause of my emotional epiphany, the experience was really, really good. I'm more intrigued by her than ever. More tied to her than I ever thought possible.

This, though—this is the only way I can have her. In a bed. With my body. Because I have nothing else to give to her. I have nothing else that I can share with her. The want to be with her elsewhere is fantastical. It's a whim, a silly impulse that must be controlled.

And since this is all we will have that is real, I cling to it in a way that makes me think of a little child clutching a security blanket. It's overdramatized and slightly pathetic but genuine all at once.

I whisper into her skin, needing to share this feeling with her in whatever way I can. "I knew sex with you would be like that. Powerful and intense and fucking incredible. I knew it."

It's a lie, though. I had no idea it would be *that* good. No fucking idea at all.

— CHAPTER —

TEN

S he's sleeping.
  I went to the bathroom to clean up and came back to her gentle rhythmic breathing. The softness of it—of her skin, of her hair, of this moment—it makes me yearn for something I can't name.

I tug the blankets from underneath her and cover her.

Alayna struggles to sit up.

"Sleep, precious." I like the idea of her sleeping in my bed. Even though it's not the bed I tend to spend many nights in. It almost bothers me to see her in this place where I've had other women. She seems out-of-place.

But where else would I have her? Certainly not at The Bowery where I live. I bring no one there. Still I can't help but picture her in *that* bed...

The strange yearning is about to take over, and I refuse to let that happen. Though there's a part of me that wants to explore it and study it the way I've studied and explored the emotions of others, I know this isn't the time or the place to do so. It's not fair to Alayna. I want her to come out of this unscathed, and these notions are not healthy for either of us.

I need to focus on that, focus on the real, and abandon thoughts of the impossible.

I brush a kiss on her forehead. "I need to order dinner. Chinese okay?"

"Sounds delicious."

She stretches and her tits pop out from under the covers. They're gorgeous and are distracting me from food, but Alayna works later and I need to take care of her. "I'll call it in."

I feel her eyes on me as I leave the room, and I very nearly let them pull me back to her. Except I'm a man of discipline. I can abstain from the things that I can't have and Alayna Withers…I can only have her in this way—in measured doses. In fragments of time.

But when I *am* with her, I will be with her completely.

I make the call to the Chinese place on the corner. They're on speed dial and know me well.

Then I take a few minutes to gather my thoughts, to remind myself of the games I'm playing and the games I refuse to play. When I return, I need to distance myself from her. This evening can't be construed as anything but what it is—a simple fuck. She can't believe there is anything more to my desire than that.

Because there's not. I won't let there be, no matter what ideas are shaping in my mind.

I collect the clothes we'd discarded earlier in the living room, not letting my mind recall the details of the hot memory. When I return to my room, she's half-dressed. It should be a good thing—she understands exactly what this was supposed to be and she isn't cleaving to the physical act, making it something meaningful, like most women would.

And I'm disappointed.

"You're getting dressed?"

I've startled her. She covers herself with her arms, hiding from me. I don't like her hiding.

But that's not a fair thing to want. Not when I'm hiding. From everyone. From her.

Still, I can't let her go.

I throw the shirt and tie onto the laundry basket and strike a stern pose. "Are you in a hurry to leave?" My gaze travels the length of her body—her well-toned legs, her trimmed pussy. My cock twitches with arousal.

She shivers and I wonder if she's cold or if she can sense my want.

Then she looks away and I realize she has no idea how she affects me. It's insane that a woman so intelligent can't see the obvious.

"Guys don't usually want me to hang around after sex," she says.

I'm ripped apart by her words. "That statement brings up so many issues for discussion that I don't know where to begin."

She's perfect and men have turned her away? I step toward her on impulse. "What is wrong with men to not…?" I can't finish the statement. Because *I* should be turning her away. Because sentences like that are too close to sharing emotions. Because thinking of her with other men makes my gut twist.

Yet, I have to say something. "Alayna, please don't group me with other guys you know. I'd like to think I'm not like most of them. And I don't want to know or think about you having sex with other men. I don't share."

She doesn't meet my eyes, but I can tell she likes what I've said.

"That sounds awfully relationship-y to me. I thought you didn't do relationships," she says as she tugs on her shorts.

It's not a challenge—she's feeling out the boundaries of what's going on with us. I admire her for that. "I don't do *romantic* relationships. Sexual relationships are another thing entirely. Why are you getting ready to leave?"

She reaches for her shirt, but I beat her to it. "Stop," I say, holding her shirt out of her reach. I put my finger under her chin, tilting her to meet my eyes. It's an intimate gesture—almost too intimate. Lost in her eyes, I say the words I shouldn't but that can't bear to be held inside. "I want you to stay." I add my addendum so that my plea doesn't get misconstrued—by her or by me. "And, if you are so inclined, I'd prefer that you not be dressed."

She's stubborn. Or cautious. "*You're* dressed." She crosses her arms over her chest again and thrusts out her lip in such a way that it takes all my energy not to lean forward and nibble on it.

"As soon as the food's here, I'll be happy to lose the clothing. Would that make you feel better?" It would help me to be naked with her. This strange energy between us is wearing on me. The physical is what I have to give her. I need to bring that back to the forefront of our relationship.

"Yes," she answers, and I'm relieved.

But then she changes her mind. "I don't know."

I brush my hand against her cheek. Other women are so easy to read, so easy to manipulate because I understand what they're thinking. But Alayna—she's different. And all I know is that I have to have more of her. "What's going on inside your head, precious? Are you going to run off every time we have sex?"

She turns away from me. "I hadn't really thought this would be more than a one-time thing, Hudson."

Honestly, I'd thought that I could get her out of my system easier than this myself. But I can't. I need her in a way that I can't fully understand.

And something about the way we connected makes me think she feels the same. So why is she running?

I grab her arm and pull her to me. "Alayna." I search her eyes. "If you don't want to have sex with me again, you need to tell me."

"I do! I do."

She throws her arms around me and buries her face in my chest. I shouldn't do what I'm about to do, but my arms have a mind of their own, my body needing to protect her and hold her and comfort her. I return her embrace.

"What is it?" I stroke her hair. "Tell me." I want to know her thoughts, her reasons, her worries. Even though I can't give her the same in return.

"I'm not good at relationships. Of any sort. I have…issues."

"Like what?" I know more about her past than she realizes. Her issues are nothing compared to mine. I shouldn't let her know that I've researched her. I should let it go, let her secrets stay inside her. I'm not going to share mine with her.

But there are other parts of me—parts that want her to share with me and darker parts that want to force her to open up. Those parts take over and I ask, "Does this have anything to do with that restraining order?"

She stills in my arms. "You know about that?"

A rush of satisfaction runs through me. I'm addicted to this power—this thrill of being able to make someone feel a certain way. She's uncomfortable, humiliated.

She tears out of my arms and buries her head in the blankets.

And I hate myself.

This power isn't the power I want. It's not who I want to be with her. I want the light, carefree Alayna back—the one that yielded to me with pleasure, not discomfort.

I should let it go. But I have to fix it.

I lie on the bed next to her and force a laugh. I put my hand on her back and massage her shoulders. Her naked skin beneath my fingers feels incredible and warm. I can't stop touching her.

I bring us both back to the thing that we have, the only thing we share—our physical connection. "I know intimate things about you, precious—the way you look and the sounds you make when you're about to come—and you're concerned about *this*?"

She groans and my dick throbs.

"It was a big deal. The biggest deal. Like my biggest secret. I thought my brother had buried it." She rises on her elbow and turns to eye me. "And are you saying I should be embarrassed about how I look and sound when…you know?"

It's the last part of her statement I want to react to, but I still have mending to do. "I needed to know anything that might come up about my pretend girlfriend. It wasn't necessarily easy to find, but not incredibly hard. It's been buried now."

With that out of the way, I cup her cheek and lose myself in her brown eyes. "And never, never be ashamed of how you look or sound at any time, especially when you're about to come." I circle her nose with mine. "I'm honored to be acquainted with you in that way." I'd like to be acquainted with her in that way right now, in fact.

"I'm mortified." She falls back onto the bed. "About the restraining order, I mean. I don't know how to react to the other."

"Why?" Her past is nothing like mine, and in many ways, her restraining order is silly and frivolous in comparison to the lives I've ruined.

But I understand her regret and her compulsions. They intrigue me and I want her to see that I can relate even though I can't tell her how. Instead, I run my hand across her face and through her hair. I shouldn't be touching her like this—it's too near showing affection—but I can't help myself.

"Because it makes me feel all weird and tingly. And turned on."

"Fantastic." I should take her again, right now.

I don't. "But I meant, why are you mortified?"

"Oh." She flushes and my dick hardens. That color on her face is so beautiful—she looks the same way when I'm fucking her, when I'm driving inside her. The urge to ravage her deepens.

But I want to hear her other answer. It's important.

"Because it's evidence of my crazy," she says. "You know when I said I love too much? The restraining order is part of that, and I like to pretend it never happened."

Like to pretend it never happened. I can't get to that point. The things I've done are still real in my mind—every moment, every day. They consume me and eat at me, and even though I have learned to regret them, I can't move away from them. What I'd give to pretend they never happened.

I suspect that, despite what she says, it's the same for her—that she can never escape the things she keeps running from. I admire her for trying.

So, as if I have any power to make it true, I give her this wish. "Then it never did." I kiss her nose, and for this one moment, I let words wash away past sins—both of ours. Mine and hers. "We've all done insane things in the past. I'd never hold it against you."

In this time and space, I'm captured by her—connected in a way that goes beyond the physical. I *know* her at a depth that she can never understand.

And that's when I return to reality. I can't keep this connection. I have to let it go, have to push her away. Alayna Withers cannot belong to me. "Just another reason romantic love holds no interest for me. People get crazy with it."

Why does my stomach twist from this reminder? This is all that can be between us. What else would there be? Even if I can feel something for her—which is far-fetched in itself—I am incapable of any emotion she deserves.

I force myself to relax and focus my attention on her. "But going back to the heart of this conversation—why does that have a bearing on a relationship between you and me?"

She sits up suddenly. "I freaked out, Hudson. About a guy. Several guys, actually, but it was the last one that ended not well."

I sit up next to her. "And do you think you're going to 'freak out' about me?" I'm afraid of her answer. I don't want to freak her out. I don't want to break her.

Yet I can't deny that there is a part of me—a very sick and disgusting part of me—that wants exactly that. Not because I want her to fall apart or because I want Celia to win, but because I want Alayna's attention. I want her focused on me.

Whatever she says, I realize, it will be a disappointment.

I hold my breath while she answers.

"I really can't honestly tell you. I've stayed away from any relationship for a while so I wouldn't have to deal with it. Trying to have something now with you—it's uncharted territory for me." She looks up and meets my eyes. "I haven't freaked out so far. With you. And I don't want to not have sex with you again. I mean..." She turns away, blushing.

I see her struggle, and I wish to God that I could let her go. For her sake, not mine. If I could simply walk away, this would be so much easier for her. Even if I followed through with Celia's game, I understand that it is this—the pursuit of her outside the game—that will do the most harm to Alayna.

But I can't let her go. I'm too much of a selfish ass.

I wrap my arms around her and nibble on her ear. "You're adorable when you're flustered. I don't want to not have sex with you again either. So we won't do that. We'll have tons of incredible sex instead."

She surrenders into my embrace. "I'm not saying yes, yet. I have to take this one day at a time."

If I had a conscience, I'd be more supportive of her declaration. "Alayna, you might have to take this one day at a time, but I already know there will be tons of fucking between the two of us." I pull her closer. Holding her like this, talking to her so intimately, it's made me hard. "In fact, I'm going to have to be inside you again before you leave for work."

She glances down at my erection and then peers back up at me. "Like right now?"

The way she's looking at me with big lust-filled eyes, it takes everything I have not to pull her beneath me and plow into her. But I only succumb to a kiss. Then the intercom buzzes and dinner has arrived.

In the few minutes that I'm away from her—getting our food and paying the deliverer—I gather my wits. When I return to the bedroom, I'm more together. She still drives me crazy with her long fantastic legs and her perfect pouty lips, but it's manageable. We flirt and I feed her and we banter about. It's nice, actually. Comfortable.

Then we swing around to the topic that has both of us on our toes—our relationship. Our wants are actually very much the same. She wants to be with me sexually without any attachment. I want to be with her sexually without any attachment. Yet, we both fear it's not possible.

Pretending that I have any self-control when it comes to her, I tell her that sex in the future is her decision. I mean it at the moment, but I'm not sure I'll be able to resist pushing her if it comes to that. I can't resist her. I already know this. My intent, though, is what matters now, and she seems to appreciate it. We make headway, setting boundaries and terms. Just talking about it relaxes us both.

Until she brings up fidelity.

Alayna will not fuck others while she's in a relationship with me. It's not debatable. The mere idea of her touching another man makes my chest tighten, and I finally understand what it means to see red. And I'm back to feeling out of sorts and out of control. Because I've never felt this possessive about a woman I'm fucking. I've never demanded faithfulness. I've never offered it from myself. For the most part, I have been loyal to one lover at a time, but only because it was easier. Never because a sexual commitment actually meant something to me.

Alayna has agreed to fidelity, thank God, but she wants to know my intentions. Any other woman and I'd dodge the question. Or I'd find ways of making her forget she'd even asked. I don't do that now.

Meeting Alayna's eyes, I brace a palm on each of her legs. "I'm not a slut, Alayna. This loft has been used for sex, yes, but I have it so I can be close to my office, not for fucking." I brush a strand of hair off her face, mostly to distract myself from the weight of what I can't stop from saying. "I will be as faithful as I expect you to be."

It feels right to give this to the girl in front of me. To say these words. They're a promise that I know I'll have no trouble keeping, but they scare the ever-living fuck out of me.

Apparently they scare the fuck out of her too, because suddenly she's up and gathering her clothes. "I can't think about this anymore right now."

I stand as well, recognizing the emotion etched in her features. "Why are you panicking?" Though I haven't had much experience with this type of scenario, this is certainly not the reaction I expected.

She turns on me, her eyes blazing with rage. "You know, it's all very good and fine for you to say you want a committed sexual relationship. You'll have no problem remaining unemotionally involved—that's your default. It's not my default. Don't you see what you're asking of me might be impossible for me to deliver?"

She's on the verge of tears. I've seen tears—many, many times. I've gloried in them. They are often the sign of a victory on my part. I've also studied them. They've fascinated me and intrigued me.

Though not a single tear has escaped her eyes yet, I know that I do not want to see Alayna cry.

I reach for her, but she pulls away.

"The more we have sex, Hudson, the more I'm likely to latch on, and even if you were into that, you wouldn't be into the level that I latch. So, trust me when I say this has bad idea written all over it. Let's call this a wonderful—oh, my God, such a wonderful evening—and now we need to move on."

My moment of compassion—if that's what it was—disappears and I am left hardened. "If that's what you need."

"I do. And I need a shower. Do you mind?"

"Not at all. In there." I point out the way. "I'll bring you some towels."

She disappears into the bathroom, and I head for the linen closet. As I pile two fluffy towels into my arms, I consider my mood. A few minutes ago, I was unbalanced and apprehensive. Now, I'm...numb. Like I am most of the time. Honestly, it should be an improvement. The strange way I've been acting around Alayna is unsettling.

Yet underneath the numbness, there's something else. Something tugging at the corners of my guard trying to get out. Feeling of some sort. It's pleasant, in a way. But also not at all.

Suddenly I want that more than anything. The something else. It's a compulsion that impels me into the bathroom where I set the towels on the counter. I strip and then I'm sliding in the shower to join her. It's not what she wants, she said she needed time, but here I am, unable to help myself.

She turns into me with no surprise on her face. Then her lips are on mine and any doubt I had about my actions disappears. I kiss her long enough to let her know I'm in charge. When I've left her breathless, I wash her. I explore her body in all the ways I haven't yet. I speak to her like this. I have so much that I need to say to her, and this is the only way I can. The only way I know how—rubbing her, caressing her, learning her. I leave no part of her untouched.

When I brush my fingers past her clit, she moans and leans into me.

I suppose it was a bit manipulative—getting her to this point. I've aroused her and wound her up. For once, though, my actions were not purposeful. I'm here because I can't *not* be.

"Hudson." She says my name and it's infused with as much confusion as I feel.

None of this has been planned or premeditated. I don't know who I am in this moment. I rely on instinct, thrusting two fingers inside her pussy. "Is this what you want?"

"Yes!" She gasps. "I mean, no. I want you."

There's a part of me that wants to sit on the bench in the walk-in shower and figure out everything going on in my head. I ignore that part and focus on the other part of me—the new part that wants only to please and tease and adore the woman in my arms.

"You'll have to wait," I tell her. "I'm enjoying making you wait."

I work her, squeezing her clit and fucking her with my fingers until she's moaning and writhing and digging her nails into my shoulders. Just as she's about to come, I pull away. "I need to be washed too."

I'm playing with her now, but it's in fun. When was the last time I played like this? Without any malice? Without any need to examine? I'm not sure that I ever have.

She plays back, and I wonder if it's new for her as well. Something about the way her hands touch me, the way she tentatively brushes my cock—I'm certain it is new for her. She strokes me once, twice. At the third stroke, I can't take it anymore. Playtime is over.

Or it's just beginning.

I lift her up. Her legs wrap around me and I press her back against the shower wall. I take her mouth in mine as I thrust inside her. I'm not gentle. I'm fierce, I'm forceful. Because those are the things between us. Those are the things we share. Vague intangible energy that pulls us both toward each other, into each other.

I pump her like this, quick and hard, even as she clenches down around me. I come fast after her.

We're quiet as I towel her off and help her dress. She has to go now. She has to get to work. I wrap a towel around my waist and walk her to the door.

Despite our silence, it's not awkward between us. I sense that she's...*absorbing*. As I am. There's a lot to take in. Though I can't begin to even process any of it. So after I've kissed her and sent her on her way, I decide to *not* process. I turn my brain off and simply let the evening settle around me.

I've never stayed overnight at the loft after having a woman here. I prefer to be in my own bed without the lingering scent of sex and female. With Alayna gone now, however, I can't make myself leave. I throw on a pair of boxers and climb into the sheets that still smell like her.

— CHAPTER —

ELEVEN

Before

Christina swept her tongue along my crown, sending a shiver down my spine. "Stop fucking teasing," I hissed. A blowjob in a hidden alcove at Cipriani 42nd Street hadn't been in my plans for the evening. But when my one-night fling from the summer arrived at The Pierce Industry Annual Thanksgiving Eve Charity Gala with her lips painted in *Fuck Me Red*, my agenda had been altered.

"Tell me what you want then, Mr. Pierce?" She was playing at some hot fantasy where she was my employee and I was her boss. It wasn't necessary as far as I was concerned, but it got her mouth on my dick without much work, so I went along.

"I want you to fucking suck it. Like a good girl." I flicked my finger at her cheek. "Open up." She complied, shaping her lips into an "O" before wrapping them around my hard cock. "Yeah, like that."

I closed my eyes, relishing the feel of her warm, moist mouth cocooned around my dick. There were few things that I enjoyed in this world as much as getting head. It was the only situation where I could sit back and think completely of myself. I didn't care if the girl was turned on or enjoying it. Examinations of human nature were put on hold. Fellatio was about simple pleasure—*my* pleasure.

With one hand pumping the base, Christina drew her mouth up and down over my swollen cock. Her other hand reached below to fondle my balls. She wasn't very original with her play, but she had spirit. And honestly, even mediocre blowjobs are fucking fantastic.

As for her tempo…it was on the slow side. That could be remedied. I tangled my hands into her hair, messing up her carefully coifed bun. It took her a moment, but soon she relinquished control and that's when things got good. I drove into her at an aggressive speed. With each thrust I hit the back of her throat, the tickling on my crown sending me closer to the brink. I glanced down at the erotic sight—her eyes watered as my cock fucked her mouth. Even as I pounded harder, faster, she allowed me to control the experience.

"Keep up, Christina. Fuck me with your greedy little mouth."

Her lips tightened around me. She was so willing, so submissive. How strange that she didn't find it completely debasing. She struggled to catch a breath and the hard floor had to be a bitch on her knees. The demeaning nature of the situation only added to the eroticism. My climax came rushing toward me. I had time to warn her, but I didn't want to give her a chance to pull away. I spurted into her, holding her head in place so that she had no choice but to swallow.

"That's a good bitch. Swallow it all."

Like a champ, she even licked me clean.

I took a deep breath and exhaled. Jesus, that had felt good. A perfect distraction from my parents' dismal casino night.

After I'd tucked myself back into my tuxedo pants, I helped Christina to her feet. "Very good, Ms. Brooke. I suppose I'll have to approve your vacation request after all."

She wiped at her lips before giving me a seductive smile. "Thank you, Mr. Pierce. Is there anything else I can do for you this evening?"

"I think that's all, Ms. Brooke." If she wanted me to return the favor, it wasn't happening. I'd been there and done that, and there were plenty of fresh cunts at the event to choose from if I decided I wanted to get off again before the night was over.

However, it was never good to burn bridges, so I tugged her close and whispered at her ear. "I have to get back to this boring party. But if I find another chance to get away…" I bit at her lobe.

"Right. Got it." She was smiling when I released her.

Mission accomplished.

She pulled at the few pins that I hadn't already dislodged from her hair, gathering them into a pile in her hand. "You need to get out there and practice for when you're hosting this event. It won't be long now, I'm sure."

I did have plans to work for my father over Christmas Break. He'd already given me preliminaries on some of his accounts. "When I'm in charge, I'll own the nightclubs we party at." Made much more sense than spending a fortune to rent out another venue. Especially when the evening was for charity. I'd seen the event expenses. It was hard to imagine there was anything left to donate after all the bills were paid.

"Smart thinking, boss."

I cringed. Now that we weren't immersed in the fantasy, the remnants of it left a bad taste. It was time to excuse myself from my date of the moment.

"Have you heard anything from Celia?"

That question, however, kept me interested in Christina for a bit longer. "Not since summer." Not since that night she'd fucked my father. I'd made sure to avoid her until she'd gone back to school in California a few days later. Having been at school myself, I'd heard little of her and had often wondered how my experiment had affected her semester. This was a chance to find out. "Have you?"

"I went to see her a couple months ago," Christina said, picking up her handbag from the floor. She tucked the pins into a side pocket. "She was a fucking mess."

Now that was interesting. "What do you mean by mess?"

"Partying. Drugs. She was doing a shit-ton of cocaine when I saw her. And talk about slut—she spread her legs for any guy who gave her the time of day."

I wiped at my mouth, trying to decide how to evaluate the information. It was probably a coincidence. Her behavior couldn't have been because of me. Could it?

"That's too bad." I actually meant it.

"Rumor has it," Christina narrowed her eyes at me, "that she was nursing a broken heart."

"Are you blaming her self-destruction on me?" The idea didn't sit well. While I'd never cared what happened to my subjects after I'd concluded my experiments, Celia was different. She was family, in a way. Again I resolved myself not to scheme anymore with people I knew.

Christina chuckled. "She's a big girl. She's responsible for her own destruction. I just thought you'd want to know."

I shrugged. I *did* want to know, but I didn't need Christina knowing that.

"She's in town for the holiday."

I shrugged again.

"You know, Hudson? You're kind of an asshole."

It was my turn to laugh. "And you're just figuring this out now?"

"No. I knew." She pulled her fingers through her tangled hair. "And I still let you fuck me. So obviously I don't really care."

Too bad I didn't give a shit about people. Christina and I might have made a good team.

As it was, I was done with her. I paused, devising a way to escape. In the end, I simply nodded toward the restrooms. "You should clean yourself up. Have a good Thanksgiving if I don't see you again." I left her before she had a chance to respond.

Back in the main room, I found myself scanning the casino tables for Celia. It was silly to think she'd be at the event. Her parents weren't even there, and Celia wouldn't have come without them, but I wanted to see her. Wanted to know if she was really *a mess*. Something in me needed to know that she wasn't.

I wasn't expecting to find the answer I was seeking. My survey of the place, though, led me to another sight I hadn't been expecting—my mother, climbing onto a blackjack table.

Goddammit.

She'd been a drinker most of my life, so I was used to all her modes of intoxication. Usually, she kept her shit together in public. Whatever made her go overboard tonight, I wasn't sure I wanted to know. But someone had to rescue her, or at least keep her from embarrassing herself or the family.

My father was already helping her down when I arrived at the scene. He smiled, like it was all in fun. "Sophia, now how many times have I told you that isn't the way you play twenty-one?"

The handful of spectators laughed. Jack Pierce, shithead that he was, always did have a way with a crowd.

My mother blinked a couple of times, as if trying to clear her vision. "There you are. I was climbing up there to get a better view of the room so I could figure out where you'd wandered off to."

She could still speak without slurring her words. So she wasn't as intoxicated as I'd imagined.

My mother pinned her stare on the blonde standing next to my father. "Is this the latest? I should have known. When you disappear, it's usually with a tram—"

I stepped in before she could finish her sentence. "Mother, walk with me, will you?"

"And leave him alone with his bi—"

My father cut her off this time. "It's okay, Hudson. Of course you won't be leaving me, sweetheart. I'm going with you." He wrapped an arm around her waist and began escorting her toward the exit.

While my mother has been known for false accusations, the glance he threw back at the blonde gave him away. Not to my mother—she already knew. But now I knew too that the woman at his side was not just an acquaintance. The look he gave her said he'd be back later for her. In other words, he was just putting my mother in a car before returning.

No wonder Sophia Pierce felt the need to get a little too drunk at her husband's company party. *Fucking asshole.*

I rubbed my hand across my jaw and considered whether I wanted to stay any longer myself. Though there was plenty of room for me at the penthouse where my parents lived, I'd been staying at the Plaza, so if I left, I wouldn't have to deal with my mother. But maybe I should go to the penthouse anyway. It wasn't the newest nanny's job to take care of a drunken employer. And Sophia might get to keep a shred of dignity if I were the one to attend to her.

I was already at the coatroom when I'd made my decision to leave. The clerk had just handed me my coat when I found a reason to stay. Celia Werner had just walked in, hands thrust in her jacket pockets, her attire nowhere near formal.

She walked toward me. My surprise at seeing her kept me glued to my spot, my mouth slack as I looked her over. Though she wasn't dressed for the event, she didn't like the mess that Christina had suggested. Either Celia had cleaned up in the last couple of months or the rumors about her had been exaggerated.

I couldn't decide if that made me happy or disappointed.

"Do you want to check your coat?" the clerk asked when Celia reached us.

She shook her head and fixed her gaze on me.

I'd had enough time now to gather my wits. "You're too late, Celia. My father just left. But if you want to wait, I think he's coming back. He already has a leggy blonde picked out for the evening, though. Do you mind threesomes?"

"I'm not here for Jack, asshole."

I tensed at the familiar use of my father's name. "That's too bad. No one else is going to look at you dressed like that."

"You want to stand around and throw insults at me all night? Or can you zip it a minute so I can talk to you?"

"I have nothing to say to you."

"Awesome. Then you can shut the fuck up and listen while I talk."

I hesitated, wondering what her angle was. Then I decided I didn't care enough to find out. "While that sounds like a whole hell of a lot of fun, Celia, I think I'll pass." I tipped the clerk and started out.

"Hudson." Her tone was more commanding than was typical for her. Still, I kept walking. "Fine," she said, running to catch up to me. "I'll find your father then."

That stopped me. Though they'd already been together, I detested the idea of a repeat performance. I'd rather imagine my father fucking anyone else—the blonde waiting for him in the event room, even. Just not Celia.

I'd never let on how much it bothered me, but I would try to prevent it any way I could. "What is it you want, Celia?"

Her eyes darted toward the clerk. "Not here. We need to be in private."

"I'm not—" A noise at the door down the hall stole my attention. It was my father returning from "taking care" of my mother. He hadn't seen us yet, so I grabbed Celia's arm and tugged her toward the men's room. At the door, I said, "Stay." I went in and checked to make sure the room was empty then I pulled Celia inside.

As I locked the door behind us, there was a brief moment where I considered how different our lives could have been if it hadn't been for my experiment that summer. How I could have been sneaking away with Celia for a bang in a stall instead of hiding her from my slut of a father. Or maybe not that. I hadn't ever wanted that, had I?

Something different, though. Not this.

But as Thoreau said, "Never look back unless you're planning to go that way." And I was not going that way. Come to think of it, Celia was the one who'd told me that.

I turned back to face her. "You have three minutes. Then I'm taking you out to the curb and putting you in a cab. I'll even give you some cash, if that's how you're used to getting paid."

Her eyes blazed with the heat of my insult. "Did I mention *fuck you*, Hudson?"

"I don't get off on my father's sloppy seconds. Sorry." I looked at my watch for effect. "And now you're at two minutes forty-five."

She crossed her arms and leaned back against the counter, her eyes narrow with challenge. "I'm willing to bet that I'll have your attention for longer than that."

Again, a glance at my watch. "Two minutes forty."

"I knew I should have talked to Jack instead."

She'd realized that mentioning my father was her power card. She'd laid it down several times now. Each time it worked.

But I was losing patience. This was the last time I'd ask and my tone let her know that. "What the fuck is it, Celia?"

She brushed the hair off her face and swallowed. "I'm pregnant."

I opened my mouth to make some smartass remark—it wasn't *my* kid after all—and then I realized whose kid it was. I did the math as I glanced at her belly. It had been three months. Would she be showing? Did she look rounder than she had before or was I making it up?

Or was *she* making it up? All of it could be a lie.

"Are you trying to figure out if I'm lying? Oh, my God. I can prove it if you need me to. Trust me, pregnancy is not something I'd be able to lie about for long."

While my trust in people was limited, I knew Celia well enough to believe she told the truth. I didn't like what she had to say, but I believed her.

I ran a hand through my hair. "You're sure it's his?"

She shot me an ice-cold glare. "I didn't sleep around, Hudson."

"That's not what I heard." I tilted my head, recalling Christina's earlier tales of a Celia gone wild. "Actually heard you were quite the slut these days."

"From who? From *Christina*? And you believed that fucking whore cunt?" She closed her eyes, cursing more under her breath. "Whatever. Fine. Yes, I was a little wild this semester. Before I found out I was pregnant. *After* you." It was a slip—what she meant, but not what she meant to say. She quickly corrected. "After Jack, rather. But the timing is…It's your father's, Hudson. There's no one else that fits the time frame. And the condom broke."

"I don't want to hear that." I covered my eyes with my hand. As if that could hide me from what she was saying. Not just the condom talk, but the whole conversation—I would have preferred to not have it continue.

"I'm sure you don't." A trace of regret laced her words. "But you get to hear it because I blame you."

Now I was incensed. "For faulty birth control? Or for your bad decision?"

"Oh, don't even play like you have no comprehension of your culpability. You drove me to him. You gave me no choice."

"Pathetic, Celia. Take responsibility for your own actions."

"I am. That's why I'm here. Now it's your turn to take responsibility for your actions." She pointed a finger at me. "And tell me what we're going to do."

"What *we're* going to do? This is not my problem." But I already knew it was. Not just because of the reason she'd given, but because this affected my family. Affected *my* life. It didn't mean I knew what should be done about it.

Celia straightened. "Then I'll take it to your father. I'm sure he'll step up. He'll have no choice when I get a DNA test." Again laying her power card. She straightened and started toward the door.

I could have let her go. It would serve Jack right.

But Jack wasn't the only person who would suffer from this. And Celia knew it.

I pounded the wall behind me with a fist. "*Fuck.*" Forget Christina as a good partner. Celia had manipulation down to a science. "What do you want from me?"

She flung her arms out to the side in exasperation. "I want you to tell me what to do!"

It was almost funny. As if we were a real couple discussing their unplanned pregnancy. The situation had much that would intrigue me under normal circumstances.

I banged my head against the wall behind me. "What are our options?" I scolded myself for using the word *our*. It gave her too much power, thinking of us as a partnership.

"Well." She returned to lean against the counter again. She needed the support, I realized. The conversation was tough. I'd give her that. "I'm not having an abortion. I might have been able to, but I saw the ultrasound. I saw its heartbeat. I can't do that."

"So no abortion." I was glad for that, actually. It didn't feel right sentencing my unborn sibling to death.

My sibling. Jesus, was this really happening?

"I'm not opposed to adoption." She talked as if she'd already been through all of this on her own—and she probably had. For me, though, it was new and there was a lot to take in. A lot of different aspects of the situation to absorb.

"My mom will want to keep it." She let out a single chortle. "Can you just see my mother as a doting grandmother? Either way, my parents will want to know who the father is. My father would kill me if he knew."

"More like he'd kill my father if he knew." My father was Warren's friend. And he'd knocked up his daughter.

Celia sighed. "Let's just say it wouldn't be good for either one of us."

"It would destroy my mother." *Not just my mother.* "And my brother and sister."

She nodded, biting her lip. "I can't tell him it's Jack."

She was right. That much was clear.

And there was only one thing I could think of to make sure that information never came out. "You'll tell him it's me." I set my jaw. "Tell him I'm the father."

"What?" She lifted her head as if in surprise, but something about her tone was false. "Are you really…would you really do that?" It was more gleeful than hopeful. More triumphant than incredulous.

"Now you're the one pretending." I could read her like a book. "You came to me because you knew I'd offer. Don't even fucking try to convince me you didn't plan this."

"I hoped," she whispered. "Not that I'd get pregnant. But after I did, I hoped you'd offer."

"Finally we're getting somewhere." I leaned back, bracing myself on the wall as I rocked back on my heels. "Then that's what we'll do. We'll say it's mine." I worked it out as I spoke. "You can finish this semester. Come back at Christmas and I'll go with you to the parenting classes or whatever. I'll play the supportive sperm donor. If you choose to keep it, I'll set up a trust fund or something. Dad's money will be my money anyway when I take over the company."

"Okay." She took a deep breath. "What about fathering?"

"You want me to have a relationship with it?"

"Don't talk like it's a stranger. It will be your brother or sister."

"Right." I'd already realized that, but my stomach dropped at the reminder. And since it really was my sibling, could I just abandon any contact with it? If it were Chandler or Mirabelle, I would want to be involved. Even in my own cold, stoic way. "Sure. Fine. Minimal relationship though. I don't want custody. But that also means I get to help make parenting decisions. Are you going to be okay with that?"

She shrugged as she shook her head. Then said, "I'll be okay with whatever." Her eyes glazed like she was overwhelmed. "I don't even know if I'm keeping it yet."

Another thought crossed my mind. "I'm not marrying you, Celia." I straightened to show my seriousness. "This in no way makes us a couple."

She looked at me with stark unbelief. "I never thought for a moment it did." But her tone was layered with the subtext of our past. Of a time when she would have wanted exactly that from me. "Nor would I ever expect it. You, I've discovered, are incapable of anything remotely like a relationship."

Perhaps she'd meant to hurt me with her statement. She didn't. She'd made our new situation easier. I looked her straight in the eye. "I'm glad you know."

She held my gaze for several seconds. Then her eyes fell to the floor. She shook her head again, as if she were bewildered. As if she were at a loss for words. Finally, she looked up again. "Hudson, why are you doing this?"

I studied the light smudge on the tip of my right shoe as I tried to figure out the answer to that. It wasn't for my father. I was disappointed that he didn't have to face up to his actions. As for my mother...I'd begun to understand that the biggest contribution to her drinking was my father's infidelity. My relationship with her was strained, at best. Yet I did feel an urge to protect her. Was she the reason?

Then my mind flew again to my siblings. Chandler. Mirabelle.

Ah, Mirabelle.

She was a girl who believed in love and rainbows and happily-ever-after—all the things I detested. The breakdown of my parents' marriage would strip her of those convictions. And that thought felt like a kick in the stomach. I realized I would do anything to prevent that from happening to her. So the why was for Mirabelle then.

There was another reason, and that reason was standing in front of me—her face thin and ashen. Her eyes heavier than I'd remembered them, her smile not as easy as it had once been. I'd chided her for blaming anyone but herself for her predicament, but wasn't I also culpable? If I hadn't set the dominos in motion, she'd never have gone to Mabel Shores that night. She'd never have climbed into my father's bed. She wouldn't be pregnant now.

Did I care that I held responsibility? Maybe. Maybe I couldn't care for people in the way that others could, but I did have some sense of duty. I couldn't explain it, even to myself.

I'd never try to explain it to anyone else.

"Hudson?" Celia prodded me for an answer since I'd been quiet so long.

"I heard you." I swallowed and raised my eyes to hers. "The family name." And because I was uncomfortable with the course of my self-examination, I turned spiteful. "Pierce is my legacy. I wouldn't want it poisoned by my father's mistakes."

She sneered and opened her mouth to likely deliver an equally caustic jab.

But I jumped in before her. "Let's give our families Thanksgiving. We can tell them on Friday. I'll call you tomorrow to arrange the details of our announcement." I turned and straightened my bow tie in the mirror. There would be no going back to the event for me, and I wasn't going to leave Celia behind. "I'll walk you out."

We didn't say another word to each other until she was seated in the backseat of a cab and I was about to shut the door.

"Hudson?"

I bent toward her. "What?"

"Thank you." Her lip quivered and her eyes glossed, and I remembered that Celia wasn't like me. She had emotions, she had feelings. This situation was probably more to her than the inconvenience it was for me. A rush of...*something*... swept through me. Something not quite comfortable. Like I was listening to Schubert's *Adagio for Strings* while battling the flu.

More and more lately, the depth of my own ability to feel surprised me. I didn't like it.

I nodded once and looked for the thing she needed me to say. "Congratulations, Ceeley," I managed. "Everything's going to be just fine."

I didn't have to try to sound sincere. I was.

— CHAPTER —
TWELVE

After

Alayna's hand on my back—even through my shirt and jacket—stuns my skin to life. I turn to look at her, wishing we were elsewhere, anywhere but here at my mother's charity fashion show. This event has been planned for weeks to be the kick-off for the charade within the charade. It was Celia's choice, not mine. I would have preferred a private introduction for Alayna and Sophia Pierce. Not this extravaganza of people. Celia wanted it for exactly that reason—it gave her the excuse to be present. She wants to see the game in action; I get that. It was always the best part. But her nearness reminds me what this really is. Reminds me that my relationship with Alayna is an experiment.

No, that's not correct. My relationship with Alayna is *not* what happens here—it's what happens in private. That is our reality. This is only a show. And both of us know that.

But it's hard to remember that when she's running her hand across my shoulder like this. I should tell her to stop, even though I don't blame her. I have the hardest time concentrating on anything that isn't her when she's near. Even when she's not near, actually—all I think about, all I long for, is her.

Her touch has awakened my constant desire for her. I don't care who might see. I don't care where it will lead. I don't care that I'll likely regret the hard-on I'll get from kissing her luscious mouth. I place my hand on her thigh and lean in to take her lips.

"Oh, you don't need to be all PDA on my account," a familiar voice interrupts me. "Remember, I know."

I stiffen. I shouldn't be as angry as I am at Celia's arrival. I'm surprised she hasn't shown up sooner. There's no reason for her to interact with us though. No reason for her to take the seat next to Alayna as she is now. I'm not happy about it, and the look I share with my old friend doesn't hide my irritation.

Alayna removes her hand from my body and I'm instantly disappointed. I can't withdraw so easily, strengthening my grip on her leg, maintaining our connection.

"I'm Celia," she says to Alayna. "I thought we should probably meet. Though it doesn't look like Hudson's too keen on it."

Celia's trying too hard. What is she trying to prove?

And what do I care? If she screws this up, the experiment's over, and I can concentrate on my real relationship with Alayna instead of this farce. That thought perks me up. "No, you're right. You should meet." I stroke Alayna's thigh as I speak, claiming her as mine. "Now you've met."

"You aren't getting rid of me that easily, you oaf." Celia smirks. She turns to Alayna. "Believe it or not, we're actually friends."

Friends. Is that what we are? It's how I've always referred to her. She knows my secrets; I know hers. We share a bond. I suppose it's the closest thing to friendship that I know. Perhaps that's why I tolerate her as I do—for the sake of friendship. Except it's more than that. We're tied together. I tolerate her because I have no choice.

Sighing, I enter into the game. "What do you want, Ceeley?" It's a double-edged question that fits the scene we're playing, as well as our personal play.

"I wanted to personally thank Alayna for this whole charade." There's a gleam in Celia's eye and I find myself worrying for Alayna. She held her own against my mother's bitchy insults. Can she handle Celia as well?

I tense as she leans toward Alayna. "You can't know how dreadful the idea of marrying that pain in the ass has been," she says with a teasing grin.

Alayna returns a nervous smile. "Um, I can imagine. He's not the settling-down type."

Her statement bothers me. It shouldn't, because it's true. This strange connection with Alayna has made me forget who I am. I take my hand from her leg. Maybe that will make it easier to remember.

"Wow," Celia laughs. "You already know him so well."

"It's nice to talk to someone else who knows," Alayna says.

"But isn't Hudson amazingly good at pretending?" Celia's line is for me. It's a game within a game within a game. She's pushing my buttons and I have no idea what her motive is.

And Alayna's caught in the middle. "He is. Quite good."

I don't like Alayna's subtext. Does she think that what we have isn't real? I can't defend our relationship. Not here in front of Celia. But I can't get us out of here.

"I'd love to continue this wonderfully entertaining conversation, but I see someone I need to talk some business with." I stand and hold my hand out. "Alayna?"

She doesn't move. "Go ahead, H. I'll hang with Celia."

"We'll be fine," Celia insists. "And we'll end our conversation with a pretend catfight if you want to up the charade."

What I want is to pull my lover out of her chair and drag her away from my so-called friend. Can I really leave them together? "No catfight. In my script, you're friendly toward each other."

"Then she and I should sit and chat, since we're supposed to be friends." Celia winks at Alayna, and my fist balls at my side. "Right, Alayna?"

"Right." Alayna returns the wink. "And since we're friends, you should call me Laynie."

Aw, fuck. Celia's good—I forget that sometimes. Why wouldn't Alayna fall under her spell?

I have no choice but to leave them. Together. Alone. "Friendly, not friends." I take a deep breath but it doesn't help. "Fine. I'll be back shortly."

Since I hadn't really spotted a business associate, I make my way to the lobby bar. It's crowded and I have to stand in line. While I wait, I send a text to my assistant to get some gourmet coffee and leave it at Alayna's door. She's wearing an elastic band to remind herself to get some, and if things go as I plan, she'll be too worn out to get any later. Plus the gift will keep her thinking about me while I'm in Cincinnati the next few days.

My chest clenches at the thought of time without her. I consider asking her to come with me and quickly dismiss the idea. She has a job and I have my own work. I've never taken a woman on a business trip with me; why would I start now?

And what the fuck is Celia talking to Alayna about?

I'm anxious and on edge. When I get my Scotch, I down it quickly. The burn feels good, feels appropriate. It also does what I mean for it to do—it calms me.

Why am I worried about leaving Celia and Alayna alone anyway? Maybe it's even a good thing. Celia will feel like she's a part of the scheme. She'll feed

Alayna details that make our story more believable. There's nothing that could go wrong.

Still, I can't shake the feeling that everything's at risk. Celia is the only person who can expose me. That's never been a concern for me before. I've never cared what people knew about me. If someone discovered my sadistic experiments, what did it hurt me?

With Alayna, I care. I don't want her to know my secrets. I want to protect her from that hideous side of me. I *will* protect her.

But then I see Alayna rushing toward the exit. I try to convince myself she's simply looking for me, that my mother came back and delivered a snide remark. Except my mother is standing on the other side of the foyer and has been there the whole time I've been at the bar.

I reach out and gently take Alayna's arm. "Where are you going?"

She throws me off of her. "Don't touch me!"

"Whoa." I put my hands up in surrender. There's no way this can be what I imagine it to be. No way would Celia tell her this was all a scam. So I just have to figure out what really happened and then I can make it right. "What's wrong with you?"

"What's wrong with you would be the more appropriate question." Alayna's eyes dart to the door.

"Alayna." I hush my voice and step toward her. "I don't know what you're talking about, but you're making a scene. You need to calm down and save whatever this is for later."

I start to take her elbow, but she pulls away. "There isn't going to be a later—I quit." She runs past me and out the doors.

"Alayna!" I don't care that I'm shouting as I follow her outside. I don't even care that my mother is watching all of this. All that matters is stopping Alayna.

I'm about to reach for her again when she turns to me on her own. Her eyes are filled with tears and my stomach tightens. What has hurt her? I know somehow that it's me and I can't bear to hear it from her lips. Yet I need to know.

"Tell me, Hudson, did you pick me because you thought my obsession issues would make your game more fun? Because really, where's the challenge in that?"

Rage travels through me like a bolt of lightning. "Fuck Celia and her big mouth." A million questions flood my mind—how much did Celia say? Why would she reveal our scam? How the hell do I fix this?

I step toward Alayna. She backs away. I soften my approach, reaching out to her with words. "Let's talk about this in the limo."

"I don't want—"

"Alayna. It's not fair of you to listen to a stranger tell her story and not give me a chance to explain." I don't know how to beg, so I command. "I'm telling you we will talk about this in the limo which is parked in the lot next door. First, because my mother is watching, I'm going to bend down and kiss your forehead. Then I'm going to walk over and tell her that you aren't feeling well. I will meet you in the car."

She peers over my shoulder, likely confirming my mother's standing at the doors behind us. Then she gives a slight nod. I lean in and kiss her on the forehead and wonder if this will be our last kiss.

No. I will not allow that. "The limo, Alayna," I say. "I'll meet you there."

Alayna heads to the lot. I pull my phone from my pocket as I turn back toward the doors and text Jordan. *Get Alayna. Meet me in front.*

My mother meets me as I walk in. "Trouble with your plaything already? That didn't last long."

My eye twitches and all the anger I feel toward Celia makes it hard to remain civil with my mother. "Alayna's not feeling well. She hasn't built up a tolerance to the poison in this environment like the rest of us have. I'm taking her home and putting her to bed." I let her assume what she wants about that statement. "I'll be back in time to present your precious Pierce Industries donation check."

I'm gone again before she can respond.

Jordan reaches the curb just as I do. I climb in the back, and the car pulls into traffic.

Alayna presses into the corner farthest from me as if she's disgusted with me. As if she's frightened of me.

I wish she knew I'd never hurt her. But how could she possibly know that when I'm not even sure of that myself?

I pressed the intercom. "Jordan, drive around until I say otherwise. Or find someplace to park for a while."

We sit in silence as Jordan drives around. I don't know how to begin the conversation. If I knew exactly what she was upset about, I'd fare better, but I have no idea what Celia said or did. Whatever it was, I have to figure out how to make things right.

It occurs to me that the best move might be to come clean about everything. Alayna's already said she's quitting the scam. She's already walking out of my life. Yet, I hold out hope that I can change that. If I confessed everything—there would be no making that right.

Instead, I'll have to tread carefully. Figure out what I can from Alayna and repair the damage as best I can. I keep my voice low and pray my desperation isn't transparent. "What exactly did Celia tell you?"

"Oh, just how you fuck with vulnerable women's emotions. Is it true?"

Every hair on my body stands on end, and I feel as though I've just stepped into a landmine. How could Celia…? Why would she…? I can't gather my thoughts. I can't reason what or why or how much of our game Celia has exposed.

"Alayna—" I slide closer to her and reach for her knee. I need her touch. That's the way I communicate best with her.

But she isn't having it. "Don't touch me! And stop saying my name. Is it true?"

"Will you calm down so I can explain?" Though I have no idea yet what my explanation will be. I'm doing my best to keep calm, but energy gathers inside me, wanting to explode.

Her eyes blaze and she looks as worked up as I feel. "Is. It. True?" she demands.

The panic rising in my chest escapes in a burst. "Yes, it's true!" And oh my God. I've said it out loud. I've disclosed the worst thing about me. I take a deep breath and attempt to regain control. "In the past, it was true."

I can't look at her, can't see the disappointment that I feel shooting from her eyes. I shouldn't say anything else, but now that the confessing's started, I feel compelled to complete it. "I did…things…that I'm not proud of." My admission is slow. Painful. "I manipulated people. I hurt them, and often it was deliberate." I'm speaking as if my faults are in the past. And they are. At least they were. Is that still true?

I vow right then that it is true. *I will not hurt Alayna deliberately.* I may be trapped in this game, but I will do everything and anything to make sure that my actions with her are sincere. I meet her eyes and make the promise I will try my damndest to keep. "But not now. I don't do that now. Not with you."

I pray that she believes me.

She doesn't. "Really? Because it seems completely obvious that you did exactly that with me. The way you picked me out at the symposium, and you tracked me down and gave me a spa vacation, and Jesus, you bought the club!"

I shake my head. "It's not like that. I explained the gift, and I was looking at the club anyway." I'm already breaking my promise, already manipulating truths. "When I found out you worked there, yes, it helped me make my decision—"

She cuts me off. "And you 'hired' me and seduced me. And when I told you I needed to not have sex with you, you somehow got me to do exactly that. You *are* manipulative. You're a bully, Hudson."

She wraps her arms around herself, and more than anything, I wish it were me wrapped around her. But her words are ringing in my ear—*manipulative, bully.*

"No, Alayna. I didn't want that with you." But, God, she's right. I've tried to have my cake and eat it too. Tried to get near her with my games, and then tried to protect her from them at the same time. It was a ridiculous plan. "I don't *want* to be like that with you."

But it's the only way I know how to be with her. With anyone.

"Then what do you want to be with me, Hudson?" She wipes at her tears, and I have to hold myself back from kissing them from her face.

"Honestly? I'm not sure." It's the truest thing I've said. I lean back against the seat, and though I'm physically here in my limousine, I'm also completely lost. I've never been so without answers. Not just today with the mess that Celia has created, but since the very first day I saw Alayna.

Why her? Why now? Has therapy actually changed me? Is that why she makes me feel the way she does? Because as scared as I am to admit it, that's exactly what's going on with Alayna—I'm feeling. *She makes me feel.* What, I can't say. I'm not familiar enough with these sensations to explain any of it.

It strikes me as funny. Why, after all my life of never feeling anything for anyone, this woman shows up and throws all my truths out the window. It's ironic. Comical even.

So I laugh. Then I attempt to put it into words, for both our sakes. "I'm drawn to you, Alayna. Not because I want to hurt you or make you feel a certain way, but because you're beautiful and sexy and smart and, yes, a little crazy maybe, but you're not broken. And that makes me hopeful. *For me.*"

And, God doesn't that feel fucking good to say? It's raw. It's real. It's the freest I've ever been.

I glance at her and know from the way she's watching me that I have her attention. I have her sympathy. At another time in my life, this is the moment where I'd inwardly celebrate. This is the prime moment to take advantage of someone else.

I could reach out to her, and I'm willing to bet she'd let me do what I'd like with her. Only a day before, I probably would have. I regret that now. "And maybe I've been a bully. But I'm a dominant person. I can try to change things about me, but the fundamentals of my personality are never going away." That acknowledgment brings another rush of freedom, and I realize that Alayna likely gets this as well as I do. "You of all people should be able to understand that."

"I'm sorry." Her voice cracks. "I'm sorry. You didn't judge me and I judged you."

Her apology returns me to my prison. The reprieve from my guilt was brief. Now I remember that no matter what I feel or intend or wish to have happen between her and me, we got here because I set her up. My remorse is so heavy, I can't speak. All I can do is nod once.

She assumes my response is acceptance. "And I exaggerated when I called you a bully. I haven't done anything I didn't want to. And your whole confident, domineering thing is actually kinda hot."

I want to smile. But I won't let myself. There's still too much at stake. I squeeze my eyes shut, focusing all my strength and will on the thing I want—*need*—most. "Alayna, don't quit. Don't quit me."

And I don't mean the scenario I've hired her for. I mean *me*. I want her to have as much faith in me as I do in her. It's the most ridiculous thing I've ever desired, and I've never desired anything more.

She looks away, and I already know her answer. "Hudson, I have to. Not because of this, well, not only because of this, but because of my past. I'm not well enough to be with someone who has his own issues."

"You are, Alayna. You only tell that to yourself because you're scared." It's me I'm talking about, but I suspect she feels the same.

"I should be scared. It's not safe. For either of us. You should be scared, too."

If she only knew how scared I am. I'm terrified of what I've done—of what I'm doing—but more than anything, I'm terrified that I will lose whatever it is that I have with her.

But maybe she's right. This is what I want for her—to be strong like this. I let out a heavy breath and think about what she's said. And I realize I don't agree. "I don't believe that. I think spending time with another person who has similar compulsive tendencies can provide insight and healing." Because in this brief time with her, I've had more insight and healing than I've had in three years with Dr. Alberts.

Alayna leans her head back against the seat and stares at the ceiling. I've given her a lot to think about, I'm sure. I've given myself a lot to think about. But the only word that keeps repeating in my head now is *please*. *Please don't let me lose this. Please don't let me lose her.*

"I won't quit." Her words jump-start my heart. She turns to face me. "But I can't have a relationship with you, Hudson. All I can give you is the fake. I have to protect myself here."

I'm sick with disappointment. "I understand." I say it again to myself, hoping this time I accept it. "Thank you."

And since she's ended us—ended the only part of us that matters—I pull myself together, closing myself off. Shutting her out.

Then she places a hand on my knee and leans in. "Hudson, you're not broken."

I begin to falter when I catch sight of her cleavage. What I see under her dress surprises me. "What are you...? Is that...?" I swear she's wearing the corset I'd admonished her for the day we'd first properly met. Though it was inappropriate for work, I'd mentioned how much I'd love to see her in it again, privately.

She blushes. "Yes. I'd worn it for you."

"Wow. That was...that was very thoughtful of you." The moment is inopportune, but I'm instantly hard. Actually, I suspect that everything I've bared and everything she's said has helped contribute to how much I want her now. She always turns me on. But now I need her in a way that is all-consuming.

Yet, I can't have her. Even though her eyes flicker with the same need, I know that I'll hurt us both if I don't respect what she's asked for.

"I'm sorry," she says.

As if she has anything to be sorry for. "I know. I am too." I remain caught up in her gaze for a minute. Everything I want to see is there, including the way she sees me.

But it's not real and it can't last. I have to move on. "This may be poor timing, but I need to get back to my mother's show."

"Sure."

"And since you're supposed to be sick, you will need to go home."

I direct Jordan to drive to Alayna's apartment and discover we're nearly there already. It's a good thing—I can't be with her much longer without going crazy. But I also wish I could gather every second until she leaves me and stretch them infinitely.

"When is our next show, boss?" she asks.

Celia and I had planned the symphony to be the next event on our agenda. She went off script today, so I don't feel obligated to stick to our plans. Even though the damage has been done, I'd also like to keep Alayna and Celia as far from each other as possible.

So I don't mention the symphony to Alayna. "I'm not sure. I have to fly to Cincinnati tonight." I frown. "And I am not your boss."

"Cincinnati? Tonight?" She sounds disappointed.

"Yes, tonight. I have a meeting first thing in the morning. My jet's leaving early evening." My mother has invited us to the beach house later that week. That I'll be unable to get out of. "I'll text you later to arrange the Hamptons. We'll leave Friday afternoon."

"So you'll be gone all week?"

"I'm not sure yet." I'm supposed to be back by Wednesday, but I don't tell her that. It's best for both of us if she thinks I'm not in town.

"Oh." She sounds disappointed. But I've turned everything off now. Years of not feeling and it's old hat to return to numb. So it doesn't hurt when we arrive at her place and she gets out of the car.

Or maybe it does hurt, but it's so deep inside, buried so far, that I find a way to ignore it.

I can't ignore her pain though. It's written all over her face, all over her carriage. I call her back before she's gone too far. "Thank you for today. I think you've truly made an impression on my mother. Good work." It's nothing of what I want to say, but it's all I allow myself.

Then Jordan drives away, and instead of thinking about all that I'm leaving behind, I concentrate on what is waiting before me until all my emotion—all my rage and anger and bitterness—is focused on Celia.

<hr />

The fashion show has started when I return to the Manhattan Center. I know where Celia's sitting, thank God, and I'm grateful that it's near the back of the room. When I reach her, I tap her on the shoulder to get her attention then not so gently assist her up from her chair. She doesn't fight me as I escort her to the lobby and to the coatroom. It's summer, so it's not in use.

I can't help but think of the last coatroom I was in. It was with Alayna at The Sky Launch—I'd barely been able to control my passion with her. Now it's my temper that's barely controlled.

After locating the light and shutting the door behind us, I turn on Celia. "What the fuck did you do?" My tone is threatening and wild.

She rolls her eyes at me. "Oh, chill out. I hadn't had a chance to get to know our subject. I was simply feeling her out." She takes a seat on the bench in the middle of the room.

"You told her *my* secrets." Her lack of concern, her docile temperament, fuels me. She's fucked me over and isn't at all afraid of my retaliation. I search for something she'll find meaningful. "You practically ruined your own scheme by telling her something that we aren't even supposed to talk about. Ever!" I'm yelling. It's very unlike me. As if I'm not only feeling new emotions because of Alayna, but feeling old ones deeper and with less inhibition.

With only a mildly surprised look on her face, Celia starts a slow, exaggerated clapping. "Wow, Hudson. You're angry. I'm impressed."

She's pushing my fury. But her recognition of my temper puts me in check. Emotions, I remember, make people weak. I'm extremely vulnerable in this situation, and Celia is not the person who should witness this.

I throw a hand through my hair and rein in my rage. "I get angry. This isn't new." I'm noticeably calmer, playing off my outburst.

"You never get this angry. If you do, you don't let it show." She places her palms on either side of her and leans back to study me. "Did that therapist of yours finally teach you how to feel?"

She's poking at me, needling me, and in a flash of clarity, I understand what it's like to be on the other end of a manipulative attack. The realization weakens me, and I have to sit. I fall on the bench next to Celia.

I have to get myself together. Get myself in the dominating position. I take a deep breath, and let it out slowly. "I'm just…out of practice at this. And you're changing the rules without consulting me. I'm frustrated." Another breath in and out.

"Understandable, I suppose." She's watching me with eagle eyes. "But I didn't change the rules. I saw a flaw in our scenario and I improvised. Same as we always do."

I'm cautious, but this piques my interest. "What flaw?"

She shifts so she's angled toward me. "The girl is doe-eyed about you, Hudson. It's obvious she's going to fall apart over you, and while that's the expectation, this was going to be entirely too easy." She runs a finger between her brows. "So I injected a little challenge. That's all."

Another rush of emotion washes over me. I'm angry again. Angry that Celia is playing with Alayna like this, molding her, bouncing her back and forth. "Making the experiment more challenging? Since when was that something we'd aspired to?"

She shrugs. "This is your first game in a long time. I wanted to make it good for you."

It's plausible. Her motives could very well be to keep me interested. God knows she's been trying to reel me back in for years.

But I know Celia better than that. The challenge is for her. And I'm still not entirely sure that was the reason for exposing me to Alayna. I just can't determine her true aim.

More composed now, I attempt to figure it out. "That was quite a risk you took. She almost quit the whole thing."

Celia delivers a confident smirk. "But she didn't. Did she?"

"Only because I convinced her not to. If it hadn't been for me, she would be gone." A tug of guilt—I should have let her walk away. Whatever happens now between Celia and Alayna is my fault.

But wasn't it always?

Celia crosses a leg over the other and clasps her hands at her knee. "If it hadn't been for you, she wouldn't be so enamored in the first place."

"What's that supposed to mean?"

"Just that the scheme would have worked more objectively if you hadn't fucked her."

There it is—her true motive. She's not happy about my personal relationship with Alayna. Is it jealousy? Or just pure spite? "You've never cared if I fucked them before."

"And I still don't. Except when it messes with the hypothesis." She stands, straightening her skirt as she does. Then she turns to face me. "Your extracurricular activities are your own business. Keep up your fun if you prefer. But realize that what you do with Alayna Withers outside our plan has the power to affect the outcome."

"It's a little late for that sentiment. You've effectively ended any extracurricular activities, as you like to call it." I know that despite Celia's animosity or jealousy or whatever, she's actually done Alayna a favor. There is a connection between her and me, and Celia's right that our sex life is only hurting Alayna's chances at remaining strong. I've known this for quite some time, yet I didn't have the strength on my own to end things as I should.

This is for the best, as devastating as it is for me to live with.

Celia recognizes my disappointment. She crosses behind me and strokes a hand through the hair at my temple. "I'm sorry, Hudson. I really am. I probably shouldn't have intervened as I did. I just know that you have faith that Alayna will come out of this strong, and with the road you had chosen, that was simply not going to happen." She leans down and hugs me from behind, her mouth at my ear. "I did it for you. To give your thesis a fighting chance. Forgive me?"

I tense under her touch. We've had physical contact over the years, growing comfortable enough with each other to kiss and embrace when scenarios called for it. But now, her arms around me feel like shackles. She has a hold on me, I realize. And I have no idea how to break free.

Pushing out of her embrace, I stand and spin to her. "Don't pretend this was for me, Celia. You forget I know you. You wanted to make the game more challenging—well, you did just that. Good luck with the rest of this going the way you'd like."

I head to the door, but she calls after me. "The symphony on Thursday? It's still our next outing, correct?"

I'm still committed to my vow to keep Alayna from Celia, but an outright refusal will only goad my partner. "I'll see what I can do, but I'm making no promises."

Later, in the limo as Jordan drives me home to change before my flight, I have my first taste of loneliness. I miss Alayna. I want to see her, to touch her, to hear her voice.

But mixed in with the loneliness is a measure of affection. It's not anything I understand. All I know is that I care more for Alayna's well-being in the moment than for mine. So when her text arrives, I ignore my impulse to respond. I need to help her let me go.

I read it one more time. *"Thanks for the coffee. And for everything else."*

And then I push delete.

— CHAPTER —

THIRTEEN

The next few days are painful. I work punishing hours, throwing all my energy into solving the problems at Plexis. But the nights are long and lonely. Neither alcohol nor jerking off relieves any of my need. If I were a subject in one of my own experiments, my point would be proved—affinity toward another person makes one flawed. Still, as miserable and weak as I am now, I wouldn't give up the moments I've shared with Alayna.

I'd planned to fly directly to Chicago on Wednesday for another meeting regarding Plexis on Thursday morning, but I come back to Manhattan late Tuesday night instead. It's harder to fight my desire to run to her, but I find comfort being in the same city. I spend the night in the loft, and thoughts of our time together accompany me as I drift in and out of a fitful sleep.

First thing Wednesday morning, I receive a report from Jordan. He's still driving Alayna and, more importantly, still reporting back to me. His report is somewhat banal, except that I note Alayna's stopped by Pierce Industries the last two days. Her behavior might be written off as meaningless to someone else, but I understand things about her that others don't. I wonder if her visits are an indication of falling into past habits.

The idea worries me. It's a minor win for Celia.

At the same time, I'm blanketed by a warm tingle that is almost comforting. It's a shitty thing to take joy in, but I'm not triumphing in her setbacks. I'm hopeful, instead, that her actions indicate something else—that I mean something to her. That I'm on her mind. That she feels some affection toward me as I feel toward her.

Though why it matters is beyond me.

It's after an impromptu lunch meeting with one of my advertising teams that I see her. I've walked my associates to the elevator, one of the men finishing a joke as the doors open.

And there she is.

"Alayna." Even saying her name is a treat I've denied myself. I'm dizzy at the sight of her, but I'm aware of where we are and of what our relationship is, and I manage to keep much of my surprise to myself.

She's frozen, a deer-in-the-headlights expression written all over her face. I hold a hand out to her. She takes it and I'm elated. How simple to be thrilled at only the touch of a woman's hand? It's ridiculous and wonderful all at once.

I turn to my team. "Gentlemen, my girlfriend has decided to surprise me with a visit to my office."

The men make some wisecrack that I miss because I'm completely absorbed in her smile. Completely absorbed in her.

The next few minutes are a blur, but finally, I have Alayna with me in my office. Alone.

Nothing about this is a good idea.

With great strength, I drop my hand and distance myself from her physically and figuratively. "What are you doing here, Alayna?"

She doesn't look at me. That helps.

As she works out her answer, I study her. I understand her, I think. The feeling of wanting to be near someone and knowing you shouldn't be. Yeah, I get that.

After a while, she hugs her arms around herself and takes a deep breath. "I, uh, I wanted to see if you were back."

This is difficult for her. It's difficult for me too. "I got back late last night. You could have called. Or texted." It's impressive that I can seemingly remain so cold about her presence when in reality I'm spinning with elation.

"You don't answer my texts."

"I didn't answer one text."

A tear runs down her cheek. "It was my only text."

Our eyes remain locked, and I find myself slipping into examination mode. I'm collecting data—the vulnerability in the way she stands, the frailty in her voice, the weight of her tears. But unlike the other times I've studied women in the same position, I'm moved by her. I can't stay hard with her, even if it's what's best for both of us, and I falter. "I didn't realize it was important to you. I'll make a better effort to respond in the future."

She gapes.

I've surprised her as much as myself, and I fear my softening has done irreparable damage. I straighten, assuming a commanding position. "But you can't just come here like this. How do you think it looks to have my girlfriend wandering around the lobby, riding the elevators when I'm not even in town?"

"How did you...?"

"I pay people to know things, Alayna."

More tears fall. "I...I'm sorry. I couldn't help myself."

"Please, don't do it again." I'm ripped apart. I want to pull her in my arms, not admonish her.

Her forehead wrinkles in confusion. "Why are you being like this?"

"Like what?" I'm as confused as she is. Was I too stern? I thought I'd been gentle. Well, as gentle as I could be without betraying us both.

But she's sobbing now. "I've fucked things up, Hudson! You should be calling your security to escort me out. I'm a mess, and you're taking it all in stride."

I step toward her, hating the space between us. "No." God, how I want to touch her. "That's what I meant about being around someone who understands. I know about compulsion. I know about having to do things you know you shouldn't."

Not able to help myself, I reach forward and wipe a tear from her cheek, my hand lingering there longer than necessary. "When you feel you can't help yourself, talk to me first."

Am I deluding myself? Thinking that somehow we could be like this together—healing each other, fixing each other? Is it really that far-fetched? If I forget about Celia and the game and only concentrate on us—on me and Alayna—it almost seems...possible.

She meets my gaze, and I think she feels the same. Where could this take us? I wonder...

But then my secretary's voice echoes over the intercom. "Mr. Pierce, your one-thirty is here."

Reality enters and I remember that the space between us is for her own good. I sigh and drop my hand from her face. I miss the warmth of her skin already. "I apologize for cutting this short, Alayna, but I have another meeting now. And I'm leaving again this evening."

She doesn't hide her disappointment, though I'm not sure which part of what I've said bothers her. Then she says, "I hate that you're leaving. It makes me feel a little distraught."

I feel like a Christmas tree the way all my nerves light up at that small admission. "I'll be back tomorrow." I squeeze her hand. "Join me tomorrow night for the symphony."

I'm selfish. I'm sadistic. I'm sending her to slaughter. But I'm elated because it's less than thirty hours and I'll be with her again.

The euphoria follows me through the rest of the day, and when Alayna texts me later, I answer. When her message asks, *"Are you thinking of me?"* I don't hesitate and answer honestly, *"Always."*

<hr />

My plane is delayed leaving Chicago, and I'm late for the symphony. I'm anxious as I rush through the lobby at Lincoln Center. Not only am I eager to see Alayna, but I'm going crazy imagining all the shit Celia could have stirred up in my absence. Luckily, Madge and Warren are also in attendance. Hopefully their presence will keep their daughter in check.

I enter our box just as the lights go down. Alayna's back is to me, but even just the nape of her neck and the curve of her shoulders is enough to make my cock twitch and my chest warm. I can tell that she's wearing the dress I requested. Though I can't see how she looks in it now, I know from memory how the long black gown hugs her curves, how the corset ties that lace up her back are going to be a bitch to untie when I strip her later.

Except I'm not stripping her later. I have to remember that's not what she's asked for.

My phone buzzes with an incoming text and I glance at it. It's from Alayna. *"Where are you?"*

I slip down the steps to my chair and lean toward her to whisper in her ear as I sit. "Right beside you."

The music begins as I nod a greeting to the Werners, but all I'm aware of is Alayna. The look of her, the warmth of her, the smell of her—it's all consuming. She doesn't want anything but the pretend between us, but I take her hand and justify it as a part of the show for Celia's parents. I hold it, clinging to her touch until intermission. If this is all I have of her, I'll soak up every last bit.

We do well with our performance as a couple. The Werners seem to buy our relationship. I'm concerned when Alayna accompanies Celia and Madge to the restroom, but I can't do anything to prevent them from using the facilities. My eyes dart from Warren to the box entrance the entire time they're gone.

Warren notices. "Ah, young love," he says. "I remember when I couldn't stand being without Madge. In fact, forget young—I still feel that way."

I nod. *Love,* he said. I spin the word in my head. It has no meaning to me. The way he seems to feel about his wife is nothing I've ever witnessed between my parents. And, yes, I'm keen to have Alayna by my side again. But that's not called *love.* Is it?

When they return from the bathroom, Alayna seems on edge. She's needy, touching me as often as she can. She slides her hand under my suit jacket, and I'm hopeful that it means she may be willing to give us another chance.

But if she is, it's a bad idea for me to pursue it, and an even worse idea to let Celia know. So I limit my contact with Alayna to hand-holding, even though I am just as desperate to touch her as it seems she is to touch me. As the music plays, I convince myself a million times that I will not take her back to the loft. And just as many times, I convince myself I will. Whichever will win, I don't know, but at least Celia won't be privy to it.

After the concert, we all walk to the parking garage together. I keep my arm around Alayna, but I can't look at her. The touching is supposed to be show, but if she peers into my eyes, I'm afraid she'll see how very real this all is for me. I'm afraid it will be witnessed by my partner in crime. It's a balancing act that I manage but only barely.

At my car, I put Alayna in the passenger seat and then say goodbye to the Werners. Celia leans in to hug me. "You've backed off. I'm impressed," she whispers in my ear.

"I could say the same." I whisper back, though I doubt that she's backed off anything and I'm not at all impressed. She laughs. My gut constricts at the sound. She takes such pleasure in this game while I'm struggling, playing both sides.

But I don't want to think about Celia any longer. Now I get to be alone with Alayna, and I have to decide what that's going to mean.

We're quiet as we drive out of the garage, snippets of the symphony replaying in my mind. I use this time to let go of the tension the evening has caused. I also resume the internal war—do I take her to her home or to the loft? From what I can read of Alayna, she's equally conflicted. Since she's unaware of all the risks involved in our relationship, it's up to me to make the informed decision.

I've made up my mind by the time we've gotten to the road. It's not a decision that makes me completely comfortable, but it's the only one I can live with.

While I'm working out how to tell Alayna, she breaks the silence. "So you knew Celia would be there tonight."

Her tone is harsh, and it surprises me.

"I knew Celia would be there with her parents, yes." I throw a glance at her, trying to understand her angle. "Her parents, whom are friends with my parents, remember."

She's upset with me. I'm not sure why. Or she's upset with herself. She knocks her head softly against the window, and I catch her dabbing at a tear.

"What's wrong?" Maybe there was more to the restroom trip with Celia and Madge than I realized. I'm already making plans of what I'll do to Celia next time I see her.

But Alayna surprises me again. "I want you," she whispers into the glass.

She's said it so quietly that I doubt what I heard. "Alayna?"

"I know what I said." She wipes her eyes. "But maybe I was wrong. I mean, I don't know if you're right—if spending time with you can make me better. But I know that since we've been apart, I've been worse." She looks at me and there's the light again. The light I've been longing for that shines only in her eyes.

"I miss you." She giggles. "Told you I get attached."

I'm relieved. I'd made the right decision, and even more comforting is that she's admitted she's attached. I don't even care what that means for Celia's scam. Because what it means for me is everything.

I can't hide my delight. "Where do you think I'm taking you?"

She looks out the window. I can tell the exact moment she realizes we're headed for the loft. A blush shades her cheeks. "Oh."

Then she thinks about it more. "I told you no more sex, and you were taking me to the loft without asking?" Irritation's spun with her words.

"Alayna," I sigh. God, our situation is frustrating. *She's* frustrating. "You are a bundle of mixed signals. At the symphony, you seemed to indicate—"

"And you totally blew me off. Don't talk to me about mixed signals!"

Of course that's what she thinks. She didn't understand my motives. How could she?

I rest a hand on her knee. "I was trying to avoid mixing business with pleasure. A difficult task with you, precious." I need her to know how she affects me. I would prefer to show her, but since I'm driving, I have to try words. "Especially with your wandering hands and how hot you look in that dress."

She softens. "Oh."

"If you want me to ask, I will, though you know it's not my style." She stares at me, wide eyed, so I force myself to ask what I never ask. "May I take you to my bed, Alayna?"

"Yes," she moans, and I've never been so grateful for a traffic light. I pull her to me. I'm greedy with my kiss. Forget manners or niceties. I'm going to fuck her how we both need to fuck tonight—with desperation and need. This kiss is the prelude.

A horn interrupts us, prodding me to drive. My dick is as hard as stone, and I can barely concentrate, but somehow I manage to get to the Pierce Industries building without killing us. I hand my keys to the valet. Then we're in the elevator. We tease each other on the ride up, and as soon as we're in the loft, I have her pressed against the wall. I cradle her face with my hands, and I kiss her. Greedily, hungrily, with abandon.

While I worship her with my mouth, she strokes me through my clothing. Then she works my cock free, stripping me of my pants and briefs. She sinks to her knees, and before I can think about it, she has me in her mouth. I gasp, tugging on the strands of her hair. "God, Alayna. That's so…ah…so good."

And it is. It's pleasure upon pleasure the way her tongue licks my crown, the way her mouth sucks my shaft into her warmth. I'm dizzy, my thighs clenching as I get harder and my orgasm gets closer.

But while she's amazing, while everything she does to me is amazing, I don't want this from her. I've been blown so many times by so many women. I've taken from them—taken, taken, taken. I don't want to be like that with Alayna. I want to give to her. I want to pleasure her. At the very least, I want to come with her, in her. I don't want to be the only one on the receiving end.

So I stop her.

She's bewildered, disappointed, maybe. "Did I do something wrong?" she asks.

It's part of her beauty—how naïve she can be without being innocent. This is about me, though, and I need to alleviate her fears. "No, precious. Your mouth is amazing." I kiss her again, the salty taste of my pre-cum still on her lips. "But I need to come inside your cunt. I've been thinking about it for days."

Then we're lost in each other again. By the time we've struggled through stripping each other of the rest of our clothes, we're both so eager and impatient that we can't wait any longer. I lift her, urging her legs to wrap around my waist. I pause, my cock poised at her pussy. I'm sure she's not wet enough, but she invites me to take her anyway.

I can't help myself—I do, driving into her with a deep thrust. She's raw at first, and so tight, but I ram into her over and over until she loosens and I slide in her easily. It's insane that I can fuck her like this—holding her while pounding into her so intently, and I have to credit pure adrenaline and lust. The erotic sounds of her moans and our thighs slapping and the fuck-hot sight of her breasts bouncing in front of me fuel my desire. "So…damn…good," I tell her. "You feel…so…damn…good."

I'm close, so close, and if she doesn't go over with me, I'll be wrecked. I turn her to the wall, using it as a brace to hold her up while I help to get her there too, rubbing her clit as I continue to pound into her with my cock. "Come with me, Alayna," I urge. "Come."

Her thighs shake around me and that's how I know she's at the breaking point. Then she throws her head back and lets out the most beautiful sound—a euphoric sort of keening. Her nails dig into my back as her cunt milks me. It's so goddamn hot and I'm there too. I call her name as I come inside of her, and in those simple three syllables, I give her credit for all that she does to me, not only physically but emotionally.

She can't possibly understand everything I mean by the stating of her name. In that post-orgasmic state, while the whooshing is still in my ears and my legs are still numb, I hope that one day she will understand. That she'll know how much she means to me, how much she's changing me. How much more I'm willing to change for her.

We're both still panting when she says, "Can we do that again?"

Does she even have to ask? Of course we can do it again. I make a show of telling her, though, looking at my watch before I respond. "You have to be at work at one? I think we can manage to do that again twice."

I take her mouth again, not trying to start things up, but rather to cool me down. Her lips are swollen, and my kiss is tender. When my heart rate resumes a normal speed, I break away.

After leading her to the couch, I start toward the kitchen. "Water or iced tea?" I call over my shoulder.

"Water, please."

I grab a bottle and take a long swallow before returning to her. She's curled up in the corner of the sofa, hugging her knees. I hate that she still hides her nakedness from me, but it's adorable at the same time. As if she can actually hide anything from me.

I hand her the bottle. She nods a thank you as she takes it, her forehead wrinkled as if she's thinking. She has a sip then asks. "Could you really do that? Go again twice?"

"What do you think?" I could go all night with her. She's the first woman that I can say that about. I can never get enough of Alayna.

Her brown eyes flash with sass. "I think you'd like to think you can."

My eyes narrow. "You don't have to challenge me to get me to prove it, precious." I'm semi-hard already.

"Oh, really?" Her eyes dart to my cock and it grows harder under her gaze.

I take the bottle from her hand and set it on the coffee table before I pounce on top of her. She squeals but easily obeys when I urge her to stretch out her body beneath mine.

"Be careful who you're playing with, Alayna." I nip at her jawline. "I assure you, I'm the one who will come out of this on top."

I prove it by pinning her hands above her head while I kiss her senseless. Her hips wriggle to meet mine, but I keep my pelvis slightly off of hers, taunting her. Just as I'm about to get swept away with my teasing, I back off. There's something I need to ask her, and I can't wait any longer for the answer. "Why did you decide to resume this?"

It takes her a minute to understand my question. "The sex?" She blushes, moving her eyes from mine. "Well, besides the obvious reason—"

"Which is?"

"It's fun." Her blush deepens.

"Yes, you're right. Quite obvious." *And quite fun.* It's her other answer I'm interested in, though. "And...?"

Now she meets my gaze, her dark browns penetrating me with their transparency, with their honesty. "And I trust you," she says.

My throat goes dry and my heart feels like it's dropped to my stomach. It's not what I expected her to say in a million years, though what *had* I expected her to say? That she'd jumped back into bed with me because I'd bullied her? Because she couldn't resist me? Because she was in love with me?

Most anything she could have said would have had its own repercussions to face, but any other answer would have been easier to take than this one.

It suddenly seems like there isn't enough air, and I have to sit up. I gently maneuver her legs so I have a place to sit. And then, because I'm a masochist and I have to hear it all, I say, "Go on."

"Well..." She curls her knees again as she thinks, but doesn't use them to hide her breasts like she did before. She's more comfortable—quite ironic considering how uncomfortable I feel at the moment. Thankfully, she doesn't seem to notice.

"You said you were different now," she says finally. "Different with me. And I realized that it doesn't matter if it's crazy or stupid to believe it. Because I believe it anyway. I believe you. I trust you. About this, I trust you."

Again, she hits me with those piercing browns, and I feel like someone who's standing before a judge waiting for his sentencing. It will either be freedom or execution, but the strange thing is that the verdict will be decided by me. By how I choose to respond to her frankness.

I already know what decision I'll make, even before weighing my options.

There are so many reasons she shouldn't trust me, of course, and not the least of which is that I'm currently lying and scamming her. This is a perfect opportunity to confess, and if I were decent at all, I would, even though it would certainly be the death of me.

But it's not what I choose. Because in a very real way, I've been more honest with her than anyone in my entire life. Even with Celia, I smothered any emotion that ever began to creep into being. With Alayna, I'm letting that go, letting feelings slip into my existence. It's changing me into someone who *can* be trusted. *She's* changing me into someone who deserves those words—*I trust you.*

It moves me—her words, her presence, my transformation. It robs me of speech.

So I pull her into my lap and take up telling her in the way I know best—with my body. With our physical connection that transcends any connection I've had with another human being. I kiss her face, her eyelids, her cheeks, the curve of her jaw. Then, as my mouth travels along her neckline, I trail my hands down her sides, memorizing the lines of her ribs with my fingertips, gliding the slope of her hips with my palms.

I speak to her like this. My gestures in place of words. *I'm learning for you*, I say when I lick the rise of her shoulder. *Your trust gives me a reason*, I say as I tug her nipple to a peak. *Don't give up on me*, I say as I slide my hand between her thighs to rub at her clit. *I feel for you*, as I lift her up and settle her on my cock.

Though I know nothing of love, I make love to her. Wholly. Completely. Undeniably.

She steadies herself with her hands on my shoulders as I buck into her and glide out. She's warm and tight, and my crown knocks against her in a place that makes her writhe and makes my cock grow harder. She's on top, but I control all the movement—the tempo, the force of my thrusts, the depth of my drive. It's a love song that I sing to her, the way I hold her and kiss her and send her to a state of ecstasy, her breathy gasps the underscore. I make sure she comes—twice, even—before I grip my fingers into her hips and chase my own orgasm, reaching it when I least expect it with a sudden burst of euphoria.

It's the sweetest sex has ever been for me. The most poetic. The most transformative.

As we settle together, spiraling down from bliss, I land in a space of clarity. I stop worrying if it's going to be Alayna that falls apart from this affair and start accepting that it's going to be me.

— CHAPTER —
FOURTEEN

Before

Trying to ignore the Christmas music my mother had playing, I concentrated on entering some figures into a spreadsheet from one of the companies my father was letting me work on over the break. Plexis, a Pierce Industry subsidiary with a great outlook. If my modifications to the business plan were successful, the earnings for the coming year would far exceed what had been predicted. It was exciting enough to make spending time with my family over the holidays bearable.

"I don't see any diamond ring size boxes under here," my mother said behind me.

I glanced back to see her arranging the presents under the tree in the living room for the fifth time in an hour. There were more gifts than I'd ever seen growing up, and I bet that at least half of them were for *the baby*.

"There's not going to be a ring, Mother. I'm not marrying Celia. I've told you that."

"I keep hoping you're trying to surprise me with a Christmas engagement." She'd talked nonstop of marriage plans since Thanksgiving. I'd thought it would have been Celia's parents driving a union. Turned out Sophia was even worse.

"I really wish I'd known what color to buy." She added another gift to the heap. "I saved all the receipts though. In case you and Celia get sick of green and yellow."

When I'd arranged for limited fathering of Celia's child, I'd neglected to factor in my mother. Since we'd announced our news, Sophia had been a buzz of excitement. Every conversation stemmed around our child. Every day was another chance for her to dote on her unborn grandchild. It seemed she might not be drinking as much too, though that was hard to prove, especially when I'd been away at school for much of the last few weeks.

She moved a present from the back so that it was more visible. It was one I hadn't seen before, the package shaped very much like a rocking horse. How long would it be before a kid could even use that? With a sigh, I turned back to my computer.

"I'm so glad Celia's not going back to school next semester. I wish you were staying here."

This was another conversation we'd had repeatedly. By phone and then at least twice a day since I'd come home for break. "Boston isn't far. I'll come up for every prenatal exam. I'll make sure I'm here for the birth."

"That's what you keep saying. But labor can come on quickly. What if you missed it?"

I didn't answer. Honestly, I'd be glad to miss it. Seeing Celia in a delivery room did not rank high on my-fun-things-to-do list. The rest, though—the exams, the ultrasounds, even the damn yellow and green layette—that I'd begun to look forward to with surprising enthusiasm. I was going to be a father. It didn't matter that it wasn't biologically mine. Because I'd claimed it, it was mine in every way that would ever matter.

Sophia didn't seem to care that I hadn't responded. "You know, we don't have to wait until after Christmas for the gender reveal ultrasound. We could probably get in with one of those 3D ultrasound places. Should I call Celia and arrange it? My treat."

"No." I paused while I finished entering the formula I was working on. "Madge doesn't trust those things. She wants to wait for her scheduled exam."

"We don't have to tell Madge."

"Even if you are capable of keeping a secret from Madge, I don't think Celia would want to go without her mother."

"What I don't understand is why you're not more excited about it?" My mother's voice came nearer as she spoke. Then she sat at the table next to me. "It's your first child, Hudson. Take some more pride."

Perhaps I needed to do a better job at mustering enthusiasm. My father, though, hadn't shown much more excitement than me. No wondering why there. We'd never talked about it, but if he didn't assume the baby could be his, then he was an idiot. Even if he believed I actually was responsible for Celia's pregnancy, he had to be at least a little uncomfortable with the idea that he'd shared a woman with his son. It would bother *me*, anyway. But my father and I had obvious differences in what was socially acceptable and what wasn't.

"I'm not very expressive," I said, not looking up from my work. "It doesn't mean I don't feel things." It was a line I'd stolen from some movie. Wouldn't it have been something if it were actually true?

She put a hand on my arm. "I'm glad to hear that, Hudson. I used to worry you didn't."

My mother had never given any indication that she noticed my lack of emotional response. I typed in one more figure and shut my laptop. "What exactly worried you, Mother?"

"You, Hudson. You worried me." She dropped her hand from my arm to the table. "Do you remember when you were twelve and you had those entrance exams for Choice Hill?"

I nodded. Choice Hill had been the elite middle school I'd gone to. The admissions process was a rigorous six-hour session of various IQ and personality tests. The children accepted were not only the wealthiest in Manhattan but also intellectually gifted.

"One of the psychologists that worked with you—" She furrowed her brow as if trying to remember something. After a few seconds, she waved her hand dismissively. "His name escapes me, but anyway, he suggested that you struggled with emotions. He recommended we had you tested further to rule out sociopathic tendencies or schizoid personality disorder or Asperger's Syndrome. Because you had a blunted affect. Or experience avoidance. Or something like that. I don't remember the terms."

My heart thudded in my chest. This was the first time I'd heard any of this. "But I don't remember being tested for anything."

"Oh, no. You made it into the school, so we didn't see any reason to pursue the issue further."

I sat back in my chair, incredulous. "I made it into the school," I repeated, "and so you didn't see any reason to find out if your child might be suffering from a major psychological disorder?"

She rolled her eyes. "Don't act like it's such a big deal. You're obviously fine."

How on earth did she think I was fine? I'd never been anything but fine. While I wasn't particularly eager to experience the volatile, irrational emotions of my peers, I at least wanted to know what the fuck was wrong with me. What the hell made me so different?

My parents' casual dismissal of a potential problem disturbed me most of all. Whatever my issues were, I at least knew how to feel anger. And I was exceptionally angry at the moment.

I hadn't finished deciding whether or not to express my rage when the phone rang, making the decision for me. The housekeeper had the day off, so Mother got up to get it. By the tone of her "hello," I knew it must be one of her friends.

I tuned her out, opening my laptop instead to do some internet searching. I'd just typed in "blunted affect" when my mother gasped. I looked across the room to her. She was shaking her head, her hand raised to clutch her chest. For a good second, I wondered if she was having a heart attack.

Then her eyes met mine. "Okay. Okay," she kept saying into the receiver. "We'll be there. We're coming. See you soon."

She hung up, and I saw that all the color had left her face. "Hudson. Hudson. Oh, no."

My forehead creased. Was it Dad? He'd taken my siblings ice-skating at Rockefeller Center earlier. Or Mirabelle? Or Chandler?

Mother rushed toward me, and I stood to catch her. She was crying already as she buried her face in my shoulder. "It's the baby," she said into my sweatshirt. "Celia's losing the baby. She's at the hospital. We have to go."

I never pushed return in the search field. The results for *blunted affect* never made it to my script. I didn't need the internet to tell me whether or not I could feel. At that moment, all I felt was numb.

I watched the drip of the IV in a daze, the measured beeps of the heart monitor the only sound in the quiet, darkened room. Celia was sleeping. She had been for several hours. I hadn't spoken to her or seen her awake since I'd arrived.

When my mother and I had gotten to the hospital, Celia had been in labor. The baby, we were told, was dead already.

After, she hadn't wanted to see anyone. Madge and Warren gave us what little information they'd had. They'd gone to the ER when Celia's water had broken. There, an ultrasound had failed to find the fetus's heartbeat. The doctors guessed it had passed sometime two weeks before. Celia was admitted to the obstetrics ward. Labor continued naturally, and a few hours later, she'd delivered. It had been a boy.

I spent the evening comforting my mother in the waiting room. Eventually, my father arrived and took her home, where I guessed she'd mourn in the way she knew best—with a bottle of vodka. Though Celia still refused to see me, I stayed.

Around midnight, the Werners said goodbye, promising they'd return first thing in the morning. That's when I snuck in her room. I spent the night awake in an armchair by her bed. I had no reason to be there. I had no reason to go.

"Why are you here?" Celia's voice drew me from my stupor.

I wiped my mouth and cleared my throat before trying to speak. "You're awake."

"I am." She pushed a button, and the bed tilted her into a sitting position. "And you don't need to be here. The façade is over. You can go." Her tone was straight, empty of expression.

"I'm not leaving."

"Why?"

I answered honestly. "I don't know."

She leaned her head back into the pillow, accepting my answer. She didn't ask me to leave again, and something told me it was because she really didn't want me to go.

Though I knew that conversation wasn't necessary, I asked all the same, "How do you feel?"

She shrugged one shoulder. "Numb."

That was an emotion I knew well. "That's natural."

"Is it?"

Who the fuck knew what natural was? Certainly not me. "I don't really know, Celia. I assume it is." She stared at me with blank eyes. So I said more. "I imagine it's some sort of defense mechanism to the trauma. Do they know what happened?"

She started to shake her head and stopped. "One of the doctors told me—in private, when my parents weren't in the room—that there appeared to be developmental issues. I asked if it could have been because….because I'd partied early on. I, uh, drank a lot. And there was drug use. Before I knew I was pregnant, of course. He said that he couldn't be sure, but it was probably a contributing factor."

Her voice was raw with the honesty—or perhaps it was the fact that she'd just awoken and the day before had been more than rough. Either way, I sensed I was the only person who would hear this truth.

And I had nothing to offer her in terms of comfort. I didn't even try. I wondered, though, in the quiet that followed, if she blamed me. It seemed a reasonable reaction from what I'd learned about human behavior. She'd lost her child because of drug and alcohol use. She'd used because she'd been broken. She'd been broken by me. It was fair to say, then, that she'd lost her child because of me.

She wouldn't have even been pregnant if not for me. It was easy to say her actions were her responsibility, but I had manipulated her for the exact reason of studying how she'd react. I did have culpability.

I didn't feel guilty or even regretful, necessarily. I simply wondered if she blamed me. Even here in this inappropriate moment, I searched to understand the nuances of human psychology.

Celia broke the silence. "I'm sorry."

"Why are you sorry?" Coming after my internal dialogue, her apology was particularly out of place.

She blinked several times, and I realized she was crying. "You aren't really the father, but I feel like I need to say this to someone. So I'm telling you I'm sorry. I'm sorry I killed our baby."

Her tears flowed in gentle streams that she wiped at with the tips of her fingers. She was silent and her body still as she grieved. I watched her, taking it in. Not completely heartless, I did notice a certain melancholy wrap around me. It was refreshing almost, to feel something other than even. Though, it appeared to be much less comfortable of an emotion for Celia. That was unfortunate.

When the crying let up, she threw a glance at me. "It was fun for a moment, wasn't it? Pretending it was ours."

I tilted my head as I contemplated that. Our scheme had been easy to fall into. People had been ready to believe, and that had inspired a kind of secret delight. Celia had been in California for the majority of our ruse, but in the days before she'd left, I'd recognized her own euphoria. She'd tried to hide it behind the pretense of embarrassment and guilt, but I could read her too well.

"I feel like I understand you better now, Hudson." She waited until I'd met her eyes with a questioning brow raise. "Why you play those games. Why you played that game with me."

My heart stilled for a beat. I had to have misunderstood her allusion. I clarified. "What game?"

She let out an exasperated sigh, throwing her head back onto her pillow. "Let's not do that right now, Hudson. Please? Be honest with me for a minute."

Maybe it was the circumstances surrounding us or the lingering melancholy. Or perhaps the darkness of the room. Or the lack of sleep. Or finally a chance to speak with someone who was willing to hear. More likely it was the combination of all of the above that allowed me to step onto sacred ground and bare my secrets.

In a steady low voice, I let down the first wall. "They aren't games."

"What are they then?" She matched the tone and timbre of my voice, as though she understood as well as I did that this moment was unusual. That this conversation was unique.

"They're experiments." I trained my eyes on the steady blip of her heart monitor. "I don't...understand...people." *Blip. Blip.* "What makes them feel. I experiment to understand." *Blip.*

"You don't feel things?" *Blip.* Her heart rate didn't alter.

Blip. "I don't think I do. Not the way most people do." *Blip.*

"That explains a lot."

I met her stare. "Does it?"

"Yeah. It does." She wasn't accusatory. Simply matter-of-fact. We were alike, in a way. She understood things about people. She understood things about *me*, at the very least. "You've done it with more than just me then?"

I nodded once slowly.

"Have you learned anything?"

"I've learned a lot."

"But you still don't feel things?" She was curious but accepting.

"I don't." I gripped the arms of the chair and let them go again. "I don't think that's something that will ever change. It's not why I do it. If anything, the more I experiment, the less I feel. Except with you. You...I don't know." It wasn't that I didn't want to share. I just didn't have the words. "You're too much like family, I think. So I have...I did feel...*something.*"

"You don't know what, though?"

"No." I'd tried to figure it out so many times. "Obligation, maybe. Responsibility."

She fiddled with the edge of her bedsheet but kept her focus on me. "But with the others, you didn't feel anything?"

"No."

She let go of the sheet, turned and propped her head up on one hand. "Do you ever feel anything else?"

God, we were actually doing this, then? Examining all the pieces, letting all the walls down. *Might as well get comfortable.* I crossed an ankle over my jean-clad knee. "Not really. Anger sometimes. Disgust."

"You're never happy?"

"I'm often content." I didn't mention that the only excitement I felt revolved around the manipulation of others. I was stripping myself in front of her, but I didn't need to be vulgar.

"What about sorrow?"

"It's more like disappointment." I cleared my throat. This was the closest to sympathy she'd get from me. "Right now, I'm disappointed for you."

Though, there had been a moment—the moment that I'd learned Celia's baby was dead—and the disappointment had been something else. Something more intense, more intolerable. It seemed to start in the center of me, the sensation so strong it sounded in my ears. Soon it reverberated in my bones, in my skin, until every part of me had...*ached.*

But all it took was a straightening of my spine and a decision to not feel it anymore. And with a *whoosh*, it was silent. Gone. I was hardened.

It had been a unique incident. One I'd never experienced. Perhaps it warranted a relabeling for Celia's benefit. "*Very* disappointed for you."

She bit her lip as if she were fighting a fresh set of tears. "What about guilt? Or compassion? Or love?"

I shook my head.

"You don't love your mother? Or Mirabelle?"

"That's more complicated." It was difficult to explain my lack of emotion to someone else when I barely understood it myself. "I have a fondness for them. I feel an affinity toward them. But that's all."

She took in a ragged breath, and I could only assume this revelation disturbed her.

"Don't get me wrong," I added, "they do mean something to me. But it hardly measures the depths that I believe others feel for people they care for."

"Does that bother you?"

"It intrigues me. Bother me? Not really." I was grateful for the semi-dark room. It made the honest conversation less intense. "It actually makes me strong, I think. No one has the power to hurt me."

This idea had itched at me for a while, but had never fully formed. Now that I'd said it out loud, I sat back in the chair and soaked in the revelation. This incident had actually been the best test of the notion. This had *almost* hurt me. Not quite, but almost. And watching the Werners and my mother and Celia bear the pain like a terrible fever with no relief was exhausting in itself. If I'd ever thought my impassivity was a curse, I didn't now. It was my blessing.

Accepting this didn't change anything—didn't change me—but perhaps it propelled my interest in studying the human psyche. It gave me a mission. Because in learning why others behaved the way they did, I discovered more of my own strength.

"Hudson." Celia's small voice drew me from my reverie. "Teach me, Hudson."

I raised a questioning brow.

"Experiment with me."

"What? Why would you want me to…?" I didn't know how to react to the insane request. "I'm not experimenting on people I know anymore."

"Not *on* me. *With* me." She sat straight up. "I want to learn how you do it. Teach me."

Understanding her real intent didn't make the request any less strange. "No. That's absurd."

"Please."

"No." But now she'd planted the thought, and I couldn't help but explore it. "Why?"

"Because I want to be like that."

"Like what?"

"Like someone who doesn't feel." She fell back into the bed. "I don't want to feel anymore. I said I felt numb, but there's worse hiding underneath that. Jagged spikes of pain. I wanted that baby, Hudson. And before that, I wanted *you*. Not anymore, but I did. All that's left from all that want is hurt. I tried to hate you, and I do a little. But mostly I can't help but admire you. Your methods are impressive. Maybe you're an example of evolution. Maybe a lack of emotion is what it takes to move the human race to the next level. Because I think you're right—it is your strength. And I don't know if you were born that way or if you turned into this over time because of your fucked-up family—sorry, but it's true—but I think I could learn that. Or at least try. What's the harm in letting me try?"

Her voice had strengthened as she talked, and now her words echoed in the quiet room. Honestly, there was little to refute. And the possibilities her monologue had inspired…

"Okay."

She perked up in surprise. "Okay? Really?"

My mind was already swimming with plans. I never went looking for experiments. They'd arise out of situations and relationships around me that were interesting, that I wanted to explore. As it happened, there was a newly married couple that had just moved into my parents' building. Though they'd recently pledged their lives to each other, I couldn't help but notice the way he eyed other women. There was a lot I wanted to study there. Celia would actually prove helpful. "After Christmas. If you're up to it."

"I'll be up to it." She was excited.

My pulse kicked up a notch. How sick was it that her enthusiasm was a mental turn-on? I stifled my adrenaline rush by adding practicality. "There will be rules. Some we'll have to make up as we go since I've never worked with a partner."

"Of course. What's the fun of a game without rules?"

"They aren't games." It came out harsher than I'd intended, but it was important to me that she understood the difference. "They're experiments. It's science."

"Whatever you want to call it, Hudson. It's semantics. There's nothing wrong with having a bit of fun with it. I know you do."

So it didn't matter that I hadn't told her the games excited me. She already knew.

And Jesus, I was already referring to them as games myself. If I weren't so looking forward to the new phase of my research, I might have been irritated.

"Maybe," I conceded. "There is an enjoyment at correctly predicting how people will react."

She smiled—the first sign of joy since she'd awoken in the cold, sterile room.

"What have I agreed to?" But I genuinely smiled back.

She took a deep breath. Then her expression eased into something more solemn. "Thank you, Hudson."

"You're welcome." Also genuine.

We settled into a comfortable silence. My mind swirled with ideas and notions. Perhaps good really had come from all of the Celia mess. Though somewhere deep inside of me, a warning bell sounded, and while it was quiet enough to ignore, it was persistent and left me with the slightest niggle of doubt and dread.

After a moment, she chuckled. "You're so ridiculous, you know. You're like the Tin Man in *The Wizard of Oz*. All the time he doesn't think he has a heart and yet he really does."

"An interesting comparison." I'd always identified more with Hannibal Lecter from the famed Thomas Harris series about a psychologically curious sociopathic serial killer. Though I wasn't a serial killer, the way the character molded and manipulated others, studying and predicting their behavior—reading him had felt like looking in a mirror. "Except I don't really have a heart."

Even in the dim light, I saw her roll her eyes.

I tapped a finger on the arm of the chair and considered the basis of her analysis—she saw kindness in things I'd done, I guessed. Though she may have perceived benevolence, it wasn't sincere. "You realize, Celia, anything that appears like an act of compassion on my part is simply that—an act."

"Why act at all? I mean, with me, for example. Why claim to be my baby's father? Why let me bully my way into your 'experiments?'" She used quote fingers when she said the word *experiments*.

There were a handful of answers I could have given, some with a bit of truth, some downright lies. The fact of the matter was that I felt obligated. It was the one emotion I owned, and as such, I owned it well. If my sense of duty was going to be the reason for most of my existence, then I'd make sure I lived up to it with all I had. I was responsible for Celia's predicament—there was no doubt in my mind of that—and for that alone, I was obligated to her, no matter how strong the alarm of doubt in my gut.

"I see you formulating a response over there, Hudson. Don't bother. If you aren't going to answer honestly, don't answer at all." She looked up at the ceiling. "I'd prefer if you just said you didn't know."

So that was what I chose to say. Because it was easier. "I don't know."

The nurse arrived then, and I slipped out. It was near seven and I had to get home and changed before heading into work. A night with no sleep was going to make for a miserable day at Dad's office, but worse would be a day with my mourning mother.

The nursery was on the way to the elevators, I told myself, when I found my feet heading in that direction. A lone male figure dressed in a suit and tie stood peering in the windows, and even down the hall, with his body half-turned away, I recognized him.

I didn't say anything as I approached the windows next to him. I forced myself to look in, forced myself to gaze at the newborn babies. Forced myself to recognize that there had been a loss in this world—in *my* world—and there should be at least a moment of grieving.

The disappointment from earlier returned. But that was all.

For my dad, though, there was more. Tears streaked his face, and I realized I'd never seen a grown man cry, let alone my father.

Without any greeting, without looking at me directly, he asked. "Was it mine?"

Perhaps it was appropriate that he was the one in mourning. But the facts surrounding his bereavement—the too-young daughter of a friend that he'd knocked up, the wife he'd driven to drink, the secrets that required him to be there incognito in the early hours—angered me too much, overwhelming all else.

"I didn't sleep with her," I said, confirming his suspicions. "But that child was never yours. Don't ever speak like it was anything but mine again."

He closed his eyes as a new wave of pain furrowed his expression.

I left him there at the windows and headed for the elevators. Left him to struggle through his regret and guilt and sorrow and heartache—all those ridiculous emotions that made him weak.

— CHAPTER —

FIFTEEN

After

I only have a few minutes before Alayna returns from the bathroom. I'm supposed to be waiting for her naked on the bed when she returns, and I will be.
I'm already half-undressed and full-hard. But as I finish shucking my pants and
briefs, my mind sifts through a vacation's worth of thoughts at lightning speed.

This room, this place—I'm overwhelmed.

Mabel Shores holds a lifetime of memories, yet the prominent ones right now
are the summer with Celia's experiment. It taints every wonderful thing that has
happened here in the Hamptons this weekend with Alayna. It buzzes in my ear as
a reminder of my faults, of my flaws, and there's very little I can do to silence it.

My father's presence here this weekend doesn't help. While I should be grateful that he is a counterbalance to my mother's bitchy welcome, I don't trust his
motives with Alayna. I don't want him to befriend her as he has. Though she
would never betray me the way Celia did, though he's never made a move on
anyone I've known in the years since, I can't stand the idea that he might try
something with Alayna. It frightens me, and I've never been one to scare.

The memories haunt others too. My mother is constantly reminded, and
she takes it out on Alayna. Her unwillingness to move past Celia's miscarriage
and embrace Mirabelle's pregnancy as her first grandchild makes me suspicious.
In the back of Sophia's mind—does she know? Does she suspect the secrets that
surround Celia's baby? Probably not, but how can she not feel that there is something *off* about it?

I suspect that's why she brought it up again today, throwing it in Alayna's
face. I understand that the recollection doesn't let my mother go—it doesn't let

me go either. But it's no excuse for the way she hurts Alayna. The way she hurts me. It's another new emotion that has cropped up in my repertoire in the last few days, but I'm not sure of its name. Sympathy? Compassion? It's a pain that digs deep into my chest whenever Alayna is hurting, and I'm desperate to prevent it—not for my sake, but for hers.

And the way I had to dig myself out of that revelation with Alayna...

I've vowed to be as honest with her as I can despite the one lie—the *huge* lie—that I carry with me always. So when she asked about the baby, I told her what I could. For the first time, I wanted to tell her all of it, but I didn't know how I could without exposing the worst parts of me. Yes, she knows of them, but she doesn't truly know how awful I've been. Where does Celia's baby's story end, anyway? At her miscarriage? When she asked me to teach her how to be like me?

The only thing I could do was beg for Alayna to trust me. She'd given me her trust before, and I had no right to it then or now, but she gave it to me again. It's another brick in my pack of guilt. How long can I drag this around before it weighs us both down?

And it's not just the guilt pulling me down. There's more—the emotion. There's so much of it wherever Alayna's concerned. It's all new and intense, and it feels like a smear of colors on a painter's palette—all of it so blurred that I can't identify any colorful emotion for what it really is. Sometimes from the look in her eyes and the soft pressure of her lips and the way she gives and gives and gives—I wonder if she doesn't feel it all too. I've told her, I've warned her that this can't be real. But is she as powerless as I am in all of this?

Isn't that just the question Celia's putting to the test?

Alayna's more experienced with feelings. I can only hope she's unaffected. But if she *is* unaffected...

God, that might kill me too.

I hear her stir in the bathroom, so I rush to get in place on the bed. Suddenly I'm struck with a very different memory of Mabel Shores. *Mirabelle's wedding day.* While I didn't put any faith in romantic relationships, I knew she did. Her deeply rooted trust in Adam perplexed me so entirely that I eventually had to ask her how she could be so certain about marrying the man.

"Because when you love someone," she'd met my eyes and answered without a flicker in her confidence, *"their world interests you more than your own."*

I don't have time to examine why that memory came to me now because the bathroom door opens and Alayna's standing there, ready for me. She's wearing a red lace nightie that draws attention to her gorgeous tits. Her hair spills around her shoulders, and she looks so incredible. My breath catches.

"Jesus, Alayna. You're so goddamn beautiful," I say, surprised I can speak. I kneel, my cock standing at full attention between my legs. "I might have to let you wear that while I fuck you."

She blushes, and I wonder if I'll be able to last until I touch her. "Come here," I growl.

She starts toward me and then halts. "Wait, I'm in control, remember?"

I'd forgotten I'd agreed to that. I'm not usually comfortable giving up the reins, but for Alayna, I'm actually looking forward to it. She might not understand it, but this is my way of saying *I trust you too.*

I sit back on my heels and invite her to take the power. "Then take charge."

A spark flashes in her eye. She bites her lip and then issues her first command. "Sit back against the headboard."

Fuck, she's sexy. I can't help grinning as I follow her orders.

She climbs up the foot of the bed and crawls up the length of my body. Her breasts are on perfect display and they steal my attention, but I'm also drawn to her eyes. They're on fire with lust and something else. Something soft and beautiful that I can't quite make out.

Then she's licking my cock, and I forget all else but her wonderful tongue. "Do it again." I haven't forgotten who's in charge, but she needs to know what I want.

"Maybe I will," she teases.

Jesus, she's so goddamn adorable.

She bends to my dick again, kissing and licking my crown before she takes me into her mouth.

I groan. "Oh precious, you suck me so good." She teases me—licking and sucking and fondling without taking up a steady rhythm. Soon I have to take over or I'll die. I tangle my fingers through her hair and hold her still as I thrust into her mouth.

She doesn't let me get away with this for long, and when she resumes control, she releases me. I moan at the loss of her warmth.

"You want more?" she taunts. "You'll have to wait."

I do want more, but I'll take anything she's giving. She climbs further up my body and straddles my waist. My cock nudges against her ass. Fuck, it's pure torture. I'm in heaven.

She spreads her hands across my chest, and as my skin burns from her touch, she bends down for a kiss. She tastes so good. I cradle her face with my hands, holding her in place so I can devour her.

But she shakes her head free, and I'm reminded how out of my comfort zone she's put me. I don't know what to do when I'm not directing the scene. "What do you want?" I ask, though I wonder if it sounds more like begging.

"Touch my breasts."

Gladly. I slip my hands inside her nightie and fondle her tits. I'm rough because I know it's how she likes it, but also because I'm so turned on I can't be gentle. I pull down her gown and sit up to take her breast in my mouth. I suck and bite at her nipple, and I'm rewarded by her cry. "Hudson, oh, God."

I love her reaction, and I have to have more. I slip my hand under her panties and swipe across her clit, through her folds until I find the opening of her pussy. "You're already so wet, precious." I lick across her peaked nipple, and she shudders. I'm about to shove my fingers into her hole when I remember she's in the driver's seat. So I urge her to drive. "Shall I put my fingers inside you? Tell me."

"I want your cock inside me." She's tentative with her request, and it only makes me harder.

There's nothing more I want than to bury myself in her warm cunt, yet I force myself to hold back. I suck on her other breast until she moans. "But you aren't ready for me, precious."

"I'm ready enough." She's demanding. "I want to ride you."

That's all it takes. I rip the sides of her flimsy panties open and throw them aside. She grasps my cock, and I jerk in her hand. She balances over me. I'm so close to being lost inside her.

"I can't imagine why I deserve this," I say, palming her breasts. I know from our times before how it will be, how I'm going to feel when her pussy clenches around me. Not just physically but emotionally.

And I spook.

So I say something shitty as a reminder to both of us that none of this can be real. "I should be rewarding you for your very believable girlfriend act today."

She stills, and I realize instantly that I've hurt her. And the implications of why that statement would hurt her tell me what I didn't necessarily want to know—she *is* feeling it too. All of it.

I'm not sure how to deal with that knowledge. A bubble of euphoria has burst in my chest and spreads through my limbs. But my brain tries to halt it.

She can't fall for me, it says. She cannot. Because if she does, it's going to hurt her more when all this comes to an end, and it has to come to an end. And that will destroy me.

I just don't know what will destroy me more—that it ends or that she's hurt. Shit, I'm so fucked.

Her eyes seem to recognize everything going through my mind. Then, with a defiance that almost makes me proud, she lifts her chin and slides down on my cock. She's tight and raw. She wiggles, trying to work me in deeper. It's a metaphor, I think, how she's trying to slip further into my life and how she meets resistance from me time and again.

Though there's nothing to be done about the metaphor, I can help her with the literal. I place my hand on her belly, pushing her back slightly until she opens up and glides down until I'm buried completely.

"Fuck," I groan. "You're so tight, Alayna. So good." They're sex words, but in my head, the meaning is hazy. Is it her clenched wet cunt that feels so good? Or is it everything else about her that feels so fucking good?

Or is it all of it?

She lifts up and down my length. I try to command the tempo, but she maintains her steady pace, sliding up and down. Up and down. It's the most erotic sight, and my inability to direct any of it makes me restless. My hands wander over her body, touching her, caressing her, finally settling my thumb on her clit where at least here I can take some control.

"God, oh, god," she cries, squeezing my cock with her pussy. She's close, and I'm caught up in the way she writhes and squirms on top of me. Her skin glistens with sweat, and her cheeks are flushed so beautifully.

She talks as she rides me, her words mixed with broken moans. "I'm happy, Hudson. You've made me happy." She's not usually a talker, and I absorb every single sound she makes, every sentiment she shares.

All of it heightens the confusion of desires within me. I don't want to hear these things. I want her to say more.

She does say more. "And I've made you happy too." *I want her to stop. I want her to go on.* "We're falling in love. This is us, falling in love."

Those words are the death of me. They're beautiful poison, and I can't listen anymore.

"Enough." Instantly, I flip her underneath me. I bend her legs and push them back while I pound into her with a rebellious force. I drive to silence her words that still echo in my head—*in love, we're falling in love.* She shouldn't have said that. I thrust into her, punishing her for voicing the ridiculous thoughts. If there's any truth to it, I refuse to acknowledge it.

But I know. As Alayna comes undone underneath me, as I spurt my own release into her with long, hot pulses, I know that she's right. That this can't be thrashed out of our systems with desperate, frantic sex. That this can't be forgotten or buried or ignored. There is emotion between us, and if that's what it's called—if it is actually love—it isn't going away.

And what the fuck do I do with that?

I roll off her and fall onto the bed. As much as I want to be, I'm not angry with Alayna. I'm angry with myself. And Celia. Angry that she has any part of my relationship with Alayna, of what might be the most genuine moment of my entire life.

Most of all, I'm affected. When I've never been affected by anyone, and that means I'm also confused and maybe a little afraid. Or maybe a lot afraid.

Not knowing what else to do, I pull Alayna into the crook of my arm, close my eyes and pretend to sleep. I wish that I could fall into the bliss of unconsciousness, where thoughts and feelings can't bite and nip at me as they do as I lie here wide awake. It's not like there's anything new to dwell on. The same thoughts recycle through my mind: *We're falling in love. Can I actually be in love? I have to end this game. I have to tell her everything. But then I'll lose her. And won't I lose her anyway? Eventually doesn't all love end?*

Or what if it doesn't end? What if this door she's opened, if the flood of sensation she's unleashed, is a permanent part of me now?

It's nearly an hour later before her breathing settles into a deep rhythm, and I know she's asleep. I slip out of her embrace and throw on some sweats. Even with clothing on, I feel stripped naked. Is this what love feels like?

I take a seat in the armchair next to the bed and watch her as I try to sort it all out. Mirabelle's wedding-day words return to me: *When you love someone, their world interests you more than your own.* Everything about Alayna interests me more than myself. That's why I'd thought of that memory. Because somewhere in my fucked-up psyche, I understood that what I felt for her was love before she even named it. I'd avoided the acceptance of it, knowing that this amazing, wonderful birth of love inside me couldn't have come at a worse time.

Whatever I do next—and I still have no idea what it will be exactly—I do know that there will have to be a denial. Either I'll deny this emotion and all that this woman brings to me, or I'll deny Celia and her fucked-up game. Denying this love would be painful for us both, but admitting my hand in deceiving Alayna…I can't even bear to think about how much she'd despise me for that.

I spend the rest of the night hours looking for any other way out of this mess I'm in. I come up with plan upon plan that involves further manipulation and lies. But I don't want to be that person anymore, so I abandon each one and am left without a strategy. This is another first for me, another newness I can credit to the beautiful creature sleeping in my bed.

When the pale light of morning starts streaming through the window, I imagine for a moment waking her up and telling her I love her too. With words and then again with my body. I can picture the warmth in her gaze as I say it. I can hear the way she'll say it back to me. Again and again we'd pass the declaration back and forth with our lips, with our tongues.

This fantasy doesn't go far though, because of all the decisions I've yet to make, there is one thing I know for absolute sure—I can't tell her how I feel without telling her all of it. My definition of love is still forming, but I am certain it includes transparency and honesty, and I can't give either without shedding all my secrets. I can't truly proclaim my love to her while keeping this dark curtain closed over one of the most important parts of us.

It's an ache in my side. A double-edged sword. I can't claim her without releasing her. So I let her sleep.

Needing a distraction, I pull out my laptop and look through my emails. I'd turned everything off the day before, taking the day off work at Alayna's request, and now I have a slew of unread messages to sift through. Quickly, I realize that many of them are from Roger and other members from my Plexis team. Despite my attempts to stall, the board is taking a vote to sell at noon Monday. Which is today. My personal life is in an uproar, but this—my company—this I can do something about. It's business, it's familiar. It's where I can make a difference.

It only takes a couple of texts and a handful of emails to arrange my departure later this morning. I shower and pack my things, careful not to disturb Alayna. I stare at her for long minutes before leaving. There's so much I want to tell her, so much I want to be with her. But I don't know how. So, though I'm fearful this could be the last time I see her naked in my bed, I slip out without a goodbye.

Leaving her is the hardest thing I've ever done. It's also the only thing I *can* do.

Downstairs in the kitchen, I find fresh coffee. And Celia.

She's sitting alone at the counter bar, as if waiting for me.

I don't speak to her or acknowledge her in any way until after I've poured myself a mug and taken a long swig. I need the shot of caffeine to deal with her. I wish it were something stronger.

Glancing at the clock on the coffeepot, I say, "It's barely eight." I set my mug down. "To what do we owe the pleasure of your presence?"

Her voice meets my back. "I'm talking with Sophia about some redesign she wants me to do."

Yes, that. Right. My mother had announced that the day before. Celia may legitimately be working for us, but I know her well enough to know that her visit was purposefully planned to coincide with my own visit.

I turn to face her, scanning the kitchen for signs of others. "Where is she then? My mother."

Celia shrugs. "She went to go get some magazine with a picture she'd like to use as inspiration." She props her elbows on the counter and rests her chin on her clasped hands. "What about you? Why are you up and dressed for business during your Hampton vacation?"

"An emergency at work. My vacation is over."

"Oh, Hudson, I'm sorry to hear that." My mother sashays into the room, a stack of magazine clippings in one hand and an orange juice in the other. "Are you and Alayna both leaving?"

I eye her drink as she takes a sip. My mother never drinks OJ pure. "No. I didn't want to wake her." I throw a glance at Celia. She can take that as she'd like—it doesn't really matter at the moment.

If she thinks anything of it, she doesn't let on.

"I'll leave my car for her to take back to the city if she'd like," I say to my mother. Though, I'm not exactly sure Alayna drives. "If she'd prefer a cab, you can give her this for fare." I pull out my wallet and hand my mother a hundred. She has money she could give Alayna as well, but it wouldn't surprise me if she claimed she had no cash just to give Alayna a hard time.

"Okay." She takes the cash with a pucker of irritation in her brow that says that she hates to be bothered. "How are you getting to the city?"

I stick my billfold back in my jacket. "I need to get to the East Hampton airport actually. My plane is already set to meet me there. I just need Martin to take me, if you don't mind."

"He's not here until later, I'm sorry to say." She isn't sorry. Her smile is too sweet, the sparkle in her eye too bright. She loves it when she's in control of a situation. Loves it when other people's plans don't work out the way they'd like.

Not for the first time I wonder, did she teach me? Or did I teach her?

But I don't dwell on the question. I don't have the energy or the mood to cogitate this morning.

"I'll take you," Celia offers.

My jaw tenses. I can sense the trap I'm about to be caught in. "That's not necessary," I say, as politely as I can. "You have a meeting with my mother. I'll take one of the other cars."

I nod a goodbye and start to leave.

My mother steps in front of me, stopping me. "Don't be silly, Hudson. Let her take you. Our business isn't a rush. We can meet later. Can't we, Celia?"

"Of course." Celia's grin makes me ill.

I run a hand through my hair. Between the lack of sleep, the tension surrounding Celia's presence, my mother's early morning drinking, and my inner turmoil regarding Alayna, I don't have the strength to argue. "Fine."

Besides, leaving Alayna alone with my mother is bad enough. Leaving her with Celia as well would be very unwise.

We're ready to leave within ten minutes. At the door, my mother makes a show of saying goodbye, even though there's no one to watch as Celia's already waiting outside. Then she excuses herself to the kitchen, likely to refill her drink.

Mirabelle descends the stairs just before I depart. "Where are you going?"

I don't have time to explain the whole situation, but I'm fearful of my mother's version, so I get Mirabelle up to speed as succinctly as possible.

When I've finished, she doesn't seem happy. "But you aren't even going to say goodbye to Laynie?"

I shake my head. "I'm in a rush."

She puts a fist on her round hip. "It will take you two minutes. Get the eff upstairs and tell your girlfriend what's going on."

"Mirabelle, I don't have time for this." I pull my shades from my briefcase pocket and put them on. I don't need my sister peering into my eyes right now. I'm not sure what she'll see.

"Hudson, this is…" She searches for what she thinks *this is*. "It's terrible, is what it is. I'm usually on your side, and you know that, but I'm rather ashamed of you at the moment."

You're not the only one, I think. There's nothing to say, so I start to go. The air feels tight leaving like this though, so I say over my shoulder, "Make sure Alayna…" I pause. I don't know how to finish the statement. "Make sure she gets home okay."

I escape before she has a chance to respond.

Celia's waiting in the driveway. After setting my briefcase in the back, I get in the passenger seat and buckle my belt. The feel of it across my chest is confining. I release it again and try to convince myself that I'm better now, as though the small width of material is responsible for my inability to get a good breath. My stomach lurches as Celia's car pulls down the long drive to the main road. I don't glance back. I feel shitty enough as it is. This isn't how I wanted to leave Alayna—with Celia, driving away without even a goodbye.

The thought gives me pause—is that what I've decided then? That I'm leaving her?

It's unbearable, but it's possible that it's inevitable.

Only a few minutes have passed after Celia turns onto the highway before she speaks. "How long are you going to keep me waiting?"

I scrub my face with my hands. "What do you want to know, Celia?"

"Don't be a fucking dick, Hudson." Her glare is apparent even behind her dark sunglasses. "You know what I want."

I do know. She wants a progress report, so to say. How can I answer? I'm still reeling from my recent self-discoveries. I'm lost. There's nowhere I can turn in this maze without hitting a wall. I have no hope of escape. The question is—does Alayna?

I'm not an impulsive person, but I make a spur-of-the-moment decision. And though there is nothing ideal about it, I know it's the best choice I can make. So I commit to it with everything I have. "It's over, Celia," I say. "The game is over."

She groans. "Not this bullshit again."

"No, not this bullshit. That's not what I'm saying." I turn my head to face her profile, letting her know the fullness of my sincerity. "I'm telling you that I've put my time in. Like you wanted. And now it's over. There isn't anything else that you need to complete your experiment."

Her brow rises above the rim of her glasses. "What do you mean?"

"I mean…" I hate myself for what I'm about to say—for sharing something so intimate and private between me and Alayna—but I'm familiar with self-loathing. I force the words. "I mean that she's already emotionally invested in me.

I don't need to spend any more time with her. I can end the business arrangement I have with Alayna, and you'll be able to study her reaction like you wanted to."

Celia's still skeptical. "Game over means all of it, Hudson. That means the personal too."

"I know." Just like that, I let go of every possibility of anything more with Alayna. I'm walking away.

My chest constricts, and it's hard to breathe. It feels like I've been caught under a giant boulder. My limbs are numb, I can't move, and the pain…it's sharp and persistent. Crushing.

With the severity of my agony, it's not easy to explain why I'm doing this, even to myself, but I try to reason through it anyway. Alayna says she's in love with me, and while I'm wary that anyone could possibly feel any affection for me, I *feel* her love. It pulses through my veins as if she injected it into my body with her kiss, with her nails on my back, with her pussy when our fluids mingled in the heat of our lovemaking.

But the reality is that Alayna doesn't really know me. Not all of me. And if she ever found out, not only would that love vanish, but she'd be hurt. I'm almost certain that would break her more than my abandonment now.

It's a gamble, I suppose, but it's the best chance she has. Her credit cards and student loans have already been paid for, and the confirmations will be sent tomorrow. It's the perfect time to end the charade, and then I won't see her again. I'll let our private affair seemingly fade away. Perhaps I can spend some time working at our overseas headquarters. It will be a good excuse to be gone from her life. Then I'll hope—pray, even, and I'm not a praying man—that she doesn't fall into past behaviors.

And if she does, I'll offer whatever support I can anonymously. Celia will win her experiment, but I won't let Alayna be damaged permanently. She'll recover. I'll merely be a bump in her road.

Celia stares at me. She's trying to read me, trying to identify my angle. Finally, she asks, "Are you su—"

I cut her off. "Do you doubt my experience in these matters?" It's hard enough as it is to stick to this plan. I don't have the conviction to convince Celia too.

Fortunately, she backs down. "No. I don't doubt you. It's just so soon. I had expected we'd need more time."

She's almost there. Just one more push from me ought to do it.

So I push. "It is soon. Alayna gives her heart easily, it seems." I have to look out the passenger window at this. It's a lie, and I know it. Alayna doesn't give her heart easily—she gives it fully. She doesn't fall for just anyone. When she does, it's her everything. That's the reason behind her obsessive tendencies. I've learned that about her.

I won't let Celia know that though. I've betrayed Alayna enough.

"And you?" Celia's question hits the back of my head, but I feel its blunt force. *And me...*

I've given my heart as well, though Alayna can't possibly know. She owns it, fully and completely. Each beat that it spends away from her is the cadence of a death march. If there was anything to my life before her, its substance has faded in my memory. This—leaving her—this is a darkness that I've never witnessed.

But why did Celia even ask? She's always been fully aware that I lacked heart. Does she sense something's changed? Does she know I'm no longer the man she used to play with?

Or is it simply another one of her tricks?

I pull out my phone and busy myself with flipping through my screens as I answer her. "I'm not sure what you're implying. But it doesn't matter. I don't have time for this charade anymore. I have a business I'm trying to run and a subsidiary company that I'm on the verge of losing. If you don't mind, I need to focus my attention on that right now and not this silly game."

Knowing Celia will assume I'm doing something for work, I type out a text message to Alayna. It's painfully brief—*Plexis crisis. I'll call as soon as I can.*

I won't call. I'll see her again to end things more formally, but it won't be by phone.

We ride in silence for several minutes before Celia says quietly, "Maybe I was wrong about you."

Her cryptic statement pulls my attention from my morose thoughts. I spend a few seconds trying to track the source of her remark and come up empty-handed. "What does that mean?"

She shrugs. "You're too grown-up to play, I guess."

I don't believe that's what she meant, but I don't push her. I'd rather capitalize on the opening she's just given me. "Too grown-up because I have a life and responsibilities? Yes, I am too grown-up. These experiments don't have a place in my life any longer."

"I don't know about that," she says as we turn into the airport. "We'll see."

Her words are ominous, but I don't let them in. I'm cold. I'm steel. I've put on my mask now, the one I've worn for as long as I can remember. I used to wear it to hide that I don't feel. Now I wear it to hide that I do.

— CHAPTER —

SIXTEEN

I throw all my energy into saving Plexis, and it isn't enough. The company is sold out from under me. I'm not surprised. My proposals were spot on, but my presentation was mediocre. I'm off my game, my attention divided. I wonder how long I'll be split like this—half of me in the current moment, half of me always with her. While all of this is unfamiliar to me, I've studied enough breakups to see that there is recovery for most individuals.

I'm certain that I am not most individuals.

I linger in Cincinnati for most of Tuesday, not wanting to go home to Manhattan. Eventually, I have no more reason to stall, and I head home. I land in the evening. I'm disheveled and exhausted, but instead of heading home, I ask my driver to take me to The Sky Launch. There's no use delaying seeing Alayna. I need to get our dissolution over with so I can move on.

I note the time when I arrive. It's a little early for Alayna to be at work, but that's better. If I'm already here when she arrives—going over business with David, perhaps—then my visit will appear casual. It will seem like my meeting with her is an afterthought. It should help her see that I believe anything that exists between us is mundane. Ordinary.

I'm not sure she'll buy it. Honestly, I'm not sure I want her to.

But she has to. Because this is how things are now. This is how things have to be.

The club is dark as I enter. I head for the office—if David is here, that's where he'll be. The door is open when I approach, but as I enter the frame, I'm not prepared for the sight that meets me. David is here, but in his arms—Alayna.

They're embracing, and it's far too intimate to be a hug between friends. I can't see her face, but the expression on his is one I can relate to. It's adoration. It's affection. It's maybe even love.

Emotion shoots through my body at the sight. Jealousy, astonishment, scorn—the emotions mix into a toxic cocktail of rage. I've never been this worked up, this livid. My blood is boiling, my skin itching, and my gut feels like it's been punched.

But I wear my mask. So David sees none of it when he sees me. Instead he sees cold and steel, which can be very intimidating, I've found.

Instantly, he lets Alayna go and backs away. "Hey, Pierce."

Alayna spins, and her eyes meet mine. Hers are sparked with worry, with fear, and the blood drains from her face. Her concern softens the slightest bit. Not enough, though. I'm still consumed with my fury.

The bitch of the whole thing is that I have no right to feel this way. To feel any of the way I do regarding her. I've made my decision. I've chosen to walk away and to bury any emotion she may have stirred in me. She's allowed to embrace any man she wants. She can kiss and fuck anyone she pleases. Because she isn't mine.

My stomach clenches. All I see is red.

I'm vaguely aware of David speaking and then the sound of the door closing as he leaves. At least he was smart enough to know he should go without being asked. I realize I'm angry with him as well—he's an employee and he's making moves on his boss's girlfriend. My feelings toward him are such a small part of my turmoil though, and I'm glad for his departure. Now I focus on directing the torment brewing inside. If I have to feel this pain, at least I can use it to push her away.

"Hudson." She says my name, and it sounds like a broken chord—each syllable hanging in the air with distinct weight. She steps toward me. "I read about Plexis. I'm so sor—"

Like I give a fuck about Plexis at the moment.

I cut her off. "What's going on with you and him?" It's not my place to ask, but though my voice is controlled and even, I have no authority over my actions. I need her to answer. I need her to alleviate this fear that she feels for anyone the way she feels for me.

It's insane. It's irrational. And I can't stop *needing* it.

"Nothing." She sighs. "David was, um...it was a friendly hug, that's all."

Her answer only makes the sting worse. "The expression on his face was much more than friendly." I step toward her, demanding with my body before I've even voiced the question I have to have an answer to. "Have you fucked him?"

"No!"

I study her with narrowed eyes. There's more she isn't saying—I can read her face, read her posture. There's *something* between them. "But almost," I guess.

"No." Her tone is adamant, but her eyes shift.

This, her lie, tears me apart more than anything. "Why don't I believe you?"

"Because you have some serious trust issues. What is your fucking deal, anyway?"

There is a rational voice in my head screaming that this is not how I should behave. That her relationships are private and not my concern. That this is not my place. She. Is. Not. Mine.

I want to listen to it. I want to calm the blistering storm that is traveling through my every nerve. But it's impossible.

So I give up, letting the tempest swallow me as I step toward her and growl. "I told you before. I don't share."

Whatever plans I had for our paths are suddenly null and void. Because though I cannot have her, though I'm supposed to let her go, I've just claimed her.

There's a flash of acceptance in her eyes. It's brilliant, and I cling to the light of it long after it's lost to the challenge that follows. "But I have to share you with Celia?"

"Goddammit, Alayna. How many times do I have to say it? There is nothing going on with me and Celia." I convince myself it's not a lie because she's questioning a romantic involvement. In my bones, I'm sure that she senses the truth—that there is some sort of connection between Celia and me. Alayna can read me too well to miss this.

Still, I refuse to shed any light on my secrets.

So she uses the only weapon she can. "And there's nothing going on with me and David."

"Really? That's not how it looked when I walked in here."

"Just like that's not how it looked when you left with Celia while I was still naked in your bed?"

Anger surges through me like lightning. How can she not understand? I grab her by her upper arms and pull her into me. "Leaving you that morning was the hardest fucking thing I've done in a long time. Don't treat it lightly."

Then, because she has to know how I feel and because this is the only way I know to tell her, I crush my mouth to hers. I bite and tear at her lips. I'm brutal and bruising. *This,* I tell her with my kiss, *is how it felt to walk away.*

She pulls away. "Hudson, stop."

But I can't. I have to get through to her. Or maybe I just need her body to calm the fury inside of me. I don't know anything anymore except this fervent urgency to have her.

"Stop." She pushes at my chest.

"No. I have to fuck you. Now."

"Why? Are you marking your territory?"

Her question startles me. Is that what this is? Is this action merely an extension of my irrational jealousy? It's not what I wanted this to be.

My pause allows her to wrestle free of my grip. "You don't own me, Hudson! Stop messing with me like I'm one of your other women. *Not with me*, remember?"

It's the truth I try not to face, slapped at me with such force I can't deny it. "Don't you think I know that? Every minute of every day, I remind myself that I can't conquer you. That I can't do that to you. But it doesn't mean that I don't want to."

The words rush out of me so quickly, I can't digest them until they hang in the air around us. In them is clarity. I *have* wanted to conquer her. As much as I've refuted Celia's plans and defended my actions as benevolent toward Alayna, there has always been a part of me that wanted to own her. To master her. To win her. Was this the real reason I agreed to the game? Because I can't help myself from playing?

The possibility pains Alayna as much as it does me. Tears spill down her cheeks. "So I am just like the others."

"No. You're not." I wanted to manipulate her—it's a desire that will never go away. But it was faint with Alayna. It lingered in the background behind so many other more prominent desires. "I told you before," I tell her. "I don't want to hurt you more than I need to win you."

She's sobbing as she says, "You've already done both."

Horror washes over me like an icy shower. "Fuck!" This was not what I wanted. It was everything I'd tried to prevent. And even though I knew—I *knew*—that I had hurt her, the reminder of it, paired with the reminder that she's declared her love, overpowers me. The reality of her emotions bring all of mine to the surface. I've fucked everything up. There is no possibility of either of us walking away from this relationship like it was a bump in a road. There is no good decision to be made. I've made our story so that it can only end in pain.

I step backward, away from her, as if I can distance myself from the hell I've put us in.

But she follows, charging into my arms and kissing me with the same determination that I'd earlier thrust upon her.

I can't resist. And there's no point, really. We're both damned no matter what.

"Alayna." I take what she's giving me, take it greedily. My hand kneads her breast as I lick into her mouth. My other arm pulls her closer. She says my name. She tells me she needs me. I don't need to hear the words. I feel it in her kiss, in her body as she yields to me.

I'm quick to remove her panties and lay her on the couch. My gaze never leaves her as I undress. She's gorgeous like this—all spread out for me, her cunt glistening with her arousal. And even beyond the erotic visual, there's beauty in the significance of her capitulation. Even in her pain, she looks to me for comfort. Just as I look to her.

I can't delay our connection any longer. I lower myself on top of her and drive in. I'm relentless with my speed, with my force. I'm focused only on release, mine and hers, my thumb rubbing against her clit as I pound into her. Our sex is primal and raw. It's a mirror of our circumstances—we shouldn't want each other, but the pull that draws us together is stronger and baser than anything we can control or contradict. I have no words for this connection, and so I shower her with the only sound that makes any sense—her name, spilling from my lips, repeatedly, reverently. Then it's the word that announces my release as I come inside her in a savage explosion. She echoes my climax with her own, crying out while she clenches around me.

I collapse onto her, burying my head into her neck. My cock twitches inside her as it calms. She's warm and safe, and as our breathing settles, I relax into her. This is the first time in my life that I can remember being completely at ease. Despite the lack of resolution in our predicament, I'm free in her arms.

In the sanctuary of this moment, disclosure comes naturally. "I wanted to win you. But I didn't want to hurt you." I tighten my grasp around her. "That's the last thing I wanted."

With this simple admission, my load lightens. There's so much that I still carry in guilt. I can almost imagine what it would feel like to relieve my entire load, brick by brick, confession by confession.

Alayna runs her hand through my hair, her fingers sending sparks of electricity through my scalp. "That's part of relationships, H. People get hurt." She kisses my head. "But you can make it better, too."

Though her relationships may have been atypical, Alayna has much more experience at this than I do. I realize that many of the questions I have can be answered by her.

I'm not used to asking for help, but I lift my head to meet her eyes and plead, "Tell me how."

She cradles my face in her hands, her thumbs skimming across my skin. "Let me in."

"Don't you see I already have?" I've let her in further than anyone's ever been. She's broken walls that I didn't even know were standing. She doesn't even realize.

Or it's just not enough.

She closes her eyes and swallows. When she opens them again, a tear runs down her cheek. She moves out from underneath me, pulling her panties on as she stands up.

There's my answer, then. It's not enough. But this is all I can give—for her protection as well as for mine. And I'm still stuck between a rock and a hard place. Where does this leave me with Celia? Where does this leave me with Alayna?

I sigh as I tuck myself back in and zip up my pants. I'm back where I was to begin with, where the best decision is to end this.

And I can't.

So I fight for her instead. Even though I don't know how. Even though it's the worst possible thing I can do.

I stand and cross to her. I wrap my arms around her from behind and can feel her pulling against her desire to lean into me. She stays put though, and I speak gently in her ear. "Why do you act like I'm running?"

"Because you shut me out. Isn't that the same as running?"

It's exactly the same. I'm hit with the sudden recollection of Alayna in our bedroom at the Hamptons. I'd been asleep, and she'd been out swimming. When she returned, she'd been upset. "What about you? What about how you showed up in our bedroom crying and couldn't even tell me why?"

She tenses in my arms. "That was different."

What could be different? I wrack my brain trying to come up with a scenario that had hurt her. Then with sickening certainty, I know—my mother.

I turn Alayna toward me. "What did she say to you, Alayna?"

She wars with herself for only a moment before answering. "That I was insignificant. She called me a whore."

Fuck. My anger is reignited, directed at my mother now. Time and time again, I've come to Sophia's rescue. Now I can't think of a single reason why. "My mother's heartless and cruel." For so long I would have added *like me* to that phrase. In this moment, I don't feel anything like her.

I lift Alayna's chin up to meet my gaze. "You're not a whore, Alayna. Not even close. And the magnitude of your importance in my life can't be put into words." It's the nearest I can come to a declaration of emotion.

As if she can read my subtext, she adds, "She also said that you can't ever love me."

My hand drops from her face. I'm stunned. That my mother would tell her that, for one, is appalling to me. And enlightening. But more importantly, I don't know how to respond. I can't refute the statement, not without admitting that I'm learning how to love because of her. And I can't say that until there aren't any lies between us.

So I say the only thing I can. "I've told you that before."

She pulls out of my arms. "Well, she told me again." She spins back at me. "So there, I opened up. Are you happy?"

I've hurt her. Again. It's not what I'd meant, but I'm torn. I'm helpless. "Alayna…"

But there's nothing I can add to make this better. I'm drowning in my secrets, and I feel all of it coming to a head. If I can't walk away, I have to tell her the truth. Every bit of it. Yet the words stick in my throat.

With tears smearing her face, she implores, "How could you not think I'd fall in love with you, Hudson? Even if you didn't mean for it to happen, how could I not? Does that mean anything to you at all?"

I feel like she's slapped me. "How can you ask that?" That she loves me means *everything*. It's the reason I'm here with her now, floundering with no direction. Her love is the only beacon of hope I've encountered in my dark world. I cling to it. I hold it like a lifeline. "Of course, it does. But, Alayna," always that *but*, "you don't know that you'd still say that if you knew me."

"I *do* know you."

"Not everything." Secrets push against my lips, begging to be released.

"Only because you haven't let me in!"

I spread my arms out in frustration. "What is it you want to know? About what I did to other women? About Celia? I'm the reason she got pregnant, Alayna. Because I spent an entire summer making her fall in love with me when I felt nothing for her. For fun. For something to do."

The words spill like the tears that still stain Alayna's cheeks. With them, the pain and anguish that I didn't feel then sprouts within me. The horror of what I did takes root. The disgust at my actions, the regret, the guilt—all of it overwhelms me with each syllable I pronounce. Yet I can't stop them. "And then, when I'd completely broken her, she became destructive—sleeping around, partying, drugs. You name it, she did it. She didn't even know who the father was."

The last part is a lie, but I'm not about to implicate Jack right now. It's not the point, anyway. The point is that it's out there now, one of my biggest secrets. And while there's relief in the admission, a blanket of uncertainty hangs in the air like a heavy mist that cloaks my vision. Before I could read Alayna so well, every expression, every thought that darted across her eyes. Now I see nothing. I'm certain this story turns her off, disgusts her—how can it not? But I can't *see* it on her face.

She takes in a shuddering breath and wipes her eyes. "So you claimed it was yours."

"Yes." I narrow my eyes, studying her as she works through this.

"Because you felt responsible." Her voice is even, void of any inflection.

"Yes. She lost the baby at three months. Likely from the drinking and drugs she'd consumed early on. She was devastated." And I'm devastated now, as if the loss has just happened. There's a familiarity in the pain, and I remember feeling a hint of this ache back then. I'd been convinced that Alayna had taught me sensation, but now I wonder, have these emotions always been inside me, locked away, waiting for someone to set them free?

"That's awful," Alayna says, and I leave my introspection, returning my focus to her. I still can't read her, still can't figure out what awful things she's thinking behind those beautiful brown eyes.

"It's awful," she says again, her voice tinged with confusion, "but I don't understand. You thought this would make me not love you...why?"

I fall onto the arm of the sofa, baffled by her lack of concern. "Because it changes everything. I did that. That's who I am. It's my past, and it's very ugly."

Finally, her face breaks, but it's not disappointment that I see on her features—it's compassion. She moves to me and settles her hands on my shoulders. "Do you think your ugly is any different than mine?"

Her touch, her words—they're hard to bear. She's making too light of my sins. They're nothing like the things she's done. "This isn't like following someone around or calling too many times, Alayna."

"It was an unforeseen tragedy, Hudson. A game that got out of hand. You didn't set out for Celia to get pregnant and have a miscarriage. And you can't diminish the things I've done to a simple statement like that either. I hurt people. Deeply. But that was before. Less than ideal pasts, remember? It doesn't mean it defines our future. Or even our now."

Her words reach deep inside me, through my skin, into my bones, and I *hear* her. Really hear her. She's voicing an idea I've played with since I've met her. Can I—can *we*—break free of our pasts and step into the future unchained?

I let out the breath I've been holding and brush a tear from her eye. "When I'm with you, I almost believe that."

"That just means you need to spend more time with me."

That almost makes me laugh. "Is that what that means?" Maybe that is what it means. I entertain the idea with more sincerity than I have previously. Could I be with Alayna like this? For real? Put another way, could I ever find the strength to *not* be with her like this?

I slide my thumb down to caress her cheek. "Yesterday morning, when I got the phone call that required me to be in Cincinnati—I couldn't even let myself look at you, sleeping in that bed. If I did, I wouldn't have been able to leave."

Her face lights up. "I thought you left because you were freaking out. Because of the love stuff."

"I wasn't freaking out." Not about the love stuff. That I'd welcomed. "I was surprised, that's all."

"Surprised?"

"That that's what we were feeling." I hedge around an actual declaration. "That it was love."

"It was," she says with certainty. "It is."

"Hmm." I let her affirmation settle around me. This thing I've felt for Alayna began when I first met her, the first spark igniting at the moment I first saw her. Since then, it's remained constant, growing and brightening, refusing to take a shape that I could identify, but always strengthening in intensity. Love, she calls it. It's new. It's amazing. "I never felt this before. I didn't know."

I sweep my hands down her sides to rest on her hips. "But, Alayna, I've never had a healthy romantic relationship. Every woman who's loved me..." My throat clenches as I recall the pain I caused Celia and others who claimed they'd fallen for me. "I don't want to break you too."

"You're not going to break me, Hudson." She's so sure. "I thought you might, at first. Turns out you make me better. And I think I do the same for you."

"You do." She's the only thing that ever has.

"If you decide to not…follow through…with whatever this is that we have, it will hurt. But I won't be broken."

"But it would hurt?" I'm already committing to a new plan, one that hasn't fully formulated in my head.

"Like a motherfucker."

I don't want to hurt her. It's why I can't admit everything to her, but it's also why I can't leave her. She's confirmed it now. And while I fully realize that there will be pain at some point in our relationship, I decide that it's not going to be right now. "Then we better follow through."

It's wrong, I'm sure. It's definitely selfish because I want this more than anything.

I pull her closer, wrapping her in my arms, and say the words I came here to say. "Alayna, you're fired. You can't be my pretend girlfriend anymore." Then I add the new ones that I've only just chosen in my mind. "Be my real girlfriend instead."

Happiness flares in her eyes. "I kind of think I already am."

"You are."

"Can I still call you H?"

"Absolutely not." That ridiculous nickname for me of hers. It's somewhat endearing. I'll never tell her that.

I kiss her then, sealing our new deal. It's here, as I mold my lips to hers with tender passion, that my plan solidifies. I'll love her like this, without words, but with my life. I'll let her in as far as I can. I'll commit to her completely. Her world will be mine. And I'll do everything I can to protect her from being hurt, including hiding the one secret from my past that will hurt her more than any other—the one involving her.

All of this I tell her in my kiss.

She's the one who pulls away, but only far enough to ask, "What now?"

I feel her trepidation. She has no idea all that I'm offering her, and I have a feeling it will take a while to make her understand. Soon, hopefully, she'll be able to hear everything I tell her with my nonverbal cues.

For now, I'll try to use my words. I smile slightly. "Come to my place after you finish here."

"I'm not off until three."

"I don't care. I want you in my bed." I want her in my life. I'll move her into my penthouse as soon as she'll let me. And more, when she's ready.

"Then, yes."

Am I moving too fast? I'm nearly thirty years old and feeling for the first time in my life. I think that by most standards I'm far behind the curve.

She helps me up, and I reluctantly let go of her to straighten my clothing. I miss her touch already, but it won't be long until I see her again. My eyes catch sight of the furniture behind me—we just fucked there, and it only occurs to me now that it's new. "Nice couch," I say. Really nice couch.

She laughs. "Thanks."

I study her, untangling her sex-mussed hair and straightening her dress. God, she's amazing. She's everything that I never knew I wanted. I'm addicted to her—she's my drug and I can't get enough of my fix. But she's also just the opposite. She's my cure. She's a balm that eases and relieves me. She's rehabilitation. She's remedy. She's reason.

I take her hands in mine, surprised to find that I'm not shaking. Inside, adrenaline is pumping, not with fear, but anticipation. "Tell Jordan to take you to The Bowery. He knows where it is."

"Not the fuck pad?" Excitement sparks her voice.

"No. My home. I'll leave a key with the doorman."

She laces her fingers through mine and giggles. I love the sound. Almost as much as her words. "We're really doing this, aren't we? Moving forward."

"We are." I pull her into my arms, wanting her to know how completely I am doing this, hoping this embrace tells her.

Her mouth is at my ear, and she whispers, "I'm going to rock your world." Then she sucks on my lobe.

I nip at her neck, already thinking about how we'll christen my bed later tonight. "I can't wait."

"Neither can I."

I leave her to her job and head home, a list forming in my head of all I need to prepare for her. She'll need clothes and bathroom products. I have almost seven hours until she'll arrive. That's more than enough time for my assistant to make my home presentable for my girlfriend.

My girlfriend.

Mine.

Since I was born, I've had everything I could want. Money has bought me my every whim. I could never begin to fathom all that belongs to me, and still I know there's never been anything as beautiful and special and precious as Alayna. And she *is* mine. As much as I am hers. I know I appear stoic and steady, but inside, I'm delirious and dizzy with this knowledge. How could I ever believe that my strength was in impassivity? This—this never-ending rush of love and joy and vitality—*this* is real power.

I'm not fooling myself—this won't be easy. There will be obstacles. Celia. My mother. My past. Her past, even. But none of that feels as monumental as what's going on inside of me. Alayna is reason enough to fight every foe and more.

So, while much of my night is filled with preparing for Alayna's physical presence in my life, it's also spent formulating a plan to protect our love. I'll find a way around Celia. I'm the one who built her; I can surely outplay her.

And Alayna…I'll keep my secret from her. Whatever it takes, whatever the cost. She'll never know the betrayal that brought her into my life. For her sake, I'll hide this truth. Only for her.

— CHAPTER —

SEVENTEEN

Before

Opening the door to the loft was tricky with my mouth lip-locked to the curvy brunette I'd brought home, but somehow I managed. Inside, I pressed her against the wall and held her hands above her head, my torso digging into hers, trying to find some comfort for my raging hard-on.

I licked her lower lip and pulled my head away. "Monica, I'd like to be a gentleman about this, but there's just no polite way to tell you how much I'm going to make you come tonight."

She gasped, and I leaned in to nibble on her ear. The moans elicited from the sharp nip of my teeth on her lobe made my cock pulse.

She gasped again, but this time it wasn't quite as sexy. She pushed me away from her and with an angry look over my shoulder asked, "Who the fuck is she?"

It took me a second to follow her gaze. When I did, I had to fight against the smile that tried to crawl across my lips. "Celia. I didn't realize you'd be over tonight."

I was as surprised as Monica to see my guest. Good thing I was excellent at winging it.

"Yeah," Celia said, feigning embarrassment. "I guess I should have called first." She was dressed only in a white fluffy towel, her hair wrapped in a second towel on top of her head. Even without the blush that would add to the authenticity of the moment, her speech and gestures appeared genuine.

A small burst of pride spread through me. I was impressed.

"Hudson," Monica said, reminding me she was still there—like I could forget with my dick still throbbing in my jeans. "Who the fuck is she?"

"She's…" I ran a hand through my hair and looked from one woman to the other, as if searching for an explanation.

"I'm Celia. A friend." She tugged her towel higher over her lithe body. "I'm really sorry to interrupt your date. I'll just go get dressed. Excuse me." She apologized again as she ran to my bedroom.

"Hudson?"

I took a deep breath, removing the delight from my expression, before turning back to my date.

"She's no one, Monica. An old friend. I didn't know she'd be here."

I moved back in to kiss her again, but she turned her face from mine. "Why is she here then? Does she have a key?"

Her suspicion delighted me. The entire setup of the scheme with Celia was to make my latest "girlfriend" doubt my fidelity. The experiment was meant to examine how long the subject—Monica—would stay with me if given repeated evidence that I may not be faithful. This was the first time in our relationship I'd given Monica any cause for doubt. We'd only been seeing each other for a week. I hadn't even fucked her yet, an activity that had been on the evening's agenda.

Until Celia had shown up, anyway. Now I was even more interested in getting it on with Monica, because, though I hadn't expected my partner in crime to show up on this particular night, the fact that our game was proving fruitful made me very happy. Turned me on.

"Yes, she does have a key." I did my best to sound like I was ashamed of this admission. "But only because she stays here now and then. When she's fighting with her boyfriend. I didn't know she'd be here." The excuse was made up on the fly since I hadn't been given a chance to prepare for this scenario.

Monica's eyes widened. "She's naked, Hudson!"

"Obviously she didn't know I'd be here either." I pulled her into my arms, and leaned my forehead against hers. "Come on. I'll make her sleep on the sofa. Or we can get a hotel room."

She melted into my body, her hands resting on my forearms. "I can't believe I'm even considering this."

"Monica, come on. Stay. I want you to stay." This was easy to say because it wasn't a lie. I'd been looking forward to burying myself inside her since the moment we'd picked her out for our experiment two weeks before. I kissed down the side of her face. "You know you want to stay too."

"I do want to, but I don't know."

God, she was so close to being convinced. I rocked my pelvis into hers as I descended upon her mouth for a kiss she couldn't say no to.

But before my lips met hers, she pulled away. "No. I can't. Maybe this is innocent like you say, but I think it's a cue to take a step back."

I dropped my head with an only slightly exaggerated sigh. "Okay. I understand." I grabbed my cock through my pants. "I'm crazy hard for you right now though. I'm going to be thinking about you all night."

"Good. I'll be thinking about you too."

I escorted her out to the hall with a mixture of satisfaction and disappointment. On the one hand, she was going to present quite a challenge. That was a thrill I was looking forward to. On the other hand, she was leaving me with an ugly case of blue balls.

While we waited for the elevator, she turned to me with doe eyes. "Call me?"

"Tomorrow." I planned to call her, but I already knew it wouldn't be the next day. I'd make her sweat first. It would plant more seeds of doubt. "Goodnight." I kissed her seductively, letting her know what she was missing out on.

After, I put her on the elevator. I kept her gaze locked with mine until the doors closed.

Then I went back to my apartment to deal with Celia.

She was lounging on the couch when I returned, sipping a bottle of Diet Coke. She was dressed now, or more accurately, no longer in a towel but in my bathrobe. Her hair was also no longer wrapped up, and I saw it wasn't even wet. I suspected she had underwear on under the robe as well.

"How did it go?" she asked.

"Considering that I'm hard as stone, I'd say not very well." I adjusted myself as I walked to the bar to make myself a drink.

"But she still wants to see you again?"

My back was to her, but I could tell she was eager for a progress report. It was understandable, though I imagined she'd listened to a good portion of it from the bedroom and already knew what had happened. Plus, it was fun to taunt her, so I delayed answering.

"You don't seem to care that you cock-blocked me," I said instead as I poured myself two fingers of Scotch, a recent discovery of mine.

"I don't. I care about whether she'll see you again."

I turned toward her and took a sip of my drink. "She'll see me again."

Her entire face lit up, and she clenched her fists in a sign of victory.

While I was also feeling triumphant, there was a bone to pick. "But what the fuck, Celia? It wasn't in the plan for you to be here tonight."

Celia had shaped into being a great component of the experiments I conducted. She made variety possible, and I'd studied many new emotions and situations since she'd joined me nearly three years before. But as long as we'd played together, I'd always been the driver. I dictated the parameters of our research. I wrote the script. Of course, there was always a fair amount of ad-lib required, but as much as could be controlled was. And it was controlled by me.

This had been the first time Celia had surprised me in our ploy. It had been a good move, but I wasn't ready to tell her that. Wasn't ready to concede any of my authority.

"It was awesome improv though, wasn't it?" She already knew she'd played well, whether I was ready to say so or not. My reprimand did nothing to shake her confident grin.

"I'll admit no such thing." I played smug as I joined her on the couch.

She swatted at my shoulder with the back of her hand. "Come on, it was perfect. I'm supposed to make her jealous and suspicious, and trust me, old friend naked in boyfriend's apartment is the perfect way to do that."

I rested an arm on the back of the sofa and studied her. "You're extremely happy about this."

"And you're not?"

"Do I need to remind you of the cock-block?"

She threw her head back in frustration. "Oh, my God. You and your dick. Go whack off in the shower. You'll be fine." Then she curled her legs up underneath her and leaned toward me, her eyes sweet yet demanding. "Now admit that I did good."

I hesitated. Finally, reluctantly, I conceded. "You did good." I took another sip from my drink, letting the burn of it relax me and melt away the desire to hold onto the reins. "Actually, you did really good, Celia. Nice job."

She wrinkled up her nose in glee as she soaked up my approval. Her pure joy somehow made it easier to continue the acknowledgment.

"You're a lot more flexible with the experiments than you used to be," I said. "You've come a long way." There'd been quite a few in the early days that we'd barely survived. I'd never realized how naturally that scheming came to me. How hard it was to teach someone else. Yet, even with the difficulties, Celia had been born for it.

"I'd hope I'm better. We've been doing this now for…what? Three years?" She rolled her soda bottle in between her hands as she spoke, like a stick she was trying to rub into fire. "It's about time I finally got a Hudson compliment."

She was nervous, and I suddenly realized how much my acclaim meant to her. Was this the first time she'd received it?

I finished my Scotch and set the glass down on the coffee table, then peered at her with narrowed eyes. "I've complimented you before. Haven't I?"

She shook her head. "I'm not complaining. I haven't deserved it."

I shrugged half-heartedly. She'd made mistakes, but overall I'd been pleased with her as a partner. More than pleased. I'd also been glad for her company.

She pursed her lips now, as if thinking. "Remember that couple in your building? The newlyweds?"

I nodded. How could I forget? They'd been our first experiment together.

Celia dropped her bottle into her lap and propped her elbow on the back of the couch, leaning her face onto her hand. "I'd been so nervous when I first approached him. Tim was his name. I was supposed to drop that bag of groceries, remember? And see if he'd help me with it. That was all there was to the first contact. You'd coached me and coached me. I swear I stood in that alcove of the lobby watching him flick through his mail for, I don't know, an eternity before I had the guts to go out there. Then dropping my bag was easy because I was shaking so hard."

"But he noticed you. He helped you with the groceries."

"He brushed my hand even. On purpose, I think. And it was only our first meeting." Her eyes narrowed as she lost herself in the memory. "He kept staring at my cleavage, and I remember how amazing it felt to have his attention, but at the same time, I thought he was a bit of a smarmy asshole." She laughed. "Obviously, I got over the smarmy asshole part."

I chuckled. "Obviously."

It had been a great study. Celia had seduced Tim, the husband, while I'd worked my charm on the wife. My subject had resisted me, deeply devoted to her marriage, but Celia had succeeded in getting her subject in bed. Repeatedly. They'd had an all-out affair. Even when the wife had found out, she still refused to sleep with me, though she'd shown more than once that she was attracted. It had not been what I'd hypothesized. More surprising was that she forgave him for his infidelity.

I'd filed the entire experience as another attestation to the detriment of love. Why the fuck would any sane person forgive a spouse for that kind of gross unfaithfulness? It was weakness. Devotion made people stupid. There was no doubt in my mind.

"I still get nervous the first time we start any new game." She leaned back into the corner of the couch and bent her legs up in front of her, her bare feet perching on the edge of my thigh. "And this is the first time I've felt comfortable changing things up without talking to you first."

"Well, we don't need to make that a habit now." I pulled one of her feet into my hands and started rubbing it.

"We'll see how it goes, I guess."

I tried not to let that bother me. Things would morph just fine, I told myself. Whether I was in control or not.

We settled into silence. I continued my massage as I thought about how we'd both changed in the last years. Through our games, we'd become comfortable with more than just improvising. We'd found an ease in our relationship as well. We frequently staged kisses and embraces without any residual sexual tension. The undercurrent of emotional pull that had once existed between us had dissolved into something less fraught, less physical, yet intimate. We shared a rapport with each other that we had with no one else. We were…close. Friends. Partners.

I dropped her foot in my lap, ready to move to the other. The first brushed against my crotch. Celia's forehead rose. "Is that your dick?"

"I told you I was hard." It was actually a semi now, but certainly not flaccid, and the reminder of my pent-up lust for Monica had me stiffening again.

"Still?" She poked at my bulge with her toe and waggled her brows. "I can do something about that if you want."

"Are you serious?" The idea alone already had me softening. We'd become close, but the idea of taking things to a physical level still seemed wrong.

"Why not?" She flicked her tongue along her lower lip. It was meant to be sexy, and any other man would probably have taken it as such. Not me.

I had to look away. "Uh, thank you, but no." I pushed her feet off my lap to further enunciate my lack of interest in what she was proposing.

"You're such an asshole." Her scowl was present in her voice. "You're a total man-whore, but you won't let me suck you off?"

"It would ruin our relationship."

"Whatever."

I studied her, trying to determine if she was pulling my leg. A side effect of knowing how well a person can pretend is that you don't know when to question their sincerity. "Are you really serious about this?"

She shrugged. "I'm excited about how tonight went. It made me horny."

"I get the excitement." But I wasn't having sex with Celia. "I'll buy you a vibrator."

"Fine." She folded her arms over her chest. "I'm not really interested in sucking your hairy little prick anyway."

I couldn't decide if she was really fine with my refusal or if now she was pretending. Either way, I was happy for the lighter turn in the conversation. I kept going in that direction. "Little? Did you just call my dick little? Maybe you need to put your foot back here again."

"No, no, no!" She screamed as I grabbed her foot, pretending to want to pull it back to my crotch.

I held her foot in my hands while she scrambled to get away. "Just a minute ago, you were willing to put your mouth on me, and now you can't even touch me with your foot?"

She put her hands up in surrender. "I was joking. I wouldn't suck you, Hudson. Or fuck you. Ever. It would be…weird."

"Very weird." I let go of her foot, and she casually pulled her legs up under her again. "And it would mess up this." I gestured back and forth from her to me.

She smiled. "Agreed. And this is nice."

"I do like this." We didn't talk about *this* often. Or at all actually. We'd let our relationship evolve without commentary, but this felt like it needed to be said. Especially after her strange sexual innuendo. I had no intention of going there with her, but *this*—what we did have—it meant something to me. And that was interesting in itself—that any relationship I had meant something to me was unusual.

Still, if things got strange, if Celia tried to be something more than what we had, I'd be able to walk away. And I would walk away. Without looking back. Funny, then, how the idea bothered me.

It was more than I wanted to contemplate at the time. I stood and stretched, feigning a yawn. "Are you staying?"

Celia often stayed over at the loft with me, sharing my king-size bed like two school kids having a sleepover. It was never an issue, but this night I hoped she would say no. Some distance after our conversation might be needed.

But she didn't seem to agree. "I'm staying," she said. "Do I have any clothes still here? I couldn't find any in the closet, and I usually have some items."

"I hid all your things in case Monica stayed over. They're not that hard to find. Back of the armoire, in the closet. If she snooped, she would have found them."

"Smart."

Celia found some of her yoga pants and a tank and went into the bathroom to change. I wondered at that as I stripped from my clothes. She usually dressed and undressed in front of me. Perhaps she also noted a lingering strangeness from our discussion. I certainly did. Normally, I'd be sleeping in boxers. Tonight I'd chosen sweats and a T-shirt.

I was already in bed when she slipped in on the other side. Without speaking, I leaned over and clicked off the lamp. I stayed on my side, facing away from her, and waited for sleep to take me over.

We lay like that for several minutes in the dark. I could tell from her breathing that she was also still awake, so it didn't completely surprise me when she spoke.

"Do you think you'll ever stop playing?" Her voice was smaller than usual. Thin and unsure.

Or it was just the dark messing with my senses.

I lifted my head so I could talk over my shoulder. "The game?" There was nothing else she could mean, though. "No. I'll always play." It wasn't a question I'd ever even considered asking. The experiments were part of me. Even when I didn't try, I was constantly manipulating the wills of those around me and gauging their reactions. "I don't have a choice."

"Of course you have a choice."

Though I didn't know if she could see it in the dark, I shrugged, not agreeing but not wanting to debate it further. "What about you?"

"It's good for now." She cleared her throat. "But I could see myself quitting one day."

Her answer bothered me. I didn't like that she'd thought about quitting. I didn't like that she believed it was a possibility for her.

I rolled to my back so I could look at her and found her also laying on her back. "You're fooling yourself. You could never quit. You love it too much." Perhaps I was speaking for myself. But I wanted those words to be true for her. Needed them to be true for her.

She turned her head to face me. "I do love it. Parts of it, anyway."

Parts of it. Yes, there were parts that were better than others. My favorite part was correctly guessing how a person would react to a situation. I'd gotten so good at reading people that I rarely failed to predict the outcome of the schemes we created. But even as I could anticipate results, each experiment taught me something new about human emotion—about the things I didn't feel. I grew more and more interested in studying further. And more and more alienated from the world around me.

Except not from Celia.

The experiments had brought me closer to her. We were friends now in the way we'd always been meant to be. It occurred to me, though, that I didn't know what it was that Celia liked about the game. I'd always assumed she'd liked it all, and I'd never thought to ask her.

So I asked her now. "Which parts?"

"Hmm," she pretended to think about it, though I was sure she already had an answer. "The pain," she said finally. "I like seeing people in pain."

Her answer baffled me. I liked seeing an outcome of an experiment, and very often it was pain, but when it wasn't, I was just as satisfied. This desire of hers intrigued me as much as any other person's desires.

I turned toward her, propping my head up with my hand. "Why?"

"I don't know, really. I can't explain it."

"Try."

She was quiet for a while, but eventually she spoke. "It makes my own pain feel diminished somehow."

I laughed. "What pain can you possibly have?"

"Hey, even spoiled little rich girls can have things that hurt them." She paused again, but I waited. I knew how the dark could draw things out that hid in the light. Wasn't that where Celia and I always met? In dark rooms? In dark situations?

Seconds ticked by in silence, but eventually she did give more. "Don't ask me what my pain is specifically, though. I haven't felt anything in so long that I don't remember. But it's there somewhere—I know it. Waiting for me. And every time someone else cries and falls apart, it gets smaller. I keep thinking if I just hurt enough people, break enough hearts, then eventually it will all go away. And I won't have to play anymore. I can go back to feeling."

Her monologue was slow and burdened. As though it was hard to say, or like it was the first time she'd ever thought the words. I wasn't even sure if she was finished speaking or not, but her last statement begged for response. "Why would you want to do that?"

"Because I remember what it's like to be in love." She pulled the covers up to her chin, tucking herself away. Hiding.

But she exposed herself once more. "I'd like to feel that again, I think. Someday."

"Again, I ask, why the fuck would you want to do that?"

"You've never been in love, Hudson. You couldn't understand." She turned to her side, her back to me. "Goodnight."

It was clear the conversation was over, so I didn't push her. Besides, I didn't want to continue it, not really. Though I was very much interested in whatever it was that kept that hope of love burning inside of her. Even now, after all the time she'd spent with me—how could she possibly still feel that pull? I was dying to understand.

But there were other thoughts that were swimming through my head that I didn't want to explore. Like, why now? Where did this come from? Was it connected to our playful banter earlier on the couch? Was Celia still carrying a torch that I had effectively ignored?

If I had to make a guess, I'd say that she wasn't so much still enamored with me but with the emotion in general. Both ideas were perplexing, but I couldn't believe that I'd missed signs of her affection for so long.

There was something else that kept me awake long after Celia had slipped into rhythmic breathing at my side. If she really did stop playing the game eventually, where would that leave me? Alone again. It had never bothered me before, but now...

Now, I'd grown accustomed to Celia's companionship. The experiment had evolved with her help, and I'd found considerably more joy in it since she'd joined. If she didn't continue to play, we'd have no bond between us anymore. Our friendship would fall away. And for reasons I couldn't explain, that wasn't something I could live with.

So I wouldn't let it happen. We'd keep playing, and she'd see how ridiculous it was to want a happy ending. There weren't happy endings. Not really. There were only those who got that and the fools who didn't. Celia and I would not be the fools.

EIGHTEEN

After

We're quiet as we drive to the restaurant for my mother's birthday. Alayna's nervous—I'm sure that's the reason for her silence. Mothers in general are intimidating, I hear. My mother beats them all.

I'm nervous as well, for more than one reason. First, I'm worried about subjecting Alayna to this evening with Sophia. It's partly why I hadn't told her about tonight. Alayna was supposed to be working, so I used that as an excuse not to bring it up. Then her plans were canceled, and I had to make a decision. She thinks she wormed her way into an invite, but, honestly, I wanted her with me. I always want her with me.

Now I'm left with a bigger problem. Celia. I'm certain she'll be there. Her family has joined us for my mother's birthday dinners for as long as I can remember, so the scenario isn't unlikely. And that brings up so many potential issues. Alayna, for one, may not be happy if Celia is present. I've promised her I won't spend time with Celia without her. It hadn't even occurred to me that this evening would break that promise until I realized Alayna would be with me.

I should tell her now. But I can't bring myself to say it because I'm hoping to God that it isn't an issue, that Celia doesn't come tonight. Not because Alayna will be upset, but because I don't want to see Celia. At all.

Even the thought of it causes sweat to bead across my brow.

As the limo pulls up to the curb, I wipe my forehead and laugh inwardly at myself. I'm a man who's generally self-assured and confident, and now, at the thought of my petite, demure childhood friend, I'm frightened. It's my own fault. I should have contacted her before now. It's been three days since I completely left the experiment, and I've yet to tell Celia. I've avoided it, not knowing what to say. All my focus has been on Alayna, making her part of my world, inviting her to live with me—it feels like a lifetime since Celia drove me to the airport in the Hamptons and I told her I was done. I'm not that man anymore. I'm completely new.

Stepping out of the car, I casually glance around for sight of her before reaching back to help Alayna out. Celia's nowhere to be seen, and it shouldn't matter if she was. She likely won't be surprised to see us. She knows I haven't broken things off since she showed up at my penthouse while Alayna was there. The game was supposed to have ended before that. But she can only guess what the circumstances are to have made me change the plans. I'm sure she suspects something's different—I've never had a woman at my house before. Not one I was in a relationship with. Not even one I was pretending to have a relationship with. It's a change in my pattern that Celia will not have missed.

Yes, there's a lot to be said to Celia, a lot that's past due. When I finally do tell her the truth, she'll retaliate. It's not a question.

I gesture to Alayna to go ahead of me while I make arrangements with Jordan for our pickup. A last minute urge to flee seizes me. I could call Alayna back, take her somewhere else, enjoy the evening with her to myself. My mother will throw a fit and drink more than usual, or maybe exactly as much as usual, which is already too much. But I won't care because I'll be far away from all of it.

Our problems wouldn't be solved, though. Simply postponed. Which is why I decide to continue with this horror of an evening. It will be worse because Alayna is with me, but I'm strangely comforted knowing she'll be beside me through it all.

I step into the lobby after her and look at my watch. We're a few minutes late. This shouldn't be a problem. I called my mother earlier to let her know I was bringing Alayna, so the table should already be prepared for us. In the elevator up to our floor, I take her hand. I need to touch her even if it's only in this simple capacity. It gives me strength. It reminds me my power lies in her.

The tension in my neck and shoulders tightens as we ascend. I realize that I don't know what Alayna will do when she discovers Celia is here, *if* she's here. Maybe it won't be a big deal. But if it is…? Will Alayna be tight-lipped and cold? Will she lash out? What will I say when she questions me about it? The truth is safest, but what exactly is that?

More than once I lean toward Alayna with the intent of telling her that Celia may be here. Each time I stop myself. Finally, I start praying for the improbable.

Don't let her be here. Tomorrow, I'll contact her. I'll start making things right with her. Though I have no idea how.

Much too soon, long before I'm prepared, we are led by the host to my family's table. Everyone's there—Chandler, my parents, Mira and Adam, the Werners. Celia.

My stomach drops.

I know the moment Alayna spots her. She releases my hand and looks at me with pain-stricken features. "I thought you said this was family only," she mumbles. And she bolts.

Well, that wasn't a reaction I'd expected.

I nod to my family, catching my mother's scowl as I make an apology. "She left something in the car. Excuse us a moment." Then I follow after my date. While she may just need a moment to calm down, she has to know she can't run from me. I will always come after her.

She takes the stairs. I pause at the door, trying to discover if she's gone up or down. Her shoes echo on the concrete, but when I peer over the rail, I don't see her below me. So I head to the roof.

At the top of the stairs, I open the heavy door and spot her rushing past the lounge area to the far edge of the space. There's not many people here—a couple absorbed in each other on a couch, a small party conversing around an unlit fire pit. Not wanting to make a scene, I slow my pursuit. Alayna's trapped in my sight. I can't lose her.

When I'm close to her, I stop. Her back is to me, taking deep breaths. Her body rises and falls with each new lungful of air. I want to reach for her, but I'm tentative. Though I'm ready to move everything in my life to be with her, our whole arrangement is new to me. I'm making mistakes already, and I'm desperate not to make more.

I should have told her.

Now I have to say something, so I settle on the only thing that comes to mind. "The Werners are practically family."

She doesn't turn toward me. "Right. Uh-huh."

"What, do you think I didn't tell you on purpose?" Okay, I didn't tell her on purpose, but not for the reasons she thinks. I'm in defense mode, and my phrasing tends to get manipulative when I am.

She chortles. "You don't want to know what I'm thinking."

"Actually, I do."

She spins toward me. "No, you don't."

I watch her as she backs away from me, stopping when she meets the wall. She should be angry at me. Aggressive, not retreating. There's more to this than simply jealousy, but I don't understand what.

And I *want* to understand. "Trust me when I tell you I do."

"Hudson, you can't say that when you don't know what I want to say." Her voice is strained, as if she's holding back. "It's not good. In fact, you need to leave me alone. Or I'm going to blame you for things. Things I'm probably overreacting about, and you're going to be offended. And I'm going to lose you."

The light goes on, and I feel like an idiot. She's told me that she makes things bigger than they are, and here she is, afraid that that's what she's doing. She's not, of course. I deserve her accusations, misguided as they may be. I deserve blame.

But, asshole that I am, I don't tell her that. It will push her away, and I need—*she* needs—to be pulled in. So I do everything I can to make her see that her issues don't scare me. Make her see that I'm not going anywhere. "You aren't going to lose me." I take a step toward her to prove it.

Her face is anguished, disbelieving. "You haven't seen this side of me, Hudson. You don't know."

I don't know what she's like, what she can be like. I've seen glimpses of her obsessive tendencies, but nothing substantial. She's been so strong, hiding her weaknesses from me.

I'm selfish because, even though I won't show her all my darkness, I want to witness hers. "Then I need to stay. I need to see every side of you."

Because I'll love her through it all.

She shakes her head and bites her sexy red-painted lip, and I can tell she's fighting tears.

But she's also considering. I see it in her eyes. So I press her. "Go ahead. Ask me."

"It won't be asking; it will be accusing." Her voice is smaller, and I can tell her resolve is weakening. It won't take much to coax her thoughts out of her.

Am I a bully because I'm pressing her like this? Am I a masochist because I'm eager to hear what she has to say? Her accusations won't be accurate, but I deserve to be questioned and grilled. I deserve to have to fight for her.

That's not why I push her. I push her because I can't live without her, and that means all of her, even this. "Do it," I say. "I want to hear it. I need to know what you're thinking. Trust me."

She lets go. "You didn't invite me tonight because you knew she'd be here." It's barely a whisper.

I nod in understanding. It's not the reason I didn't invite her, but if I'd known this morning that Alayna didn't have to work this evening, I don't know if I would have invited her then, either. And Celia would be the reason.

That admission would lead to things I don't want to talk about, things I don't want to face, and so I say, "That's not true. I told you why I didn't invite you. And I did invite you in the end. You're here."

"But you didn't want to at first." Though she won't meet my eyes, her posture is stronger. "That's probably why you had to doll me up. To show up Celia, whatever your game with her is. It wasn't about your mother at all."

This punches me in the gut. "You're right."

Her head whips up.

"You're right that it wasn't about my mother. It was about you. I wanted everyone to see how beautiful you are. How beautiful the woman who loves me is." It's hard for me to even say these words because I know that she really does love me and I don't deserve it.

Worse, she doesn't understand how much her affection means to me.

"Celia. You wanted to show Celia, you mean."

I shake my head, not knowing how to get through to her.

"She's here, Hudson!" she shouts. "She's here with free rein, and I had to beg to be here. And you told me you wouldn't see her without me. What is she to you?"

"Nothing. An old friend." An enemy, maybe, depending on how things play out.

"Bullshit." Her voice cracks. "Otherwise you would have told me about this dinner from the beginning. You were hiding it from me." She points an accusing finger at me. "Because you knew she would be here too."

"I didn't know." I close my eyes and take a breath. Will I always have to live like this? Skirting the truth? Dodging the past?

My only hope is to give as much honesty as I can. "I suspected," I admit. "But she's not here because of me. Her mother is my mother's best friend. You know that."

"Fuck that. She's twenty-eight years old. She's old enough to not go to every goddamn function with her mother. She's here for you."

There's truth to this. Though our relationship hasn't ever been romantic—not really—we've clung to each other like two orphaned hatchlings, birds of a feather. Our circles always entwined. If it were her mother's birthday, I'd be there.

I'd called it friendship. Now I see it for what it really is—habit. And obligation. And fear.

That ends now. It doesn't matter if Celia's here for me. It only matters who *I'm* here with. "And I'm here with you," I tell Alayna. It's raw. It's honest. It's the most important thing I've said to anyone in quite some time.

"She's still in love with you." Her jealousy and fears are evidence of her claim on me. It turns me on.

"And I'm with you." I can't stand our distance anymore. Not literally or figuratively. I need her. I need her to obsess about me, to love me so deeply that it rocks her world, because it's how I love her. I cross to her, bracing my arms on either side of her. "I'm with you."

Her hands reach for my jacket as I move closer. I press into her, and she responds by leaning into me. She notices my erection, and her eyes spark with questioning want.

"I'm hard for you and only you. It's you that I adore." I kiss along her neck. She moans, and my cock jumps.

This isn't about me, though. This conversation is about her—about soothing her, pleasing her, showing her that she owns me in every way.

I crash my lips to hers, stroking and caressing her mouth with my tongue. I kiss her in a way that I know will make her wet. Make her drip with her desire.

"I'm with you," I say again when I break the kiss. I repeat it to her over and over like a mantra, like a soundtrack to the love scene we're performing. A love scene that's about to get fucking hot.

I gather the skirt of her dress up and tuck it into her panties, slipping my fingers inside. The smell of her cunt drifts up, and my dick turns to stone. The faint laughter in the background reminds me that there are people nearby, but I can't stop myself. In fact, their nearness fuels my lust.

Alayna doesn't seem bothered by them either. I rub against her clit, massaging her in the ways I've learned she likes. Her hips buck into my hand.

"That's it," I coax her between kisses, my fingers working her. "Relax. Let me be with you."

My hand moves down her pussy, and I slide two fingers into her hole. She's warm and tight and wet. The sounds she makes as I fuck her with my fingers—whimpers and breathy little moans—drives me mad. My cock is throbbing, begging for release.

But I have more to say. More I need to tell her. I drop to my knees and pull her panties to her ankles. I leisurely drag my tongue down the length of her cunt. "It's you that I'm about to go down on," I tell her. "It's you I'm going to make come with my mouth, so that when we go back down there and you start to feel insecure, you will still be wet and you'll remember my lips were on you and no one else."

My words alone make her squirm. Now I'm going to make her writhe.

I lift her foot from her panties and toss her leg over my shoulder. Then I go down on her in earnest. I suck and lick and nip at her clit, thrusting three fingers into her hole. I bend a finger, rubbing against the spot that I know will make her come. And she does. She rocks forward as she gushes over my hand, into my mouth. God, she tastes so good.

She's still coming when I stand and press my erection against her hand. "Take it out," I demand. Even if I could manage to settle down enough to return to dinner with my family, I'd still have to fuck her first. This is a crucial part of what I have to say to her. I'm here with her—I told her that with my mouth and my hands—but she's also here with me. This I'm going to tell her with my cock.

"We're not alone." She's just noticed.

If I wasn't so goddamned hard, I'd take a moment to savor the knowledge that I'd sucked her into oblivion.

But I'm pulsing with need. "Take it out. I don't care about anyone or anything but being inside you right now. I have to be inside you."

She does as I've asked. I lower my pants only enough to free my dick. Then I lift her, bracing her against the wall, and thrust into her cunt. Hard.

"Goddamn, your pussy is so good." I move in and out of her with quick jabs. "Do you hear me? Your pussy makes me this hard. No one else's."

Her whimpers move in time to my drives. It's so hot, and I'm about ready to explode, but I keep reminding her as I continue to pound into her. Keep reassuring her. "When we go back down to dinner, I will smell like you and you will smell like me. And you'll remember that we are together. I am with you."

I don't have to tell her to come with me. She does anyway, and I take it as a sign I've gotten my point across. She bites my shoulder, muffling her scream as my release rips into my words "No one but you."

No one but you.

No one but her, never before, never again. My commitment runs deep, and there's no end to it. She's inside me, wrapped around me like a tumor. There's no way to cut her away without cutting into me. Without killing me.

When we join my family for dinner, we're both calmer. Mirabelle greets Alayna warmly, as does my father. The latter doesn't please me, but I remember the rooftop—I'm with Alayna, she's with me. My father is not a threat.

My mother's her usual self—drunk and bitchy. For the most part, though, she's manageable. Celia's the one I'm most concerned with. I steal a few glances at her throughout the evening. She's unreadable. She's good.

By the time dinner arrives, I've relaxed considerably. Whatever Celia is planning, there won't be a scene. Not here, anyway. I may even get away without speaking to her at all tonight. Maybe there actually is a God.

I've just taken my first bite of duck crepes when Warren strikes a conversation. "I'm very sorry to hear about your Plexis deal," he says around a mouthful of steak au poivre.

We'd bantered business earlier, but nothing personal until now.

"You win some, you lose some." Though I'm still disappointed with the loss of Plexis, I'm in the process of getting the company back, thanks to Alayna. It's too early to share this type of news with others, so I don't mention it.

Besides, there's another plan I've been toying with, a plan that might insure me some leverage, but a lot needs to line up if I'm to pursue it. Part of that includes information that I can only get from Warren. "Is GlamPlay still looking to buy into Werner Media?"

Warren shrugs. "They're toying with me. Haven't made up their mind." He takes a swallow of his wine. "It would be a great advantage for both corporations, but I can't quite convince them of that."

I nod, digesting the information. Pierce Industries has heavy influence over GlamPlay. They're a company I've considered purchasing for a while. For my plan to work, GlamPlay needs to buy shares in Werner Media first. I'll have to get Norma to see how we can make that happen.

Meanwhile, I need to shore up my own investments in Werner's company. "How much is GlamPlay looking to buy?"

"Thirty percent is on the table. Any more than that would put me at a liability."

"Of course." With the ten percent I already own, plus the thirty percent that GlamPlay could own, I would be at forty percent total holdings. I'm not sure that's enough. "Is the portion on the table from your shares or from the other investors?"

He offers me a grin. "All from me."

It leaves Warren with forty percent as well. It's a risky move on his part, leaving himself with less than fifty percent of the ownership. But he's right that GlamPlay will bring benefits that will increase the overall worth, and as long as he has the majority shares, he's in a good position.

So I just need to make sure he doesn't have the majority. I'll need to convince another investor to sell. Another star that has to align.

As if he can read my mind, he says, "Are you interested in further investing? Bishop is looking to sell his two percent. Great time to buy. Prices are going to go up if GlamPlay invests."

Bingo.

"I'll have my people contact Bishop tomorrow." This idea of mine is working out better than I thought. The prospects excite me for many reasons, not the least of which is because it's a version of the game. Making good business deals always is. Just like chess. It's strategic and secretive and often manipulative, but much more ethical. Work is where I exercise my need to play. It's thrilling.

But not as thrilling as life with Alayna. I tuck away the newfound information and turn my attention to her. Loading my fork with a piece of my crepe that doesn't have any mushrooms, I offer her a bite. Her lips slide along the silver, and all I can think about is how beautiful she looks when her lips curl around my cock.

"Divine," she says.

"I could say the same thing." I'm not subtle about my meaning.

Madge reddens and clears her throat. I guess I'd spoken louder than I'd meant to. Oh well. Maybe this will make her forget her silly ideas about me marrying her daughter. Though whether it does or not, I'm not really concerned.

Talk turns to Mirabelle's pregnancy. The whole table joins in. It's hard to ignore the excitement of a new baby. I know this from experience.

Also from experience, I recognize the tension in Mirabelle's voice when she suggests hyphenating the baby's last name to Sitkin-Pierce. It's a ridiculous idea, and I know she's only saying it for my mother's benefit. Even more ridiculous is how my mother makes Mirabelle think she needs to say it.

"It's not the same." At least Sophia isn't encouraging the idea. "Sitkin-Pierce is not Pierce. So the bloodline continues, but not the name."

It's that one statement that makes me fear for this conversation. If I know my mother—and I do—it won't be pretty. I watch the pieces line up for the accident that I'm certain is about to take place: Adam reminds us that Chandler could have a Pierce child. My father slips in his doubt that Chandler really is a Pierce.

Then Sophia says it, the thing I've been dreading. "Hudson and Celia's baby could have been both."

It's at this moment that I realize how my lack of emotion has enabled me to survive a life with my mother. Her drunken antics, her caustic comments, her cold indifference—none of it has ever fazed me. They've skimmed off the surface of my shields, leaving only faint scuffs and shallow dents.

Now, though, with Alayna in my life, my armor is down. And I feel every hit.

I'm angry. She has no right. She's not only hurting Alayna but Mirabelle and Celia. Probably the Werners as well. While my mother can't know all the memories and pains that she dredges up with this casual statement, she isn't so ignorant as to not realize its inappropriateness.

I plan to say something, but I want to be in control of my rage before I do. I'm unused to having to rein in emotion, and it takes me a minute. Meanwhile, it's my father who speaks out. "Not this again, Sophia. Really? Goddammit, I won't listen to this." He tosses his napkin down and stands. "Thank you everyone, I wish I could say it has been a lovely evening, but, well, I'll leave it at that. I'll take care of the bill on my way out. The rest of you stay and enjoy. Order dessert. As for my wife, I'm not going to invite her to rot in hell, as I probably should, because I think she already lives there. At least hell is where anyone who spends time with her feels like they've been sent."

My father's outburst surprises everyone. For me, I find that within the surprise is lucidity. Jack hasn't had the emotional shelter that I have had. Perhaps I've placed too much blame on him for my mother's behavior. Maybe it's her that drove him to infidelity in the first place. Maybe the situation is more complicated than I've realized. Even with all my study, I couldn't realize how easy it was to get hurt and be hurt in a relationship until I was in love with someone myself.

Sophia's unaffected by his departure. "What a drama queen." She takes a bite of her food. "I was merely pointing out that we had a chance at a Pierce grandchild and now it's gone."

Adam makes a snide remark, but I don't pay any attention. I'm collected now. I'm ready to have my say. "I could have a child with Alayna."

Admittedly, the main purpose of my comment is to goad my mother, but it doesn't change its truth. I've never given much thought to children except for that brief moment of time that I almost became the father of Celia's baby. I've had no desire to continue my line, and, to be fair, I'm sure my mother had understood that about me. It's likely encouraged the notion that her one and only chance to have a Hudson Pierce child has slipped away. Babies were not in my future.

Now, with Alayna, it's suddenly possible.

Without looking at her, I sense her astonishment. She's not the one I meant to shock, and I feel a bit guilty. This should have been a conversation first discussed in private. A second rush of fury washes over me at being put in this position in the first place. I smother it by focusing on my plate, taking another bite of my dinner.

Despite the unfortunate timing of my declaration, it hits its mark. "Are you talking marriage and children already? It's early for that, Hudson. Incredibly early."

"Oh Mother, don't be so old-fashioned. You don't need to be married to have children." I take a swallow of my wine. "And what Alayna and I are discussing is frankly none of your business."

Sophia's eyes narrow. "You brought it up."

"I was stating that *I* could father a child, and that would continue both your precious bloodline and your precious name." I'm calm, in control, even as I reveal myself. "And the only person I could ever imagine wanting to have a child with is Alayna."

Before when we were with my mother, my relationship with Alayna was a ruse. Though much of what was supposed to be pretend was actually very real, this is the moment where Alayna has to know exactly how sincere I am about us. Because I'm very serious.

After everything my mother has said and done this evening, it seems it's this pronouncement that has caused the most tension.

"Hudson, I…" Alayna stiffens at my side, and I'm afraid I've gone too far. Scared her off. For the first time, it occurs to me that she may not be as invested in me as I am in her.

No, I can't think about that. She's probably just uncomfortable with all the eyes pinned on us.

I place my hand on her leg to reassure her—to reassure me—and apologize with my eyes before turning to my mother. "The point is that you need to let the past go, Mother. There is still a future to look forward to. For all of us." *For me and Alayna.*

I turn my focus back to my girlfriend. As my hand strokes up and down her thigh, I tell her with my eyes words I wish I could say. *Our future is bright, Alayna. You are the only one who matters to me. I'm with you. I love you. Always.*

My gaze is locked with hers, so I notice her eyes fill. God, please let those be happy tears.

She excuses herself to use the powder room.

My mother barely waits until Alayna's out of earshot before she starts in. "Well, look, Hudson. You scared her off with your talk of a future. She's smart enough to know there's no such thing with a man like you."

"Oh, stop it," Mirabelle says. "If anyone scared her off, it was you."

Warmth spreads through my chest. I do have a great kid sister. This isn't a revelation, but rather a reminder. I'll have to remember to tell her thanks sometime.

As for everyone else, I'm ready to be done with them. I wipe my mouth with my napkin and stand. "Actually, Mother, *powder room* is our code for *DTF*."

Mirabelle and Celia gasp while Adam tries to hide a laugh. Chandler even looks up from his phone, his eyes wide in admiration.

I cross to my mother's chair, and before she can ask what it means, I say, "Google it. You'll learn something." I bend to kiss her cheek. "Happy birthday, Mother. Perhaps next year you can manage to make it through the meal without running anyone off."

"You're charming as always, Hudson," she says, her words drenched in sarcasm.

"Aren't I?"

As I head to the bathrooms, I hear Chandler laughing as he explains to my mother, "It means *down to fuck*, Mom. He means he's meeting Alayna for a booty call."

I'm still smiling when I make it to the restrooms. I use the facilities, taking time to clean up a bit from our earlier tryst on the roof. When I leave, I notice Mirabelle heading into the women's restroom. And Celia heading out.

She sees me and starts toward me. I realize that this is it. I can't avoid talking to her any longer.

Fortunately, she doesn't look angry. A tiny smirk rests on her lips. It's playful. As if she's going to scold me, but that's all.

I'm hopeful.

"So…?" she asks.

I glance behind her toward the women's room, afraid Alayna may walk out any minute, or that I've already missed her.

"She's still in there," Celia says, guessing at my worry. "She's fine. Now spill."

I run a hand through my hair, wishing I'd dealt with this earlier. "I'm sorry. I should have called you."

"Probably." She folds her arms over her chest. "Did you decide you needed more time with the game, then?"

It crosses my mind that I could let her believe that. I could explain that this time with Alayna is just a chance to further gain her affections. That doesn't sit right, though. Not only will it cause more problems in the future, but I don't want to lie about my feelings anymore. Especially my feelings about Alayna. "No, the game is over. This is…this is real."

Her brow furrows. "Are you…? I can't tell if you're kidding or not. Did you… "she pauses as if she can't believe the question she's about to ask "…fall in love with her?"

It's a betrayal to say it out loud to someone before telling Alayna, but it's necessary. "I did. I am. In love with her."

The scene is surreal—Celia and I discussing love in a nonclinical context. She's as baffled by it as I am. "But you've never—"

I cut her off. "No, I haven't ever. It's the first time. I'm…I'm…" I don't have the words for all that I'm feeling. It's partly why I haven't reached out to her before this.

"You're speechless." Her eyes are wide but also bright. She lets out a laugh. "God, I've never seen you like this."

"Neither have I."

"Wow." She brings her hand to cover her mouth, suppressing another awkward laugh. "I'm so surprised. Forgive me if I seem flustered. I'm just really, really surprised."

"You're not the only one." My eyes dart back to the restroom as another woman goes in. Alayna still hasn't emerged.

"And she's in love with you too?" Celia calls my attention back with this question.

This I don't hesitate to answer. "I really think she is." I know she is. There's not a doubt in my mind, and I want to shout it from every rooftop.

"I think you're right. The way she looks at you…" Celia sighs. Then her eyes crinkle in distrust. "You promise you aren't trying to pull one over on me? You really feel something for her?"

It's funny how she's as suspicious of me as I am of her. "I promise. This is the real thing." *Now, the most important thing.* "Which is why I can't play this game anymore."

I brace myself for her reaction, holding my breath as I wait.

"Of course not." Her expression says she's appalled that I even mentioned the game. "I mean, I knew you were into her, but I thought it was just sex and that's why I was pushing you to keep playing. I had no idea it was serious."

I'm not sure what she's saying. "Are you…okay…with this then?"

"Why wouldn't I be? You mean because of the scheme? Is that why you were so distant during dinner? Did you think I'd be upset about this?"

It's my turn to be shocked. "You've never been one to drop an experiment."

"No, I haven't. But this is a totally different situation." She bites her lip. "I'm worried it's too late though. We've already pushed her too far."

I tense. "What do you mean?"

"In the bathroom just now. She…" She closes her eyes and takes a deep breath. "It's probably nothing, but she cornered me. Verbally attacked me."

My stomach knots. I'd thought I'd eased Alayna enough regarding me and Celia, but apparently I haven't. "What did she say?"

She shakes her head dismissively. "It doesn't matter what she said exactly. But she was possessive. It seemed to be a repeat of behavior straight out of her file. I think she may already be relapsing."

I don't believe this in the least. Alayna's issues all stem from my own secretive relationship with Celia. It's a natural response, not a relapse. "I'm not concerned about it."

"You're not concerned? But if she needs therapy—"

"If she needs therapy, I'll get it for her. What she really needs is reassurance." I can see that Celia is skeptical. "Look—you're the ex-girlfriend in her eyes. Isn't it common to have some jealousy in that arena?"

"Yes. I suppose you're right. Forget I said anything. She loves you, and she's protecting what's hers." She dabs at the corner of her eye, and it's then I notice she's teary. "I'm sorry; I wasn't prepared for all this. I'm a little flustered."

I'm equally unprepared. I'd expected lashing out and defiance. Not tears. I place a hand on her upper arm. "Celia…are you okay?"

She waves a hand at her face. "I'm fine. I'm touched. Jesus, what's going on with this world? Hudson Pierce falling in love, and me getting touched by it. Who would have thought?" She looks down at her shoes. "This is a good thing, though. Surprising, but good."

The relief that fills me spreads through every fiber of my body. I'd been convinced Celia would not approve of my recent emotional developments. She was as die-hard about the game as I was.

Wasn't she? Or had I simply assumed she shared my own commitment?

I remember back to the night she told me she was still holding out for a man to sweep her off her feet. It was five years ago, possibly six. I haven't thought about it in some time, and now I wonder if she'd been holding onto that desire all this time. And if she has been, what's the reason that she hasn't looked for it? Is it me? Have I been holding her back, keeping her bound to this ridiculous romance-free notion of a life?

Fuck.

How many times have I ruined this woman's life? Can the mess I've made ever be undone? It's small retribution, but I give her the permission that I suspect she's waiting for. "Maybe it's time for you to let love in as well."

She rolls her eyes. "Pssh." Then she considers, letting the suggestion settle over her. "Maybe," she concedes finally. She thinks about it another few seconds before shaking her head. "But let's not talk about me right now. Does Alayna know about...?" She looks around to make sure no one's listening and then lowers her voice. "You haven't told her, have you?"

I know what she's talking about without her spelling it out. The game. The experiment that brought Alayna into my life in the first place. The weight of this secret slumps my shoulders. "No. I don't think I can."

"You can't." She's adamant, her eyes ablaze with her insistence. "Not if you want to keep her. Trust me on this. I've been scammed by you before. There's no way she'll love you after that."

This isn't news. But the confirmation coming from the one person who could possibly understand Alayna's position is jarring. I don't want to hear this. I don't want to believe that there is anything that could make me lose Alayna's love.

Celia steps toward me, her expression regretful. "I'm not saying that to upset you. I just—"

"I know." I don't need Celia to feel bad about this. "It's the truth. I have to keep it from her. It's only you and me that know—"

"And I won't tell her."

It hadn't crossed my mind that she would, but now I have to secure that she won't. "I hate to ask this, but do you swear that?"

"I swear, Hudson. Not only because you asked me not to, but because it's the code. We don't speak about the game to anyone. Even if we're not playing anymore, old rules apply."

"Thank you." I look again toward the restrooms, but my thoughts are on Celia. She has a streak of darkness in her that I can't deny. She's a sadist. While my experiments were always a sterile study of human behavior and emotion, she repeatedly felt glee at the expense of others. It's made me wary of her.

Yet, even though I'm the one who taught and nurtured her perverse nature, she's never turned it back on me. Time and time again, she's stood by me, been my only confidant, shared the deepest bond in the keeping of our ruthless secrets.

And now, she's supporting me in a way that I'd never expected. Letting me move on when I always held her back. "You've been a better friend than I've given you credit for."

"Back at you." She squeezes my hand. "A really good friend, Hudson. You saved me, you know."

I meet her eyes. They're still watery, and she blinks several times, probably trying to keep her tears from spilling. It occurs to me that I owe Celia the same acknowledgment. If not for her pushing me to the game, I wouldn't have Alayna now. I don't have the time or the words to explain the extent of my gratitude, so I simply say, "You saved me too."

She squeezes my hand once more before letting it go. "I have to go back. Good luck, Hudson. I mean that." Then she leaves.

Alayna and Mirabelle appear with impeccable timing. The ache that always fills me when Alayna's not with me eases at the sight of her. But my mind is tied up in the encounter with Celia. Long after we've left the restaurant and are buckled in the back of the limo, I'm replaying phrases, coming to a fuller understanding of truths that were exposed in our brief conversation.

I dwell most on what I've done to Celia throughout our friendship. And also on what I've done to Alayna, what I'm still keeping from her. These thoughts send me into a spiral of self-loathing and deprecation that I haven't ever experienced. Not at this level.

When we arrive at the penthouse, I'm so consumed in myself that I send Alayna away, telling her I have work to do. I can't be with her when I'm like this. She doesn't deserve this. I don't deserve *her*. Still I won't let her go. I can never let her go, no matter how unworthy I am.

But how long before she discovers the worst of me and leaves? More and more, I feel the inevitability of that day. And then will it destroy her like it destroyed Celia? I can't bear the thought.

The cursor blinks on the empty document open on my computer screen, keeping me locked in my pitiful trance as the night passes. I'm aware of Alayna in the background—always aware of her. She runs on the treadmill, her music blaring through the house stereo as she does. She showers. Then the house quiets, and I assume she's gone to bed.

Lyrics from one of the songs she played stays with me—a woman's voice singing about her darkness, wondering if her lover could love her dark side. It's apropos, and I wonder if Alayna realizes it. I wonder if my distance tonight has pushed her away already. I don't want to push her away; I want to pull her in.

Then what the fuck am I doing sitting alone at my desk?

I shake my head at my stupidity. I'd told her earlier that I was with her. Always with her. It was a promise that I've already broken because here I am wrapped in my self-hate, and that's miles away from her and her love.

I turn off my computer and go to her. Undressing quickly, I slip into the covers and spoon behind her. She's naked, and I know that it's an invitation. So, though she's sleeping, I wrap my hands around her torso and kiss along the angles of her body.

She sighs into me, opening her legs for me so I can slip my cock into her warmth. We make love like this, quietly, intently. In this silent act of passion, she brings me back—back to the man that can be trusted and loved and present.

Afterward, when we've found our breathing, when we've found each other, she asks, "Where did you go? Earlier."

I nuzzle against her. "Does it matter? I'm here now."

She wants more, words that I can't give, promises that she's not ready to hear, walls to crumble that are too strongly built. There are things I can't tell her—not yet, not ever—but there are also things I *can* say. I pull her underneath me, stretching my body on top of her so she can feel the weight of my company. So that everywhere our skin meets, she can *feel* I'm with her.

I rock into her and begin whispering in the language of love. *"Mon amour. Mon précieux,"* I say at her ear. *"Mon chéri. Mon bien-aimé."* My love. My precious. My cherished. My beloved.

I tell her this over and over in between kisses as I roll in and out of her. I tell her that I'm with her. Always with her. With all that I can give her. With every part of me that matters—the places that she's awakened, the dark corners that she's lit with her love.

I can't give her all of me, but I can do this. I pray that it's enough.

NINETEEN

"Hudson."

Celia's voice on the other end of my office line surprises me. I haven't spoken to her since my mother's birthday four days before, but it isn't the length of time between then and now that throws me. It's the tone in her voice. There's something I can't identify beneath that one word. Something…off.

My body tenses immediately. "What's wrong?"

"I need to see you. Now."

I have a business meeting and two phone calls left before my day is over. Then I hope to convince Alayna to join me on my trip to Japan to try to win back Plexis. "Now's not good, Celia. Can I call you tonight?"

"No. It's urgent." Her voice is tight with emotion. "It's Alayna."

She won't tell me more than that, insisting that she has to see me face-to-face. There have been many times that Celia has snapped her fingers expecting me to jump. I rarely obeyed. This time, I do. Not only because she's said the magic word—*Alayna*—but because her demeanor is so completely foreign. It's fragile and fearful. These are traits I haven't seen from my old friend since she lost her baby ten years ago.

I ask my secretary to cancel my afternoon and am out of the office within seven minutes. My mind wants to jump to conclusions, wants to settle on the worst possible reasons for this impromptu meeting, but I don't allow myself to think about anything but getting to The Bowery. Celia's riled me up so completely that I didn't even argue when she declared the meeting place as my penthouse. Though, as I take the elevator up, I remind myself once again that I need to take away her key.

Inside my apartment, I find she's not alone. My parents are there as well, and a man that I recognize from pictures in Alayna's file as her brother. I suddenly wish I'd tried to contact Alayna on my way home. Has she been hurt? Has there been an accident? Is that why everyone's here, to tell me something I don't want to hear? Something I *can't* hear?

I'm on edge now, but I hide it.

I hold a hand out to the stranger. "Hudson Pierce."

"Brian Withers." His shake is firm enough, but I can't help resenting him for the troubles he's given Alayna. "Good to finally meet you."

"You as well. Though you'll pardon me for not being privy to the circumstances in which we're gathered." I direct this last comment to Celia. She's the one who holds the answers.

"I was just getting to that, Hudson. Why don't you sit down?" Her voice is heavy, as though she's a doctor about to deliver a terminal diagnosis.

It's unnerving, and again I'm struck with a cold bolt of fear. *Please, God, let Alayna be okay.*

Then I remind myself that though she sounds sincere, I've heard Celia use that tone many times when she's not. So I remain wary. "I'll stand."

"Whichever you prefer."

"I prefer you explain what's going on." There's an edge to my words that I recognize as completely unwarranted. Celia had surprised me when she declared her support of me and Alayna, but I didn't doubt her earnestness. Why am I so ready then to battle her now?

It's because I'd rather a battle than any other news she could give me. I'd rather fight her than find I have no reason left to fight.

"Calm down, Hudson." My mother is the last person who can calm me. Her presence alone is a distress. "Pour yourself a drink."

"Of course that would be your solution," my father mutters.

It's the usual banter of my family. Normally, I would echo the sentiment. Right now I only want to hear what Celia has to say.

She senses I'm losing my patience and clears her throat, preparing to deliver what I can't help but assume is a show. "There's no other way to say this except to just come out and say it. Alayna has been…well, she's been harassing me."

I'm instantly relieved. She's okay. There's been no accident. No body waiting to be identified in a morgue.

But the respite is short-lived as a new storm of emotions overtakes me.

"Not just harassment," Celia clarifies. "She's been—I hate to use the word, but it's the one that fits—stalking me. Calling me. Following me."

"Stalking you, Celia?" I'm incredulous. Alayna knows not to spend time with Celia. She wouldn't break that vow, would she?

"Stalking, Hudson," she confirms.

Brian pinches the bridge of his nose. "Not this again."

I want to punch him. Because even if I didn't know to question the source of the accusation, I would not jump to believe anything spoken against Alayna.

But more than that, I want to punch Celia. I realize now why she's included my family here. It's the only way she can say these lies and stand a chance of being heard. "This is bullshit. Get the fuck out."

"Hold on, Hudson." Celia crosses to me. "Before you decide not to believe me, listen to what I have to say. I have proof."

She hands me a stack of papers. I consider tossing them to the ground, but there are other people in the room. Throwing a tantrum will not win them to my side. My eye twitches, but I focus on the page on top. It's a call log. Celia's, to be precise. Several phone calls have been made to her from the same number. Alayna's number.

"This proves nothing." Celia must have stolen her phone somehow. Or paid someone to use it. Maybe someone at the club? I shove the papers back at her.

She doesn't take them, ignoring them to answer the ding on her phone. My mother grabs the log out of my hand instead. She can have them.

"And look at this," Celia says, turning her phone toward me.

On her screen is an image that seems to have been sent by text. The woman in the picture has her back to the camera, but it's clearly Alayna.

"This is at the job site where I've been working this week. Fit Nation. She's shown up there so many times to bother me that I asked the front desk guy to document it the next time she came in. This is from today, Hudson. Twenty minutes ago."

I shake my head. "This is ridiculous."

"You just don't want to hear it." She returns her phone to her slack pockets.

I get it now. I see her angle. She never meant the kind words of support she delivered at the restaurant. She meant to throw me off guard. It's the next play in her game.

It doesn't surprise me, but it stings. I'd wanted to believe that we shared something beyond the hateful schemes we concocted. I'd wanted to think that she actually...*cared*...for me. The way that I suspected that I cared for her.

No more. The blinders are off. If we're meant to be foes, so be it.

I step toward her. We're face-to-face now. Close enough that she can see I'm serious when I say, "Drop it, Celia. Let this go." There's no mistaking that this is a threat. She may hold things over me, but she can't forget that I hold things over her as well.

She doesn't back down. "There's more. Besides the calls, Alayna's shown up at restaurants while I was dining, left messages with my office, followed me on the street."

"It's a bunch of goddamned lies." I narrow my eyes, accusing. "This is what you wanted to happen, and when it didn't, you made it up."

"I didn't want it to happen, Hudson." Celia leans in so that I'm the only one who can hear her. "Not anymore."

Her expression is not only genuine but desperate. It's not a look I've seen before on her. She can be cold, calculating, but this…this is different. Why does she care so much that I believe her? She can cause her trouble without me. She's never cared if we were on the same side. So why this time?

My conviction wavers.

What if she's telling the truth? I'm fully aware of how "proof" can be fabricated. I'm also aware of how past addictions can call to you. How easy it is to fall into old patterns. Has Alayna really fallen off the wagon, so to say? We pushed her toward this. Did we achieve our goal?

"Why would Celia make it up?" My mother, ever the clueless, pipes up from her place on the couch.

I could school her on that, but it would break every rule of the game. Or has Celia already broken every rule by making up this entire scheme? I'm suddenly uncertain of everything.

"Because that's what she does." Jack's snide remark reminds me that he too has been played by Celia. He'd been old enough to know better when she'd shown up on the doorstep of the guest house, but she was manipulative enough to fool even the wise. "Ah, and many of these questions can now be settled because the subject at hand has arrived."

In sync, every eye in the room turns toward the newest occupant.

"What's going on?" she asks, her gaze pierced on me.

"Alayna—" God, I wish I could steal her from this moment. It's going to be a bloodbath, and all of it, whether there's any truth to Celia's accusations or not—am I really considering that there is?—all of it has come about because of me.

I wanted to protect her. I thought I had succeeded. I was wrong.

The room is abuzz around me as Alayna is brought up to speed. I don't hear most of it, lost in my own battle. The urge to dwell on my fault in this scene is overwhelming. I try to deny it, but it freezes me. Coupled with the desperate plea from Celia, I'm reminded that there is more to this than simply believing her or not. How I choose to handle this will have repercussions. Repercussions for all of us.

I want to dismiss everything Celia's claimed. It would be the easy thing, to cross the room and stand by the woman I love. But will that be the right decision? I'd have to explain why I think that Celia is lying. How far can I answer that without exposing the game? Without acknowledging my own part in it? And if I am able to save myself from blame, will Celia point the finger at me instead?

As Alayna defends herself, I realize a worse truth—she's broken her promise. She was seeing Celia behind my back. She's lied to me, and it's not the first time. She kept her past relationship with David a secret that I only just recently worked out. Then her ex who had saddled her with a restraining order, reentered her life, and she kept me in the dark there as well.

Now I find that she was seeing Celia covertly on top of all that—what does that mean for our relationship? Can I stand by her when she's so unwilling to stand by me?

Yes. I can. I will.

But can I so easily assume that Alayna has betrayed me? Perhaps she hasn't at all. Maybe all of Celia's claims are true, and I'm ignoring the bigger picture, the mental illness that resides in her. It isn't what I want to face, particularly when I'm aware that if she's fallen into old habits, it's my fault. Yet, if she has—I'll do anything to help her. Anything to keep her sane and with me. She has to know that I'm on her side.

So which is it? I'm with her no matter how she needs me, but which way is that?

Celia rests a hand on my arm, pulling me back to the present conversation. "I told you that night, remember?"

What night are they talking about? I replay the last few seconds of conversation in my head. There was something about my mother's birthday. What had she told me that night?

Oh yes. Celia had said that Alayna had harassed her then. Had that been an early sign that I'd ignored?

I pull my arm away from her. "I don't need a reminder."

"He refused to believe me then too," Celia tells the room.

I hadn't refused. I'd chosen to believe the harassment was born of a different cause. Is this twisting of the truth evidence that Celia's fabricated it all?

"He's blinded by the sex. It's not real." My mother's snips don't faze me. She's irrelevant in this situation.

Alayna though…

"She told you I harassed her?"

I feel her try to meet my eyes, but I keep them pinned on the floor. She'll too easily be able to read me. She'll see the war I'm waging, and she'll misunderstand what I'm battling. She sees this as Celia versus her. She's waiting for me to choose sides. There's only one side—Alayna's. I just can't figure out the best way to fight for her.

"Why didn't you say anything to me, Hudson?" Her voice is pleading.

Why didn't you say anything to me? I ask silently. One thing I can say for sure—the two of us have to work on our communication. I've blamed myself for the gaps in our connection, assuming I've had the bulk of secrets between the two of us, but now I'm learning she has secrets too.

More accusations fly, more heated words. Celia brings up Paul. The fact that she knows about Alayna's recent interaction with her ex is another detail that baffles me. Does Celia know because she's been tailing her? Or because Alayna told her? And if the latter is the case, I'm again struck with the knowledge that Alayna left me in the dark while letting others in.

Honestly, if it's because she's sick again, it will feel like less of a betrayal.

I turn away, hoping to shut it all out while I work through the facts. But tempers in the room rise, and soon I find I'm unable to zone out the conversation any longer.

"Do you hear her, Hudson?" my mother says behind me. "She threatened Celia. In front of everyone." She isn't helping.

"Mother, stay out of this."

"Hudson, you have to get rid of her. She's dangerous. Celia tells me she has a record. Why on earth would you let her into your life when you knew these things about her?"

I won't hear this. "Shut up, Mother."

I spin around and brush past Celia and Sophia, stopping in the center of the room to finally meet Alayna's eyes. Though I'm torn and uncertain, there is one truth that does not waver—I am in love with Alayna Withers. I will do anything for her. She is my light, and I will fight like hell to keep her from my darkness. Whatever that takes.

I tell her this silently through my stare, and I feel her acknowledgment pass back to me. She knows. She has to know that I'm here for her.

I'm barely aware as my mother prattles on behind me. "It makes sense why she'd be obsessed with Celia. She knows you belong together, Hudson, and she's jealous. Celia was pregnant with your baby. She can't compete with that, no matter—"

"Aw, shut the fuck up, Sophia," my father cuts her off. "It wasn't even Hudson's baby. It was mine, you ignorant bitch."

And then all hell breaks loose. My rage, already bubbling just under the surface, ignites in a blaze. "Goddammit, Jack."

"It's my business to tell," he says, "and I'm tired of this lingering lie."

"It wasn't a lie we told for you." For as much as I've resented that I had to keep his secret, I guarded it wholly. There are too many people who will be hurt by this unveiling. My mother. Celia's parents. Alayna, because I never told her. It was a secret best kept to the grave.

Now the room swarms with the aftermath of this. Sophia's crushed. Celia's embarrassed. Jack's...relieved, it seems. I'm surprised to realize I don't care as much as I once would have. Everything in my world is dimmed next to the spotlight of my precious Alayna.

In the bustle, she slips away. I rush to follow her, not making the elevator before the doors close. I take the other elevator down and find her in the lobby.

"Alayna," I call after her. She waits for me, but when I reach her, I realize I don't know what to say. So I settle on, "Why did you leave?"

"Isn't it obvious? That was a madhouse, and I didn't want to be there anymore."

"Yes, that it was." There are words sitting at the tip of my tongue. So many of them. Which do I choose?

"I, um...why didn't you defend me up there?" she asks before I've decided how to respond. "Are you that mad about the David situation? It's me that's supposed to be mad at you, remember?"

Was it only this morning that I transferred David to my club in Atlantic City? It seems like a lifetime ago that I was worrying about her and him. I don't regret my decision to move him from The Sky Launch—that club belongs to Alayna—but I admit that I was underhanded in my dealing with it.

Now that feels benign in comparison to the malignancy that I'm about to inflict upon our relationship. But if we have any chance of working past our issues, I have to be sure we're both mentally able to handle the task.

"Wait—" She realizes it before I have to say it. "You believe her."

My jaw twitches. *I don't know.*

"Hudson?"

I put my hands on her upper arms. "I believe in you." They're the truest words I've ever spoken. "And whatever you need, I want to give it to you. If you need help—"

"Oh my god, I can't believe this." She backs away from me. "I can't fucking believe this."

I clench and unclench my fists as if it will somehow help me hold onto her. "Tell me that you didn't do it. Tell me you didn't call her. Tell me you didn't see her." If she tells me she didn't—I'll believe her.

But she doesn't.

It's confirmation that she's lied to me. I can't bear to think that she's done it willfully. She has to be acting out of her illness. It's the easiest thing to believe.

She shakes her head. "It's not how it looks, Hudson. I didn't stalk her or harass her or whatever she's claiming. Are you on her side or mine?"

"I'm on your side. Always, your side." How can she not know this by now? Everything I do, everything I say, it's always for her.

"Then you believe me?" Her eyes are soft, pleading.

It's not that simple.

I stick my hands in my pockets. If I don't hide them away, I'll pull her into me, and then I'm afraid I won't ask her the hard questions. "Did you call her?"

"Yes! I said I did upstairs!" She pulls her phone from her bra and shoves it toward me. "Here, you want to see? Take it! You'll see all the times I called her since that's what you seem to be concerned with."

I ignore her outstretched hand. "I don't want proof. I want to help you."

"I don't fucking need any help!" She throws the phone across the lobby. It shatters when it lands.

She stares at it while I stare at her. She's hurting. She feels like I've let her down.

But she let me down as well. *I'm* hurting too. I'm new to this pain, and I don't know how to deal with it. Her constant betrayals are wounds that I know I can learn to ignore, but I'm not sure how or if they'll ever completely heal.

She turns and runs. Out the front door.

I follow. "Alayna, come back here." I catch her by her wrist. "I'll cancel my trip. We'll find the best treatment—"

"I'm not sick." She yanks her arms from my grip. "Go to Japan, Hudson. I don't want to see you."

Jesus, Japan. I'm supposed to be leaving in a couple of hours. "I'm not going to Japan now." I'll cancel everything for her. There is *nothing* without her.

Still, she walks away. "Go to Japan," she calls back to me. "I don't want to see you for a while, if not ever. Got it? If you're at the penthouse when I get home, I'll find somewhere else to sleep, and I don't mean for just one night."

She keeps walking. I let her.

I watch after her for long minutes though. I chose wrong; I know that. I probably knew that as I was pushing treatment on her. She's not sick. She didn't do the things Celia accused her of. She was in her right mind when she went behind my back.

I have a new decision to make. I can either choose to let this pain weigh me down and ruin our relationship forever, or I can choose to make my own transgressions right.

The decision's easy. I won't lose Alayna. Before I can try to win her back, though, there is an obstacle that must be dealt with—Celia.

Crying and yelling meet me when I return to my apartment. Celia and my father are in a screaming match, my mother's sobbing. Or pretending to sob. There's no actual tears. Brian is studying the artwork on my walls, seemingly trying to be invisible.

I almost feel bad for the guy.

I don't feel bad for anyone else. In fact, they need to leave. "Thank you everyone for the chaos in my living room. It's time for all of you to go now."

Brian heads first toward the elevator, as if he'd been simply waiting for permission before he bolted.

I stop him. "Not you. I'd like you to stay, if you don't mind. Alayna has asked me not to be here when she returns, but I'd rather she isn't alone."

Brian's mouth opens, his eyes darting. "I suppose that would be fine."

"Where are you staying? The Waldorf?" I surprise him with my accurate guess, but he simply nods. "I'll arrange to have your things moved over here. The guest room is down the hall. Make yourself at home."

He nods and heads to where I've directed him, happy for the escape.

Celia's tried to sneak past me while I was speaking to Brian, but I catch her before the elevator arrives. "And I didn't mean you should leave. We have to talk."

Her eyes are red and tired. "Hudson, I'm not in the mood."

"Oh, let's not talk about mood." My delivery is even and cold. I'm actually surprised I have as much patience as I do for her. Inside, I'm boiling.

"Do you not realize what just happened here?" Her voice is low, but she's seething. "My parents are going to fucking kill me. They were never supposed to find out about me and Jack."

"It's called karma, Celia. You reap what you sow. And today you sowed a lot of bad karma. Would you care to explain?"

"I've done all my talking. I have to be somewhere now, so pardon me." She brushes past me into the waiting elevator.

She won't get away this easy. I step in after her. "I'll see you down."

Celia rubs at her temples. She's not happy about this, but she has little say.

"I'm coming too." My mother sticks her hand in just as the doors begin to close.

I may actually snarl when I say, "Take the next elevator."

But my mother isn't fazed. She slips in despite my command. "I'm not staying another minute here with that man."

That man is standing behind her, a surly expression on his face. "*I'll* take the next elevator."

I suppose expecting Jack and Sophia to travel down to the lobby together is a bit much at the moment. "Fine," I concede. I wait for the doors to close before adding, "Though I'm surprised you don't mind being with *this woman.*"

Celia throws me a glare.

My mother throws me a glare as well. "I know Jack. He's the one who's responsible. It wasn't her fault." She wraps an arm around Celia. "He took advantage of you, honey. I understand. He was the grown-up. You were the child."

Unfuckingbelievable.

Celia leans into my mother's embrace, putting on the full victim act. "Thank you, Sophia. That means more than you could know." She even dabs at her eyes, which, as far as I can tell, are dry.

"Jesus Christ," I mutter. They're more alike than I'd ever realized.

My mother scolds me as she affectionately pats Celia's arm. "I'm not happy with you either, Hudson. Covering for that cheating bastard—"

"I wasn't—" I don't finish the sentence. It's not worth it. She'll never understand. "Whatever. I'm not going through this with you, Mother. Work out your feelings about this on your own."

"I don't know why I expected sympathy." Her terse tone is well-practiced. "I forgot who I was dealing with."

I roll my eyes. "Like mother, like son."

"That's not how the saying goes."

Celia straightens and pats Sophia with the consolation I've denied her. "This must be so hard for you, Sophia."

As if she wasn't the exact cause of all the *hard*.

My mother takes the inch and yanks it a mile. "It is. It's devastating." She continues as the elevator doors open in the lobby and we step out. "God, it feels like so much of the last ten years have been a lie. The baby. The baby wasn't even mine at all."

This time it seems tears might actually be forming in her eyes. Somewhere deep inside, there's a piece of me that acknowledges this is a big loss for her. As unhealthy as it was to do so, she'd focused so much of her energy on her dead grandbaby. The child that would have continued her union with Jonathon Pierce. Today's revelation had to shake her to the core.

But frankly, at the moment, I don't give a fuck. "Save it for your shrink. I said I didn't want to hear it."

Meanwhile, Celia has tried to sneak away again. I trot after her, abandoning my mother. "Hey, hey, hey." I grab her by the arm and escort her across the lobby and out the front doors. "We aren't done. I'll see you to your car."

"I didn't drive."

"I'll wait with you until your driver shows up."

"I was planning on taking a cab."

"We'll cab together." I don't let her interject another excuse. "Celia, we're having a conversation whether you want to or not. And we're having it now, though you are welcome to choose our location."

Her shoulders fall as she surrenders to defeat. "Cab, then."

We hail a cab and slip in the back. I dive in the minute she's finished giving her address to the driver. "This scam of yours, Celia—it's not cute. It's not even clever. It ends now."

"I love how you immediately assume that anything I say is a scam. You can't ever give me the benefit of the doubt?"

"I did give you the benefit of the doubt. I believed you when you stood there and told me you were happy for me. That you would give up this experiment with Alayna. Blatant lies is your trick now?"

She stares away from me out the window and shrugs. "I changed my mind."

"And now you're changing your mind again. Alayna is not your subject. Your experiment is over."

Her head spins to face me. "Is there a threat buried in there? Let's not forget that I know things you don't want shared."

There's not a question of what she's referring to. Yesterday, I could have said the same about her. But the biggest secret I had over her has now been revealed. I have little to hold over her at the moment, though I plan to change that. And fast.

In the meantime, though, I'll have to gamble on her loyalty. Not to me—to the game. "You won't tell Alayna that I played her. You won't tell anyone. It's against the rules."

"You're concerned with the rules? The game is over for you. What do you care about the rules?"

Her nonchalant attitude incites me. "How dare you?"

"I beg your pardon?"

"You heard me. How the fuck dare you?" It's too much. All of it. Not only what she's done to Alayna, but the insinuation that the way I taught her meant less to me than it did to her. It was *my* way of life, for Christ's sake. How dare she act as though I had no respect for it? "I always adhered to our law. I did everything exactly as I said I would, even with Alayna. My only sin was to fall in love. And that was never against the rules."

"It was certainly implied."

I ignore her caustic remark and continue with my attack. "You're the one who's gone off plan. You've even changed the goal."

"I changed nothing. The goal was to make her break."

I pause, my head tilted toward her. "You mean the test was to see if she *would* break. There was no goal to *make* her." Studying her reaction, I realize that I'm wrong. Celia's goal *was* to make Alayna break. Not to simply watch what happened.

I'm baffled by this revelation. "When did our aim become to hurt people? We were scientists, not executioners. We weren't malicious. We didn't set out to hurt people."

She looks at me incredulously. "You're so fucking clueless, Hudson. We've been hurting and destroying people since the game began. You always pretended like that was just an unfortunate side effect, but even pursuing an experiment that might hurt someone is malicious. It's like performing harmful research on humans. Scientists don't do that as a rule. You know why? It's not just unethical; it's against the law."

Shaking her head, she faces forward. "I get it, Hudson, I do. You didn't want to face how fucking cruel you really are, so you told yourself what you had to in order to live with yourself."

She was wrong. I did know how fucking cruel I was. I knew I was an asshole. I knew that, before Alayna, I had no heart.

But I had been a man with no comprehension of what it felt like to experience real pain. I hadn't understood the damage I could do to people. Dr. Alberts had likened it to being a blind man asked to describe the color blue. While it didn't excuse all my actions, it did make them less willful.

"It's not the same at all." *We* weren't the same. All this time, I'd thought we were. "And the fact that you think so shows what a cruel bitch you really are."

She claps her hands together with mock enthusiasm. "We've resorted to name-calling now, have we? How fun!" Her expression grows sober. "You can't fucking be serious."

"I'm dead serious, Celia. You will end this. And us…" I pause, not because the words are hard to say, but because I want to make sure she hears their emphasis. "We're over too. I want you out of my life. Don't call me. Don't stop by. Do you understand?"

She sneers. For a woman so about grace and appearances, she can sure put on an ugly face. "It's not that easy to just cut me out of your life, Hudson. Our families—"

And there's a blessing about the recent disclosure of our baby lie. "I'm not so sure our families will be a problem after today. I'd bet our parents are not going to want to spend much time together from now on."

The reminder of her parents and the afternoon's revelation seems to shake her. She regroups quickly. "Well, we run in the same social circles."

"And you will steer away from me when we show up at the same event. Do I make myself clear?"

Her nostrils fume, her eyes calculating. But she concedes with one word, "Perfectly."

For good measure I add, "You do not want to make me your enemy."

"Funny, I thought you'd already made me yours."

That truth lingers in the air around us, irrefutable. She may mean I made her my enemy when I dropped out of the game with Alayna. Or when I left it three years ago and entered therapy. But I think instead it's more accurate that she became my foe that summer ten years ago—when I decided to break her heart.

I'd told her she was suffering from karma. Wasn't I as well?

We've arrived at her apartment building. The cab pulls over to the curb. "Farewell, Hudson. This is for good, I suppose. The taxi's on you."

She gets out of the car. I don't watch after her.

I instruct the driver to head back to The Bowery. There's just enough time to collect my luggage before heading to the airport for my trip to Japan. If it were only the Plexis deal at stake, I'd cancel. But there's something else now, something more important. It's time to act on the information that Warren Werner gave me about the vulnerabilities of his company, and that will begin with a source in Japan.

When I return, my energy will be thrown into repairing my relationship with Alayna. There's been serious damage done on both our parts, but we can move on, I think. I have to believe that. Because without her, there's no reason for anything else.

Though much is in turmoil about me, I feel oddly at peace as we return to my penthouse. Celia is gone from my life, and there's a freedom with that knowledge that I hadn't expected. Like a long-growing tumor has finally been removed. There will be a scar, I know. I'll rub at it and scratch at phantom aches. But it's gone, and, with Alayna, we can finally begin the process of healing.

— CHAPTER —
TWENTY

Before

"Why can't I just ditch tonight after the actual rehearsal? That's the important part, right?" Chandler had been trying for twenty straight minutes to get out of Mirabelle's wedding rehearsal dinner.

My mother tested the temperature of the curling iron, her mind clearly more on her task than on her son's complaints. "I don't understand why you're so eager to abandon us."

He's fifteen, I wanted to tell her. That was reason enough.

"Because it's boring!" He flung his hands out, exasperated.

"Chandler!" my mother warned, covering my sister's ears as if she might be offended by the word *boring*. As if blocking the sound after the fact could undo that it had been heard.

But *boring*...that I could agree with, even though I hadn't been fifteen for nine years. The entire family had spent the last week of August at Mabel Shores preparing for Mirabelle's wedding weekend. Five days of nothing but social interaction. I was close to going insane. At my sister's insistence, I'd agreed to not bring any work. It was a mistake. With my mind unoccupied on business, my thoughts returned again and again to my other addiction—the game.

Celia and I were between schemes at the moment—part of the reason I was so eager to concoct a new one. Every guest that walked through our house that week, every visitor, was a potential subject. *What could I learn from her?* I'd ask myself. *Or him? Or them?*

Somewhere I recognized that my obsession was getting out of hand. Our experiments had grown more and more complex, more intense, more frequent.

Often even my work hours were infiltrated with daydreaming about the next project, the next scam. The week away had made me realize just exactly how consumed I'd become. I felt like a junkie who hadn't scored in a while—jittery, agitated. On edge.

Needing something to occupy my time, I'd resorted to joining Mirabelle in my mother's room as Sophia made her presentable for the evening's rehearsal.

Chandler leaned against the doorframe. I could sense he was on the verge of giving up but not quite. "No one will miss me," he said quietly.

"I'll miss you." My mother didn't even try to make it sound like she meant it.

My brother and I exchanged a glance. I wasn't close to Chandler—eleven years of separation made it difficult, not to mention I wasn't the type to bond. But we were still family, and in that we shared the basest parts of our existence. We had the same parents, the same upbringing. We both knew that he could sneak away from the dinner and our mother would never notice.

Mirabelle knew this as well. Having remained quiet for the bulk of the conversation, she spun to face Chandler now. "*I'll* miss you! So for one night, Chandler, can you forget about your friends and stay? For me?"

There wasn't a person in the world who could say no to Mirabelle Amalie Pierce. The subject was dropped. Chandler left the room with a huff, but he'd stay for the night's extravaganza.

It occurred to me that Mirabelle could have simply asked him to stay from the very beginning and saved the entire debate. I supposed she'd been giving Sophia a chance to be the mother. It was amazing, really, that she continued to do so. I started to wonder what it would take for Mirabelle's faith to be broken and then caught myself. Those were the kind of thoughts that led to experiments. And no matter how desperate I was for a fix, I wouldn't play on Mirabelle. I couldn't.

I forced myself to concentrate on the scene at hand for distraction. Mirabelle sat at the vanity, my mother stood behind her, working on her hair. She was even, near as I could tell, sober. A memory flashed through my mind, or rather a collage of memories. Times that my sister and I had sat around my mother's feet as she primped in front of that same mirror. She'd sit there for ages, dolling herself up. I'd watch as she applied her rouge, plucked her eyebrows, straightened her hair, and every time, I'd think how beautiful my mother was.

Though it had been a frequent occurrence, I'd seemed to have forgotten. Those had been good moments. *There* had *been good times.*

The memory inserted a warmth to the present, like a light had been focused on us, brightening the ordinary moment into something meaningful.

"Good thing your hair only hits your shoulders. We'd never get ready in time otherwise." Even my mother's complaining seemed less dreary.

"I should have cut it. Then we wouldn't have to worry about this at all. I'm thinking I'll get a pixie as soon as the honeymoon's over. Thoughts?"

I bit back a smile. My mother hated short hair on girls.

"Are you trying to kill me?" But I noticed the hint of a smile on Sophia's lips as well. "I still don't know why you didn't hire someone to do your hair and makeup tonight."

Mirabelle shrugged. "I didn't think I'd need to get made up tonight. I'll have enough of that tomorrow."

I studied her in the mirror, and I saw her lie. She'd hoped for this—for Sophia to insist on making her up instead. She remembered those times too, and Mirabelle, forever romantic that she was, had hoped to recapture it. She'd succeeded.

Perhaps I owed my sister's optimism more credit.

"Thank you for being here, Hudson," Mirabelle said when she caught my eye with her reflection. "It means a lot that you can share this time with me."

Normally, I'd shrug her off. But the nostalgia made me strangely willing to chat. "I have to admit, this isn't my thing. Yet, I'm glad I'm here too." I hadn't realized it until just that moment. She didn't need to know that.

My mother took a strand of Mirabelle's hair and wove it around the curling wand, seemingly oblivious to our conversation as she concentrated on her work.

"I'm sure you have a spiel waiting on the tip of your tongue, though," Mirabelle said, touching up her lipstick. "How love is a myth and marriage the bane of all evil."

I chuckled at the accuracy of her statement. "Not to mention that you're barely old enough to drink. Quite young to be signing off your entire life."

Her face fell slightly. She'd wanted me to deny my disdain for the practice of romantic union, and I'd enforced it instead. Oh well. It was honest. What was I supposed to do? Lie?

So I wasn't the type to put on niceties. But I could find another way to be supportive. Mirabelle had always been a bit of a Pollyanna. She'd make the best of anything. Maybe marriage actually would work for her. "I trust you know what you're doing, Mirabelle. Don't mind me."

"I usually don't." Her grin was back, and I felt my shoulders relax. I hadn't even realized I'd been tense. "And I do know what I'm doing. Adam is the best thing for me. He makes me happy. I make him happy. You know. It's all a bunch of happy."

Blah, blah, blah. It was what all the lovebirds said. Then a bump in the road, and everything fell apart. Love was so easily manipulated. So easily redirected. How could it ever be real? How could anyone be willing to give up their life for something so unreliable?

How could Mirabelle?

She must have read my thoughts in my expression because she added, "I mean, I know it won't always be top of the world. There will be hard times. But none of that matters as long as we have each other."

"Excuse me while I roll my eyes."

"You won't know until you find it yourself, Hudson." She was the only one who ever spoke like I might find my own *one true love.* It was kind of charming, actually.

"But did you have to get married? Couldn't you shack up together for a while first?" Like, until the euphoria faded, and she realized the ridiculousness of the notion of happily ever after.

"Nope. I have to get married." She widened her eyes as she applied mascara to her lashes.

"Mirabelle!" So my mother was listening.

"Is there something you aren't telling me, little sister?"

Mirabelle laughed, pausing her makeup application. "I'm not pregnant, you ass. I'm in love. And yes, I still *have* to get married. Because when you love someone," she met my gaze in the mirror and said without a flicker in her confidence, "their world interests you more than your own. So much so that you disappear into them, and the only choice you have is to merge your life with theirs. Because otherwise, you cease to exist at all."

It was more mumbo jumbo. But it struck me—somewhere deep inside me, a place that I didn't recognize, reverberating in my bones and tingling through my nerve endings. So I let it sit and settle and didn't refute.

A few silent moments later, it was my mother who spoke. "I couldn't wait to marry your father. Did I ever tell you that?"

I froze, and I sensed Mirabelle did too. My mother never spoke about the past. Never anything pleasant, anyway. We'd grown up assuming that her marriage to our father was based on business. Jack's father's company had just gone under, but the Pierce name still held weight, and my father was an innovative thinker. The Walden family, on the other hand, had money and investments with no one to groom for takeover. Sophia Walden's union to Jack solved a lot of problems.

We'd never been led to believe that there was love involved.

"No, Mom, you haven't told us," Mirabelle said quietly, and I could feel her silently urging Sophia to go on.

"We were more in love than anyone should have the right to be. It scared my father, I think. When we announced our engagement, he nearly had a heart attack. 'How will he ever provide for you?' As if my trust fund didn't give me enough money to provide for myself."

Sophia didn't look up as she spoke, her focus pinned on a lock of hair that refused to lay the way she wanted it to. "But Daddy took Jack out for 'a talking to.' And when they came back, it was decided that we could get married as long as your father took over the Walden companies. It was a win-win as far as I was concerned. Our worlds were becoming entwined in every way possible."

I noted her use of the word *worlds* and realized that had been what had spurred her trip down memory lane. My mother had also moved her world to be with Jack Pierce. Or Jack had moved his world to be with her. Such a strange thing to try to comprehend. It was easier for me to imagine my parents having sex than to imagine them being in love.

"My father wanted Jack to take over as soon as we were married. Since I wanted a short engagement, Jack spent a lot of that time at the office with Dad. I didn't see him nearly as much as I would've liked. Our wedding day, though." She sighed softly. "It was the happiest day I could imagine. There Jack was, in his tux. So handsome. I kept wishing the ceremony would hurry and get finished so I could jump him."

"Mother!" Mirabelle feigned embarrassment. It was the sort of story she got off on. Even if it was coming from her parent.

"I was young once too." Sophia's face was bright, happier than I'd ever remembered seeing it.

"Then I hope you had a wonderful honeymoon."

My mother's wistful smile vanished at Mirabelle's words. "Well, it started out well. But Jack had to leave the day after we arrived in Bora Bora. Company problems. He was in charge now. You know. If a wife had to be left alone on her honeymoon, then that's what had to be done. The story of our lives after that."

Mirabelle dropped her gaze. If I had to guess, she was fighting back tears. She was an easy crier.

Interesting, though, was how my mother's words affected me. I'd always seen my mother encased in a hard shell of bitterness. Now, she seemed to shift in my view, and from this new vantage point, I saw something else surrounding her— something warm and tender. Approachable, even. A woman that she once was.

How fascinating would that study be? To examine where she came from to how she ended up. Maybe it was another scenario Celia and I could recreate. Another game we could try to play.

God, always the game…

My mother set the iron down. "But the wedding day was beautiful. And yours will be too." She combed her fingers through the last curls she'd made then took Mirabelle by the shoulders. "Look at yourself. You're just lovely."

Mirabelle did as she was told. She smiled at her reflection, apparently pleased with her appearance. Or she was pleased with the experience. She reached up and patted one of Sophia's hands. "Thank you, Mom. For everything."

For the smallest space of time, while I watched as this mother and daughter shared a seemingly ordinary moment that was anything but ordinary, I sensed that there was something to life that I was missing. A color adjustment, perhaps. A flavor that I simply hadn't been introduced to. A sound that hadn't found its way to my ears. Something…*more*.

But that was mumbo jumbo too. If I needed proof, I only had to look back on the results of my experiments. How I lived—emotionless and free—that was all there was that was real. There was nothing *more*.

I discovered that evening that rehearsals were as draining as actual weddings. Though I'd attended a few out of obligation, I'd never been involved in them as Mirabelle had involved me. She'd convinced Adam to make me the best man. I was in the damn wedding party. It was the most hypocritical situation I could imagine myself in. All night I was asked, "Aren't you so happy for Mira? Doesn't she make a lovely bride?"

As happy as I can be and *she's lovely all the time* could only be said so many times before responding grew wearying. In between the fake conversations and polite smiles, I imagined the schemes I could work. That one in the too-tight skirt—would she still be drooling over the dick who'd brought her if I convinced her the best man was into her? The waiter who kept flirting with Adam's sister—would he cheat on his wife (he clearly wore a wedding ring) if she returned the attention? I knew I could get Mirabelle's bridesmaid to slip away with me—we'd fucked occasionally in the past—but could I arrange for her fiancé to catch us?

It was maddening how many times I had to remind myself that Mirabelle's wedding was off limits for my experiments. So many times, in fact, that I stopped listening to myself. And when the bridesmaid in question took a seat next to me, the tug to attempt my play was too strong, the buzz overwhelming all reasonable thought.

I placed my hand on the back of her chair and leaned in. "You wouldn't have chosen that seat, Melissa, if you didn't mean to get something from me."

She twirled a ringlet of hair around her finger and sat forward so I could easily peer down her dress. "And what exactly would I want from you, Hudson?"

"From the way you're shoving your chest at me, I'd say you want me to fuck your tits in the pool house." Under the table, I slid my hand up her skirt. "But don't worry. I'd give your cunt proper attention as well."

Her breathing picked up, and her eyes dilated. "I'll go out first. Wait five minutes to follow."

Perfect. "Be naked when I get there."

I waited until she was out of sight before I tracked down Timothy, her fiancé. He was an intern in a law firm that would fall all over themselves to get Pierce Industries business. "Timothy, I have some off-the-record legal I might want some help with," I told him. "Would you mind meeting me in the pool house in fifteen minutes?" An image of Melissa pushing her porn-size tits together while my cock thrust between flashed in my head, and I amended my request. "Make that twenty minutes."

He agreed. Of course. And I was off for a night of what I loved best—scheming and sexing. My dick stiffened as I snuck away from the stage where dinner was soon to be served. I'd barely made it five feet, however, before a familiar voice called to me.

"Hudson?"

I spun right around at the sound of Mirabelle's voice. "Uh, yeah?" Even though she couldn't have any idea what I was up to, I felt guilty all the same. Thankfully, it was dark enough here that she couldn't see the bulge in my pants.

She stood just at the edge of the stage. "Where are you going?"

"Just stepping away for a bit of a breather."

"The fuck you are."

If I didn't catch that she was angry from her swearing—Mirabelle rarely said anything coarser than asshole—then I'd surely be able to tell from the bright fury sparking from her eyes. "I'm not sure what you're talking about."

"Like hell you don't. I've been watching you. I saw you talking to Melissa. And I know you've been with her before. Then she goes off, and you get all whispery with Tim? This is my wedding weekend, Hudson. I can't even look at you right now."

She knew, she had to. There was no other reason for her to be outraged. Honestly, attempting to play her friend was shitty on my part. But, like any addict, I continued to deny. "Mirabelle, I really don't have any idea what this is about."

"You know what? Fuck you." Her small frame shook as she crossed her arms in front of her. "Fuck you, and I don't want you here anymore right now. I want you to leave."

The pool house counted as leaving, right?

"But so help me God, if you fuck with my friends tonight or tomorrow or during any of my wedding stuff, I will never be able to forgive you."

"Seriously? I—"

"Yes, seriously!" Her voice cracked. "I don't want you here right now. Go."

I wanted to argue more, but what exactly could I say? She'd pegged me correctly. And it wasn't my intention to ruin Mirabelle's rehearsal. "Fine. I'll go."

She kept her eyes on me, so heading to the pool house now was out of the question. I pushed past her instead and snagged a bottle of Scotch from the bartender before storming toward the house. I didn't allow myself to think. Not until I got far enough away that I didn't do anything I'd regret.

Getting off the premises, however, proved problematic. The driveway was too packed to get my car out, so it looked like I was on foot. There was nowhere for me to go if I went toward the highway. So taking a path on the side of the house opposite from the party, I crept down to the gazebo at the edge of our land. Though it had a nice view over the ocean, it was rarely used. Too far from the convenience of household help, I supposed. Mirabelle and I had used it a lot growing up though. It had made a nice escape when Sophia grew too difficult— or drunk—to tolerate.

It seemed fitting that I ended up there.

The stairs creaked as I climbed in the rotunda. I settled on the wood bench and undid my tie. The breeze came in and out like the waves of the ocean below. I nursed my Scotch and let the shit settle in my mind.

God, Melissa with her double G's and tight pussy. Right about now, she was probably pissed and about ready to throw her clothes back on. Then Timothy would show up. They'd likely think I set it up that way, for them to find each other and fuck each other's brains out. I'd never thought I'd be jealous of that prick of a guy.

But disappointment and irritation at the forced end of my fun didn't last long. Their disappearance left space for a heavier emotion—shame. I felt certain that Mirabelle wasn't aware of the extent of my games, that she thought she'd just caught me fucking around with an engaged woman. It wasn't really the biggest of deals. Except I'd let her down. I'd hurt her. That realization was not one I wanted to dwell on. It was too raw, too uncomfortable. Like an ice-cold wind slicing across my skin, stinging and chafing.

I let the Scotch burn through the chill and searched for something else to occupy my mind. Soon I found my thoughts returning to the disclosure from my mother earlier. It was strange to think about what her life had been like once before. That she'd been a happier woman. That she'd believed in her future with my father. Was it so simple to say that her entire life had been ruined because her father had wanted her betrothed to prove himself? That, in turn, Jack—out of love for his new bride—threw himself into doing just that? That the time apart the work caused led to the estranged relationship, the drinking, the cheating?

And if events had been different, if they'd managed to find the balance in their worlds and maintained a healthier relationship, would I have still been the way I was?

It was pointless to dwell on it. There would never be an answer.

Likely, my parents would still have been fucked up even if he'd stayed for the whole honeymoon. And I would still be exactly like I was. Why was I complaining, anyway? It was my superpower, wasn't it? Not feeling.

Lately, though, it didn't seem like a superpower. It was more like a distraction. A constant whirring in my head that begged for explanation. Pushed me to examine and study and scheme. Drove me crazy. Or was I already crazy to begin with?

Wasn't that the question of the century?

"Hudson?" Mirabelle's soft call startled me out of my spiraling speculation. I didn't answer, but she continued toward me anyway, climbing up the stairs and then leaning against the arch of the entry. "Here you are."

"Here I am." Though her demeanor was calmer than it had been, I wasn't happy to have been found. It surely meant there'd be *talking*. Fuck, how I hated that. I couldn't exactly send her away though. And it had been my actions that led to this. Consequences.

The light was out in the gazebo, and Mirabelle blocked the moon behind her, so I couldn't make out the expression on her face. Was she still mad? Hurt? Or did she come to apologize?

Finally, she tucked a stray curl behind her ear and said, "Mother's drunk."

Huh. Not even focused on me, then. "Are you surprised?"

"No. I was hopeful, though. She'd had a good day." Her tone was melancholy, and I knew if I could see her eyes, they'd be sad.

I didn't understand sad. But I didn't like it when Mirabelle was. I tried to be consoling. "Parties are the easiest time for her to drink without anyone noticing. Everyone's drinking."

"True."

She stepped forward and sat on the bench next to me. That meant she was staying. It didn't leave much chance of escaping more reprimand from the earlier incident.

"You should be with your guests." I took a sip from the bottle of Scotch and tried to appear nonchalant about my suggestion to leave.

She wasn't biting. "You're my guest."

"You have more important guests than me."

"I don't think so." She mirrored my posture, looking out over the ocean. "Besides, we need to talk."

I pretended not to know what topic she thought should be discussed. "If you need last-minute marriage advice, you know what I'll say—don't get married."

"You're an ass. And no. I'd never come to you for marriage advice. You'll come to me, though. I'm calling that now." She swung her foot in a rhythmic sway that seemed in time with the ocean waves.

"Uh-huh." The hell I was ever getting married. Though marriage seemed more likely than falling in love. Telling that to Mirabelle would be another impossible conversation. Really, any way I looked at it, there was an uncomfortable discussion about to take place.

I decided to dive in and get it over with. "Look, we don't need to talk about earlier. Lapse in judgment. That's all."

It was so quiet I could hear her swallow. "No. We don't need to talk about earlier," she agreed quietly, much to my surprise. "But there's something else."

Well, that had been easy. With her soft disposition and her somber mood, I had a pretty good guess at what she wanted to say instead. The typical, *I love you, you're a good brother even though you tried to drown me when I was seven and screw my bridesmaid at my wedding rehearsal,* all the bullshit things that sweet, naïve sisters say to their siblings on the eve of superficially important occasions like their weddings.

But she stunned me again. "Hudson, I need to talk to you about an intervention."

Really? Tonight? I'd wondered how long before someone tried to sober up our mother. I did not think it would happen in the middle of my sister's wedding. "Shouldn't Chandler and Dad be here? They have just as much effect on our mother as I ever would. If not more."

"Not for Mother." She stopped the swing of her feet. "For you."

I laughed. "This probably seems unconvincing when I'm drinking straight from the bottle, but I'm not an alcoholic." Sure, that was what all alcoholics said. Still, I'd never gotten drunk or sloppy. It was hardly believable that Mirabelle really thought I had a problem. I laughed again. Seriously? "Besides, aren't there supposed to be lots of people at these things?"

"Well, they're supposed to be formed of a group of people that the addict— that's you—loves and will listen to. I happen to think that I'm the only one who could possibly say anything that matters. At least, I'm hoping that I can say anything that matters." She was so solemn, so intense.

I sighed and tried to address her with equal earnestness. "I don't have a drinking problem, Mirabelle."

She chuckled politely. "I don't think you have a drinking problem, Hudson. Get real." Her somberness returned. "But I do think you have a problem. A very different kind of problem."

My heart skipped a beat, my mind immediately jumping to the game. There was nothing else that I did, nothing else that I had in my life. But how could she even know about that? There were occasions that my experiments had come back home. Tonight, for example.The result of a few bad choices on my part. Perhaps that's what she meant?

I played ignorant. I *was* ignorant. "I don't know what you're talking about." I took another swallow of my Scotch. It didn't calm me the way that I'd hoped.

"Let's not dance around it, Hudson. I don't know the word for it anyway. There might not even be one. But I'm aware. I see it. I see what you do to people. How you...*handle* them. Like earlier tonight, but this is hardly the first time. Or the fifth. Or even the fiftieth, I'd bet. It's cruel behavior. It's destructive. And I don't just mean to the people you do it to. But to you. It's destroying you."

They were the only words I had, so I repeated them. "I don't know what you're talking about." My voice was weaker than before, though. I had zero conviction.

"You do know. And you don't have to say anything. I don't need to hear excuses or details. What I need is for you to hear me." She fell down on her knees in front of me and grasped my empty hand between both of hers. "Hear me, Hudson. You are not who you think you are. There is more in you than you suspect. More to you than the mind games that I think absorb your life. I see it. I *feel* it. And not because I'm a hopeless optimist, but because this other part of you is very, very real."

I started to pull my hand away, a jerk reaction, but she held it steady. "Don't. I won't let you break away from me, Hudson. You can't. I'm invested in you, even if you aren't invested in yourself. And I'm about to start a new life. One that might possibly push me further away from you, and here's the thing—I can't go if I don't know you're okay. I can't move my world from yours until I know you aren't going to destroy your own."

My throat tightened. It felt like I should say something, but there weren't words. And inside, where I usually felt empty, my chest burned. Uncomfortable, like indigestion, but even more constrictive. Like something was stirring around in there, stealing the space to breathe, about to explode out of me.

Mirabelle dug her fingers into my skin, her nails pleading as much as her words. "So will you do it? Tell me you'll do it. Tell me you'll quit. Tell me that you're going to try. For me, if for no one else. Please, tell me."

I could tell her to fuck off. I could tell her whatever she wanted to hear just to get her off my back. I could try to explain to her what the game really was, so that she could understand that it wasn't actually a problem.

But the truth was that it was a problem. The experiments had become an obsession. I lived and breathed for them. And none of them, not a single one, ever taught me what I really wanted to know, which was why the hell I felt so goddamned empty.

So I said the only word I could. "Okay."

"You mean that?"

I nodded, speech not easy through my clenched throat.

Her face crumpled, tears forming at the corners of her eyes as she bit her lip. She nodded a few times. Finally, in a choked voice, she said, "Thank you."

She crawled up into my lap then, her legs to one side, and hugged me, like she used to when we were younger.

I let her.

I even hugged her back. Reluctantly at first, and then with a bear-tight grip.

"Thank you," she said when she finally broke away. She scrambled off my lap to the bench beside me. She dabbed again at her eyes. "I'm sorry. I didn't want to cry. I figured you'd take me more seriously if I remained together. But, that's not me, I guess. Anyway. You have an appointment tomorrow."

"An appointment tomorrow? With who?"

"A psychiatrist. Dr. Alberts. He's an expert in experiential avoidance and a bunch of other big words that basically mean 'aloof.'"

Other big words like *sociopath*?

"He's situated in the city," she continued, "but he makes house calls, and he agreed to come out here to meet you at ten. I arranged it before tonight even happened, Hudson. So don't think I'm just reacting to this one incident."

That she'd had this planned all along left a sour taste in my mouth. I hated that she'd formed an opinion about me, and then I'd proven her right. It was almost as though she'd played her own game, formed her own hypothesis, and she'd guessed correctly. Having the tables turned wasn't my idea of a good time.

Besides that, I'd agreed to being intervened, so to say, but I'd thought it would be on my own terms. I could decide the course of my treatment. Not her. I used the obvious for my protest, "It's your wedding day."

"And this is my wedding present. From you." She was even giddy about it.

"My wedding present was to not work all week." But I already knew I'd meet with her specialist.

"This is another wedding present. You got me two." She swiftly pecked my cheek. "Thanks, big bro." And *I* was the master manipulator.

"What have you done to me, Mirabelle?"

"Good things, Hudson. I've done good things. Just wait and see." She stared at my profile for several seconds. I felt her gaze like it was her hands that touched my skin. When she seemed satisfied with what she saw, she said, "But I'm going to go back to the party now and let you stay here and mope or mull or whatever really boring antisocial thing it is you like to do. Brood. That's what you do."

"I don't brood."

"Well, whatever you do, I'll leave you to it now." She stood, her skirt swirling in the light breeze. At the stairs, she looked back. "Ten tomorrow morning. In the study. Dr. Alberts is coming. Be there."

"Where else would I be? Organizing the flowers with Mother?"

"Good point." She gave me another bright smile, this time adding a wink. "I love you, brother. Thanks for making my wedding everything I ever dreamed."

There it was. The typical words for the occasion. It made me smile a bit as well.

She blew me a kiss then skipped off into the night.

I sat on that bench for a long time after. I sipped my Scotch. And I cried. Sobbed for the first time that I could remember. There was no feeling behind the tears, just release. It was cathartic. It was a start.

Maybe it was even the beginning of the road to more.

TWENTY-ONE

After

I wake to an empty bed. I should be used to it by now, having woken up the last several days alone. Each of those nights had been restless, sleep hard to come by without the warmth of the woman I've come accustomed to wrapping around in slumber.

Except I came home from Japan earlier tonight and reunited with Alayna, so my bed should *not* be empty. I'm so in tune with her that, despite several days apart, her absence can be felt even in my sleep.

I find her in the bathroom, staring in the mirror, her face pale and eyes wide. "What's wrong?"

She jumps slightly at my voice, then peers over her shoulder at me. I don't miss that she scans my naked body. My dick thickens a bit at her eyes, yet I ignore it, crossing to her. "Are you okay?"

There's a moment of hesitancy before she says, "I just had a bad dream, and now I can't sleep."

Her reluctance to say more worries me. It's only a dream, but after everything we've just been through, we have to be more open with each other. I need her to share this with me, if for no other reason than to feel like we are making progress.

I prod her gently. "Want to talk about it?"

She shakes her head then says, "Yes. But later."

That, I can live with. Meanwhile, I start her a bath and agree without pause when she invites me to join her.

A few minutes later, we're settled in a warm tub, Alayna sitting between my legs, her back to my chest. I hold her and think for the first time in my life that I understand happiness. It's a truly different feeling than being sexually sated. We are naked, and I'm definitely aroused. I'll have to be inside her before our bath is over. I'll need to lick the wet drops of water from her breasts, need to fill her tight pussy with my cock. But it's not a requirement. Touching her, holding her, being in her world—that's where this peaceful bliss originates.

Also, we talk. We connect with words. It's a strange thing for both of us to communicate openly, without fear of judgment, without regret. It will take getting used to, but we begin to try. I'm profoundly excited about this new start.

I even begin to forget about the one secret that I've held from her. I've worried whether I should tell her, then I've worried she'd find out. Now the worry starts to fade. Perhaps it's not that big of an issue. I can keep it buried, and, as I learn to live with it, I can maybe stop letting it affect the way I am with Alayna. Possibly I could tell her how I really feel. Tell her that I love her without the guilt preventing the words.

But then Alayna asks a very unexpected question. "What happened between you and Stacy?"

"Stacy?" It takes me a minute to figure out who Stacy is. Then I realize she means the girl who works with Mirabelle at her boutique. "Nothing happened." I'm baffled she'd think there was anything between us. "What do you mean? Like did I date her? I took her to a charity event a year or so ago. But after that, nothing. And I didn't sleep with her."

Alayna doesn't seem to be comforted. "Is there a reason she'd have a vendetta against you? Or reason to distrust you?"

I shake my head. "Not that I can think of."

Except that's not true, because suddenly I can think of a very valid reason why she wouldn't trust me. Celia had played her. And when she did, she had used my persona for her scheme.

I should tell Alayna. There's no reason to keep it from her. It wasn't even me who played her. Well, that's not entirely true either. I'd *let* Celia use my persona. And, in the end, I'd participated. I told myself it was to put an end to the scam, but I had enjoyed the rush of the game, just as Dr. Alberts had led me to realize.

Whatever the reason—the guilt of my participation, the newness of being so open—I'm not ready to share it with Alayna. Not yet. Not until I understand the reason for her interest. "Why are you asking?"

She takes a deep breath. "The last time we were at Mira's, Stacy told me that she had some sort of video. A video that proved something or other about you and

Celia. She didn't have it with her, so I gave her my phone number so she could contact me later."

And just like that, the peaceful place I'd discovered is disturbed. What the fuck video could Stacy have? Something from that night? Something after? Did Stacy know about our plot with Alayna? There was no way she could, but if Celia had given her something…recorded a conversation or something…

These were paranoid thoughts. Liars and schemers learn that's the only way to stay a step ahead of discovery. I'd believed I was past this. I'm disappointed to find that I'm not.

I stall the conversation as much as I can as I try to get my balance. Then she asks point blank, "Do you know what she's talking about?"

"No idea." And I don't. Not really. "She didn't tell you what the video was of?"

"No. Just that she had it, and that it would show me why I couldn't trust you. And she texted me again tonight. Or sometime this past week when I didn't have a phone, and I didn't get the message until tonight."

Though the water is still warm, the hairs on my arms stand straight up, as if I'd been thrown into ice. It's possible that Stacy has proof of something in the past which Alayna is already aware of. But what if it's something else? "What did her text say?"

"That the video was too big to send over the phone but to contact her if I wanted to see it."

I'm frightened. I would never say that aloud, but I can admit that to myself. I'm scared that I will lose Alayna. I don't know how to deal with that fear. I'm not one who cowers.

What I do know is that Alayna can't see that video. Not until I do. It's with self-loathing that I resort to my greatest skill—manipulation. "Do you want to see it?"

There's no way I'll let her see it first. Letting her believe I'm indifferent will take away her need to pursue it.

"No." She hesitates. "Yes." Then, "I don't know. Should I?"

She's conflicted. It's right where I want her. Now to push her to the answer I want her to choose but gently. Too forceful, and she'll see right through me.

"Well." I rub my hands up and down her arms, taking advantage of the distraction our intense physical connection provides. "You know that Celia can't be trusted already. And there is nothing that Stacy could have on me that you don't already know. You know more about my secrets and my past than anyone. You know me, Alayna."

"I do."

"Then unless you don't trust me..." The words taste so sour in my mouth. Yet I chew through them.

"I do trust you. If you say there's nothing I should be concerned about..."

Direct eye contact is the best way to sell a lie. "There isn't."

It may be the worst thing I've ever done, misleading her like this. Worse than my actual participation in the game. Because then I didn't know her. Now I'm doing this to someone I love.

I hold my breath as she makes her decision. Though I'm sickened by my betrayal, I'm desperate for her to choose as I wish.

After what seems like a lifetime, she smiles and says, "Then I don't need to see it."

A mix of emotions overcomes me. Relief is the most prominent, but there's also a heady rush. Not from the successful conning but because Alayna has just given me her trust. It's delusional to think that I deserve it. But oh, how I want it. It's a gift I can't ever begin to repay.

I vow that I will try. Whatever it takes, I will work to finally earn it.

I lean forward and kiss her chin. "Thank you."

"For what, exactly?"

There's no way to explain my true gratitude. I make it simple. "For being open with me. You didn't have to tell me about that, and you did anyway."

"I'm serious about being more open and honest."

"I see that. I'm serious about it too. The only way we can move on is to decide that we're committed to each other first and foremost." These words are more than my attempt to erase the lie I've just told. They're the beginning of the most important promise I plan to ever make. It's because I'm so devoted to her that I've hidden what I have. It's for her. It's for *us*. "Are we?"

"I am."

It's only two words, but they're musical. When I marry her—and I will, one day—that vow of forever will only be a repeat of this moment right here, right now. "So am I."

I make love to her. I need her like this, need to blot out the horrible thing I just did with the beautiful thing that we are together. I pretend that the weight of my love for her can drown out the buzzing of the lies.

My hands and mouth take over her body, a body I know by heart. Quickly, I send her toward orgasm. It's selfish, really. I need to be inside her. Need her ready. She intervenes, though, deciding to stall her release. Straddling me, she lowers herself down my cock, moaning as I take rest inside her.

God, she's so fucking tight. She feels so incredible. Every time, it's a surprise. Every time, I have to gather myself so I don't come too soon. She rides me slowly but with force. It's hot—her tits bouncing, her forehead creased with exertion, the breathy moans of pleasure that slip out of her mouth with each slide down. So mother-fucking sexy.

But this won't get her off. She needs me to thrust. My girl likes it hard. I wrap my hands around her ass and hold her still so I can drive into her the way she needs.

"Do you always have to take over?" She's not complaining.

I smile slightly. "If you want us both to come, then yes."

She laughs and it causes her pussy to tighten. I twitch inside her. I'm close. She's close.

"And who is it that wouldn't come if I stayed in control?"

Does she even have to ask? "You."

I push deeper into her, angling toward the spot that always seems to send her over. It works. Instantly she's gasping and digging into my skin as she soars through her orgasm. In this position, I can see her face clearly. She's completely transparent in this moment. I see everything in her expression—her love, her trust, her ecstasy. It's beautiful.

God, what I'd give to deserve her.

I finish after her. Then I kiss her along her neck and jaw and lips. When I pull away, she has tears streaming down her face. "Alayna. What is it, precious?"

But she doesn't answer, and soon, her tears are sobs.

She pushes me away and fumbles out of the tub. I'm right behind her. I grab a towel and wrap it around her. "Alayna, talk to me."

Again, she runs from me.

I'm baffled and worried. I have no idea what is bothering her. Did I hurt her? Was there something I said? Always, I wonder, does she know somehow?

Worst is that she's running. When we just said we were committed to each other. When we just vowed we wouldn't do that anymore. Did I expect too much from her too soon?

If so, she has to tell me. I follow after—I'll always follow after her—and spin her toward me. "Talk to me. What is it?"

Her breaths are deep, her entire body shuddering with her sobs. "You. Really. Hurt me." Her words are broken, but I understand them.

"Just now?"

"No." She tries to calm herself enough to talk. "You really hurt me. With Celia. When you believed her. Instead of me."

There's a weight on my chest, crushing against my heart, making it hard to breathe. "Oh, Alayna." I pull her to me. That I am the cause of such deep pain— it wrecks me. I wish that I could take it all from her. "Tell me. Tell me all of it. I need to hear it."

She tells me. All of it, in short, broken sentences. Each word another knife through my own skin. "It hurts, Hudson. It hurts so much. Even though you're here. Now. And we're together. There's a hole. A deep, deep hole."

I can't say what I want to say, the magic phrase that will take it all away. So I tell her what I can. "I'm sorry. I'm so sorry. If I could take it back, if I could change how I reacted...I would have chosen differently."

"I know. I do. But you didn't choose differently. And you *can't* take that back." She straightens in my arms. "You can never take that back."

"No. I can't." For all the things I've accomplished in my life, they will never outweigh the burden of this one failure.

"And that changes things. It changes me."

I'm afraid to ask, but I do. "How?"

"It makes me vulnerable. Exposed. And you know now. That you can hurt me. You can hurt me real bad."

"Alayna." I pull her back to me. "My precious girl. I never want to hurt you again. Will you ever be able to...forgive me?" My voice is thick and unrecognizable, and I realize that I'm also on the verge of a breakdown. If this has the power to hurt her so much, what would my other secret do?

If I'd ever wondered if our love could survive my deceit, I know the answer now. It will not. She will not.

Maybe Celia had the experiment pegged right all along. Alayna could be broken.

I rock her in my arms, kissing her, apologies on my tongue. Eventually, I carry her to the bed where she finishes her tears wrapped in my arms.

While she cries, I think how there was a brief space of time there where the whirring had stopped, where my mind was quiet and my skin didn't itch with regrets. I'd cut Celia from my life, and though I expected that she wasn't finished with me quite yet, I'd begun the work to ensure that she was. In Japan, I'd met with GlamPlay and convinced them to purchase shares in Werner Media. I'd even got back Plexis.

Then I'd returned home to fight for Alayna.

And I'd won.

We'd won, I thought. Our demons hadn't come between us. We were still together. Still in love.

Then in the course of an hour, I'd realized that not only would my lie always be on the verge of discovery, but how important it was to keep that secret buried. While I'd always expected, now I knew. The truth would destroy us.

When she's calm, we talk, we start to mend. We move on.

We'll be fine, I know that. I'm not worried that we can't recover from the mistakes we've made. The ones in the open, anyway. And I vow yet again to never let her know the truth of how she came into my world. It's this battle that may kill me, but better me than her.

After the words are said and our hurts confessed, I make my promises again to her, silently, with my lips. I kiss her, I cherish her. From her head to her toes, I leave no space untouched. My mouth adores each square inch of her skin, each freckle, each finger, each toe.

I lavish her in love that I can't speak. I claim her body, her life, as mine.

———

I tap the side of my cheek with my pen in rapid tempo, deep in thought. Has it really only been five days since I returned from Japan? It seems like a lifetime has happened in this week.

"If you purchase GlamPlay under any of your American subsidiaries though, the press is going to get a hold of that information, and it won't be covert like you want. Hudson, are you even listening?"

I halt my pen mid-tap and throw my gaze to Norma Anders. She's frustrated with me. With this project. I'm frustrated too. But whatever it takes, we have to make this purchase happen. "I heard you. So we need to find a more indirect way to buy GlamPlay."

I work my jaw as I try to come up with a solution to our problem, but my brain isn't working. Running a hand across my face, I let out an exasperated sigh. "Fuck. I don't know. Do you have a suggestion?"

"I'm not sure." She shakes her head as she thinks. "Actually…what if we use Walden Inc. to purchase GlamPlay? Pierce Industries still holds controlling interest there, right?"

When my father took over Walden Inc. for my mother's family, he left a small portion of the company outside the Pierce Corporation. As a safety net, he'd said. Over the years, Pierce Industries had ended up being the lifeline for Walden Inc., purchasing shares and investing when the small financial company needed it. Now it holds its own, though Pierce Industries does own the majority of the stock. Norma's idea is a good one. As long as Walden has enough liquid funds to pay the price—and I'm certain they do—it would be a way to move under the radar.

Walden Inc., though, is the one company that my father still actively runs. Any such purchase will have to go through him.

I'd prefer not to involve Jack. But if I have to…"It's our only shot, isn't it?"

"The only one I can think of. Will you have trouble convincing your father?"

Considering how Jack feels about Celia, I'm sure that won't be a problem. "No. He'll do it." I push the intercom to my secretary. My meeting with Norma was early, but it's gone long enough that Patricia should be in by now.

"Yes, Mr. Pierce?"

"I need my father on the line in about fifteen minutes, please."

"Yes, sir."

"Okay then," I say to Norma. "Anything else?"

Norma scratches a note on her legal pad then looks up. "Not that I can think of. If all this goes well, we will need to be in L.A. next week for the final signatures. And no, I can't do this for you. You'll have to be present."

"Great. Thank you."

She stuffs her pad in her briefcase and sits forward as if she's about to stand. But she pauses. "Hudson, are you all right?"

I don't have to guess why she's asking. I've been grumpy and distracted for the past few days. The sources of my stress can be broken down into two things—or people, to be precise: Celia and Stacy.

The former has begun stalking Alayna. I'm sure it's simply a scare tactic—that Celia won't do anything to physically harm my girlfriend—but I won't take any chances. This deal with GlamPlay should end any interaction with Celia at all. Now if we can just survive until the deals are signed.

Stacy, on the other hand, is still an unknown quantity. The video she's sent me…

"Hudson," Norma prods. I've left her waiting too long for my answer.

"I'm fine. I just have a lot on my mind." Understatement of the year.

I stand, hoping that will prompt her to as well. I have other business to take care of, starting with a heart-to-heart with my father. "Thank you for meeting with me early. I appreciate all your work on this project."

She stands and nods at me. "Of course."

"I don't need to remind you that this all must remain confidential?" Keeping this purchase secret is vital. I haven't even told Alayna about these plans. I wouldn't want to get her hopes up, in case something falls through.

"Completely." Norma says. "Oh, by the way, I wanted to thank you for hiring Gwen."

Alayna had officially hired Norma's little sister at The Sky Launch only the night before. "I can't take any credit. Thank Alayna." I suddenly remember something Alayna had said about her new manager. "Norma, may I ask why Gwenyth was so eager to leave the Eighty-Eighth Floor? I thought she was happy there."

Norma sighs. "She was. Long story. Let's just say there was a man."

"Oh." I give a tight smile letting her know she needn't say more.

"But on that subject, Gwen would really like to not be found. Do you have any suggestions how we might make that happen?"

It was almost comforting to know I wasn't the only one with secrets. "We'll need to pay her under an alternate social security number. That's illegal." I pause to make sure she's with me. "But I could arrange it."

"I'd very much appreciate whatever you can do."

"No problem." There are few people who I'd ever make this sort of offer to. But Norma has been with me through thick and thin, and has navigated more than one not-so-legal deal in our time together. I trust her. I make a mental note to get Jordan on the task.

It's only a few minutes after Norma's left that Patricia has Jack on the line.

"Hudson. What a surprise. Is it my birthday?" His charm has never worked on me. Not since Celia, anyway.

I should just ignore his play, but for whatever reason, I don't. "Your birthday is in December. It's July seventh. So no."

He *tsks* through the line. "Always so serious. How on earth can you possibly be my son?"

"Come on. We know you're my father. The physical resemblance is irrefutable. The real question is: who else on earth is your son?" I have no idea why it feels so fucking good to be an ass to the man, but it does.

He chuckles. "So far only three are taking claim. And at least one of them would probably prefer not to." There have been rumors that Chandler isn't Jack's, but he's referring to me.

I think about that for a moment. Would I really prefer not to be Jonathon Pierce's son? It's a hard question to answer and not one that serves any purpose in dwelling on. I am his son, for good or for bad. With all that I've done to further his legacy and Pierce Industries, I'd like to say I've made the most of it. But now as I start to see the world differently through Alayna, maybe there's more I could gain from Jack. Something not measured in stocks and bonds.

Anyway, it's not for today. What I need from him now is much more tangible. "While I'd love to consider the pros and cons of being a Pierce further, I called for another reason." I hesitate. It's harder for me to ask than I would like. It's the only choice I have, so I plow on. "I need a favor."

"Ooh, that's intriguing." There's a creak in the background. I can picture him in my head, sitting back in his chair, his feet crossed on his desk in front of him. "Do tell me more."

Where in the world do I begin? There's no good place, so I just start talking. "It may not come as any surprise to you, but it has become necessary to remove Celia Werner from my life."

"No, really!" he gasps in mock astonishment. "Glad you've finally come around to see the light. That girl is fucked up."

It's strange that there is still a part of me that wants to defend Celia. Except for her most recent actions, she'd done nothing worse than I'd ever done. And, as always, I can blame the way she behaves on me.

Stranger is that my father, who I would never describe as intuitive, seems to guess at my feelings. "She's not like you, Hudson," he says. "I know that you think she is, but she's different. She wants to hurt people. You just want to understand them."

I'm stunned at his insight, but I try to hide the shock from my voice. "You're right. She's not like me." It's a big admission, and I could spend more time trying to evaluate how I feel about this. But it doesn't really matter. "Celia's been stalking Alayna."

"Fuck. Are you kidding me? Jesus." He curses some more, things I can't make out, then asks, "Is Laynie okay?"

I grit my teeth. "She is. A bit shaken, but I have a bodyguard on her. She's safe."

"Thank God." My father's always been fond of Alayna. It's bothersome. Is his attraction to her fatherly or something else? Even if he came right out and told me, I'd likely have a hard time believing it.

But it's because of his fondness for her, and because of his loathing for Celia, that I know he'll help with my plan. "Celia hasn't broken the law yet and talking to her has done no good. I need another way to convince her to stop her game."

"And I'm sure you have an idea already in the works. Hit me with it."

As succinctly as possible, I tell him how I've already convinced GlamPlay to buy into Werner Media, and how, if combined with the shares I already hold, it would be possible to own the majority stock in Warren's company. "If I purchase GlamPlay—"

"Then you'll be able to boot Warren out," my father finishes.

"Right. I don't want to actually take control of Werner Media, I just want to have the power to do so. And since I need it to be covert, I need to buy GlamPlay under a different entity."

"You want to use Walden Inc." My father catches on quickly. I shouldn't be surprised. He was the one who taught me. "Of course. Tell me what to do, and it's done."

I spend the better part of the next hour working out the plan with Jack. He's smarter than I remember, quick to solve problems that come up during the conversation. It's…nice, actually. A bit like coming home.

Before we finish, another idea strikes me. "Anyone using the cabin this weekend?"

"In the Poconos? Not me. Mira's the only one who goes up there really, and she's so busy with her opening, she's not going to want to leave town. Are you thinking about going up?"

"Yeah. I think I'll take Alayna." The stress of the past few weeks is taking its toll on me. On her too. We need some time alone.

"Good idea. Do you need a key? I can have mine couriered over."

I have one somewhere, but rather than try to search for it, I take him up on the offer. "Thanks. I'd appreciate it. And Dad," I pause, not sure how to say what else it is I want to say. Finally I settle on, "Thanks for everything else too."

After I hang up, I stare at the phone for several long minutes. After the years of tension and resentment between us, I wonder, did we just reconcile? God, is there nothing that Alayna won't have a finger on in my life? I'm not complaining.

With Celia shit handled for the moment, thoughts return to the other major weight on my mind—Stacy. I'd had Jordan find her contact information first thing on the day after I learned about the video. Then I emailed her. And called. When she didn't respond, I emailed and called again. Every day. My messages were, well, threatening. Finally, yesterday, she sent me the video.

Today, I'm still processing what to do with it.

I turn to my computer and open the file. I've watched it several times now, but I'm compelled to watch it again. It's both worse and better than I thought it might be. It's not exact footage of my conversations with Celia regarding Alayna, for instance. But what it does show is also damning if a person put together the pieces.

I try to see it the way Alayna would. First, she'd be hurt. It's me kissing Celia. I wouldn't want to watch her kiss another man, and if it were someone I knew she had a history with—David, for example—it would be so much worse. So there's one reason why she should never see the video.

After that, she'd want to know *why* I was kissing Celia. I'd always said I was never in a romantic relationship with her. I wasn't. I could say that I lied before, that Celia and I actually did have a fling. But I've never been a fan of lies, and that's what it would be. If I told her the truth, that I was helping Celia with a scam, then Alayna will think I was still playing then. Even if she understands that I truly wasn't, she won't miss that the video takes place outside the symposium where I first saw her. She'll know Celia was with me that night.

How far of a leap would it be for her to go from Celia and me at the symposium to Celia and me playing a game with her?

Again, it's paranoid. But *I* would leap to that conclusion. I'm more analytical, sure. Still, Alayna's smart. I wouldn't put it past her. And that's just a risk I can't take.

Alayna can never see this video. Whatever I have to do, I'll have to convince Stacy to get rid of it. It has to be destroyed.

— CHAPTER —

TWENTY-TWO

T he bar at Lester's is much different than the type I usually frequent. There's a pool table and darts in the back corner. The patrons wear jeans. I'm the only one in a suit, let alone a suit that probably costs the entire amount that the register will take in tonight. The music blares from an old jukebox—hits from the nineties that seem familiar. I'd prefer a live band. Jazz or a piano player would be nice. But I'm not here for the ambiance. Lester's fulfills the two requirements I have at the moment—they have a good bottle of Scotch, and it's only half a block away from the loft. I'll be drunk when I leave here. Hopefully, the short distance will ensure that I pass out on my own property.

I shake my head at myself. Me, turning to liquor for comfort. It's quite comical. To think that only yesterday I was curled up with Alayna in the mountains, making love under the stars, flirting with the topic of marriage. Tonight, I'm here. What a difference a day makes.

I'd known something was wrong the moment I'd walked into the penthouse. I found her outside on the balcony. Drunk. Ha. She'd chosen the bottle as her friend as well. I hadn't realized the irony until right this moment, when I've just ordered my third this hour. We're so alike, she and I. And so different. She's made mistakes with us, but I fully believe hers have been with the best of intentions. I can defend my own evil ways—and I will if it comes to it—yet my excuses really hold no weight. How could I ever explain such a level of deceit?

I don't have the answer. That's why I'm sitting here, alone, in this fucking bar. I don't have the answers.

She saw the video.

I have to say it over and over to remind myself that it's not just a nightmare of what might happen, but is the actual fact of the matter now. She's seen it. And worse, she knows the lengths I went to in order for her not to see it. I'd practi-cally bribed Stacy to get rid of it. I'd lied to Alayna. Outright lied. I thought I'd covered my ass, that she'd never find out. I was wrong.

God, was I wrong…

So I was unprepared.

I'm usually good on my feet. Preparation isn't mandatory. But I had no words for Alayna. Snippets of our conversation replays over and over in my mind. *Looks can be deceiving*, I told her. *I'm not admitting anything. You haven't figured out anything.*

Fuck, I'm such an asshole. What else could I have said? Nothing. *I have no answers*, I said. *The subject is closed.*

And then…Jesus, I cringe at the memory of this…I blamed *her* for the lack of trust. Did I mention I'm an asshole? Worse than that. I'm a horrible person. Willing to throw her under the bus to hide what I've done to us. What I'm still doing to us.

The bartender checks on me. I gulp the last of my glass. "Another," I say.

I stare dazedly into the mirror behind the bottles. The reflection that meets me looks like fucking death. What does Alayna even see in me? How does she not see me for the vile creature that I am? I don't blame her for pushing me further tonight. I would have pushed her if the roles were reversed. Because it's evident that I'm hiding something. I'm hiding everything. I can't even tell her how I feel about her because it's all tangled up in this lie. I'm drowning in this charade, and I don't know how to get a breath.

I did the only thing I could do. I called a timeout.

A fucking timeout.

What am I supposed to do with that? Do I believe that hours away from her will help me come up with a bigger and better lie? Do I think it will give me the balls to come clean about everything? Or am I hoping that the break will make her forget all her questions? I laugh out loud at the absurdity.

"Something funny?"

The question comes from the woman on the stool to my right. I hadn't noticed her come in. I barely notice her now. "An inside joke," I say, dismissively. Which is stupid. I know that engaging at all, even at a minimum, only encour-ages more conversation.

I'm correct in my assumption.

"Tell me about it, sugar. Lola's got a good ear."

She refers to herself in third person. I roll my eyes.

"Come on, honey. You wouldn't be here if you didn't want to talk to someone."

I snort—the alcohol is definitely taking effect. "I'm here because I want to get loaded."

"But that's not all. Otherwise, you'd be drinking alone somewhere."

I look her over now. She's older than me, forties, I'd guess. Not bad looking. Her hair, nails and boobs are fake. Her skirt is too short, but she has nice legs.

The bartender returns with my drink, and Lola places her own order. I can tell she's hoping I'll offer to buy it for her. I consider it. Not because I'm thinking of hooking up with her—even if she were the hottest supermodel, I wouldn't bang her. I'm with Alayna. Even with a timeout, I'd never be unfaithful. Besides, no one else does it for me anymore. The only woman I'll get hard for I left in tears in my penthouse apartment. I broke her fucking heart. When I promised myself I never would. When I told her that I'd never leave. I left.

I feel like shit. And that's why I consider buying Lola a drink. She's open, trusting—she'd be easily played. The things I could make her believe, the things I could make her do…a million different scenarios start forming in my mind.

Then they stop.

The game won't solve anything. It will be a quick high and then what? Then I'll be even less worthy of Alayna than I am now. I can't fight my demons with my demons. It's not the solution I'm looking for.

So I swallow down my drink and close out my tab.

I stagger back to the loft and spread out on the couch. I don't let myself sleep in my bed. I don't deserve to be comfortable. I don't deserve to be where she's been. I don't deserve her.

I wake the next day with a dry mouth and a fucking headache. It's an instant reminder of the miserable situation I've put myself in. After texting my secretary to reschedule all my appointments for the day, I allow myself a glass of water, but I don't take any pain relievers. I earned this discomfort, and I won't back away from it.

When my phone buzzes, I check it immediately, hoping it's Alayna. It's not, and I pretend I'm not disappointed. It's important though—a text from Norma asking me to call her. She knows not to text me anything incriminating. She also knows to be careful about her phone calls. If she's texting, she needs me.

She doesn't even say hello when I ring her. "You aren't in your office."

"No. I'm working from my loft today." I look and feel like shit. I shouldn't see people. "What do you need?"

"Stuart Reed's having doubts."

Stuart's our man at GlamPlay. I don't need this. Not today. "Did you explain to him that Walden Inc. is still me?"

"He's not having doubts about that. They're ready to sell to you no matter which company you're purchasing with. He's having doubts about buying into Werner Media. Their latest stock prices weren't as high as predicted."

"With the change in the economy, those prices were incredible. What does Reed fucking expect?" I run a hand through my hair. "You know what? I don't give a fuck about his doubts. We'll finish the purchase of GlamPlay first, and then he won't have a choice in the matter."

"Pissing off Stuart Reed is not a good idea." Norma's calm, reasonable. "Of course, you will have full power to do what you want when you own the company, but it will be much easier if Stuart is on your side."

I lean against the full-length windows that look out over the city and remind myself why it's not a good idea to punch my fist through them. "What do you suggest I do then, Norma?"

"You need to alleviate some of his concerns. I don't think it will take much. A friendly conversation off the record." There's a voice in the background. Male. I'm pissed that she's talking about this in front of anyone, but I trust Norma.

It's because I trust her that I give her the benefit of the doubt. "Do you have a plan to arrange this friendly conversation?" We're running out of time on this deal.

"I wouldn't have called if I didn't." Her gloating grin can be heard through the phone. "Stuart will be at the Breezeway Charity Ball tonight. We'll go together."

"To the Breezeway Ball? Do tell me how you plan to get me in there." The Breezeway board of directors, Alan Fleming, is not a fan of Hudson Pierce. I'd played his sister early in my history of the game, before I'd learned that the experiment was best performed away from my work and home. Not for the first time, I wonder if my past will ever let me go.

"Alan will not be there himself. And the name on the guest list is mine. So we'll have to go together. We'll go late, and we won't stay long. Pick me up at eight."

The plan sounds dreadful, but only because the last thing I want to do tonight is get dressed up in a tux and schmooze. But it's necessary. And what else am I planning on doing with the evening? Another night of drinking doesn't seem very productive. I manage to say *thank you* before hanging up.

Another text comes through before I put my phone down. This time it *is* from Alayna. Two words, a simple request—*Come home.*

I make my way to an armchair where I slump and stare at the screen, reading the message over and over. She still wants me. My throat tightens at that knowledge, and it takes everything in me not to jump to obey. But where would we be then? Nothing's changed. We're still at an impasse. And I'm not ready to do what I think will eventually be my only course of action.

I'm still sitting there when her next text comes in. *Are you avoiding me now?*

I type and delete my answer several times. I have no response. She sends more texts:

The least you can do is talk to me.

You said I was everything to you.

Talk to me.

I won't ask about it if you don't want to.

This isn't fair. Shouldn't I be the one who's mad?

Each new message stabs me in the chest, wrenches my gut. I've caused her so much pain, yet I know this is nothing compared to the pain of the truth. What do I do? Let her suffer like this or confess what will likely destroy her? Perhaps I should just walk away. Break things off and break her heart. It will kill me, I know. I'm beginning to see there's no saving us. Soon, I'll have to choose what's best for her and forget about me.

But not today. I can't yet. I'm not ready.

I send her a text of my own because I love her, and I can't bear to leave her hanging any longer. *I'm not mad. I'm not avoiding you. I don't know what to say.*

I don't know what to say. How true is that? So goddamned true.

Don't say anything. Just come home.

I choke on a caustic laugh. For the second time in twenty-four hours, I've engaged when I shouldn't have. Now I have to draw this out, repeating words she can't understand. *I can't. Not yet. We need time.*

I don't need time. I need you.

Fuck, how I need her. She has no idea. *We'll talk later.*

You don't understand. I have to talk now. I'll keep texting you. I can't help myself.

And I'll read every one. But she doesn't send anything after that, and I'm disappointed. More than disappointed. I'm shattered. Her brief words were keeping me afloat. Her absence from my phone makes me worry. Did something happen? And I think the worst—that her life can go on without me. My life, on the other hand, is at a fucking standstill.

I check in with Jordan and learn she's convinced him to join her for a run. I'd forbidden her from running outdoors, concerned about Celia and her stalking. She's defying my wishes—can I blame her?—but at least she's taken her bodyguard. At least she still cares enough about me to compromise. If only there was a way I could compromise with her. I'd give her anything she wanted, tell her every secret from my past, break down every last standing wall, as long as she could tell me she'd never leave me. That she wouldn't give up on us.

And she'd say that she wouldn't. She'd promise me forever.

But I won't let her make that promise. If she found out what I've done, she wouldn't be able to keep it.

My phone rings in the middle of the night. In a state of half-sleep, I reach toward the coffee table where I'd left it before settling down on the couch. Then I stop myself. It's probably Alayna—and God, how I want it to be her—but I don't have the strength to deny her right now. Not in the dark hours of the night when I want her so desperately that I'll say and do anything to have her.

I sit up and scrub my hands over my face. I'm awake now. Actually, I'm surprised I slept at all. I look at the time. It's almost three. I guess I slept more than I thought. I'd gotten in around midnight. As I'd said I would, I'd gone to the charity ball with Norma and even managed to chat up Stuart Reed. I think I did my job of convincing him that Werner Media was a good investment, but before I had a chance to confirm it, I'd gotten a text from Reynold, Alayna's second shift bodyguard, telling me that not only was Celia at The Sky Launch, but that Alayna had dismissed him for the night.

Needless to say, I was furious. And worried as hell.

I grabbed Norma, and we took off for the club. Unsafe as it was to drive under emotional duress and talk on the phone, I called Alayna anyway. I kept her on the phone until I arrived at the curb outside. With my own eyes, I saw Celia leave. Alayna was safe, thank God. But she'd seen me—seen me with Norma, dressed up for a night out.

How do I only seem to dig myself deeper? Of course, that's why she wants to talk to me. I should explain. The deal is so close to coming to fruition, maybe that's one thing I can share with Alayna. But if Celia has Alayna tapped or bugged...I can't risk Celia finding out about this before it happens.

So I'll have to keep this silent too.

My phone starts ringing again, and it takes everything I have not to pick it up and chuck it across the room. Possibly the thing that stops me is realizing that the screen isn't flashing Alayna's name; it's flashing Adam's.

My heart is in my throat when I answer. "Adam?" I don't wait for him to answer. "What's wrong? Is it Mirabelle?"

"She's having contractions," he says. "We're at Lennox Hill."

"The baby?" It's too familiar—this unknowing ache. A fragile being that I've yet to meet but already care so much for. And that it's Mirabelle...this can't happen. I can't bear it if this happens. Not to her.

Adam's voice is tight. "We don't know yet. God, we don't know anything yet."

"I'll be right there." I hang up and don't give it a second thought before texting Jordan. Then I push the top number on my speed dial list. "Alayna. I need you."

"What is it?" Three short words, but her love and care are evident.

"Mira. At the hospital. The baby..." I choke up, unable to say more.

"I'll be right there."

"Jordan's already on his way to get you." I hold the phone to my chest for several minutes after she hangs up. This may be as close to holding her as I get tonight, and I cherish it.

At the hospital, Adam texts that Mirabelle's been moved to the obstetrics ward, but I wait for Alayna before going up there. I can't see my sister like this. I'm weak. I'm a mess. I need my strength.

Then, there it is—my strength. Alayna walks in wearing yoga pants and a T-shirt, and she's more beautiful than anyone I've ever seen. My pulse slows ever so slightly, and air seems to finally move through my lungs better than it had just a moment before. She does this for me. She gives and gives, without knowing, even when I distance myself from her. Even when I've wounded her, she's here to repair me.

The truth of my situation is beginning to take root inside me. Everything about her is light. I cannot continue to keep her in darkness forever.

When she reaches me, we fall into step together. We head to the elevator, and I catch her up on what I know. When she reaches her hand out to me, I take it. I shouldn't. The last thing I want to do is complicate things for her. But I can't *not* touch her any longer. I hold it as long as I can before the feel of her skin against mine makes me want more of her, all of her. Then I let it go, and forbid myself the comfort of her touch again.

Before we've reached Mirabelle's floor, I've already broken that deal. I brush my thumb across her cheek. It's a habit, I realize, to hold and caress her. I have to try harder.

We find the rest of the family rather quickly. My parents, Chandler, and Adam are all waiting outside Mirabelle's room. I tense. It's too reminiscent of the last time I came to the hospital to see a woman in the maternity ward. Fortunately, the story I receive this time is very different. Adam insures us that Mirabelle—and the baby—are fine. For now. She'd gotten dehydrated, that's all.

I want to fucking kill her. Rushing to the hospital out of dead fear because she didn't bother to carry around a water bottle?

But of course I don't really want to kill her. I'm relieved. I'm so very relieved. And I have to believe that there is some sort of justice in this world, some sort of higher power that recognizes the goodness of the woman that I'm fortunate enough to call my sister. While many of the women in my life seem to be cursed for loving me, Mirabelle seems to have remained unscathed. I spend a silent moment in gratitude, thanking whoever or whatever for sparing her.

My eyes flicker to Alayna. Now, whom do I have to pray to in order to save her?

— CHAPTER —

TWENTY-THREE

I've called Adam to check up on Mirabelle five times in the last two days, and I've texted even more frequently. Of course, I'd always worry about her, but the separation from Alayna makes me even more anxious in general. Since I still can't find the words she needs to hear, I attempt to avoid all thought of her. It's impossible, but I try anyway, throwing my energy into preparing for my trip this afternoon to finish the deal with GlamPlay and worrying about Mirabelle.

I've just settled in at my desk after lunch with a cup of black coffee when Patricia intercoms me. "Mirabelle Sitkin on the line for you." Seems my sister's beat me to the call today.

"Send it back." I take a large swallow from my coffee, letting the phone ring three times before picking it up. I'm not sleeping well, and my morning caffeine has seemed to have worn off. "Mirabelle, aren't I supposed to be the one checking up on you?"

"That's exactly why I'm calling." Her voice is light and bubbly. "Adam says you've been harassing him."

"*Harassing*? That's a fine description for brotherly concern."

"And I adore the concern. I really do." She lets out a sigh. "But between you and Mom and Dad and Adam...I think a once-a-day friendly text will do just fine."

I sit back in my chair and swivel back and forth as I speak. "You know, if you'd let me hire a nurse to follow you around like I suggested, I wouldn't need to check in."

"Hudson, I don't need a nurse. I'm married to a doctor. Remember?"

I shrug even though she can't see it. "And you were married to a doctor when you were admitted to the hospital three nights ago. It's obviously not enough."

"Oh, my God. Are you serious?"

"Very." I stop my swiveling and lean on the desk in front of me. "But if you say you're fine and promise me that you're drinking and resting—"

"—I am!"

"Then I'll agree to one call and one text a day." This is a hard concession for me to make. I pinch the bridge of my nose as I force myself to accept it. Besides, I reason with myself, I have to fly to Los Angeles for the weekend, and I'll likely not have time for anything more.

"Deal," she agrees. "I'm glad we got that worked out. But that isn't really why I'm calling."

"Oh?" And now I remember why I'd done all my checking in with my brother-in-law. I was afraid of the conversation that I'm certain she's about to embark on.

"Nope. You and Laynie…"

It's kind the way she trails off, letting me fill in the blanks rather than asking me straight out. But I know that if I don't answer the way she wants, she'll become more direct. I'm not surprised that she's asking. She'd noticed we were… *strained*…when we visited her at the hospital. She'd even sent Alayna and me out of the room to repair whatever was wrong. The time alone with Alayna was hard. Still worked up over the cause for our emergency visit, the rift between us seemed so inconsequential. But, of course, it isn't. And though I wanted to do nothing but pull her into my arms and confess every secret, including how much I love her, I refrained.

For Mirabelle's sake, we agreed to set aside our issues and put on a happy face. It seemed like my sister bought it. She convinced Alayna of that, anyway. I knew better. Mirabelle has a knack for reading people. She has a knack for reading *me*. I've never been able to fool her.

So I don't begin to think I can fool her now. "I fucked up, Mirabelle." That about sums it up.

"What did you do?" Her voice is low and tense, and I momentarily regret saying anything. Not because I'm not willing to share but because I'm worried about stressing her out.

But it's out now. I don't have to say everything, but I have to say something. "I lied to her."

"And she found out?" She doesn't ask the details of my deceit, which I appreciate.

"Yes. She found out. But there's more I haven't told her, more I need to say." I'm surprised that I'm spilling my soul so easily. And it feels good. All the build-up, I think I've been desperate to talk to someone. Since I'd never initiate a conversation, I'm suddenly grateful that Mirabelle did.

"Okay." She takes a breath that's deep enough I can hear it through the line. "So you need to tell her, but you haven't?"

"No."

"Because you're afraid of...what?"

"Losing her." Just saying the words makes my throat tight.

"But you won't know that unless you tell her. Will you?"

Isn't that the question of the decade.The question of my lifetime, actually. It's been four days since I declared we needed time. Four nights that I haven't buried myself inside her, haven't felt her clench around me, haven't fallen asleep to the sound of her rhythmic breathing. Four days and nights—it feels like forever. And still I don't know what I should do.

I realize that time is not going to give me any answers. It won't be away from Alayna that I'll find the strength to make this choice.

I'm quiet too long. Mirabelle says, "Your silence leads me to believe you aren't going to." Her disappointment is heavy in her tone.

"Not true. My silence is only a product of not having a response."

"Well, then." She pauses, and I can sense her wanting to say more. Finally, she says, "Do you want my advice?"

"If I say no, will you refrain from giving it anyway?"

"Probably not." She considers. "Definitely not."

"Then by all means, go ahead." I shoot a glance toward my liquor cabinet, wondering if it's too early to spike my coffee.

"I'm not going to ask what you're keeping from her." She's pacing; I'm sure of it. She likes to walk as she lectures. "If it's something you don't want to tell her, I'm sure it's not something you want to tell me. But, I know that you could tell me anything, and I would still love you. And not just because I'm your sister. And though it's hard to admit this, I kinda get the sense that Laynie loves you even more than I do. She chose you. Out of everyone out there who she could love or who could love her, she chose *you*, Hudson. I have to believe she sees that thing about you too. That thing you think doesn't exist. That thing that makes all your bull worth it. And if she sees that, if she loves that as much as I think she does?

Then I don't think there's anything you can say that will make you lose her. Even if it's the ugliest secret of all time."

"Even if it's the worst betrayal you can imagine?" Her sentiment is pretty. But it's naïve.

She pauses, and I know she's preparing for more of her happy-ever-after spiel. For once, Mirabelle surprises me. "Did I ever tell you that I cheated on Adam?"

"Uh, no." I'm hoping she doesn't tell me now.

"A long time ago. Before we were even engaged. I slept with another guy."

I'm shocked. Mirabelle has always been the picture of loyalty and commitment. "I don't know if I want to hear this."

She plows ahead anyway. "I was stupid. But it was really shitty. I mean, he knew the guy. They were roommates in their undergrad program. And we were serious at the time—Adam and I. I just...I don't know. It was stupid. I did something stupid. And for stupid reasons too. I wanted to get Adam's attention. Can you believe that? Well, it sure got his attention. Also, almost lost me the love of my life."

"Mirabelle..." I'm not sure what to say.

"No, no, it's fine now. The point is that fidelity is important in any relationship, but even more so for Adam because his previous girlfriend cheated, and, well, that's a whole other story. Anyway." She huffs into the receiver. "Cheating is the ultimate betrayal for him. And we worked things out. It wasn't easy, but here we are. So, yeah, I believe forgiveness happens. Even in the Pierce family."

I'm still stunned. I'm also not convinced my situation with Alayna is anything like Mirabelle's. For one thing, anyone who doesn't recognize my sister is the catch of a lifetime is crazy, no matter what her sins. But I'm moved by her confession. "Thank you for telling me that. It does give some perspective."

"Hudson, don't just smile and nod and then dismiss everything I'm saying." *God, she knows me too well.* "Because here's the other thing. Lies like those? They grow. They grow between you like big black holes. Pretty soon you can't see each other through the darkness. And that part of you that Laynie loves? She won't be able to find it anymore through the cloud. In other words, you can tell her the truth and give her the chance to prove she loves you anyway. Or you can let the lie grow until she leaves you because she doesn't know who you are anymore. It may be just me, but I think you have a better shot with the truth."

Twenty minutes after I've hung up with Mirabelle, her words are still rooted in my head, clinging to my conscience like mold on spoiled fruit. I can't concentrate on anything else. I've read the same email from Stuart Reed three times now and still haven't gotten anything from it. When I notice he's copied Norma, I give up on it. If it's important, she'll fill me in on our flight.

Thinking of my flight...I should tell Alayna that I'm leaving town. I pick up my cell phone and begin a text. Then I delete it. I can't even seem to say something as simple as *By the way, I'll be in L.A. through the weekend.* She'll want to know more—she deserves to know more—and once again, I can't give it.

Instead, I text Jordan.*Checking in, how's Alayna today?*

He responds quickly. *What do you mean? Isn't she with you?*

I'm alarmed enough by this response to call him directly. "Why would she be with me?"

Jordan sounds genuinely confused. "I dropped her off about twenty minutes ago. She said she was going to surprise you."

It would have been a nice surprise. "Well, she's not here."

"She's somewhere in the building," Jordan insists. "I've been sitting out front this whole time."

There are other exits out of Pierce Industries, but they'd be difficult for her to get to. It's possible that she gave Jordan the slip, but for some reason, I don't think that's her plan. "Stay on the line while I check the loft."

Maybe she did plan to surprise me. Naked in my bed upstairs. I can hope, anyway.

While I take the private elevator up to my quarters, I question Jordan further. "You're supposed to report whenever she goes anywhere. Why didn't you tell me when you got here?"

"She asked me to give her a few minutes. After that, I figured you would have already worked it out." Jordan sounds as anxious as I feel. "Do you want me to come up?"

"No. Stay out there. Watch the doors." I'm in the loft now. Even without checking the bedroom and the bath, I know she's not here. The room feels too ordinary. I'd sense her if she were here.

God, I'm beginning to sound like Mirabelle.

"She's not here," I tell Jordan. And now I'm fully concerned. "I'm checking the live camera feeds. Contact security and have them review the last half hour's tapes. See if we can trace her."

I end the call and head back down the elevator. After checking to make sure my secretary hasn't seen her, I return to my office. The closet in the far corner houses a private media cabinet. Here, I have a system set up to duplicate all the camera feeds from the main security desk. These don't record anything except for the cameras around my office. A quick scan through all the feeds of the main hallways and elevators turns up no sight of her. Not expecting to find anything on the recordings— she'd be here if she came to my floor, after all—I rewind frame by frame anyway.

Then I see her. Getting off the elevator outside my office. Instead of coming in, though, she darts down the hallway, away from me, and toward—

My phone rings. It's Jordan. "We found her on your floor," he says. "It seems she went to another office. Uh, getting the name now. It's—"

"—Norma Anders," I finish for him. I shouldn't be surprised. Actually, I'm not really. I'm also kind of proud. And a whole lot irritated. "Is she still there?"

"There's no sign that she left."

"Thank you, Jordan. I'll take care of it from here." I pocket my phone and chew over this new development as I walk out to the hallway. What on earth does Alayna expect to gain from Norma? I trust Norma—she won't spill any secrets about our upcoming deal. But Alayna doesn't know that. Is she trying to find out about GlamPlay and Werner Media? No, she can't even know enough to ask. Then is she here for something about Gwenyth? Or is she still jealous of my relationship with my right-hand financial manager?

Goddammit, why can't Alayna just trust me?

So what if her trust isn't warranted. I want it all the same. Especially when my secrets are mostly to protect her.

And sneaking around to talk to my staff members is not the way to help our relationship. It's backhanded, which may be a case of the pot calling the kettle black, but I know that two wrongs do not make a right. She shouldn't be here. She needs to quit pushing, always pushing.

By the time she turns into my hallway, I'm boiling. She tiptoes along the way to the elevator, her eyes fixed on my office. Okay, it's adorable. My fury eases a notch. Or several.

She doesn't notice me even when she's nearly upon me, so she jumps when I say, "Alayna."

She looks up at me with her doe-eyes, and there it is—the light that I love, beaming back at me with the affection and desire that I've grown accustomed to seeing in her gaze.

Is it crazy that in the midst of my frustration, all I want to do is fall down at the feet of this woman and worship her very existence? My life without her has been so dark, so dismal. She's not just my light; she's my sun. My world revolves around her.

But right now, she's in trouble. And I'm about to let her know.

I wrap my arm around her, her skin warming me through my suit. "Let's talk in private, shall we?" I lead her to my office. I tell Patricia to hold my calls. Then I shut and lock the door behind us.

Locking the door wasn't actually necessary. I'm not sure if I do it to frighten her or tempt myself.

Alayna's certainly not scared. She's almost flirtatious as she greets me. "Well, hello, H."

My cock is already stiffening. I release her arm. "What are you doing here, Alayna?"

"What am I doing here in your office? You dragged me in here, remember?" She walks away from me with a swagger that makes me want to bend her over my knee.

I bite back a smile that I don't want to give way to. "Don't be cute. I meant in the building."

She peers back at me over her shoulder, and I swear to God her expression is screaming *Fuck Me*. "Maybe I came to see you. I tend to stalk when I feel dismissed by a man."

Feisty Alayna is quite a turn-on. It's very inconvenient.

I sigh. "You didn't come to see me. You arrived on this floor over half an hour ago and are just now coming by my office."

She spins toward me. "How the fuck do you know everything I do? Jordan? Your security cameras?"

"I'm not going to feel guilty for the lengths I go to in order to protect what's mine." I'd do so much more. I'd kill for her if I had to.

I expected my dominating male routine to irritate her. Instead, she licks her lips. Jesus, I'm half-hard.

I've wanted her for days, but now that she's here, I remember why I can't have her. It's not fair. Until I deal with the lie between us, I have to keep my distance.

Which means, I have to get her out of here. "Alayna?"

She tears her eyes from me, leaving me instantly cold. "Yours, huh? Don't make me laugh."

"Jesus, how many times do I have to go through this with you?" I can't keep up with her. She's hot one minute, cold the next. Much the way I feel, actually.

"I don't know. Maybe a couple hundred more times. Because I'm obviously not getting it."

I turn away from her and shove my hand through my hair. I'm torn between screaming some sense into her and ripping off her clothing and claiming her with my cock. Neither would be very productive, though both would feel fucking fantastic.

No. I have to remember my agenda. I turn back to her, hoping I seem more in control. "Why. Are. You. Here?"

"I came to see Norma." Finally, she's honest.

"About Gwen?"

She covers her face with her hands in frustration. When she drops them, she says, "About you, you dummy. I don't give a shit about anything but you." Her voice is tight. "Jesus, how many times do I have to go through this with you?"

Her admission renews my earlier irritation. "You came to talk to *my* employee about *me*?" Maybe irritation wasn't a strong enough word. I was fucking pissed.

And yeah, I was mostly pissed at myself. How did I let us get to this? She and I on different sides. We're supposed to be on the same side. Always.

She throws my own words back at me in defense. "Don't guilt me for protecting what's mine."

It's then I know she gets it. Or maybe it's me who finally gets it. She's fighting for me in the same way that I'm fighting for her. We aren't *against* each other—we're *for* each other.

If she's willing to keep battling after all I've put her through, maybe we do have a chance. Maybe Mirabelle's right. Maybe Alayna can love me anyway.

"I only wanted to see for myself if she was into you," she says, softer now. "If you had something going with her." Then she points a finger at me. "And don't you dare talk to me about trust because you know I get jealous about her, and you aren't around to help reassure me."

I lean against the couch and study her. How can I blame her for things I'd do? Things I've done? I can't. "Did you get what you came for?" I ask her.

"I did."

"And?"

She bites her lip. I'm so jealous of that lip. "She thinks a lot of you. She respects you and admires you, and she recognizes you're physically attractive—don't let that go to your head."

"But…"

"But she's not into you anymore. I can see it in her eyes."

Or she discovered Norma's secret affair with her assistant. Either way, I'm pleased that this jealousy has been nipped in the bud. "Good." Perhaps it was a good thing she talked to my employee after all. "Then you believe the things I've told you."

"It was never the things you've told me that were the issue. It's the things you haven't told me."

"They aren't your things to know." It's not fair, but it's for her own good. Always for her.

She just doesn't see it. "What the ever-living fuck? I could say the same thing about you—spying on me, digging into my history before you'd even met me—maybe I think those aren't your things to know. Still, you did—and do—whatever the hell you want with no regard to boundaries or personal space."

She faces me head on. "And while that's out there, let me be clear—since you aren't able to explain things to me, I'm digging on my own."

Panic streaks down my spine. How much digging until she discovers the truth?

"That's right. I've been through all of the books Celia sent. I've been to see Stacy. And Norma. I'm collecting my own facts. Don't you think it would be better to tell me your secrets than have me find them out on my own?"

"Alayna, stop digging." I step toward her. She's a smart woman. If she tries hard enough, she'll figure it out. And it will destroy her.

"You're protecting Celia again, aren't you?"

Is she so blind to not see? "Celia's not who I'm protecting."

"Who then? Yourself? Me?"

I'm close now to telling her—telling her everything. Because I hate that she doesn't understand. How can she not understand how much my past will hurt her? How I want to save her. And, God, I don't think I can.

She has to go. For her own good. Before she pushes me too far. I grab her at the elbow. "You need to leave, now."

Alayna winces like she's just gotten the wind knocked out of her. Like *I've* just knocked the wind out of her. It's unbearable to see her like this, tears spilling down her cheeks. "Shutting me out again. Like you always do. Hiding behind your thick walls." Her pain is palpable. "What's the point of me even fighting for you if you're never, never going to let me in? Who are you protecting, Hudson? Who?"

It's the end of my rope. I can't let her believe that I'm not fighting just as hard. For her. "Yes, you, dammit! I'm protecting you. Always you."

Then, because I can never tell her in words the way I feel, I have to tell her with my body. I crush my lips against hers, tasting her, devouring her. I'm so god-damn desperate for her kiss—because I have to tell her how I feel. Because I need to feel how *she* feels about me.

It's only meant to be a kiss. Or it's not meant to be anything because there's no thought involved. But when she wraps a leg around mine, when she tilts her hips against me, rubbing against my hard cock, then I have no choice but to continue. She's like a roller coaster ride. Once you get on, you're there for the whole ride.

And so I ride.

I spin her toward the couch and remove her panties. My fingers stroke inside her cunt. Christ, she's wet. She's always so fucking ready for me. I have my pants down and my cock out before I have a chance to second-guess myself. With my fingers gripped around her hips, I thrust in. Hard.

I drive into her, over and over, chasing not only my orgasm but the answers to our shitty situation. Her back is to me, her face hidden. I can't watch her like this. I close my eyes. It's reminiscent of so many other fucks with so many random women. This used to be my favorite position. It's so wrong to be with her this way. But I'm too vulnerable right now. I can't be with her in any other way without losing every semblance of control.

Except Alayna won't let me simply use her. She knows what we need better than I do. At least, she does in this moment. Or maybe she's just stronger than I am, more willing to be that vulnerable, that exposed.

She twists toward me, clutching onto my shirt. At her touch, my eyes pop open. She locks her gaze on mine, and that's all it takes to bring me back. Back to *her*. I steady my drive, and her pussy clenches around me. Then I'm coming with her, crying her name like it's an S.O.S. Hoping beyond hope that she can save me. Save us.

I collapse on top of her, holding her, breathing with her in unison. They're short minutes that pass, every second of them precious. I don't think I can ever let her go.

Eventually, I try. I step back, pulling out of her. But immediately, she's in my arms, and my lips are pressed against hers. I hold her in place, our mouths sealed in an immobile kiss. This is it, I know. My decision is about to be made, and even though my stubborn walls won't let it be made solid with words and declarations, it's forming in the center of my mind, sitting on the edge of my tongue.

I can't lose her.

When we break apart, Alayna wraps her hands around my neck, seemingly as desperate to hold onto me as I am to her. "Oh god, I miss you. I miss you so much."

"Précieux mon amour ma chérie "I run my hands down her face, memorizing the touch of her skin, the curve of her jaw. Will this be the last time?

It can't be the last time.

"When are you coming home?"she asks, bringing us back to reality, back to the things we have to deal with.

I lean my forehead against hers. I'm exhausted. So tired of this game. "I have to go to L.A. for the weekend." I check my watch. "I'm set to leave in about twenty minutes, in fact."

"Part of your big business thing? With Norma?" There's no hint of jealousy in her question. Just a need to know.

I slide my nose along hers. "Yes, with Norma. And after this, if all goes well, we'll be done." I want to invite her to come with me, but it's too risky. If Celia were to follow us across the country…

No, I have to keep her here. Safe from ruining this deal that's almost done. Then, after this, after I know I've gotten Celia off Alayna's back. Then…

I can't even say it in my mind. Because once I voice the decision, I know there'll be no going back. This first, this deal. And then…that.

With strength I didn't know I had, I push her away. I dress and face her, my fist on my hip. Already the distance is beginning to span between us, and I think of Mirabelle's words. The lie that grows and separates and builds walls. I see it. It's here now between us, forming before my eyes.

And I know I can't let it grow any wider. I can't wait any longer to begin. I can't lose her, and I only have one shot at keeping her. The choice forms into words in my head. *I'll tell her.* I *have* to tell her. Everything. All of it. Starting with this.

I reach for her, pulling her back to me with all that I am. "God, Alayna, I can't do this anymore." It's a relief saying this. A burden unleashed. "I can't bear to be apart from you. I miss you so terribly."

"You do?" She leans back to look into my eyes.

The light. Her brilliant light overtakes me. And now that the decision's been made, the confessions spill easily. "Of course, I do, precious. You're my every-thing. I love you. I love you so much."

Finally, I'm free.

I didn't think it was possible, but her light, it grows brighter.

"W-w-what?" She's unbelieving.

I'm ridiculously in love. "You heard me."

"I want to hear it again."

"I love you." It's easy now. Like I always knew it would be. It's only the beginning of my confessions, and the rest will be so much harder. But I won't think about that now. I'll let this declaration have its own moment in the sun.

"You love me?"

I brush my lips over hers. "I love you, precious. I've always loved you. From the moment I first saw you. I knew before you did, I think." I tilt her chin to meet my eyes. "But there are things—things in my past—that have kept me from being able to tell you. And now…I have to do this…this thing. Finish this deal. Then, when I get back, we'll talk."

"We'll talk?" She's glowing. God, how I wish I didn't have to steal her happiness.

But I'm committed now. "I'll tell you anything you want to know. And if you still want me, I'll come home."

"Yes, I want you home. Of course I do. We belong there together. There's nothing you could say that would make me stop loving you. *Nothing.* I stick, remember?"

I cling to her words, holding them like a lifeline. "Oh, precious. I hope that's true."

"It is."

But I know she can't make that promise. I won't hold her to it.

"Say it again."

"You're such a spoiled girl." I circle my nose around hers. "And I love…spoiling you."

She smacks me playfully.

"And I love you." I'll tell her as many times as she wants to hear it. As many times as she lets me say it. And though this may be the last time I hold her like this, the last time I get to bask in her sun, I know I'll never stop saying the words that have rested so deeply in me for so long. "I love you, I love you. I love you."

TWENTY-FOUR

Before

T herapy, it turned out, was quite helpful. My life didn't change in the course of a session or two or even five, but little by little I began to understand things about myself that I'd thought could never be understood. And though I still felt primarily numb, I also felt something else. A lightening of sorts. Like the weight on my shoulders had somehow been decreased. I was still skeptical about progress, but I was willing to give it a try.

I managed to avoid Celia for more than a month after I began my rehabilitation. I got pretty good at excuses—business, travel, family obligations. She called and showed up at the loft, and I dodged.

Eventually, I had to face her. Dr. Alberts required it. Or encouraged it, rather. He insisted that as long as I kept the option to "game" open, then I could never completely leave it. He was right, of course. Only problem was that I wasn't entirely sure I wanted to completely leave the game. Actually, I was entirely sure that I *didn't* want to.

It was at a session in my office that I finally admitted that. "It's not that I miss playing. Well, not only that I miss playing." Strangely, I didn't miss it as much as I had imagined. There were other things, it turned out, that filled my time just as easily. I enjoyed the arts—the symphony, the ballet, the opera. So much so that I arranged a number of scholarship and charitable contributions that benefited these newfound interests. And work was a more than suitable substitute. The manipulative strategies I'd perfected proved useful in the boardroom. It even gave the same rush that I'd found from my experiments.

"Then what is it that keeps you from letting go?" Dr. Alberts' approach was always kind and understanding. Never pushy or judgmental.

"I don't know." I did know. Saying it was difficult. "It's just...who am I without the game?" It was a silly crisis of identity, really. Everyone knew who Hudson Pierce was. I could do an internet search and find several biographies that summed up my life more succinctly than I could ever hope to. I expected Dr. Alberts to give me his own list of my accomplishments and curriculum vitae.

He didn't. Instead, he said, "That's what we have to figure out, Hudson. Luckily, you're young and healthy. You have plenty of time to figure it out."

There was something about his words that attracted me. He'd phrased it like a challenge—on purpose, most likely—and that was all it took to catch my atten-tion. I'd never backed away from a challenge. And what a fitting replacement self-discovery was for the experiments of my past. Rather than study the effects of certain situations on others, I could study the effects on myself.

"But," there was always a *but* with Dr. Alberts, "you will never be able to fully explore the future you if you are still firmly anchored in the past."

Everything kept me anchored in the past. My mother, who constantly brought up Celia's pregnancy. My father, who I couldn't look at without remembering his betrayal to his wife, to me. My sister, who always looked at me with innocent eyes, yet, as it turned out, knew more than anyone about who I truly was.

But that wasn't what—*who*—Dr. Alberts was referring to.

"Celia." It was hard to even say her name anymore. There was no one who anchored me more than her. And, since I was ready to set sail, I had to let her go. "I'll take care of it."

It was easier said than done. Though I could clearly define the steps in my mind of what needed to be done, what needed to be said, the truth was that I'd never broken up with anyone. And wasn't that exactly what this would be? The ultimate breakup? I'd studied breakups with other couples, of course. I'd been the cause of quite a few. I knew what to expect from them—crying, yelling. Sometimes they were less emotional.

But what would it be like with Celia? Would there be a passionate display? If she still felt things as deeply as she once had, she hadn't shown me for quite some time.

As for me, I'd thought I was immune to the whole feelings thing. Dr. Alberts corrected me there. "If you were truly incapable of affection, then how did your sister manage to convince you to see me? Was it not because of affection for her that you agreed?"

So I wasn't completely devoid of emotion, though I still believed that the typical levels of love and devotion expressed by most people were not within my reach. And what I felt for Mirabelle…well, she was surely an exception. But there was something between me and Celia. Even if it was simply a shared affinity for the same pastime, it was a strong bond.

"You are connected to her, Hudson." Without ever meeting her, Dr. Alberts had a fairly clear picture of our relationship just the same. "It may not be the form of love that you imagine when you think of the word, but there is emotional involvement. It will not be easy to cut her from your life. You need to be prepared for that."

So I prepared as well as I could. I made arrangements to see her through her assistant, and I chose the location. Not the loft—I could never have her in the loft again; I knew that without Dr. Alberts pointing that out. Her apartment was better. I'd been there once or twice, but it was never a point of meeting for us. I set the appointment for seven on a weeknight. Usually when we met, our time was generalized. *"I'll be there after dinner."* Or, *"I'll stop by on my way to the gym."* These changes to our typical behavior would throw her off, give me the upper hand. Before we were even face-to-face, I'd already set the environment to work specifically in my favor.

It didn't escape me that I was, yet again, manipulating the situation. Funny that I was supposed to be in recovery from that very thing. This time, however, I was pretty sure Dr. Alberts wouldn't disapprove.

I arrived late. On purpose.

"Hey, stranger." Celia's greeting felt strained as she seemed to debate whether to hug me or not, evidence that my setup was going as planned. In the end, we didn't embrace. She swept her arm in invitation. "Come on in."

I stepped into her air-conditioned space and then stopped. Problem with dealing with Celia on new ground was that it was new to me as well. My eyes darted around her immaculate apartment. I hadn't thought about it before, but her Gramercy Park location wasn't cheap, and she lived in a building with all the amenities. Her interior design salary didn't pull in enough to pay the premium price. She was obviously digging into her trust fund. Or getting help elsewhere. Briefly, I wondered if she was scamming people on the side.

Then I dismissed the thought. It wasn't my business. Not anymore.

"Well, are we just going to stand here twiddling our thumbs or would you like to take a seat?" She smiled, but her hands fiddled nervously with the edge of her blouse.

"Sit, of course." I started toward her living room.

"Can I get you a drink?"

"Sure." I paused. "Actually, I'll get it." Her bar was off the dining room—this I remembered from previous visits. I grabbed a glass from her dish rack.

"I don't have any Scotch," Celia called from the other room. "Sorry."

"No problem." I opened the cabinet and studied her inventory. Bourbon and vodka sat front and center—my mother's liquors of choice. Something about that thought reminded me that I needed my wits about me that night. I closed the cupboard, filled my glass with ice, and poured some bottled water. Then I joined Celia in the living room.

She was already sitting on her chaise, spread out to look casual, but her body language said she was anything but. I took a long swallow of my water before taking a seat across from her on the loveseat.

"So." She wrung her hands as she spoke. "What's up? I mean, I know something has to be up. You've been avoiding me for weeks, and all this tonight is just…weird. You're trying to throw me off balance. It's working. So what is it?"

I chuckled. Of course she'd see through me. Wouldn't I have seen through her?

Though I hadn't planned to dive right in, Celia's point-blank questioning of my agenda gave me no choice. "I came to tell you…I need to tell you…" *Just spit it out.* "I'm not playing anymore."

It was Celia's turn to laugh. "Of course you aren't. We haven't seen each other in forever. How could you possibly be playing? I'm sure it's driving you crazy. You're such a junkie for this stuff. Don't worry. I have several possible scenarios just waiting for you to choose one. We'll get you back in."

She'd relaxed, her usual demeanor returning as she ticked off situations on her fingers. "There's a new neighbor on the seventh floor. He's seeing two women, neither know about each other. He's serious about both. We could introduce them. Or you could try to seduce one. Or both. Or I could jump in as a third woman."

Her enthusiasm was contagious. The longer I let her babble on, the worse it was for me. I had to correct her misunderstanding. "Celia, I mean—"

She ignored me, speaking over me. "If that doesn't sound appealing, then I have another. I met a pair of newlyweds at the MoMA show last week. I know, we've done the newlywed thing, but I thought it might be fun for old time's sake."

"I'm out, Celia. I'm not playing anymore."

"Or wait!" Now it was apparent that she did understand me after all. She just didn't want to. "Andrea Parish has a wedding shower coming up. It's co-ed. I'm sure there's something we could—"

"Celia, stop."

She did, her face falling as she turned to meet my eyes.

"I'm done. I'm not playing the game. Ever." My voice threatened to catch, but I managed to cover it. "It's over." I finished my water, wishing that I'd chosen the vodka instead.

Her eyes fell to the floor for the slightest moment. Then she recovered. "What happened? Is there a lawsuit? We always knew that was a possibility."

I shook my head. "There's no lawsuit. I'm just...I'm done."

"That's ridiculous." She narrowed her brows skeptically. "Are you trying to pull my leg? I don't fall for your shit anymore, you know."

While I'd known delivering this news to Celia would be difficult, I'd thought the hardest part would be convincing her I was happy with my decision, not that I meant it in the first place. "I'm not pulling your leg, Celia. I'm not making this up. I'm done with the game. I'm no longer playing. I know this seems to be coming out of the blue, but I'm serious about this. No more experiments. No game. Done."

She tilted her head and studied me. "You can't be done. You said you'd never be done."

"I'd said that; you're right. But I was wrong. I've changed my mind." It occurred to me to bring up Mirabelle, but then I realized that there wasn't any way I could explain how my sister had influenced me. Even if I could come up with the words, Celia wouldn't understand. I barely understood.

She came near to assuming on her own, though. "Is this because of your mother? Jack?"

"No. Not because of Sophia. Definitely not because of Jack."

Celia stood and began pacing. "Where the hell is this coming from, then? If not your family, did you meet Jesus or something?"

I chuckled again. "No." Though ethics were beginning to take more of an interest for me than they had before. The rights and wrongs of things I'd done. It was starting to matter. "This is me, Celia. All me."

She swung to face me. "Bullshit. This isn't you. The *game* is you."

"Not anymore."

"Always! You can't even make it through a dinner without coming up with at least one play."

I shot up from my seat. "And that's exactly the problem. The game has become my whole life. To the point that I've begun to ruin the few things around me that aren't the game. And still it isn't enough. It's never enough. I need something else. Something more fulfilling, less consuming. More honest."

"Like what? *Love*? Because I swear to God if that's what you mean..." She didn't have to finish her thought. I got it. After I'd turned her off to that particular emotion, it would be the ultimate betrayal to leave her for that.

"Not love. Of course not love." Yet, wasn't that exactly what I was leaving for? Love for Mirabelle? It wasn't romantic love, though, and that's what Celia was referring to. "You know I'm incapable of that, Celia. Just...there has to be something else. If I knew what that something was, I'd tell you. But I don't know. Yet."

"Because there is nothing else."

I'd believed that. Part of me still did. But I'd been listening to new voices recently—Dr. Alberts, Mirabelle—and they said differently. "How do we know that, Celia? Have we looked?"

She scoffed at me. "I don't need to look."

"Then how do you know?"

"Because you told me!"

"Only because you begged me to teach you!" This wasn't the course I'd planned to take with Celia. Chasing the blame, passing the buck—it wouldn't get us anywhere.

I ran a hand through my hair and blew out a stream of hot air. When I spoke again, I was calmer, more even. "Look, you chose this. I never did. I thought it was my only option, but I see now that it wasn't. So I'm trying to choose something different." My pride made me say more than I should. "I stood by you when you made this choice, and now it's your turn to stand by me."

She crossed her arms over her chest and leveled me with a look that could kill. "If we're scoring points then we need to go back much further, Hudson. Your game against me that summer was what began this in the first place."

I didn't have ammunition against that. There was no denying that I'd been the one to put the current course of her life in motion. And while I'd had little guilt about the things I'd done to other people, I was beginning to. Therapy was working already. Or messing with my mind. I didn't know. Whatever it was, there was specific remorse concerning Celia. Was it because I was connected to her as Dr. Alberts suggested? Did I *love* her? Maybe I did in some way. Maybe I always had.

I sat heavily on the arm of the sofa. "You're right, Ceely. I did begin this. I wish I knew what to do now to end it."

She shook her head, her short ponytail bobbing with the movement. The look on her face said she was readying for another attack. But when she spoke, her voice was weak and resigned. "I don't want to end it. I'm not ready."

I hadn't seen her that vulnerable since that morning in the hospital. It was hard to see her like that. She'd become so much more. So strong. Unbreakable. I closed my eyes and held onto the image of Celia that I liked best—carefree and in charge. Would ending the game take that away from her? I had no idea where I'd be without it in my life, but what about her?

It occurred to me that I wasn't there to save her. I was only there to save myself. If she needed to keep playing, then so be it.

I opened my eyes and met her glossy blues. "Then you don't have to. You're free to do whatever you want. I'm not about to try to stop you."

A tear slipped down her cheek. She looked away as she wiped it with her palm. "I really wasn't expecting this."

"Honestly, neither was I."

She circled behind me and grabbed a tissue from a decorative box on the occasional table. After dabbing at her eyes, she came and sat on the couch. "I was supposed to be the one who quit first."

I slipped down from the arm to the cushion next to her. "Because you wanted to leave me behind?"

She gave a one-shoulder shrug. "Maybe a bit of that."

At least we could be honest with each other. And I deserved that. Deserved any resentment that she might have tucked away. In fact, I owed her more. "I'm sorry for…things I've done. To you, I mean. I'm hoping that one day you can forgive me."

She swung her neck to deliver me an incredulous look. "Is this like AA where you ask for forgiveness from those you've wronged? Are you in therapy?"

I thought about denying it, but, hell, we were being honest. "I am."

"Oh." She bit her lip, seeming to ruminate on this new information. "You're not supposed to see me anymore, are you?"

"I'm…" I paused. Dr. Alberts had suggested a clean break. It made the most sense. Especially if Celia still planned to keep up her schemes. But I couldn't bring myself to say it. It wasn't just her splotchy face and pleading eyes that stopped me. I was changing, but not that fast. I was still self-centered. No, it was the burn in my chest. The ache that increased with every moment that I thought about the words I should be saying.

I changed my script. "Hey, I'm quitting the game. That doesn't mean I have to quit you."

Her brow ticked up. "Even if I decide to still play? Won't I be a temptation?"

"Maybe I want the temptation."

Her expression softened, her eyes lighting up with hope. "Do you really?"

Yes. No. I didn't have the answer. "I don't know. I don't know what I want, Celia. This isn't easy for me. I'm flying blind."

"And that's not like you."

"No, it's not." Actually, it was the weakest I thought I had ever been in front of her. Except for maybe the night we'd watched my drunken mother fire the nanny. Even then, I didn't think Celia grasped the extent of my vulnerability.

Now, there was nowhere to hide. She saw.

She shifted, angling her knees toward me, and patted me once on the thigh. "Here's what I think, and go ahead and bitch at me if it's not what you want to hear. I think this is a phase you're going through. It's something you have to try. I get that. But you're going to realize that you can't stay away. The game isn't just what you do; it's who you are. So go ahead and do this, this therapy thing. And when you're ready, I'll be here."

Years ago, when I'd first accepted her request to teach her the game, I'd thought the same thing about her. That she was going through a phase. That she'd abandon me after she got bored.

She'd surprised me when she stuck with it, much as she surprised me now.

"You might be waiting a long time," I said. "Full disclosure here."

"We'll see."

I swallowed. "Then you're going to keep playing?"

"I think I am. Is that all right?"

Not really. "I said it was. I'm not your keeper." Selfishly, I wanted her to quit as well. How much easier would it be to have a companion on the road to recovery? Was that even possible, for two addicts to be helpful to each other?

She must have sensed that I wasn't being entirely truthful. "What do you want me to do, Hudson?"

If I was really going through with this, really going to make an actual effort to be less manipulative and more sympathetic, then I had to start with Celia. "I want you to do what's best for you. For once. Honestly."

"Then I'm still playing." She smiled. "And don't be surprised if I try to tempt you back to my ways."

"Hey, that wasn't part of the deal."

She batted her lashes, feigning innocence. "You said you wanted what was best for me." Then she grew serious. "Best for me is to have you with me, Hudson. With me in the game, I mean. You've said I can't have that. But I have to keep trying."

So along with my own temptations, I'd have to battle Celia's enticement as well? Goddamn consequences. "That's fair, I suppose."

"Is it?"

"Does it matter if it is or isn't? You'll go after what you want either way."

"True." She smirked. "And you just said you want me to have what I want."

We were talking in circles, and it was exhausting. I'd thought for sure that seeing Celia would make me want to play again. Strangely, it hadn't. Instead, I saw how desperate and futile the experiments were. Here we were after all of our games, and with all the data and experience we'd collected, all we had between us was the next play. It wasn't sustainable. It wasn't—to use my own words—real.

Our relationship had to change. I saw that now. I'd said I wouldn't quit our friendship, but I didn't say to what extent I'd remain in contact. It would have to be limited, I realized. Family and business gatherings. Places where we couldn't talk and scheme. It wasn't only me I was protecting. Maybe, if we didn't see each other very often, maybe Celia would quit too.

Okay, I wasn't trying to save her, but wouldn't it be admirable if I did? Stripped of my superpowers, I was grasping for something—anything—to make me special rather than just an epic asshole.

Spending more time with Celia wasn't going to help with that. "I have to go, Ceely." I stood then turned to face her. "But, yes, I do want you to have what you want. I hope that someday you want something different than this."

She followed me, getting to her feet. "How patronizing."

I sighed. "I'm not trying to patronize. I'm trying to be honest."

"If we're being honest, can I ask something?"

"Sure."

She tapped her French-tipped nail against her chin. "Would blackmail work? To keep you playing, I mean."

A chill ran down my spine. I was stunned by her suggestion. Shocked. More than a little pissed. "Well, that really is honest, isn't it?" I eyed her carefully, looking for a sign that she might be bluffing. She did know my secrets, but would she really threaten to use them against me?

I saw none of her usual tells. While I felt a smidgeon of pride—oh, I'd taught her well—I mostly felt challenged. And I didn't like to be challenged, therapy or not. "I believe I have as much on you, Celia, as you could have on me."

A satisfactory smile slid across her lips. "Then we're agreed—our secrets are safe?"

"As long as it's mutual, then my lips are sealed."

"Then mine are too."

I left her apartment with more clarity than when I'd arrived. As much as I shouldn't engage with Celia Werner any further, I knew now that I could never cut her completely from my life. For one, I wasn't certain if she was actually a friend or a foe. And there was that old adage about keeping friends close and enemies closer.

But there was another thing—without the game, losing Celia would leave me entirely alone. And loneliness was one emotion I most desperately didn't want to learn.

— CHAPTER —

TWENTY-FIVE

After

Simply making the decision to tell Alayna the truth takes away a good portion of my fear. I no longer have to debate and war with myself. I no longer have to hide, and I'm anxious to be with her again. So when I wrap up my business in L.A. earlier than I expect, I decide to fly back and surprise the woman I love. Yes, it means my secret will be exposed sooner than if I hadn't pulled my weight to get my meetings scheduled on a Sunday, aka "off hours", but I'm ready.

What I'm not ready for is the greeting that meets me when I arrive at The Sky Launch later that evening. I'd known she'd be here for David's going away party, and, eager to see her, I headed straight over after landing. It had taken a few minutes to find her. She wasn't with the rest of the guests who are mostly mingling by the bar and on the dance floor. Instead, she's tucked away in a corner. But she *is* dancing. Slow dancing. In David's arms.

I watch them, mesmerized, unable to look away like is often the case when met with something horrible. Neither of them notice me, and from my vantage, I can't see Alayna's face. But I can see David's. His eyes are closed, but his expression is tender and forlorn. He seems to be whispering into her ear—singing perhaps. If I ever doubted that he had feelings for her, I don't now.

It's simply a dance, I tell myself. *Then he's going away.* It's likely her way of saying goodbye. If I were a different man, I'd give them privacy.

But I'm not a different man. I'm this one. And I'm thoroughly possessive. So I'm still watching when they stop moving and make eye contact. And I see when he leans forward and kisses her.

It's a moment of revelation. The first moment I feel absolute pain. There's a wave of panic accompanied by this crushing weight against my chest. It takes away all ability to move. All ability to breathe.

She pushes him away, and I should be grateful. But I'm still caught in the *before*. It replays in my head as if on constant repeat—her in his arms, his mouth against hers. Against the mouth that is *mine*. He doesn't love her like I do. He can't. It's impossible. His feelings are small and inconsequential compared to the immense affection for her that travels through my body with one beat of my heart. He would have never let her go if he felt how I do.

And now another new emotion—I want to hurt David. I want him dead. For daring to touch the woman that doesn't belong to him. For attempting to steal what is so very clearly mine. My hands are fists at my side and I'm imagining the ways I want to punish him, ways that can never equate to the pain I feel inside.

And her...

The betrayal is really hers, but I don't want to hurt her. I want to pull her into me, into my very soul, so that she can see how I feel about her, see how this rips me apart. Tie her to me so completely that she can't ever be out of my control. This was why I sent David away in the first place. This is why I hold onto her as tightly as I do. This is why I doubt her when she says she means forever. If she can wound me like this, then how easily will she leave me when it's warranted?

It's a fragment of my greatest fear realized—she loves me, but she doesn't love me *enough*.

I'm barely aware of when they discover my presence. I hear her say my name. Hear her tell me that it's not what it looks like.

It doesn't matter what it looks like. I know exactly what it *is*—it's the worst moment of my life so far. And I know it's only the beginning.

"Maybe we should discuss this in a more private setting," I manage. She agrees and painful minutes later we're alone in the employee office.

"*He* kissed me, Hudson. I didn't kiss him. And when he did, I pushed him away." The regret of her action is in her face and her voice.

Yet, the pain rages on. "Why were you in his arms in the first place?"

"We were dancing. It was a party."

"You were in his arms, Alayna. In the arms of someone who has made no secret of his feelings for you. What did you think he'd do?" I don't mean to be this angry. I am fully aware that this is minor in the scheme of ways that I've betrayed her.

But it doesn't change how I feel. My inexperience with this emotion rules how I behave.

"It was innocent," she insists. "I needed someone. He was here. And you weren't." Her expression changes and her words grow bitter. "Where were you today, anyway? When I needed you?"

I was fucking saving her from Celia, that's where I was. My own bitterness shows in my words. "What was it you needed, Alayna? Someone to keep you warm?"

She presses her lips together. "That hurts."

"What I just witnessed hurts." I sound cruel. It's not the reunion I wanted. There's so much we need to be talking about, and we're stuck on this. Perhaps I'm grasping onto it so I don't have to say the other words. The ones that will hurt her even more.

She's equally unkind. "Yeah, I know how it feels."

"Do you?"

"Yeah, I do. Let me see if I can explain it. It feels like your gut has been wrenched out of your body. At least that's what it felt like when Celia told me that you'd been *fucking her* for most of the time we've been together."

I'm caught off guard by her words. "What?" This is new and all of a sudden I'm worried that I've missed something. "When did she say that?"

She tells me.

"You saw her today?" Earlier, before I'd boarded my plane, I'd checked my voicemail and discovered a message from Celia. I'd deleted it. It was something about her lawyer and Alayna. Since I'd had no messages from Jordan or Reynold, I'd figured it was another attempt to rile me up over nothing. I ask Alayna about it now.

She explains that she'd snuck away for coffee. That she'd taken her computer. That she'd encountered Celia. David becomes a conversation for later. I'm instantly concerned about *this*—what Celia did. What Celia said.

I'm tense throughout her recounting of the event, but I try to maintain my temper. It's especially hard when Alayna admits that she's the one who approached Celia. After all I've done to keep them apart, this is hard to hear. It's as if Alayna's working purposefully against me, undermining my attempts to protect our relationship. Of course she has no idea that she's doing it.

"Then she said that you were together," Alayna says finally. "That you were a couple. That you fucked her that night and it wasn't the first time and it wasn't the last."

"And you believed her?" It's a blatant lie, of course. While it's not the most horrid thing that Celia could say, it's another straw on the heap of anger I feel toward her.

Alayna straightens proudly. "It pissed me off enough that I punched her."

"You *punched* her?"

Alayna stiffens. "You know what? Keep acting like this is an interrogation and I'm out of here." Apparently, shock wasn't the right response.

Honestly, besides shock, I don't know what I'm feeling at the moment. That's not true. I do know. I'm mad. Mad at Celia. Mad that Alayna let Celia get to her. Mad that she got herself in a situation where Celia could have hurt her.

But my anger is out of worry. And I don't want to be mad at Alayna.

I walk the room as I shove my hands through my hair, trying to calm down. When I'm as in control as I think I'll get, I stop and face her. "I'm sorry if I sound a bit tense, Alayna. I assure you it's only out of concern for you."

Finally, I've said the right thing. Alayna cools and I begin to understand the situation that I walked into. She'd done something she knew she shouldn't. She was scared. She needed me. I wasn't there. She turned to a friend for comfort. He kissed her. It doesn't lessen the pain at seeing her wrapped in his arms, but now it's me that's to blame. I should have been here. I should have called her before leaving from L.A. I should never have gotten her in this position in the first place—pitted against a woman that is dangerous and unwavering.

I understand Alayna's worries. Celia might try to press charges, but I have the deal with GlamPlay and Werner Media to hold over her head now. I almost tell Alayna about it. Except the paperwork still needs to be filed in the morning, and I have to be sure everything goes through. So I simply assure her that I will take care of everything.

"Thank you." Her relief is evident. She believes me. She trusts me in this and I'm comforted.

She, however, still needs reassuring. "Hudson." Her voice trembles. "I'm sorry."

"Don't be. Good for you, actually. She deserves worse." I'm proud, really. I knew Alayna was stronger than Celia thought she was. It's fantastic that she's had the chance to prove it.

But Alayna frowns. "I mean, I'm sorry about David."

"Oh." I see them together again in my head—her face pressed against his shoulder. I have to know, so I ask. "Tell me one thing—do you still feel anything for him?"

"No. No, I don't. Nothing. I've told you that before, and I meant it, though I'm sure it doesn't seem like it seeing me tonight. But the whole time he was holding me, it felt wrong. All I could think about was you. I was missing you, H. Needing you. So much. And I didn't think about what I was doing. I'm so, so, sor—"

I fly to her, unable to stand the distance between us any longer. I wrap my arms around her and clutch her tight. "I missed you too, precious. Needed you. I was trying to get back here—"

She cuts me off. "And I ruined your surprise. I'm so sorry."

"I don't care. It hurts, but I've hurt you. And as long as you swear that he means nothing—"

"Nothing. I swear with every fiber of my body, it's only you." She kisses along my jaw. God, she's here. She's mine. And for this moment I let myself believe that this could be always—the always that I've promised her. The always that I want to live with her. Her caught up with me as I am with her.

Then she asks, "How about you? Do you still feel anything for Celia?"

And the moment is ended.

I remember now that this reunion isn't supposed to end like this. There's more to say. More to explain. And this is where I have to begin.

I lean back to meet her eyes. "Alayna…I've never felt anything for Celia."

"You mean, it was just sex?"

I shake my head. "I've never been with her at all."

"She was lying."

She's not asking, but I confirm anyway. "She was lying."

"That's what I thought." There's no relief in her voice, and that makes me nervous. She pulls away from me, leaving me chilled. "But here's the thing," she says. "I sort of wish it were true."

I know in my heart what she's getting at. She's figuring it out. She's a smart woman and the truth was always there, waiting for her to simply put it together.

I watch her as she does just that. "Not that you were sleeping with her while we were together—not that part. But the rest of it—that you were really with her when Stacy saw you. If that was the truth, I could accept it. Don't get me wrong—the idea of you with her, fucking her—it torments me. It really does. But I think I always knew you were never with her. It's in your eyes—both now and in that video."

I swallow. "I wasn't. I was never with her."

"And that means that the thing with Stacy was a scam. Of course it was. I wanted to think it was just Celia in on it, and you were protecting her. But you said you weren't and you did go along enough to stage that kiss. You were part of it."

If we could leave it here where she's paused, I know we'd be fine. But we can't. I promised her the truth. All of it. I'm just not sure if it's better to let her proceed or to jump in with my confession.

Since I seem to have lost my ability to speak, it's her that goes on. "I thought for a minute that might be your secret. Except it's not it. I mean, yeah, that's shitty that you did that to her, but I knew you had those things in your past. And *you* knew that I knew those things. If that were all there was to learn from that video, you would have told me. There had to be more you were hiding."

It unfolds like a master detective solving the crime that has teased and taunted her, threatening to get the better of her and then she finally gets the clue she needs to put it to rest.

Alayna raises her eyes to mine. "It's because of what night it was, the night of the symposium, isn't it? I considered that you didn't want me to know that you were still manipulating people for fun that recently, but now I don't think that's all of it either."

"Alayna..." It's like watching a fragile object fall from a great height. A beautiful vase, perhaps. A crystal figurine. For a moment it feels like if I move fast enough I can catch it before it shatters all over the floor. But I'm too far away. Time seems to slow and every millisecond feels like an eternity.

She pieces together the secret that I've hidden from her, the truth of our beginning. And no matter how much I want to stop her, all I can do is watch her fall.

"It's not the video itself. It's what happened after."

"Alayna," I say again. It's the only word I have. A prayer for strength. For me. For her.

"If Celia was there with you outside the symposium...then doesn't it make sense that she went in with you? And if she went in with you, she was there when you first saw me. And if you were still playing people together..."

I can pinpoint the moment that she finally lets the truth sink in. Her face goes white and her shoulders fall inward as if she's been hit in the gut. Her anguish is palpable.

It's unbearable. "I was going to tell you. I came back to tell you." The words come now. The speeches I've prepared and rewritten in my mind over and over.

Excuses that mean shit. "It's my worst mistake, Alayna." I step toward her. "The most horrible of all the things I've done. My biggest regret, although it's what gave me you and for that I'm forever grateful. But I never knew what I'd feel for you. I never knew that I could hurt you that much, and that I would care that I did. Please, Alayna, you have to understand."

I'm desperate for her to hear me, but my voice seems to roll past her. She's in her own nightmare, and I can't get to her.

"That's what I was, wasn't I? A game. Your game. Together." She collapses to the floor. "Oh God. Oh God, oh God."

"Alayna—" I fall to my knees, reaching for her. I need her, need to fix her with my touch like I always do.

But she scrambles away. "Don't touch me!"

Her scream pierces through me. I've never heard this depth of pain and revulsion in her tone. The weight of it matches my own pain, blurring my vision, causing my heart to race.

I refuse to stop fighting though. I have to reach her, somehow. If not with my touch, then my words will have to do. "It wasn't what you think, Alayna. Yes, it started as a game. As Celia's game. But I only went along because it was you. Because I was so enamored with you."

She stares at me, blinking as if seeing me clearly for the first time. And isn't she? Finally seeing the devil that I've been in disguise.

She bends over, dry heaving.

I understand. I'm just as disgusted with myself.

I'm desperate to help her, but afraid she'll push me away again. "Alayna, let me—"

She puts her hand up to stop me from coming closer. "I don't want your help." She wipes her mouth with the back of her hand. "I want fucking answers."

"Anything. I told you I'd tell you anything." Maybe if she heard all of it… maybe then she'd understand.

But as she asks her questions and as I answer, I can hear the story the way she does. It's awful. It's ugly. It's absolutely evil.

I beg her to let me try to explain it in my own words. The words that I've saved for this occasion. But they're just as bad. Each new sentence seems to shatter her in a new way. And each new crack that rips through her echoes through me with lightening pain. Even as I plead with her I don't know what I'm asking for. For understanding? For love? For forgiveness?

I know I've lost my rights to all of these. It comes as no surprise when she declares in weighted, measured words, "This is unforgiveable, Hudson. There is no moving forward from this."

She's said these words to me before, in every nightmare imagining I've had about telling her the truth. It's why I'd hid it for so long. Because these words seemed inevitable.

Yet I can't accept it. It hurts too goddamned much to let this be the end. "Don't say that. Don't ever say that."

"What is it exactly that you don't want to hear, Hudson? That I can't forgive you? I can't." She's trying to hurt me now; I feel it. "I can't forgive this. Ever."

I also know she means it. Still, I reach for her. "Alayna, please!"

She kicks at me, screaming words that bruise and break me. She tells me we're over. She tells me she can never trust me again. I have no hope—I'm already destroyed—but I keep fighting. Keep protesting. Keep promising my love. I'll do anything to fix this. Anything to take this back.

But each time I reach for her with words or my hands, she pushes me away. Shoves me down. Do I really expect anything different? I've seen love deteriorate before. I've watched it unravel before my eyes. This is something I know. It's the thing I've always been good at—destroying the fairytale of happy ever after.

Love doesn't bear all. Love doesn't endure. Love ends. It always, always ends.

For all that I've destroyed—in my past, with Celia, here today in Alayna— my curse is that my love alone goes on. My whole life I was empty. Now I'm full. Overflowing with love and anguish. Hers and mine. They are so completely entwined, so thoroughly mixed in each other that I don't believe they'll ever be separate. I love Alayna Withers. And each drop of that love is so laced with pain that it travels through my veins like acid, burning and scarring me from the inside out.

There's nothing more I can say. There's nothing more she'll hear.

There's a knock on the door and David sticks his head inside. He ignores me and directs his focus to Alayna. "Are you okay, Laynie?"

She's honest in her answer. "No. I'm not okay."

It's her cue for me to leave. But I try once more, unable to let go of her. "Alayna…"

With a simple shake of her head she ends it. Ends us.

"I'll leave." I long for her to stop me. She doesn't.

I turn to David. "I'm sorry to put a damper on your party. Thank you for looking out for her." Though it pains me, I'm grateful that she has someone to care for her when I leave. She's strong, I know. But I can't bear for her to be alone. Like I'll be.

I look at her one last time. I'm buried under an avalanche of regret. I can barely move, barely breathe under its weight.

Somehow, though, I manage to turn away. Because that's what she wants. And after all that I've taken from her, this I can give her—I walk out the door and leave.

The only thing that keeps me alive for the next few days is my commitment to making sure Alayna is surviving. I spend Monday morning getting the battery charges against Alayna dropped and finalizing details over GlamPlay with Norma. I've kept Jordan on duty, watching Alayna from afar in case Celia decides to try anything, and I check in with him often. I order a Kindle and start loading Alayna's favorite books on it so she'll have something to do besides obsess and be sad. Those are *my* tasks this time. I'll obsess about her instead of the other way around. I'll be sad enough for both of us.

I call Liesl. I'm grateful to find that Alayna's with her and not with David. I don't give excuses. I don't beg for another chance. I tell Liesl truths—that the police aren't looking for Alayna, that her job is secure, that she can stay at the penthouse, that I'm here when she wants to talk. That I love her.

Liesl seems to care enough about Alayna to let me talk, though she scoffs at my proclamation of love. "She doesn't want to hear that," she says.

"It doesn't make it any less true."

I eat, but only because I need energy to keep fighting for Alayna. I don't bury myself in Scotch, tempting as it may be. I'll be no good for her like that. I don't sleep. I ache. I feel. I try not to drown in my emotions.

When the pain gets too unbearable, I remind myself that hers is worse. I try to embrace the misery. It's justice for what I've done. Consequences.

And I text her. I'm sure she's not reading my messages, but it feels good to say the things that I want to say. I send so many that it seems our roles have reversed—I've become the stalker. I'm the one who can't help myself. I tell her anything and everything.

I miss you, I say.

I heard that Phillip Phillips song on the radio today. You make it so easy...

Jack asked about you. You should call him sometime. I'm sure he'd love to hear from you.

And so many times just, *I love you.*

God, I really fucking love her.

Tuesday, I call Dr. Alberts for an appointment. He says he'll see me that day with the same conditions as previously given—I have to meet him at his office instead of mine. I agree.

It's easier to talk to him now than it was before. Alayna opened gates in me that can never be closed again. I tell him everything. "She taught me how to feel," I say, my eyes fixed on the smooth surface of his tray ceiling. "She taught me how to have emotions."

Dr. Alberts doesn't see it the way I do. "She didn't teach you. You always knew how. You worked hard all this time trying to forget that. But you were never incapable. You created blocks when you were young to deal with the heartache that surrounded your family life. You didn't feel because it was easier not to. It was a coping mechanism."

I work my jaw as I consider this. There are memories that creep up on me sometimes, very specific ones from my youth where my feelings are so bright they show through in my mind like a color. Reds and purples and greens. They're few and far between, but they're there. Were those remnants of the days before I learned to cope?

And if so, why didn't Dr. Alberts say this to me before? I ask him.

"You weren't ready to hear it. The question is, why do you think that you decided to let yourself now? You saw this woman from afar and immediately you were ready to take the first steps. Why?"

I'm certain Dr. Alberts isn't the type to accept love at first sight as an answer. Honestly, I'm not either. I take a second to figure out what the answer really is. "She was familiar," I say, finally. "I recognized that she'd struggled. And yet she'd come out okay. It was beautiful about her and I wanted to get to know it more. I wanted that for myself."

"And you realized to get that, you had to start to feel again."

"I guess so." It's oversimplified. But isn't everything?

It occurs to me that I have other questions that are in need of simple answers. Questions that my therapist may be able to put to rest. I sit up, and meet him face-to-face. "I'd been okay without playing people anymore. Why did I decide that I had to play the game to get close to Alayna?"

He steeples his fingers and rests his chin against them. "Why do you think?"

"Because I didn't know any other way to relate to people." It's the reason I've clung to anyway.

"I imagine there's truth to that." He thinks for a moment. "And you liked to do it, Hudson. Maybe you don't anymore—it sounds like you've overcome that addiction—but you did. The rush it gave you was a substitute for the real emotions that you'd buried inside. You manipulated Alayna because a part of you wanted to."

It's hard to hear, and I start to object. But then I stop myself. Because he's right. There was a part of me that wanted exactly that. Wanted to feel the racing of my heart as I attempted to guess how she'd behave. Wanted the reward of predicting her. I'd felt a rush the moment I'd seen her, and the game was the way I knew to recapture it. That thrill had quickly been replaced with the thrill of falling in love.

But that first yes—when I'd told Celia I'd play—that was wrong. I had no excuse. I was to blame.

Dr. Alberts recognizes my thought process. "Acceptance is the first step to moving on, Hudson. It's why you could never fully recover before—because you never really accepted the blame for your actions. This is great progress. Talking about it, sharing what you've done with those close to you will help as well. I recommend you work on that next."

Since he has no patients scheduled after me, Dr. Alberts lets me stay for two hours. Since we're in his office and not mine, no one interrupts. I forget about work. I concentrate on me. With his help, I work through many life-long questions I've had about myself. It's eye-opening. Liberating.

The one thing he can't answer, though, is the one thing I want to know most: Is there any chance Alayna can ever forgive me?

TWENTY-SIX

On Wednesday, Mirabelle stops by my office. I've cancelled most of my non-urgent appointments so I'm available to see her. I ask Patricia to send her back.

My sister's face is serious. I know it's not her health—she would have called if there were any new threats to her or the baby. I have to assume she's here about Alayna.

"I'm guessing you've talked to her," I ask as she settles into the armchair in my seating area.

Her brow furrows. "Talked to who? Mom?"

"No, I meant Alayna." I grab a bottle of water from my mini-fridge and hand it to her before taking a seat on the couch. "Aren't you here about her?"

"I am now." Her eyes narrow mischievously. "What's going on?"

I'll have to tell her eventually. But I don't know if I can talk about it. Not yet. I scrub my hand over my face. "Forget I said anything."

"Uh, that's not happening." She leans forward and places her hand on my knee. "Hudson?" I shake my head, but, as always, she reads me. "Oh, God. What happened? Tell me."

"She…" I take a deep breath in and blow it out before I can go on. "She left me, Mirabelle."

"No way." She studies me. "You're serious."

How I wish I wasn't. "I told her everything she wanted to know, and she left me." It's no easier saying it this time than it was a moment ago. My voice catches on the words. Not only am I now able to feel, but it also appears that I'm unable to keep my feelings hidden.

"I'm sure you're overreacting. People fight. You'll get past this."

I don't want to argue with her. I'd rather let her hope for the best. I'm still hoping, after all. So I simply say, "Anything's possible, I suppose."

"But you don't really believe that." She tilts her head and stares at me with sympathetic eyes. "Oh, Hudson, what happened? Maybe I can help."

I know she can't help, and that's why I don't intend to tell her. But then I remember what Dr. Alberts said about opening up to those close to me. To see progression in my therapy, I have to work for it. And I want to see progression. I don't know if there's any chance at all that Alayna and I can be together again, but if there is, I know that I need to be the best man possible. The best *me* possible.

So, for the second time in two days, I tell the story. It's harder to share with Mirabelle. She doesn't hide the disappointment in her features. She frequently brushes tears from her eyes, but she listens without interrupting.

When I'm finished, she lets out a breathy sigh. Then she says, "Fuck you, Hudson."

I'm surprised—not because I don't deserve the cursing, but because I didn't expect it. Not from her.

"I love you. I really do." Her voice is heavy with emotion. "And I'm always going to be here for you, but you really fucked up this time. And if you don't recognize that, then there's no hope for you."

I bow my head. I can't look at her anymore. Her disapproval hurts almost as much as Alayna's. "I recognize it. Fully."

She won't look at me. "That's something at least."

"It's the worst thing I've ever done."

"I don't doubt it." There's a bite to her words. They're pointed and sharp. They leave marks on me.

I always thought of myself as well-armored. Nothing could get in. And now when I really look, I see the scars. Feel their jagged edges across every inch of my body. Can everyone see them? Can Mirabelle?

I'm broken and mangled, but it's suddenly important to me that she knows I'm trying to stand again. "Losing her, Mirabelle, it's...it's hitting bottom. I'm seeing Dr. Alberts again. I tried to change when you sent me before, but now—now I want it."

Finally she looks at me. There's an edge of kindness in her gaze and a pinch of pity. "I'm glad to hear that, Hudson. I really am. I only want the best for you. And I sincerely believe you can be a different man if you want to be."

"I do." I want it retrospectively. Why couldn't I have been a different man before I met Alayna? If I'd tried harder to change before, then could I have been ready to meet her as my best self?

It's hopeless to dwell on what-ifs. Yet they sneak in anyway. I let my head fall back and close my eyes.

Mirabelle moves to sit next to me. Without saying a word, she runs her fingers through my hair. It's soothing. Hypnotic.

I swallow past the tight ball in my throat. "I fucked up, but I genuinely love her."

"I know." Her voice is gentle now. "She's not the only reason you want to change, is she?"

"Possibly." It's not the right answer, but it's the truth.

Mirabelle's hand only pauses for a half second before resuming her calming strokes across my scalp. "Because I don't know that you can win her back. This is…it's bad, Hudson. There may be no moving on from this."

I force a laugh. "The queen of love-conquers-all has doubts? Man, I'm really fucked."

"I'm just being honest." She leans her head against my shoulder. "And I want you better with or without her."

I can't imagine a without her. Even while we're apart, she's still so present in my life. I know what Mirabelle means, but I simply can't let myself think like that. "It won't be a problem. I won't ever stop loving Alayna. I need to be ready in case she ever changes her mind." *When* she changes her mind.

"Hudson. I'm so mad at you." Mirabelle sits up and punches her fist into my chest. It's a heavy enough hit, though I barely feel it through the pain that already encompasses me. I wish she'd hit me again, actually. Wish she'd beat me to a pulp.

She doesn't. Instead, she lays her palm flat against me and lays her head back on my shoulder. "And I'm so heartbroken. For both of you. I love that girl too, you know."

"I know." I'm not usually the type to cuddle up with my little sister, but I don't know who I am "usually" anymore. So I wrap my arm around her tiny frame and pull her in closer. We sit like this, both of us mourning our loss.

Then she bolts up. "Ah, shit! My opening! Laynie's supposed to be a model. She'll probably back out now."

"If I'm there, yes, I'd bet she does cancel." I'd thought about this. There's nothing I haven't thought about regarding Alayna. But my next words are not premeditated. "I won't come."

Mirabelle looks at me, seeming to gage my seriousness. When she realizes that I'm completely genuine, she says. "I know I should try to argue, but honestly? I don't want to. Don't hate me."

"I understand. She's your model. You need her. I know she wants to be there for you. So please, let me back out." I also hope it's something that will get Alayna out of her shell. Something that will remind her how to keep living. It's not about Celia winning or losing anymore—Alayna has to survive because I *will not* be the person who destroyed her.

"Okay. I'll let you back out. You're banned from the premises on Saturday." The gleam in her eyes says she understands the entirety of my motivation. "I mean it though. You can't change your mind and show up."

"I won't. Scout's honor." Like I was ever a scout. Like I ever had honor.

I reach up to erase the smudge her earlier tears have left under her eye. I'm suddenly moved by this beautiful creature. Besides Alayna, she's the one person who has been able to see something more from me than what I put on display. And I'm pretty sure I've never told her as much.

So I tell her now. "I could never hate you, Mirabelle. I love you. I want you to be happy. I want you to be proud to be my sister. As proud as I am to be your brother. You've often been the only support I've had. The only one who's believed in me. I hate that you're looking at me now with disappointment."

Her eyes well, but she smiles. "I'm disappointed, Hudson. I am. But it doesn't mean I'm not proud to be your sister. I love you, too. Don't give up on her. More importantly, don't give up on yourself. I never will."

She hugs me, and I let her.

For a few minutes, anyway. I'm the one who pushes out of her embrace. It feels too good, and feeling good is not on my agenda. My mind wanders back to the person it never really leaves. "Alayna might still back out of the opening, you know. Even without me there."

"I know." Her tone says she's not concerned. If anyone can convince Alayna otherwise, it's Mirabelle. "I'm going to think optimistically. And I'm going to be optimistic about the two of you too. I don't think I'll let her know that I know what happened. She could be really embarrassed about this. Maybe she'll feel more comfortable if she isn't worried about what I think about it all."

"That's insightful." I hadn't even considered she might be humiliated. But of course she is. She'd been duped by an asshole. "I'll support however you want to play it."

I cringe at my choice of words. "I'll support whatever you say, I mean."

She catches my correction. With a sad smile she reaches up to tousle my hair. "You're a good guy, Hudson. You did a really shitty thing, but you're still a really good guy." A tear slips down her cheek. She wipes at it with zest. "God, I have to get out of here. I'm too hormonal for this crap."

"You're fine." I stand though and help her up beside me. Then I remember, "But was there another reason you came by?"

"Oh, yeah. There was. There is. I'm telling you—hormone brain is crazy." She shifts her weight on to one leg and bites at her lip. "Anyway, I hate to bring this up after all that you're going through, but there's something important, and I need your help."

I hate that she's nervous about asking. Doesn't she know I'd do almost anything for her? "Of course. What is it?"

"It's mom. She's in trouble."

Now I understand her hesitancy. "She's been in trouble for a long time." Longer than any of us.

Mirabelle nods. "And we haven't been there for her. It's time that we are."

"Are you staging another intervention?" The look on her face answers the question for me. "Ah, you are."

"You think it's stupid?"

I'm surprised we've never discussed this before. All these years we've just let Sophia live as though her drinking wasn't a big deal. As though it was normal. Because we'd never known her any other way, it actually was normal. It was the normal we knew, anyway.

But we'd grown up. Somewhere along the way we realized that her behavior wasn't healthy or sane. And still we'd done nothing.

Mirabelle's right when she says it's time we did something. "It's not at all stupid," I say. "It's beautiful."

Hope shines in her eyes. "Really, you think so?"

"I do."

"Thank you. That's really a relief." It shows. Her shoulders relax and she stops nipping at her bottom lip.

Once again, Mirabelle moves me. I draw her into a hug. "I don't know how you ended up surrounded by such broken and battered souls. We don't deserve you. But I honestly believe none of us would have made it as far as we have if it hadn't been for you holding us together. You're our glue. You're *my* glue."

Jesus, when did I develop such diarrhea of the mouth?

Mirabelle nudges me with her elbow. "That was awfully poetic, Hudson. I'd say I didn't know you had it in you, but that would be a lie. There's hope for you yet."

I'm not sure that's true. But wouldn't it be wonderful if it were?

———

That night the weight of it all hits me. I'm in the loft, sitting on the couch in the dark, when pain rips through my chest like a bulldozer running me down. There isn't a part of me that doesn't ache—my hands, my feet. My head throbs. Blood rushes in my ears. My heart pounds as if it's going to burst from my chest. It bends me over, stealing my breath. I gasp for air in huge gulps that are half sobs.

It's a death. The ending of what was and the painful rebirth that follows. I wrap my arms around myself, my fingernails digging into my ribcage, clutching as if I can hold on where I was. I will the world to stop spinning around me. I break out in a sweat. I cry the only name that gives me comfort. Her name. Over and over.

I don't want to go through this. I don't want to be without her. I don't want to miss her like I do, longing for her taste, her touch, her sound. I don't want to be reborn in this new world, a world that means nothing in her absence.

I don't want to be in this life without her.

———

The next morning I'm met with a text on my phone. I hold my breath, hoping it's from Alayna. It's not, but the message motivates me to get out of bed anyway. It's from Norma. *All the papers are in place. I'll have them waiting on your desk when you get in.*

Finally, I have what I need to get rid of Celia once and for all.

Seven hours later, I'm sitting on the armchair in the loft, swirling the ice in my empty glass of Scotch while Celia looks over the contracts for the business I've worked so hard to acquire. I've dragged this moment out, letting her argue and goad before presenting her with the facts. It's the last game I ever plan on playing, and I want to enjoy it.

Except there isn't any enjoyment in it. There's no rush. There's no thrill. Perhaps I'm too numb with sadness about Alayna, but I know that's not it. I've lost the taste for the play. That's all.

So as Celia reads, I silently say goodbye. Even through the ache, I feel a breath of peace.

I watch her as she flips through the pages. She takes her time. I'm sure some of the language is difficult for her to sift through, but I can tell when she understands. Her face goes white and her breathing slows.

Finally, she asks, "How did you...?"

"Very sneakily." I force myself to relish this moment. I did this for Alayna, and I wish she could witness it. I'm proud that I could do this for her, though she would never have needed this sort of protection if it weren't for me in the first place. "I'll admit, it wasn't easy. I had to convince another company to purchase a portion of the stock, and then I bought out that company—you don't really want the details, do you?"

She scowls. Every trace of humor has left her eyes.

"The contracts are signed now. That's all that matters. I'm officially the majority owner of Werner Media Corporation."

Celia's lips tighten as she closes the file that contains the contracts. "And you said you'd quit playing the game."

"I had one final move to make." I wonder briefly if she really thinks that this is just another game for me. She'd loved once upon a time. Doesn't she remember?

A familiar stab of guilt strikes me, low and hard in the gut.

And then it's gone.

It's been so easy to blame myself for her. But sooner or later, we have to take responsibility for ourselves—just as Dr. Alberts said. I may have taught her this life, but she's the one who chose to embrace it. Now, as I try to show her another way to live, she refuses to see it.

I'm not responsible for her. It's the final snipping of the cord that bound us together. The last strand between us, clipped and now we're both completely free.

Celia sees it too. She lets me go on a long, slow hiss of air. "It's checkmate, is it then?"

"You tell me." It's almost admirable how she plays to the very end. Once upon a time I would have been impressed. Now, I'm weary.

"What are your plans for Werner Media?"

This is a fair question. "At the moment, I have no plans. The company's doing well as it is. Warren Werner is definitely the right man to be in charge. However, if there were any reason that I felt his presence was no longer needed..." I trail off, letting her fill in the blanks.

"He'd be devastated." Her brows are pinched and her usual stone cold expression has been replaced with despondency.

I feel a flicker of relief. I'd gambled here. My entire plan only worked if Celia still had the capability to care for someone other than herself—namely, her father. It's further proof that she's only living like she's heartless because she chooses to.

Though I don't rule out that her concern may be monetary—I've been convinced for ages that Celia lives off her daddy's wealth. And while he'd still have it even if I stole his title, it's less likely he'd feel as generous. It's well known that a happy Warren is a sharing Warren.

"I imagine he'd be devastated just to learn he no longer holds controlling interest. For now, the fact is still hidden. He has no idea that he's no longer in charge. Would you like that to change?"

"No," she says.

"Do you plan on doing anything that might cause me to alter my current business plan?"

Her shoulders sag. "No."

"Then yes, it's checkmate."

We sit, silently for several minutes. It's been a long battle. And this is the official end of our friendship. It deserves some mourning. Memories flip through my mind like a bunch of stills in a photo slideshow. Some are from so long ago, I can't date them accurately. Others so imprinted in my soul I'll never forget the details. Her winning backhand stroke in a game of tennis that had been so close. The bottle of champagne we opened at the end of our first successful play. Her hand on my back and her soft, sincere confession—*I love you.*

This is all the time I'll spend grieving for what we once were. It's brief, but I let myself feel it.

Eventually she stands. "I guess it's time for me to go."

"It is. I'll walk you out."

I check my watch as we cross the floor together. I need to leave for my parents in half an hour or so. Today is Mirabelle's planned intervention. *A day of hard words*, I think. And hard emotions. It's as if I can make up for a lifetime of non-feeling in just a few days' time. It's something I hope to never have to do again.

I open the door for Celia and hold it wide for her to cross past me. She doesn't look at me as she does. Or I don't look at her. I'm not sure which. I start to shut it behind her when my gaze hits something unexpected—a duffel bag on the floor. It's Alayna's. I'm sure of it.

Or is that wishful thinking?

No, it's hers. I packed it for her on our trip to the Poconos. But what is it doing here?

A sudden burst of anticipation shoots through me and I scan the room, hoping against all hopes that I'll see what I so want to see.

I do.

My eyes lock on hers. She's kneeling on the floor at the threshold to the bedroom. Her posture suggests that she's not here to stay, that she didn't want me to know she was even here at all—the duffel is misleading. Still, I'm elated. I've missed seeing her face, missed connecting with her even on such a base level.

I'm desperate to stay and talk to her. Eager to find out why she's here. And, I realize suddenly, she's seen the ending of me and Celia. I couldn't have wished for her to witness anything else that might better prove my love for her.

But though I'm desperate and eager and so yearning to stay, I know that if I do, I'll never get out of here in time for my mother. It's an obligation I can't ignore. Something I need to do before I can say my demons are slayed and I'm able to be the man that Alayna might be able to call hers again.

I'm not the only one who's not ready—she's not ready either. I feel it deep in my soul. She needs more time to process, and rushing it will do me no good for the long term.

So I have to hold onto this moment to get me through. Hold onto the love that still shines so clearly in her eyes and hope that it can eventually be enough.

"Hold the elevator," I call after Celia without looking away from my precious Alayna. It's always so hard to leave her. But right now I'm feeling strong, and I shut the door behind me.

Celia's waiting in the elevator holding the *door open* button. I step inside and the door closes. We travel silently for several seconds before she says, "Well, this is awkward."

Honestly, I've forgotten she is even there. I'm still back in the loft, my heart and mind fixed on Alayna. I pull myself from there to the present. "Is it really? I haven't ever lost this big. I wouldn't know." I blame my condescension on the rush from discovering our eavesdropper. But I may have been just as cocky had Alayna gone unseen.

Celia, does not seem to appreciate it. "You're an asshole."

"It's a fraction of what you deserve." The smallest fraction, though, I try not to dwell on the myriad list of worse things I could do to her. It's satisfying to contemplate but more focused on the negative than I'd like to be.

Celia crosses her arms over her chest and eyes me. "You know, my father is going to retire someday. What will you have over me then?"

I roll my eyes. "Please. Your father's going to work until he dies. I give him another twenty years, at least. If you're still holding on to a revenge plot at that time...well, I don't think you could call anything you do a win then. You aren't that pathetic."

A sideways glance at her says that maybe she is that pathetic. The idea of her still perpetuating this scheme against us years from now enrages me. I level my gaze at her and steel my voice. "But if you need further reason to drop this game, let me give one to you. I tied your hands legally. I'd prefer not to use other methods to stop you, but hear this—I'd kill for Alayna if it came down to it. Please don't test me on that."

She shrugs dismissively. "It was only a question. I didn't mean anything by it. The game is over and I'm bored with you both." She purses her lips. "I certainly hypothesized incorrectly on this one, didn't I? I'd never have pegged you for a hero."

It's a backhanded compliment, and it makes me smile inwardly. She's not alone. I certainly never would have bet on me to fall in love.

But wait—why was she pegging me at all? "Who exactly was your subject on this experiment, Celia?"

The doors open and she exits without answering. Stunned by my realization, I'm a few steps behind her. I'm not about to run her down, but I call after her again. "Celia?"

Surprisingly, she turns back. "What?"

I close the distance between us, my heart that had skipped a beat a moment before, now racing. "You were never really playing Alayna, were you? It was me. You were playing me."

The spark in her eye says I've hit the nail on the head.

The pieces fit together suddenly, the reason why she was so reluctant to let this one go—Alayna was only the pawn. All along, Celia had been studying *my* emotions, *my* behavior. It was *me* that was the subject of her scheme.

It's ridiculous that I haven't seen this before, that I never expected it. Didn't she owe this to me all along? I deserved her retaliation. Sleeping with my father was punishment, but it never equated to the kind of manipulation I'd put her through. This though—this does. Questions race through my mind. How many years has she planned this? Did she want me to fall in love? Or was her goal to prove I actually couldn't? Did she want me to hurt or just know how it felt to be deceived? Would she have played me if I hadn't quit? Was this always her goal? Was our entire friendship really just a long game?

I'm blown away.

And impressed. And angry. Really angry.

And, also, the tiniest bit grateful. Celia is to credit for my relationship with Alayna, after all. I'm smart enough to know I would never have gone after the woman who enamored me if my old friend hadn't pushed me to it.

It doesn't redeem her. But it eases an ache of sorts. She'd always said I'd saved her by introducing her to my world—was that true or part of her scheme? Whether it was or not, now she's saved me. She's given me this life with Alayna.

Perhaps nobody won this game after all. Maybe we're simply, even.

She spins on her heels, leaving me reeling from my revelation. Of course she delivers parting words, thrown flippantly over her shoulder. "Take care, Hudson. If you ever decide to rejoin the game, you know where to find me."

My mind spins all the way to my parents' place. After turning over my keys to the valet, I stand in the lobby and attempt to gather myself before going upstairs. It's difficult to set aside the events of the afternoon, but I focus on Mirabelle and all I owe her. Then I step in the elevator and head up.

I'm the last one to arrive for this intervention, even though I've gotten here early. The whole family is present as well as Adam. Madge Werner is here too. She must not blame my mother for Celia's night with my father ten years ago, though she does carefully avoid any eye contact with Jack. She doesn't seem to be too happy with me either. I suppose my participation in the lie is enough to make her dislike me. She's uncomfortable, yet she's still here in support of Sophia. It's admirable.

It goes as well as any of these types of things can. There's lots of crying, mostly from my mother who sits on the sofa clutching Madge with silent tears streaming down her otherwise stone face. Everyone speaks. Chandler says he wants a mother he can bring a girlfriend home to. Adam talks a lot about the kind of environment he wants to raise his baby in. Madge reminisces about an earlier time in their friendship when neither of them touched alcohol.

Mirabelle gives the heavy ultimatum. "Be sober or don't be in my life."

It's after this that Sophia agrees to go to rehab. She'll do anything for that grandchild.

But even with her acquiescence, there are two of us left to talk, and we will not be skipped. Jack goes first. "I know the man you married disappeared a long time ago with the woman you once were. If I'm asking you to be her again, then it's only fair that I find him again as well. You've always been the love of my life, Sophia, even though the life I created for you—for us—was a shitty one. But, hell, we're still young. There's no reason we can't start a better life together now."

My mother, doesn't say a word, but she pats the cushion on the other side of her after Jack's speech. He moves to her immediately and wraps her in his arms. It's now that she crumbles, her face buried in his chest. Mirabelle and I exchange a stunned glance. We've never seen such affection between our parents. It's quite moving.

I go last. Careful not to include Celia's involvement—Madge is here and this isn't the place to unearth more secrets that aren't mine—I share the nature of my relationship with Alayna. How I became involved with her. How I fell in love and betrayed her. It's shocking and disappointing, and I can feel the anguish in the room grow heavier and for a short second I wonder how shocked and disappointed they would all feel to know that Celia had done the same to me. (God, I still can't believe it.)

But I can't go there because then I have to reveal the whole story behind Celia and me, which is neither here nor there at the moment.

So I stick to Alayna.

It's a short confession. This isn't my intervention, after all, but my tale is relevant.

She doesn't look at me, but I end directly addressing Sophia. "I no longer know what came first, Mother—your drinking or my emotional withdrawal. It's like trying to answer the age old question of the chicken or the egg. While blame is not important, I do know that our behaviors are directly correlated. That I've contributed to your addiction. That you've contributed to mine. With that in mind, I think that if I get well and you get well too, then both of us will have a better shot."

My mother shifts, raising her eyes to mine.

I feel my throat tighten, but I talk through it. "We've both been hiding our flaws behind these crutches. It's time we face them. I'm back in therapy. I don't want to be that person anymore, and I vow that I'm going to change. For myself. For Alayna. For you. Will you change too? For all of us? For me? For you?"

It's a simple nod that she gives, but it's everything. We'll never be able to repair our past. I know this. We will always be strained and awkward and, perhaps, even cruel toward one another. But we will forever have this one moment where I asked her for her love and she gave it. It's enough to last a lifetime.

— CHAPTER —
TWENTY-SEVEN

I t's the day after my mother's intervention and already that seems like a lifetime ago. I'm sitting in the dressing room of Mirabelle's Boutique, wallowing. I hadn't planned to come to the reopening—I'd promised I wouldn't, in fact.

But I was convinced otherwise. By Jack, of all people.

We'd just gotten to the addiction center to drop off my mother when my father handed me the keys. "I've called for a ride for me and Chandler. Take the car, go to Mira's and fight."

So I did.

And then I lost.

I put everything on the line, and Alayna still turned me away. I'm not giving up, but I haven't quite gotten the strength to figure out my next move yet. Maybe I'm waiting for direction. Which is why I'm still here when my sister bangs on the door, nearly an hour after Alayna's left. Frankly, I'm surprised she hasn't shown up earlier. I suppose her grand re-opening celebration kept her occupied. I knew she'd find me eventually.

Mirabelle enters without invitation peering first around the door, looking for Alayna, I assume, before shutting it behind her.

I rise from the bench I was sitting on, and scratch the back of my neck. "She left. I'm sorry." I'm pretty sure Alayna was done with her part of the show, though, so I don't really feel that bad.

Mirabelle walks up to me, places her small hands on my chest and shoves. "What the hell, Hudson? You weren't supposed to be here." She shoves me again for good measure.

I wrap my hands around her wrists. "And you're supposed to be watching your blood pressure. Stop shoving."

She wriggles out of my grasp and puts her fists on her hips. "If my blood pressure's spiking, it's not because of the shoving. It's the man who's being shoved that's causing me anxiety." She moves again to push me, but this time I catch her first.

"There's no reason for me to be causing you anything. Everything's good. Sit down." I direct her to the bench where she sits without any pushing. "Do you need me to get you some water?"

"No," she snaps. "I'm perfectly hydrated, thank you very much."

Something about her demeanor sparks a similar confrontation. Her rehearsal dinner. I'd pulled her away from her party then too. God, I'm such a fucker of a brother.

For old time's sake I ask, "Don't you need to be with your guests?"

"I'm on a potty break. It's fine." Her narrowed eyes show a hint of humor, and I know she caught my reference. Then she's animated again. "And what do you mean everything's good? Did you talk to Alayna?"

I lean a shoulder against the door. "I did. Talk to Alayna."

"And?" She's almost as eager as I am to have us back together. It's nice to have someone in my corner.

"And I proposed."

"Um…what?"

"You'd be proud of her. She said no." It hadn't been one of my finer moments. I'd been desperate and bold and brazen. I hadn't had a ring. It had been the solution I'd concocted on my ride back into town. I thought that proving the lengths I'd go for her was the answer to our problems. As if lack of dramatic gestures had been our issue.

"Which is understandable."

Alayna already explained it in hard to hear words—she loves me, but she can't stand to look at me. She can't ever trust me again. I'm an idiot to think that she'd want to spend her life with me.

But I'm feeling masochistic and think maybe I should hear it again. "Is it?"

Mirabelle's nicer about her response. "You broke her heart, Hudson. You don't fix that with a proposal."

I want to ask, *then how* do *you fix it*?

But I don't voice the question. I'm afraid the answer is *you don't*.

So instead, I slump on the seat next to her and assume an air of confidence. "It's good, though. I'm going to win her back. I'm not giving up until I do." They were the words I'd shouted after Alayna when she'd walked away from me earlier. She didn't look back. I pretend that doesn't mean anything.

Mirabelle lifts her head to study my face, surprise etching her expression. "When the hell did you turn into a romantic?"

I shake my head. "I didn't. I just remembered that I'm a man who gets what he wants." And I want Alayna. Need, actually. I need her like I need air to breathe.

"Yeah, don't use that line with her. That's not romantic at all." She makes a face to further prove her detest.

I hadn't meant to use the line, but now that Mirabelle's scoffed so openly at it, I have to know. "Why not? It's worked before."

"Maybe to get laid." She pauses for a second. "And now that I think about that…ew." She shudders. "Anyway, cocky and dominating is not what's going to win back trust and affection."

"How the fuck do you earn back trust?" I don't mean to be so crass, but I'm frustrated.

And, also, I get it. There's nothing—*nothing*—that Celia could ever do to earn back my trust. Is that how Alayna feels about me? She probably should. As she said, there's no forgiving that kind of betrayal. Now I know.

But she also told me that she still loved me. Even if she hadn't said it, I saw it in her eyes, on her face. I felt it in the way she had to fight to keep from running into my arms. If she'd said she hated me, maybe then I could let her go on with her life. Without me. But because she still has love, well, I can't give up on that.

Huh, maybe I did turn romantic after all.

"Time," Mirabelle says. I hadn't expected her to answer. "Give her space. Let her know you're still fighting for her. But don't do anything that will get you a restraining order."

Time and space. Every second away from her kills me. Every inch between us feels like miles. But I can try. If that's what she needs, I can do my best to give her that.

Mirabelle rubs a hand in small circles over her belly. "Do you have anything specific planned to show her you're still thinking about her?"

In truth, that's why I'm still sitting in Alayna's dressing room—I was paralyzed, trying to figure out my next move. So far I'd come up with nothing.

Except as I'm caught in the hypnotic rhythm of my sister's hand motion, I suddenly remember something from long ago. "Someone once told me," I say, "that the way to win a girl's heart is to do things that prove you've noticed who she really is."

I'd used that wisdom to win me girls in the past. Always as part of a scheme, and that made it hard to consider as a tactic now. Yet, it had been good advice.

Mirabelle eyes me. "You're seriously going to develop your game plan based on something I told you as an inexperienced teenager?"

I frown at her word choice. "Not a game, but yes my plan is based on your suggestion."

She raises a brow and I assume she's unhappy with my idea.

"Do you have anything better?" I hope my exasperation isn't too apparent.

"No. The idea's great. Simple. Romantic. It's really the best you got."

"Then what was that look for?"

She breaks into a grin. "You. Asking my opinion about your love life. I told you that you would one day."

Her smile is contagious. "Don't get cocky. It's not good for the baby." I poke at her ribs where I know she's ticklish.

She bats at my hand and squeals. "Stop it. You're making me laugh and my bladder can't take it."

"Go take your potty break." I stand and help her to her feet. Then I open the door and stand back to let her pass.

In the hallway, before she goes toward the bathroom and I toward the back door she asks, "Are you going to be okay?"

I pause. "Yes. I think I am." Because Alayna seemed like she was going to be okay. And that's what matters most to my happiness. Still, until she asks me not to, I'm going to keep trying for another chance.

By the time I'm in my car, I've already bargained with myself regarding giving Alayna space. I can't stay completely away, and though that's perhaps the last thing she needs, I know she can understand being all consumed. I decide that I can physically keep my distance, but only if I'm with her in other ways. A list of gifts is already forming in my head.

Most anything I'll need can be ordered online, but there is one purchase I need to make in person. I head directly to Tiffany's. Alayna said no to my first proposal, but I still have every intention of one day making her my bride. When I have the chance to ask again, I'll be prepared. I purchase a three carat brilliant cut diamond flanked by two baguette stones in a platinum setting. As soon as I see it, I know it's hers. It's beautiful and precious, just like she is.

That night I start my gift giving. I have the Kindle delivered to her at work. She may hate it. She may give it away. She may throw it to the ground like she did her phone.

Or maybe she'll accept it. Maybe she'll even love it. I don't know. I've never so easily second guessed myself. Like everything new Alayna has taught me, this is another new concept—how to grovel.

When a text comes through a short while later, it's her cell number. I close my eyes and say a silent wordless prayer before opening up the message.

Man, ur quite the talker. This is Liesl, btw.

I'm disappointed and confused for a moment. What did she mean by talker? Then I realize she's referring to all the texts I've sent. *Has she read any of them*, I ask.

No. But I read a few. :)

I don't care that she did. I'll shout my words from the top of the Empire State if there's a chance Alayna will hear what I have to say.

While I have Liesl's attention, I take the opportunity to ask more about Alayna. I saw her today, but I want to know really, *How is she?*

Good. Considering. She won't use the vibrator I offered.

I chuckle. And then I'm thinking about sex with Alayna. Missing it. I've tried not to let those thoughts enter my mind. We spoke to each other through our bodies and remembering her beneath me, her mouth on me, her tongue sliding against my own—it adds a deeper level to the constant pain I feel for her. I'm hard at the memories, but I won't touch myself. I'll suffer with blueballs because I know that beating off will only increase the loneliness.

Ignoring the ache, I concentrate on my texts. *Is she eating? Sleeping?*

She eats. She drinks. A lot. But that's getting better. She's sleeping on my couch. It's a futon.

So we've both been sleeping on the couch. Somehow that gives me comfort. *Are you home? Can you take a picture?*

A few minutes pass and then an image of a thin worn mattress shows up on my phone screen. A message follows. *You better not want this for something kinky.*

Nothing kinky. And thank you. I just want to know where she's spending her time. I want to be able to picture her as she sleeps.

If that's not completely psycho, I don't know what is.

I stare at the image a moment longer. I have the idea for my next gift now. I'll order a new mattress for her. And one for me, just so I can feel we're connected in our sleep.

Another message comes through. *R u going to keep texting her?*

I am. Do you think that's okay? God, when did I get so needy?

Yeah. I do.

She sends another right away. *I'm putting this down now. So u can go back 2 ur pining. I'll try not 2 read 2 many of ur messages.*

I know Liesl is on Alayna's side, but I let myself think that maybe it's also *our* side.

I'm restless before I even attempt to sleep. It's the couch and the sleeping alone. I haven't slept well in days.

Tonight I decide to try something different. I pull out my iPad and look for a radio station. I tend to usually listen to the classics—Mozart, Brahms, Wagner. Alayna, on the other hand, loves to listen to modern songs, songs with words, music with a beat. Tonight I want to listen to what she'd be listening to if she were here. Something like it, anyway. I don't know which label best describes what she usually plays so I select one at random from the Adult Contemporary section.

I don't pay too much attention to the first song that plays—it's halfway over and I'm settling in with my pillow and blanket. But the second song comes on and I'm caught up in it immediately. The piano is lonely, haunting. A male tenor enters with the melody. It's simple. Bluesy. Soulful.

And the words...

They tell the story of a man who's drowning in his love for a woman. Drowning, but he can still breathe fine. The woman's flawed, but to him she's perfect. She makes his head spin. She's distracting and inspiring. And he's so enamored with her that every part of him loves for every part of her. It's a song about being open, about having no barriers. About loving with "all of me" and asking for "all of you" in return.

It's everything that I feel for Alayna. Everything I want to say to her.

I sit up and look at the artist's name and song title. John Legend, All of Me. I purchase the album and put the track on repeat. I have it memorized before I fade to sleep.

As I straddle the line between consciousness and unconsciousness, I decide that tomorrow I'll go back to Tiffany's. Alayna's ring needs an inscription, and I know just what to say.

Sunday she starts returning some of my texts. I'm elated, but I think I manage to keep my cool.

I continue sending her daily gifts, reminders from our relationship. I leave each one on her desk for when she arrives at work. Thursday, though, I leave nothing. Instead, I come into The Sky Launch during her shift and take a seat at the end of the bar. She barely speaks to me, but I'm happy just to sit and watch her. It's meant to be reminiscent of the first time I spoke to her. The night before her graduation.

It seems like a lifetime ago now. So much has changed and yet so much hasn't. Her smile still lights up my world. Her eyes still draw me in and keep me hostage. She still is the most intriguing thing I've ever encountered.

I nurse a Scotch for an hour. Finally, I leave her an envelope with a hundred and a gift certificate to my Poughkeepsie spa. Then I leave.

I'm halfway to the parking garage when she calls after me. My heart pounds against my chest as I wait for her. I'm worried about the reasons she wants to talk to me. Also, I'm so fucking happy that she wants to talk to me.

When she gets nearer, she holds the envelope out toward me. "I can't accept this. I'm in charge here. I can't leave for a week to go to a spa." She lowers her gaze. "Unless you'd rather I wasn't working here."

I practically snap in response. "Don't ever think that." The only reason I have the club is because of her. "If you think you can't work with me as your owner, I'll give you the club." It's hers anyway. In my head, in my heart. Where it counts.

She blinks a few times. "I just want to keep my job, thank you."

I'm relieved. I'd been so afraid she'd quit. Not only because I'd lose access to her, but she'd lose the job she loved so much. I'm grateful she's staying. "It's yours as long as you want it."

I push her hand and the envelope back toward her, a blatant excuse to touch her. "And the certificate—keep it. You can use it anytime you want. There's no expiration." Even with just the brush of her finger, sparks travel through our skin.

She pulls away from me. "Fine. Whatever."

Our conversation seems to be over now, and I'm disheartened that she'll leave. But she surprises me. "There's another thing." She takes a deep breath. "I need to get my stuff from the penthouse."

My stomach sinks. I've been dreading this. As long as her things are sitting safely at the Bowery, it feels like we're still together. It's still our home. We still have a chance. The minute she moves out, all of that is over.

I tighten my jaw. "I wish you wouldn't do that."

She ignores my statement. "I want to come get the rest of my things Monday." Her hands fidget and she stares at a spot behind me. At least this is hard for her too. That's comforting.

"I can have it packed and moved for you, if you'd like." My packing would consist of buying a lot of new items and putting them in boxes with her things. She'd have new clothing, new jewelry...

As if reading my mind, she says, "I'd rather pack it myself."

Each no she delivers is another rejection. It's silly how they feel so personal. I plead with her, "At least let me arrange a truck."

She closes her eyes briefly. When she opens them she lets out a reluctant sigh. "Okay. You can do that."

"It's done." My lip ticks into a smile. "This doesn't mean I'm done trying to win you back."

"I didn't think for a second that it did." Was there a bit of flirtation in her tone?

I tilt my head and study her. Her features are softer than the last time she spoke with me. Her eyes have a hint of amusement, and she's on the verge of a grin. I decide to push my luck. "You say that as if you almost enjoy my groveling."

She rolls her eyes and gives me a wave as she turns back toward the club. She calls back to me over her shoulder, "I couldn't say, H. I haven't really seen you grovel yet."

The rush from seeing her and talking without fighting stays with me until I get to the car. Then all at once it leaves. I sit behind the wheel of my Mercedes and try not to let the reality of the situation pull me under. *Alayna's moving out of the penthouse.* Even though we've been apart, as long as her things are at the Bowery, as long as her bathroom products comingle with mine and her clothes hang on my hangers, then in my mind, we're still together. The house is still *ours.*

Now she wants to end that.

It feels final. Like closure. And I don't want closure.

Suddenly I have to be there. I drive to the Bowery and enter my penthouse for the first time in weeks. The first thing I notice is the quiet. The tick-tock of the grandfather clock is the only sound stretching across the expanse of my four thousand square foot condo. I walk into the living room and flick on the light.

Even with the glow of the high-wattage bulbs, the place feels cold and empty. There have been other occasions that I've been away on business for long periods of time and yet when I returned it never seemed so unlived in. It's her absence I'm feeling. It's all around me, everywhere I go, but here especially.

I slowly scan the room taking in everything. That window where she stood, moonlight streaming on her face, the first time I saw her in my home. The dining room table where we reconnected over wine and food after a long day apart. The floor beneath where we fucked like rabbits.

Every inch of space has a memory, but nothing from before Alayna. Four years I've owned this property and the only life that's ever occurred here has been this summer. After her. Was there ever anything before her? Could there ever be anything without her?

Since the truth came out, I've grieved. I've mourned and ached and felt her absence both physically and emotionally. But I've yet to let myself be angry. Until now.

Rage bursts through me, spiraling through my veins, heating my skin, tightening my jaw. I've earned my circumstances. I deserve these consequences. But I want it to not be fair. For just a minute, I want someone else to blame. My mother and her drinking. Jack and his absent parenting. Celia and the fucked up game she played. The stone-cold asshole that occupied my life until Alayna came into it. *Him.*

He's the real person to blame.

This house without her, these things, this furniture—it all belongs to him. Perfectly placed according to the suggestions of Celia Werner. The two of them. Old Hudson and Celia. Weren't they a pair? Twisted, broken narcissists who didn't give a shit about anything but their own entertainment.

To fuck with them. I don't want anything to do with those people anymore.

With a burst of adrenaline, I sweep my arms across the side table, knocking down the designer lamp Celia bought for me at auction. The fragile ceramic base shatters when it hits the floor filling the space with a sound other than loneliness.

It feels so good, I do it again. This time it's the occasional table I attack. With a hand clutched at each side, I flip it over. The decorative tea tray that sat on top clatters and clangs across the floor. I like the noise it makes so much that I kick at the pieces again, denting the pot with the force of my blow. I pull at the curtains next. A clearing of the mantle follows. Never before lit candlesticks and framed pictures of random city scenes join the mess on the floor.

Then it's the couch. I pull and claw at the cushions, throwing all my energy into this destruction. When I don't make any noticeable marks, I go to the kitchen and grab the largest knife from the butcher block. A glance at the blade made me wonder if it has ever been used. No time like the present.

Back at the couch, I thrust the knife through the leather back and pull a long slash along the length. I repeat with another slash down the arm. Then another. I'm not crazy or wild with my strokes, but the carving takes energy. By the time I've sliced up the piece of furniture, my arm is aching.

I roll my shoulder to relax the muscle and survey my handiwork. The place is a disaster. And it's the most life I've ever felt in the room without Alayna. I cling to it, holding the life as long as I can.

All too soon, the energy fades and dies.

It's then I know that I can't live here anymore. Not alone. Not again.

I find my phone and dial my assistant. He's used to requests at unusual hours so though it's after ten, my call isn't out of the ordinary. I tell him to arrange a truck for Alayna on Monday. "Also I need packers and a moving crew for this weekend. I can be here at nine on Saturday to supervise. Most everything needs to be out by Sunday night."

After everything's arranged, I head back to the bedroom. This is where much of my time with Alayna took place. I fall onto the bed, and though the sheets have been changed and they no longer smell like her, I clutch them to me pretending I'm clutching her. I let the memories of us settle in and sing me to sleep.

Sunday afternoon, I send Alayna a copy of the John Legend CD with a note that read: *This is the song that makes me think of you. Track 6. – H*

By that evening, everything in the penthouse has been packed up and removed except the few things that belong to Alayna and the mattress from our bedroom. Celia had picked out the bedframe, which is now on a truck headed to a donation center, but I'd picked out the mattress. And it has too many memories to simply toss away.

I take a look around the empty space remembering the first time I'd seen the place. I'd walked through it once before purchasing it. The next time I came back, Celia had finished designing and installing all the furniture and art. I'd forgotten how it looked in its blank canvas stage. There's so much potential to be a real home. There's ample wall space for personal pictures and mementos. The balcony has room for plants. The rarely used guestroom could be transformed into an office or a workroom. Or a nursery.

When I live here again, with Alayna, I tell myself, we'll decide together what we want our home to be.

Later, I waffle about contacting Alayna. When she finds the penthouse empty, she'll have questions. I could call her before to explain or I could wait until she calls me.

Or I could be there when she comes for her things.

It's not really much of a debate. The conversation feels more appropriate for in person, and I'll take any excuse I can to see her face-to-face. Preferably alone. There may be a way that could happen.

I decide to take a risk and call Liesl. She's with Alayna, but she's able to step away for our conversation.

"Laynie's been listening to your damn song nonstop," she tells me. "And let me tell you, *all of me* thinks you ought to buy me a pair of earplugs."

I'm so fucking elated by this information that I offer to throw in a whole new stereo as well. It doesn't take much effort to convince her to get Alayna to the penthouse alone in the morning. The gifts probably factored in Liesl's coopera- tion. Or maybe she really is on *our* side.

TWENTY-EIGHT

I wake Monday more excited than I can ever remember being. Having spent a lifetime pushing down emotions, I'm frequently thrown off guard when I experience one. I'm not prepared for the adrenaline pumping through my veins or the sweat gathering above my brow. I know Alayna isn't an early riser so I get in a few miles on the treadmill in the Pierce Industries gym before I have to head over to the penthouse to meet her. The run helps calm me.

I wonder if that's why Alayna loves the sport so much.

At the penthouse, my excitement returns. Or maybe anxiety is a better term. I pace the length of the hallway, up and down, twenty times. A hundred times. It's unbelievable that she can turn me inside out like this. That she can bring a powerful man like me to my knees. I'm helpless about her. I'm hopeless without her.

While I wait, I try to settle myself by thinking about what I expect from our encounter. It's akin to creating a hypothesis in an experiment. This time there's no manipulation though—just predictions. I often do it before an important business meeting, sorting the realistic possible outcomes from the fantastical. It was a trick that Jack taught me, actually.

The dream, of course, is that Alayna will want to try to be a couple again. She'll accept my mistakes and learn to forgive me. It wouldn't matter if we stayed at the Bowery or if we got engaged right away. The dream is that we're together, period.

But that's not a practical prediction. I slow my pace as I imagine what's likely. *She'll arrive, she'll see the empty house and she may feel uncomfortable. She'll refuse my offer to let her stay here with Liesl—she's too independent to take what would be perceived as a handout. But she'll see yet another demonstration of how my life just doesn't work without her. And maybe I'll win a pity date.*

I could handle that scenario.

There's another scenario though. One I don't want to think about. Now though, for the first time since our breakup, I imagine her without me. I test the idea softly with my mind, focusing on what that life would mean for her. *She's strong and healthy. She's in control of her emotions. She runs The Sky Launch and makes it one of the hottest clubs in town. She's happy. She finds someone to love her—someone who doesn't lie to her, someone who isn't so bossy. Someone transparent and open.*

It's a good outcome for her. But I can't hold onto that image. It doesn't resonate in my mind. Because I *know* Alayna. I know that she will settle for less than she's worth. She's too worried about her obsessive tendencies to put herself out there. She thinks she's a burden to men so she folds herself up and inward. Closes herself off.

If I could be convinced that her future would play out better without me, then I would walk away, despite the fact that it would kill me. I would let her go. I know I don't deserve her more than anyone else, but there is no doubt in my mind that we belong together. We fit together. We fix each other. We make each other whole.

It's this conviction that makes me realize it doesn't matter what happens today. I'll see Alayna. We'll move forward in some way, and whether we take baby steps or leaps and bounds, we'll be headed in the right direction. Together.

My pacing has me near the bedroom when I hear her arrive. The ding of the elevators sends my heart into my throat and my mouth goes dry. Cautiously, I duck out of sight. It's quiet so I can hear her gasp as she realizes the place is empty.

I give her a minute to acclimate. Or I give myself a minute to get it together. Either way, eventually, I find my way to her.

She's in the library, standing over the boxes of books that I've given her. We chit-chat and it's safe. The way she looks at me, though, is anything but safe. Her eyes travel greedily up and down my body and it's all I can do not to take her up on the propositions her body language is proposing.

Thinking of Mirabelle ends my contemplation of inappropriate advances. Besides that the thought of my sister is a turn-off, she had so wisely pointed out that I was not just trying to get laid. So I'm a good boy. And Alayna's a good girl with a wicked smile.

"I didn't expect you to be here," she says after another round of ogling. Her tone suggests she's not upset. If I had to bet, I'd say she's even happy about it. *Steps in the right direction.*

"You didn't say I couldn't be." *There's nowhere else I'd be today.*

"It was implied," she teases.

"You don't seem that horribly pissed to see me." My eyes meet hers and they dare her to deny it.

She bites her lip and I can tell she's warring with herself. I can read her so well, but there's still so much I don't know that goes on in her beautiful mind. If only I could know right now what she's thinking.

But she's not willing to let me in there again. Not yet. She changes the subject. "Where is everything?"

"Your stuff is still all here."

"But where's your stuff?"

I'm not sure I'm ready to let the easiness of our banter go. I take a deep breath. Then, ready or not, I tell her, "I can't live here without you, Alayna."

She attempts to hide a frown and fails. "So you're moving out?"

The idea seems to bother her. Good. It bothers me, too. "Actually, I hope I'm moving in."

"H, you confuse me enough without you trying to be confusing." Exasperation lies under her words. "Could you say something I can understand?"

"I confuse you?"

"Is this a surprise?"

I shrug. I'd forgotten how fun it is to tease her. I've missed it.

"So you're moving in?" she prompts, her hands gesturing in the air, perhaps as a substitution for throttling me.

She's losing her patience now and that's not what I want. I answer her question. "One day. I hope. But for now, I want you to live here."

"What?" Her expression turns irritated and her tone weary.

She thinks I don't understand what she wants from me. But I do. She doesn't want me to flaunt my money or give her ridiculously expensive gifts.

It's me who's misunderstood. I'm not trying to buy her love. I simply want to know that she's taken care of. And I want her in our home.

As best as I can, I try to make her understand. "I can't live here without you, precious. But I don't want to sell it, because I love being here with you. Someday, you and I will be here again. While I'm waiting for you—scratch that—while I'm groveling for your forgiveness, it's a shame to let it sit empty. You and Liesl should move in."

"I can't accept that, H." But she seems less angry now.

"I had a feeling you'd say that. Then it will have to sit." I'd known she wouldn't accept. I still had to offer.

She bites her lip as if working out a problem in her head—God, how I want to suck on that lip—then she suggests, "You could rent it out."

"I could rent it out to you."

Alayna laughs and every dark cloud in the sky scatters. I'll do anything to keep that smile on her face. Anything to keep the flirting and the warmth that passes between us. We tease like this, back and forth, her smile remaining, her eyes gleaming. The day is already worth it just because I got to see the sun in Alayna's face.

She asks me again, "Seriously, though, where's all your stuff? Did you get another place?"

I shake my head. "I gave it all to a charity fundraiser." This is true. For the most part. Minus the pieces I destroyed.

"Lifestyles of the rich and famous," she teases.

As much as we're both enjoying the playfulness—it's obvious she is as much as I am—there are still mountains between us. There are still things to say and explain. We have wounds that need dressing and scars that haven't finished forming.

I start toward her, tightening the gap that feels like a cavern between us. "I wasn't attached to any of it. This entire apartment was perfectly designed to my tastes and style, but it never felt like a home." I stop a short distance from her. "Not until you, Alayna. You made it come alive. The things that were here—they were chosen for me by someone I want completely removed from my life. Right now, the things here are the only things that made this house a place I'd want to live. Your things. You."

She starts to say something, but then closes her mouth before anything comes out.

I take advantage of her loss for words. And the fact that she hasn't kicked me out yet. "And when I move back in, we can refurnish this place from scratch. Together. You and I."

She takes an audibly shaky breath in. "You're so sure that one day I'll take you back."

I study her. I know her so well, can read her emotions from her body language better than I can read my own. Maybe I'm fooling myself now, seeing what I want to see, but her features, her expression, her carriage—it all says that the outlook for us is good. Really good.

She's looking at me with love, her eyes begging me to take her into my arms, and I'm carried away in the moment. "I'm hopeful," I tell her with a smile. "Would you like to see how hopeful I am?"

"Sure." The word falls easily, and that only makes what I'm going to do that much easier.

I dig in my pocket and pull out the ring. When I put it there this morning, I told myself it was for good luck, that I had no intention of presenting it to her today. Turns out I was fooling myself.

I hold it up in the air, my thumb and forefinger grasping the bottom so that the diamond is standing straight up. "I bought this."

It takes her a second to register what it is. Then her eyes widen. I take her hand and drop it in her palm. I haven't quite decided if I'm showing her just to let her know how serious I am about our future or if I'm actually proposing. Again.

Her eyes start to fill and her expression is confused and hopeful. It's then I decide what this will be. I'm perfectly aware that this is exactly the opposite of giving time and space. I'm prepared for a second *no*, but honestly, I'm prepared for a third and fourth as well. I can wait for her.

But she needs to know that I'm here now if she wants me. "There's an inscription," I tell her softly. I hear her breath catch as she reads what I've had added. *I give you all of me.*

I fall to my knee. "I realized something about the last time I asked this." I haven't prepared anything, but the words come easily. "I did it wrong. First, I didn't have a ring, and second, I should have gotten on one knee. But more importantly, I didn't give you the right thing. I offered you everything I had, thinking that was the way to win your heart. That wasn't what you wanted at all. The only thing you ever asked for, the only thing I would never give you, was me."

She tries to swallow back a gasp, but it comes out anyway.

"But now I do." I throw my arms open wide. "Here I am, precious. I give myself freely. All of me, Alayna. No more walls or secrets or games or lies. I give you all of me, honestly. For forever, if you'll take it." It's the most naked that I've ever been. The most vulnerable. And the absolute most honest.

I take the ring from her hand and slip it onto her shaking hand. Or is it mine that's shaking? No, I don't think so. For the first time ever I feel completely steady.

She stares at it, the reflection of the ring seemingly sparking in her eyes. She's an open book, each doubt and worry cross the landscape of her face. But in the end, it's affection that settles on her features. Love deeper than any that has ever been shown to me.

I'm certain that she can see the same on my face. My mask is down. My feelings apparent. But I'll speak them as well. "Alayna, I love you."

She moves her gaze from the ring to meet my eyes. God, how they find me. I'm forever found in her, and though I'm prepared to wait, I hope and pray that I won't have to anymore. "Will you marry me? Not today, and not in Vegas, but in a church if you like, or at Mabel Shores in the Hamptons—"

"Or the Brooklyn Botanic Gardens during the cherry blossom season?"

"Yes, there." She has excellent taste. And then it hits me what she's said. "Is that a—"

"Yes." She nods. "It's a yes."

<hr />

Alayna loves being engaged.

She's worn the ring a month and she still shows it to everyone. Even our doorman has been forced to fawn over it. The other night, I double tipped the Chinese take-out delivery man because he stayed for seven minutes after I'd paid just to listen to her go on about her diamond. If I didn't know her as well as I do, I'd suspect she only said yes so she could wiggle her finger in front of people.

But since I do know her, I understand her compulsion to cling on to the object of her affection and parade it possessively. It's behavior that drove others away from her, which is something I can never understand. I thrive on her attention. I respond to it in kind. We tangle ourselves together with our need to belong to each other. And our love grows stronger through it. More sure.

Along with my twice weekly meetings with Dr. Alberts, we see a couple's counselor every Monday. Dr. Lucille Parns. She insists that we call her Lucy. For Alayna's sake, I actually succumb to the nickname. I'd worried at first that Lucy would frown upon mine and Alayna's attachment. Call it unhealthy. Surprisingly, she doesn't. Instead she nurtures the aspects that have worked as strengths in our relationships. She encourages our high-level infatuation and our sex life as a means to connect.

Not that Lucy would have any impact on our sex life. I can't keep my hands off Alayna, and, fortunately, she can't seem to keep her hands off me either.

Despite what we have going for us, Lucy does expect a lot of work. She focuses on our lack of communication and trust. It's a mystery to me how I can be determined to share everything with Alayna now and yet, when Lucy presses us, it's still so hard to be that transparent. "Old habits die hard," she reminds us. Then she assigns us a new exercise that sounds easy and proves to be a struggle.

Tonight our assignment is full disclosure. From me. Though Alayna has figured out the basics of my games with Celia and my scheme regarding her, I've never told her all of it. Alayna's not even entirely sure she wants to hear it.

But Lucy has insisted on it. "Alayna's already forgiven you," she's said. "Use that knowledge to erase any fears you have. But there's no way for you—for both of you—to put this fully to rest without letting light into every corner of this darkness."

So this is the night we've chosen for my confession—exactly one month after she accepted my proposal. My chef prepared a dinner that we ate together by candlelight on our brand new dining table. We still don't have living room furniture, and summer's quickly flying away, so after our meal we take advantage of this warm evening and move to the balcony.

The new outdoor furniture is better cushioned than the set I'd had before, yet I can't get comfortable in my seat. Alayna offers me a drink, but I turn it down. I don't want to suppress any emotions that come from this confession. It may not be easy, but I want to feel all of it with her.

She angles her chair to face me head on and curls her feet underneath her. She doesn't pressure me to start, and we sit for several long minutes in silence. Then I begin.

I start with the emotionally closed-off young man I'd been, the man who wanted to understand the relationships he was missing out on because of his lack of feeling. I tell her how he experimented on people he knew. How he experimented on his closest friend and turned her into a hateful, bitter woman.

I tell it all—how I'd kissed Celia, how I'd fucked her friend, how she'd fucked my father, how she'd gotten pregnant. All of it.

Alayna doesn't interrupt. She listens intently, her expression changing with the particularly disturbing details. It isn't until I tell her about the night of the symposium, the night I'd first seen her and my life instantly changed that the tears start. They're sweet tears that fall quietly down her face. They make it harder for me to go on to the part where I betrayed her. But I do. I tell her all the things I thought and felt and how I convinced myself I was doing something good, but I always knew that it was wrong.

I end at The Sky Launch, when Alayna realized the truth. It's the worst part and the best part. It was the moment I almost lost everything. But it was also the moment that I was finally free to love Alayna in the way she deserved, and in that way, it was the moment I gained everything.

I don't tell her that the whole thing was Celia's game. I will, one day. But tonight is for *my* faults, *my* mistakes. No one else's. Admitting my own role as victim shifts the focus away from that.

It takes over two hours to complete my story, and when I do, I'm exhausted. Mentally and physically. And I can't hide that I'm down. It's been an evening of recalling my sins. I'm humiliated. I'm ashamed.

Alayna stares at the skyline past me, a breeze blowing her hair behind her so her face is clear and visible. Still, it's hard to read her thoughts as she takes everything in. I start to think that maybe now I need that drink, but then her eyes swing to meet mine and she speaks.

"It's not on the agenda for me to disclose anything," she says, "but I have my own confession."

I'm not worried about anything she has to tell me. The things she thinks are her flaws are the very aspects of her that I adore most. But I am intrigued.

She clears her throat. "It could be easy to listen to what you've said and focus on the heartache that you say you caused. But the part that's missing is that your experiments were done on grown-up people. Adults who are, in the end, responsible for themselves. You hurt Celia. She had a chance to walk away, and she didn't. She's culpable for what she became after that. That's all her, H. Not you."

I tilt my head and study her. "You had a chance to walk away, too."

"I did. And me coming back to you—that's all me." Her lip twists into a smile. "Though you did do a damn good job of making yourself impossible to resist."

Weakly, I return her smile. It's a small comfort against the weight of my past.

Alayna gets up suddenly and crawls onto my lap, straddling me. My cock stirs automatically from our point of contact, but I ignore it. She wraps her arms around my neck and my own hands settle around her waist.

"Here's my confession, H. It's a difficult one to admit because I don't want it to sound like I condone the things you did." She takes a deep breath. "But, honestly, I wouldn't have given you the time of day if you hadn't manipulated me. No matter how you chased me. Nothing you could have done would have made me start any sort of relationship with you."

My eyes narrow. She's told me before that she was as instantly attracted to me as I was to her. It was in her face, in her body language from the moment we first interacted. Surely if I'd approached her in the conventional method of courtship, I could have won her attention.

"Don't get me wrong," she says, apparently picking up on my confusion. "I was attracted to you at first sight. You pulled me to you inexplicably. I was instantly fixed on you. And that made you everything that I should stay away from. I'd been well for a long time before you, Hudson. I'm pretty sure I could have stayed on the wagon. It would have been difficult, but I would have avoided you like the plague."

She moves her hands around to caress my jaw. The soft flutter of her thumbs against my stubble sends shocks to my groin. "Then you waved money in front of me. And I convinced myself I needed that money enough to break my rules and do the thing you asked of me. If you hadn't done that, Hudson, if you hadn't played me..." She shakes her head at wherever her thoughts trailed off to. "Honestly, I don't think there's any other way you could have won my attention. Unless you held a promotion over my head in exchange for spending time with you, and that would have been just as shitty."

She leans down and kisses me softly then leans her forehead against mine. "I would never have given myself the chance to fall in love with you if you hadn't forced me to. It doesn't excuse you. But it's the truth. And for that, I have to say that I guess things happened how they should have. If I had the chance to rewrite it all, I don't think I would change a thing. This is the path that led to me with you like this. It's the reason I came back to you so easily. Because I realized I'd rather live through your betrayal and end up with you than never to have gotten you at all."

She kisses me again, deeper this time. Her tongue pushes through my lips and wars aggressively with mine. I'm moved. Not just my cock, which is now hard as stone, and not just from what she's doing but by everything she's said. She's way too forgiving. Way too open-minded. But I'm so fucking grateful that she is because now she's mine.

Her kiss grows more frantic, and I know what she needs, but as I'm about to take the reins, she stops me. "Let me, Hudson. You told me things that were hard for you to say. Let me show you how much it doesn't matter. How much I love you anyway."

So I do. I wait until she asks me to touch her breasts before I cover them with my palms. I let her unbuckle my belt and release my cock. She's the one who lifts her skirt and pushes aside her thong underwear. Then it's her who positions herself over me and slides down on me. She's tight, but she pushes her hands against my chest and leans back until she's seated comfortably. I fill her so perfectly like this, her pussy pulsing around me as she moves up and down over me.

I lean in and tug at her nipples through her shirt and bra with my mouth. Alayna tilts her hips forward and I can tell she's found the right angle when she starts to moan. She speeds up, talking in breathy gasps as she rides. "I love you, Hudson Pierce. Every part of you. Every flaw, every scar. Just like you love me."

She tightens, and I can feel she's close. "I love the way you take care of me." Her words are a struggle now. "And the way you accept my jealousies and insecurities. I love your cock and the way you fuck me. And the way you make love."

She's bouncing up and down in a frenzy now and we're both on the edge. Just as she clenches around me she says, "Did you say that I can't come when I'm in control? Because I'm coming."

I start to laugh, but then I'm coming too, the dark disappearing in a flash of white as my orgasm steals my vision. We soar together like this, riding the wave of our simultaneous climax, climbing higher and higher as we fall deeper and deeper into each other. I'm lost in her and found in her all at once.

And as I am every time we touch, every time we speak to each other, every time our eyes meet—I'm made new. There's a past that led me to this moment, but it's not holding me back anymore. Even in the dark of this New York City night, the only thing before me is sun.

EPILOGUE

Three years later

C lick. Click.
The camera sounds each time I take another shot. It's the only noise in the quiet hospital room. *Click.* I look at the photo counter—eighty-seven. The memory card had been empty before we arrived. I've taken eighty-seven pictures. What can I say? I'm a proud father.

I move the camera's focus from the bundle to Alayna and take another. *Click.* I lower the camera then and study Alayna. Her eyes are closed, but her breathing is irregular so I know she's only resting. She looks wiped, and rightly so. It's been a long road to this moment. Though we'd wanted to try for a baby as soon as we got married, she'd just had a birth control injection which lasted three months. Then it was more than a year of trying before we could conceive. Her doctor said it was common to have trouble after injections. Common or not, it wore on her. And me. Alayna obsessed about the reasons she wasn't pregnant. I wondered if it was a consequence of my past. Or karma, even. It felt like a miracle when Alayna finally walked out of the bathroom and showed me the stick with the faint plus sign in its display window. It had been her birthday. There wasn't any gift I could give her that could compete with the one we'd made together.

The pregnancy itself went well. She had the typical issues—morning sickness, sore breasts, moodiness. I'd wanted her to quit working at the club and leave Gwen in charge. Alayna had wanted to stay managing until she delivered. We compromised on part-time, and Alayna's last day was a month before her due date. It gave us time to finish the nursery which we'd decided to decorate in a children's literature theme. Dorothy and the Tin Man make their way down the yellow brick road on one wall. Peter Rabbit scavenged Mr. McGregor's garden on another. And the baby bedding featured *Alice in Wonderland* characters.

Despite the last few weeks off, the whole thing has been tiring for Alayna, as to be expected. She'd barely gotten any sleep the last few nights. Then her contractions started just after midnight yesterday which meant no more sleep for either of us. She labored through the day and the baby wasn't born until two-thirty this morning. I wish she would let the nursery have the baby so she could get some real sleep, but Alayna's insistent on keeping her here. Not just in the room, but in her arms. She won't let go of the sleeping bundle, which is under-standable—and adorable—but every time the little creature stirs, so does Alayna.

I shift the camera back to our baby—*my* baby. Her face scrunches up and relaxes as if still getting used to the feel of air on her skin. I take another dozen or so rapid shots, attempting to capture each and every twist of her features. She's amazing and beautiful and there's nothing like this bubble bursting inside my chest at the wonder of her.

Then why am I still holding this camera and not her?

Quietly, so as not to disturb my wife, I set my camera on the table and reach for my child instead. Alayna moves slightly at the sudden absence from her arms, but her eyes don't open. Hopefully she's finally drifting off.

Good. Daddy and daughter bonding moment to commence.

I smile down at my sweet girl, pushing away the blanket to better see her face. Her color has paled since she was bright red and squalling in the nursery during her bath. I'd studied each and every part of the tiny creature then—counted her toes and fingers, discovered the dark birthmark at the small of her back. Then had been the examining. Now, I'm simply swept away with infatuation.

I stroke her impossibly soft cheek and trace the curve of her small puckered lips. Instinctively, my body begins to sway to a melody I hear only in my head. I hum a bit. The words dance in my head and a few lines slip out in my awkward tenor voice, "*All of me loves all of you.*"

There couldn't be a more fitting motif for the moment. I'm completely and totally in love.

"Keep singing," Alayna says from her bed, surprising me.

I feel my neck warm. "You weren't supposed to hear that. And you should be sleeping."

"But I'm not sleeping. And I did hear that. So keep singing."

It's near impossible to deny any request of hers, but this one I do. "Maybe later. Right now, since the easy part of all of this is over," I meet her glance, "we should get to the hard work. It's time to pick a name."

We'd thought of many over the course of the pregnancy, and when we'd learned we were likely having a girl, I thought we'd finally settle on something. Alayna wanted to use her mother's name—Louise—for a middle name, but she could never agree on a suitable first name. "*I need to see her first*," she'd say. "*I want her to have a name that fits her.*"

And so here we are with a perfect, beautiful, nameless child.

Alayna's tired eyes narrow at my remark. "You think all this was easy?"

I gesture for her to scoot over so I can join her on the bed. "I meant for you. It was extremely hard for me to hear you call me those things that you did—especially near the end. But I was trying to not make a deal of it."

"Hudson!"

I really don't think it was easy. The doctor had used that term, supposedly in comparison to other births she had delivered, but as far as I am concerned labor at all is hell. I've always known my wife is strong and capable of anything, yet I'd never imagined the exertion and endurance that would be required to push a seven pound, three ounce human being into the world. I'd also never felt so helpless. Of all the things I can do for Alayna, this thing she had to do primarily on her own.

I settle into the space she's made for me and kiss her forehead. "I'm teasing and you know it, precious. I'm grateful and proud of everything you went through to get our baby here. It's the best gift you could ever give me and there are no words to express how amazed I am with you."

Her face softens and her eyes start to water. Again. God, I love this woman, but pregnancy turned her tears into overdrive. Today, I understand it. It's natural to cry when in pain. And when the doctor first placed our scrawny, naked baby on Alayna's chest, I admittedly shed a tear or two as well.

Now, however, I'd prefer we'd not cry—because if she starts, I'm sure to follow. I glance at the clock. "As much as I could go on with how much I adore you, Alayna, it's now almost seven. Our families are going to ascend on us soon and I'd love to have a name for her before they do. Though Baby Girl Pierce does have a certain ring to it, I'm certain she'd be made fun of at school." I lay a kiss on our sleeping daughter's nose and return her to her mother's arms before grabbing the tablet off the side table.

Alayna looks adoringly at her bundle and then leans her head against my shoulder. "Then look up the baby name site and let's get deciding. Otherwise your mother will take it upon herself to come up with a name and that's not happening."

We'd made a conscious decision not to have any family invited to the hospital until the baby was born. *Too much drama*, Alayna had said, and I agreed. Since the baby was born in the middle of the night, I'd waited until six a.m. *to* make the phone calls. Mirabelle and Adam have to get both their four-year-old daughter, Aryn, and their one-year-old son, Tyler, dressed and ready before coming over, and my parents are slow moving in the morning so that will delay them. I figure that gives us until around eight to have our last minutes alone with our daughter before she meets the rest of the *Crazies*, as Alayna likes to call my family.

From the bookmarks on the browser, I open the website we've used as our search guide and select the link for girl's names. The most popular ones pop up in a list on the screen. *Charlotte, Sophia, Amelia, Emma.*

"I heard Celia Werner got engaged."

I glance down at my wife. "How do you always ruin the most beautiful moments with her name?" I know why she thought of her—*Celia* had been a name on the screen.

"Shut up. I haven't mentioned her since before we got married." She's right; she hasn't. Celia hasn't been a part of our lives in any way shape or form since the last time I'd seen her at the loft. She'd kept her end of the bargain, ceasing all contact with me and my family. And I'd kept my end—Warren Werner is still the head of Werner Media.

For a time after our engagement, Celia's name came up in counseling. She'd been a contributing source of much of our conflict and it was inevitable that she'd be discussed. But eventually all of us agreed—Alayna, Lucy and I—that talking about Celia further kept her around when she didn't need to be. We didn't talk about her after that, and, eventually, I didn't think about her either. Well, not often.

"Anyway," Alayna says now. "Your mother told me."

"Of course she did." She told me as well. She always did love to stir the pot, even sober. Though Sophia has long lost her love for Celia—rarely mentioning her anymore, thank God—she hasn't exactly warmed to Alayna. She hasn't warmed to anyone, for that matter, except for possibly my father. The two seem to find redemption in each other, even when no one else can see it. Perhaps Alayna and I are like them in the eyes of others.

"Thoughts?" She's not testing me for an emotional reaction. There are no secrets between us anymore. Particularly not about my old partner in crime.

"Regarding Celia? Good for her." It's as much attention as I will garner the woman on the birthday of my first child. It doesn't mean I don't wonder about her on occasion or that I didn't pause when I heard her news. Part of me hopes her romance is genuine. Wouldn't that be ironic?

But it's entirely possible the engagement is simply a scam or her parents' arrangement. She's likely still cold and unfeeling. Maybe even unhappy and miserable.

I won't lie. There's a small part of me that wishes for the latter. Okay, a big part of me.

"Yeah, good for her." Alayna's tone seems indifferent, and I sense the bitterness she once carried for Celia has been replaced with other things. Things that matter. The prestige of running New York's Hippest Club of the year, according to the Village Voice. Two anniversaries celebrated with a husband who loves her more than could ever be expressed. A new born baby who coos and clicks in her sleep.

Alayna stares down again at her pink-hatted bundle. I think she could look at her baby forever. I could look at her looking at her baby forever. Jesus, I'm getting mushy in my old age.

I turn back to the tablet and click for advanced search. I enter a meaning, curious if any names will pop up. A list of over fifty does. I scan through them, my breath catching on one. I click the name to read the definition further.

"Alayna," I say, still not believing my eyes, "did you know your name means *precious?*"

She's taken aback. "Seriously?"

"*Precious; sun ray.* See?" I show her the tablet where the definition is clear as day. She blinks at the screen. "Did you know that?"

"I had no idea." I'm not sure if she realizes how often I've referred to her as the light in my darkness. Her name is completely fitting for her. For the woman that would be mine.

"It was fated," Alayna says with the sweetest grin. "I was meant to be yours. You knew what I was about before I did."

I can't stand it. She's too beautiful. Too perfect. I look back at the tablet. "You're giving me too much credit."

"No, I'm not."

And, I think, maybe she's right. Maybe we were fated or destined to find each other. Maybe everything that happened to me and Celia and Alayna was all meant to happen, each painful part playing out in order to lead us to our personal happy ending.

Or maybe it's just coincidence. And does it really matter? It's a happy ending either way.

Our baby stirs again, this time with more determination. "She's waking up." I watch her tilt her head toward Alayna, her little mouth open and searching.

"Hey, she's rooting," Alayna exclaims.

"It looks to me like she's trying to suck your breast." I tickle my baby's cheek with my finger. "I get it little girl. I like sucking her breasts too."

Alayna laughs. "That's called rooting, you dork."

"It's not called rooting when I do it."

"No, that's called awesome," she says, looking up at me with that devilish grin of hers, the one that can make me instantly hard if I'm not careful.

Again, I have to look away. "Stop it. You're going to make me horny and the nurse said six days."

"Six weeks."

I sigh. "I suppose I heard wrong."

"Yeah, that's it."

I return my focus to the screen in front of me and scan further down the list. "What do you think about the name Mina?"

"Mina? Mina Louise." She repeats it, testing it out. "I like it. What does it mean?"

"*Precious*. In SanSkrit." I gaze down at my daughter—my *daughter!*—and watch her fight to open her eyes, her little lids squeezing tight and relaxing before they pop open. "Look at her. What do you think? Does it fit?"

"She's certainly precious."

"Like her mother."

I toss the iPad to the end of the bed and wrap my arms around my wife and child. For someone who once felt very little, I am now overwhelmed with emotions. My heart is full to the brim, overflowing with love. So much love.

Sometimes it's hard to even remember that I ever was another man. That I ever was anything but this one—a man who will fill a camera with newborn baby pictures and tear up as his precious daughter opens her eyes. A man who found sunshine in his dark existence when he deserved it least.

Alayna Withers changed everything for me. I can easily divide my life into two parts—before her and after. The person I was in that time long ago and the person I became when my eyes first found hers.

Though that isn't entirely accurate. Before her I never really lived. So there is only after.

I begin and end with her. It's as simple and as profound as that. Our worlds have entwined and wrapped around each other completely. They've shaped into something new and fixed and whole. There is no longer her story or mine, but, now and always, only ours.

THE END

ACKNOWLEDGMENTS

When I was in high school, our theater teacher wouldn't block the curtain call until we were "ready". In other words, the rest of the show had to be at its best. Sometimes we didn't get our curtain call until opening night. I've always felt that same way about acknowledgements—I'm not allowed to write them until the rest of the book is finished. So I feel a bit like a naughty girl right now as I fly to Philly for a signing and I begin writing these when I still have three chapters of the book left to right. But I'm going to see friends and fans—people that I've come to cherish so dearly, people that I wouldn't have met if it hadn't been for Alayna and Hudson and my writing world. My heart is full and I think now is completely the appropriate time to try to capture a sliver of the gratitude pent up inside.

Always, though, the question is where to begin?

Tom, my sweet optimist prime, I owe you for so much more than inspiration. I love you and I'm lucky to be your princess. Keep serving me coffee and breakfast in bed for a long, long, time. Okay?

My girls, though it seems I'm absorbed in my own world most of the time, I hope you realize that I love you more than life. I put pieces of you in all I do. Though it's happening too fast, I can't wait to see the women you become.

Mom, thank you for always pushing me to follow my dreams. I wouldn't be the person who could accomplish all that I have if you hadn't been as supportive as you have been. Now you just have to move to Colorado.

Bethany Hagen, there are so many words to describe the things you are to me. You're my editor, sure, and critique partner, and book fairy, but above all that, you're my very good friend. I dream of the day we'll run away together and build neighboring blanket forts. Some place gray of course, with lots of mood and ambiance. (P.S. I hope this experience didn't require too much Scotch.)

Melanie Harlow, I feel like we've grown up together from baby WrAHMs to NAturals to agency sisters, we've had quite a run, haven't we? Though you no longer need me to internal up your manuscripts, I hope you still send me them all before everyone else. I'm proud to be able to brag about you first. Let's try to hook up more often and introvert next to each other, shall we?

Kayti McGee, you're my other half. Honestly, it's not fair that you get all the charm and wit while I'm doomed to barely crack a smile. I might even crack more than usual when I'm with you. You're a constant cheerleader and never tire of my complaints (well, you pretend to never tire). I think you may be as saintly as my husband. There's no other person I'd partner with. Thank you for letting me boss you around.

Tamara Mataya, your sexy voice and quick-wit aren't your only amazing qualities, but they are certainly two of my favorite. You keep me laughing even when I'm not in the mood. Which is all the time. You're one of my fav peeps to be miserable with. Get over that Canadian thing of yours and we'll be fab friends forever. All right, maybe you can stay Canadian. We'll see how it pans out.

Gennifer Albin, if you ever need a backup career (in between designing the world's best covers, illegitimate agenting, and writing amazeball books), then you should definitely look into life coaching. Your "hard words" are never as tough to hear as you build them up to be, but they're always the reality check that needed to happen. You think you're not a cheerleader; I disagree. You may be sparse with your pep and compliments, but when you do deliver, I take it to heart because I know you mean it. I've known you now through ebb and flow and you're just as cool when you're ebbing as when you're flowing. That's not something that can be said of everyone. I hope I can learn to be as graceful as you through my own career.

Amy McAvoy, my favorite of all twunts, your role in my life has evolved through so many phases. You were that first blogger who said, "Oh, definitely this one" when I asked for a review of my little story. As an early and passionate supporter, I know my book sales have thrived partly because of you. Your opinions are strong, like you are, and they're also so often exactly right. But aside from what you do for my writing, I'm so glad to have you as a friend. You sincerely decorate my life. I'm honored to know you.

Patricia Mint, this book only exists because of you. If you hadn't drowned me with your constant questions into Hudson's motives, I'd have never realized that there was still story to be told. Remember when this was going to be a novella?

Now it's my longest and my favorite book I've written. I owe you drinks. And spanks. Because I'm dying to get my hands on your mint ass. Holla!

Lisa Otto, I know you've gotten too busy for me and you want me to "fire" you, but I can't do it. Even when you've only got the barest minimum of words for me, they're always just what the story needed. You can't get rid of me that easily.

Jackie Felger, you've trucked along through all my projects and that is really admirable considering how all over the place I've been. I'm so grateful for your feedback and suggestions. Thank you so much for being such a faithful CP.

Tristina Wright, you were the first person to read any of Hudson and Alayna's story. You've seen them (and me) at their worst and yet you still saw story to cheer on. You may have not been that involved with the latest installment of their journey, but what you've contributed to my growth as a writer shows in every new paragraph I write. Thank you for the guidance when I needed it most. I hope I can return the favor someday.

Shanyn Day, when I was in high school, my friend had a job working as a "keeper". She was basically a personal assistant, but her boss said she was so much more than that—she kept her on track, kept her together, kept her sane. Though I introduce you as my publicist and my assistant, you are definitely my keeper. Thank you so much for keeping me. I'd be lost without you.

K.P. Simmons, you save me in so many ways. It's weird to think we have a business relationship because it doesn't feel like that at all. You do good business though! InkSlinger PR is by far the best. But you also do good friendship. I raise my full cup to you.

Joe LaRue—There's no one else who renews
my creative, spirit, mind and drive
like you do. #thanksinhaiku

Rebecca Friedman, our relationship is new, but isn't that the best part? Can't wait to see where we go together. I totally feel the "sizzle".

Bob Diforio, we've come a long way in this last two years. I'm very appreciative of all the work you've done for me. Thank you.

The rest of my team: Anthony Coletti, Sara Norris, and Danielle Nelson for keeping more money in my wallet and guiding me through the icky parts of financial success; Stacy Shabalin at Amazon, Ian and Chris at iBooks and Lauren and Carina at CreateSpace for your time and commitment to helping my books shine in your stores; Caitliyn Greer for your quick turnarounds and beautiful formatting; and Jolinda Bivins for making my books come alive in the most beautiful keepsakes. I'm grateful every day for all the time and energy people put toward making my life easier. I'm very, very blessed.

Holly Atkinson and Eileen Rothschild, my "other" editors. I love how much we "click". Thank you for understanding me and teaching me how to make my words sparklier.

Jenna Tyler and Angela McLain, thank you for everything you are. Your friendships are invaluable (as are your proofreading skills, Jenna).

Shera Layn and the Hudson Street Team, you are simply amazeballs. Your talent and drive to pimp is just incredible. I couldn't ask for a better group of people to get my book out there. Thanks for caring about Hudson's success as much as I do. Muah!

To the women in Obsessed with the Paige and Hudson Pierce! Fixed Trilogy—my days are brighter because of your love and commitment to my characters. Thank you for sharing your enthusiasm and passion with me. It's one of the best parts of what I do.

This writing community is full of the most amazing people. So many authors have become my best friends, first online and then, little by little, I've gotten to meet you. I'm certain I will miss a bunch of you, but I have to try to specifically mention a few of you who have made a particularly significant impact on me: Lauren Blakely, Kyla Linde, Melody Grace, M. Pierce, Pepper Winters, Kristy Bromberg, Emma Hart, Kristen Proby, the women of NAturals, FYW and WrAHM and Babes of the Scribe, and that other group that shall not be named (you know who you are). There's a lot of kick ass in this world of mine and you guys represent the majority of it.

I used to try to name all the bloggers who have supported my books and my career, but the list has grown too long to even attempt recognizing you all. Please know that I see you. I see what you do and I know the hours and time that you put into your work. I'm so very grateful for your pimping and supporting. I wouldn't be where I am without you all.

And I definitely wouldn't be anywhere without the readers—I wish I could send out a personal thank you to each of you every time you choose to pick up my book or recommend me to a friend. I wouldn't have a job without you. I'm so, so lucky to be able to do what I do, and even luckier that so many of you have been touched by my words and my characters. You overwhelm me daily, even if I don't always share it. Thank you, thank you, thank you.

Above all, I give my thanks to God. You raise me up. Please keep teaching me how to do the same for you.

COMING SOON

FREE ME

Available December 9, 2014
Preorder now at Amazon and iBooks.

Her story started long before she started working at The Sky Launch...
Screw fairytales.

The only reward Gwen Anders got from her rough childhood was a thick skin and hard heart. She's content with her daily grind managing a top NYC nightclub—Eighty-Eighth Floor. So hers isn't a happily ever after. She doesn't believe in those anyway.

Then she meets J.C.

The rich, smooth talking playboy is the sexiest thing that Gwen has ever encountered, but she's not interested in a night-in-shining latex. But when a family tragedy pushes her to the brink, it's J.C. who's there to teach her a new method of survival, one based on following primal urges and desires. His no-strings-attached lessons require her to abandon her constant need for control. Her carefully built walls are obliterated.

Gwen discovers there's a beautiful world outside her prison. Freedom is exhilarating—and terrifying. When she starts to feel something for J.C., she fears for her heart. Especially as she realizes that he has secrets of his own. And his secrets don't want to set him free.

This series can be read alone or with the Fixed Trilogy.

Did you know leaving a review helps authors get seen more on sites like Amazon?

If you liked Hudson, please consider leaving a review. Amazon, iBooks

For a monthly chance to win a Kindle Paperwhite plus be notified of my book releases, visit www.laurelinpaige.com, and sign up for my new release emails. You can also connect with me on Twitter @laurelinpaige and on Facebook at www.facebook.com/laurelinpaige.

LIGHTS, CAMERA…

TAKE TWO

by Laurelin Paige
Available at Amazon, Barnes & Noble, and iBooks

On the night of her graduation from film school, straight-laced Maddie Bauers fell completely out of character for an oh-my-god make-out session with a perfect stranger. Complete with the big O.

Seven years later, that romantic interlude is still fresh in her mind. That stranger is now a rich and famous actor. And she's one very distracted camera assistant working on his latest production. She might consider another tryst…if he even remembers her.

Micah Preston does indeed remember Maddie. Too bad he's sworn off Hollywood relationships. He allows himself as much sex as he likes—and oh, he does like—but anything more is asking for trouble. For the woman, not for him. Yet knowing Maddie could want more than a movie-set fling doesn't stop him from pursuing her like a moth drawn to hot stage lights.

But as the shoot nears its end, it's decision time. Is it time to call, "Cut!" on their affair, or is there enough material for a sequel?

Warning: Contains a dreamy movie star hero, a focus-pulling heroine, off-the-charts instant chemistry, steamy sex in near-public locations, and a new use for lip gloss.

LIGHTS, CAMERA...

STAR STRUCK

by Laurelin Paige
Available at Amazon, Barnes and Noble, and iBooks

Hollywood actress Heather Wainwright was looking forward to a long, relaxing break before starting her next shoot. Except her assistant volunteered her for L.A.'s annual 24 Hour Plays.

Nervous about doing a good job for such a worthy charity, Heather falls back on "diva" mode, a defense mechanism that always carries her through. Until she encounters something that *really* gets on her nerves—a lowly carpenter whose Norse god eyes pierce right through her.

Highly sought-after production designer Seth Rafferty has little patience for A-listers with superior attitudes, which is why his attraction to Heather is absurd. Yet, sensing vulnerability beneath her screen-queen act, he lets her assumptions play out.

After the wrap party, Heather awakens with little memory of the night before—except that Seth gave Her the best orgasm of her life, then disappeared. When he shows up on the set of her next movie, she winds up to give him a piece of her mind...and Seth shows her just how stinging hot "chemistry" can get.

Warning: Contains an outwardly snobby actress with a good heart, a delicious carpenter with a power drill, some much-deserved spanking, and an appropriately consensual—if tipsy—orgasm, as well as sex at an inappropriate time of the month.

ABOUT THE AUTHOR

Laurelin Paige is the NY Times, Wall Street Journal, and USA Today Bestselling Author of the Fixed Trilogy. She's a sucker for a good romance and gets giddy anytime there's kissing, much to the embarrassment of her three daughters. Her husband doesn't seem to complain, however. When she isn't reading or writing sexy stories, she's probably singing, watching Game of Thrones and the Walking Dead, or dreaming of Adam Levine. She's also a proud member of Mensa International though she doesn't do anything with the organization except use it as material for her bio.

You can connect with Laurelin on Facebook at www.facebook.com/LaurelinPaige or on twitter @laurelinpaige. You can also visit her website, www.laurelinpaige.com, to sign up for emails about new releases and a chance to win a Kindle Paperwhite in a monthly drawing.

CPSIA information can be obtained at www.ICGtesting.com
Printed in the USA
LVOW04s1500290415

436592LV00018B/877/P